"Quista is beautifully unique and original, blending familiar parts of life on Earth with fascinating aspects of realities on new planets. The story of Danay's journey is rich, full of adventure, and sure to leave you wanting more."

— Toria Spencer

"A combination of fascinating landscapes and intriguing characters keep you turning the page in Quista. Bel'Harold brought not just one world to life, but an entire universe as she weaves this tale. This is a book to get lost in. A fantastic addition to anyone's library, Quista will pull you in and leave you wanting more when you're done that last page."

— D. C. Menard

"The world is so immersive it drags you in by having a blend of new exciting alien concepts as well as having familiar things you would find on earth giving a fascinating contrast to just the setting itself."

— Connor Tisdale

"...a must read for anyone who loves travel and adventure. Love is found in the most unsuspected people and places."

— Sarah Hein

QUISTA

BOOK ONE: DANAY

Aviva Bel'Harold

EDGE SCIENCE FICTION AND FANTASY PUBLISHING
An Imprint of HADES PUBLICATIONS, INC.
CALGARY

QUISTA

Book One: Danay

EDGE SCIENCE FICTION AND FANTASY PUBLISHING
An Imprint of HADES PUBLICATIONS, INC.
P.O. Box 1714, Calgary, Alberta, T2P 2L7, Canada

The EDGE-Lite Team:
Producer: Brian Hades
Acquisitions Editor: Ella Beaumont
Edited by: Allister Thompson and Ella Beaumont
Cover Design: Brian Hades
Cover Art Elements: Tomislav Tikulin
Book Design: Mark Steele
Publicist: Janice Shoults

ISBN: 978-1-77053-108-6

EDGE Science Fiction and Fantasy Publishing and Hades Publications, Inc. acknowledges the ongoing support of the Alberta Foundation for the Arts and the Canada Council for the Arts for our publishing programme.

Alberta

Canada Council for the Arts | Conseil des arts du Canada

Library and Archives Canada Cataloguing in Publication
CIP Data on file with the National Library of Canada
ISBN: 978-1-77053-108-6
(e-Book ISBN: 978-1-77053-107-9)

FIRST EDITION
(20160614)
Printed in Canada
www.edgewebsite.com

Publisher's Note:

Thank you for purchasing this book. It began as an idea, was shaped by the creativity of its talented author, and was subsequently molded into the book you have before you by a team of editors and designers.

Like all EDGE books, this book is the result of the creative talents of a dedicated team of individuals who all believe that books (whether in print or pixels) have the magical ability to take you on an adventure to new and wondrous places powered by the author's imagination.

As EDGE's publisher, I hope that you enjoy this book. It is a part of our ongoing quest to discover talented authors and to make their creative writing available to you.

We also hope that you will share your discovery and enjoyment of this novel on social media through Facebook, Twitter, Goodreads, Pinterest, etc., and by posting your opinions and/or reviews on amazon and other review sites and blogs. By doing so, others will be able to share your discovery and passion for this book.

Brian Hades, publisher

DEDICATION

For Larissa and Roxanne—

Without you my elementary years would have been very lonely. Thank you for being my friends when no one else would and for loving me even when I didn't really like myself... and especially thank you for being the first to fall in love with Quista.

Chapter One

Coming of Age

"Oh, hey, I got this for you," Kit said holding out a small satchel.

It was the day of the Popling Festival. We sat on the dock waiting for the event to start. Kit had her feet in the water and was making ripples as she swished them back and forth.

"What's that for?" I asked as a hot breeze caught a rogue strand of my hair and blew it across my face. I pulled it back, trying to tuck it behind my ear. I wished my hair would grow past my chin like Kit's… like everyone else's.

"It's for your birthday, silly," Kit frowned at me as she dropped the satchel in my hand. "Don't tell me you forgot today's your birthday?"

"Yeah, I forgot." I lied. I stuffed her gift in my pocket and turned to stare out over the water towards the Deeps.

A flock of hooroop soared overhead, casting shadows across the rippling water.

Kit sighed, "Did you really forget?"

I wish I had. "No, not really."

Her tone became compassionate, "I understand."

I was sure she didn't. "Thanks," I said.

I continued to stare out at the water, watching small currents pull and drag so the surface danced with yellow, gold and orange hues from the three suns above.

"You know it's not fair!" Kit'Una kicked at the surface of the water.

I leaned back to avoid the splashes.

"Of all the stupid things Emperor Zigel has done."

"Hush," I said gently putting my hand on her shoulder. "You shouldn't speak like that."

She pulled away from me glaring, "You don't like him either. You can't even think about him without making a face — see!"

I shook my head trying to lose my expression. "Still, you know the penalty for saying anything bad about him. Even on our planet you need to be careful."

"Oh, stop worrying. All I was going to say is it isn't fair that every planet has to keep time according to his planet's Royal Years. It's impossible to keep track of anything."

I looked around to be sure no one else could hear us.

"Come on Danay, you have to agree with me. It's crazy making! Last Turn your birthday fell in the rainy season, this Turn mine will." She threw her hands up. "It's as if he did it on purpose just to make us miserable! Why else would he pass such a ridiculous law?"

"It wasn't *his* law," I said, surprising myself. Then even more surprising I went on, "That law was necessary when there was open trade between the planets."

She stared at me, "Whose side are you on?"

"Not his," I said with a scowl. Then I bowed my head feeling guilty. I checked again, everyone else was at least fifty paces away. They were all on the *safe* docks waiting for the day's events to start.

"Someone should tell the Emperor to change the law then. I mean it's been over seventeen Royal years since travel was banned between the planets. No travel — no trading — no communication — no reason to keep the same time cycle. No reason to mess up our birthdays. Especially *this* one," her eyes narrowed on me. "How could you forget your Coming of Age birthday?"

I knew she hadn't understood.

"You've been talking about it for over five Seasons. Just last Turn you couldn't wait for today. What…" she bit her lip before she finished asking her question.

I pressed my own lips together and turned away. She knew full well what had changed. She stayed quiet but I didn't turn back. Instead I studied the soaring flocks of hooroop. Such strange sleek creatures they were. They easily soared through the air, but if their underfur got even a little wet they drowned. Still, somehow, they thrived here.

"Kit! Kit!" Pal'Hon called. I looked at the safe dock where he was. He was frantically waving his arms making the rolls of fat on them ripple like the ocean after a rock was thrown in. Catching my eye, he deliberately pointed a fat finger at Kit; then at the railing of the safe dock. It was slowly being raised to provide a barrier of protection for the onlookers.

"I think Pal'Hon wants you to go sit with him." I said. He was one of the more popular boys in our school, and she was lucky he kept trying to show her interest.

She rolled her eyes. "Can't you see I'm ignoring him?"

"It's okay if you want to watch with him." I often wondered why she stayed with me when all the other kids would be happy to have her join them.

Kit frowned. "Unlike you, I have not reached my fifteenth Royal Year. It would be improper to accept his invitation… or anyone else's."

I nodded. She and I both knew that Pal'Hon wasn't the only admirer she had. He was just bolder than the others. I suspected that might change the closer the Seasons got to her Coming of Age.

"Your birthday isn't that far off. It's less than a full Turn away. No one would say anything." I'd seen girls flirt with potential suitors long before their fifteenth birthday. "Besides, you have so many to choose from it might be a plan to start weeding them out."

"You never did that," she said.

As if we were the same. Kit could have been the most popular girl in Tem, if she didn't spend so much time with me.

"You forget," I tried to keep my tone light, "I don't have any suitors."

"What about…"

"He left." Just saying it made my heart ache.

"But he…"

"No Kit. He left." I squeezed my eyes shut as I thought about the only boy I'd ever liked. Phillip. He was an off-worlder, like my father. Phillip had come to our village, Tem, in the middle of last Turn. But he never showed any interest in me, and he left halfway through the last Season. "I don't want to talk about him."

Kit looked like she was about to argue.

"No! I don't even want to think about him," I snapped.

Now she looked like I'd slapped her.

"I'm sorry." I thought about the gift I'd stuffed into my pocket. I didn't deserve it. I should try and give it back... but I knew she wouldn't let me.

"More people would like you if they just got to know you," Kit said.

She actually believed that. "Kit, please, we've been over this before."

"Yeah," her voice got louder, "and I think we need to go over it again. You're the best person I've ever met. Just because you happen to be a little skinny—"

"A little? Huh. That's the understatement of the Turn."

"—looks aren't everything."

"That isn't the only thing they don't like about me."

Kit shook her head.

"Kit, open your eyes. It's not just that I'm *way too skinny,* I'm also too tall. I'm taller than *everyone* in Tem by at least three finger widths! Then there's my hair, and my eyes... and my skin — they are all the wrong color. Not to mention, I don't have enough webbing on my hands and I don't have *any* on my feet. And we aren't even talking about the biggest problem... I'm... I... I get sick if I stay wet too long."

"I don't see the problem," she said.

"You don't?" She had to be kidding. "Um, haven't noticed that the whole planet is covered in water!"

"Yeah? So? You've lived here all your life, it hasn't *killed* you yet. You visit me all the time. You could make it work with a boy if you wanted to."

That really stung. "Kit, believe me. I want to. If anyone—" my voice caught, "—*anyone* showed the slightest interest in me I would do everything I could to make it work. But I've got nothing to offer the boys here and they all know it."

"You do too," she huffed, "and if they can't see it — then — then they're all a bunch of dakka." She crossed her arms and glared over at the villagers who were squeezed together on the safe dock.

I wanted to laugh; I'd never heard Kit call anyone a bunch of hoorup droppings before. "What did I do to deserve such a good friend?"

"You don't get it." She switched her gaze to me. "You don't see how amazing you are."

I felt my smile disappear. "No, I don't."

I could see she wanted to say more, thankfully she didn't.

Turning away I wondered, yet again, *what was my purpose*? At my age, girls were supposed to be thinking about dating, mating, and learning a skill for their future. There was no chance of me doing that — so what was I supposed to do?

When I was younger, I used to wish my father's relatives would find me and take me away from Uma'Three — thinking any planet would have been better than this one. I stopped wishing for that when I realized that I'd have to leave my Nan'Dah. She was a true Uma'Threeite — as hard as it was for me, a half breed, to live on this planet — it would be impossible for her to live anywhere else. Now Uma'Three was my home. Besides, I couldn't leave even if I still wanted to as all unofficial space travel was banned. Banned by Emperor Zigel when I was just a baby.

I felt my face scrunch up, like I'd eaten something sour. Of all the things I didn't understand, banning space travel was the worst.

"Don't worry. There's plenty of time for the right boy to find you." Kit patted my back, "And the longer he takes, the longer I get you all to myself."

I leaned over until my shoulder bumped hers. "Thanks Kit." I didn't bother reminding her that by the end of this Turn she would be going away for her studies.

I stared out at the Deeps again trying not to let my mood slip any lower. Slowly I remembered why today was special. *Not because it was my birthday*. But, because it was the Popling Festival.

My breath caught. I felt the energy mounting. It made my heart flutter and my skin prickle.

The burb's were coming.

I may not have fit in with the people, and the constant waters might have dampened my mood, but when it was time for the Popling Festival — I knew this was where I was meant to be.

I smiled.

"You know, I was thinking..." Kit stopped and pulled her feet out of the water as a great white shark swam by.

I reached out and dipped my arm into the warm water, all the way up to my elbow. I ran my fingers along the great white's flank. Its hide was rough but strangely soothing.

When I could no longer touch the shark, it made a quick circle to swim by again. This time it pressed itself against me. "You are a beauty," I whispered. "Kit, isn't she beautiful?"

"Yeah, sure. *Beautiful*."

Great whites were the kings of the Deeps. They were nearly twice as long as a regular shark and over double the weight. Great whites could take on a mammoth stingray and win. This one was particularly stunning, more silver than white, with smoothly rounded fins — a sure sign that *she* was female.

Kit didn't put her feet back into the water until the great white was several paces away. She sighed as if she had been holding her breath the whole time.

"Here," she offered me the sleeve of her wet'skn before I even started looking for a place to dry my hands.

I happily wiped my fingers on it feeling the material absorbing the moisture to circulate it closer to Kit's body. Everyone on Uma'Three wore wet'skns. Nothing else made sense. A wet'skn makes it easier to move through water and it wicks in moisture, keeping the wearer damp at all times. I also wore a wet'skn, only mine was inside out. As an off-worlder the reversed wet'skn kept me dry — and made it even more obvious that I didn't belong *here*.

"You know you really shouldn't do that."

"What?" I pulled my hands away. "You offered it to me."

"Not that." She rolled her eyes. "The shark, you shouldn't touch it."

I knew I shouldn't. I looked over at the docks where everyone was gathered. They were watching me. I touched sharks when no one else would. I didn't go behind the protective barriers when everyone else did. I wasn't helping my reputation. I shrugged, "It's not like I can lose any more points. I'm pretty much at the bottom of the chart."

"What about the shark. It could bite off your arm before you could even blink."

"I guess she could," I watched the shark, she was twenty paces out. "She wouldn't though. She likes it when I rub her."

"How do you know that?"

"Easy, I still have my arm." I laughed. It was funny because I knew she'd never bite me.

Kit wrinkled her nose. She was also watching the shark — warily — ready to get out of harm's way if it turned towards us again.

"Relax, Kit, I won't let anything bad happen to you."

Her worry lines disappeared, "That's true. Nothing bad ever happens to me when I'm with you. It's like you're my good luck charm." Her gaze became unfocused. "You know, my dad told me I'd like you, even before you moved to Tem. And he promised me that if I gave you a chance I wouldn't be sorry for being your friend."

As much as I loved Mr.'Una, I always hated hearing this story. It was hard to know that my one and only friend had been *told* to be my friend. It pointed a spotlight on the fact that even Kit'Una wouldn't have liked me if her father hadn't told her to. But I listened, because ever since Mr.'Una had died, Kit liked to talk about him… and I liked to listen because I missed him too.

"You know my dad single handedly got your apartment ready for you before you moved here."

Mine was the only apartment in Tem that didn't have the customary three finger widths of water lining the floor.

"I kinda helped him, as much as any three-Royal-Year-old can be helpful." She laughed. "I didn't know what to expect. I mean I'd seen an off-worlder once when I was in the city. But I'd never really met one," she glanced at me, "or the daughter of one."

I nodded.

"Anyways, my father was so excited. He spent every minute he could working on your place. And when he wasn't working on it he was talking about it with my mom. He acted like your coming here would be this huge blessing… I guess it has been. Your Nan'Dah's been a great help." She frowned then shook her head as if trying to get her thoughts straight. "Anyways, he wanted to make everything just right for you."

She scratched her head. "It was like *good* wasn't good enough. It had to be perfect — only better than perfect."

I thought about Mr.'Una. The first time we were introduced, he bowed so low he almost did a belly flop. He had always been nice to me, treating me like… like I was one of his children. Whenever he came home from the silt mines, he'd have something for me the same way he brought back things for Kit and her brother.

When he died, I cried for days. To this day I still cry sometimes.

Kit blinked as if remembering she'd been talking.

I hadn't realized she'd stopped.

"Did I tell you what he told me the last time before he went off to the mines?"

I shook my head. It hadn't been a Royal Year yet, he'd been alive for my last birthday.

"He told me that I should protect you."

"Protect me from what?"

She shrugged, "I'm not sure." Her eyes were unfocused again, "But boy do I wish I could figure it out."

"You think I need to be protected?"

She quickly focused on me, "No." She shook her head, "No, you never seem to need protection. If anything you protect me. You've saved my life at least twice this Turn alone." She smiled.

I rolled my eyes. "Don't over exaggerate."

"Have you forgotten two Seasons' back when those sharks entered the village? They attacked five people before they were caught. You heard them coming and scared them away."

"That wasn't…"

"And what about the stinging jellie hatchlings?" she cut me off. "Those things could have killed me. But you wouldn't let me leave your house. It was like you just knew something bad was about to happen. And what about all the flood waves you've protected us — protected me — from? I would have been swept out into the Deeps."

"Enough already," I held up my hand. I was prepared to hit her if she tried to mention the mi'lex I'd stopped her from stepping on. "What I did wasn't that spectacular. I heard the sharks because they were splashing too much. I felt the stinging jellies, when their electric charge made the hairs on my arms tingle. And the flood waves are easy to anticipate if you know what to watch for."

"You heard. You felt. You saw. You." Kit was looking at me the way she sometimes did. As if to say… I don't know, something like: *I was different*. I hated that look. "Danay Qwan, you've been my good luck charm ever since day one."

I shook my head feeling exasperated.

"You have. Do you think I could sit here, on the open docks, if you weren't with me? No. I would be there, with them." She pointed back at the safe dock.

She was right; anyone from the village who'd come to watch was gathered there. And anyone else who wasn't there would be locked in their homes.

The people on the dock moved away from the railings as the great white slowly passed in front of the crowd.

I scowled, "Idiots. It won't hurt them. It's this kind of blind fear that causes the senseless killing of these magnificent creatures."

"Not everyone loves sharks." Kit patted my knee, "You've gotta cut them some slack. It's hard not to be afraid of something that big with so many *rows* of teeth. I mean, what does it need all those teeth for? If it really wanted to it could swallow a person whole."

"Great white sharks aren't interested in humans. Aren't you supposed to be a future marine biologist? You should know that they don't attack people unless they're ill."

"How are we supposed to know if a shark is sick?"

"They splash too much and froth at the nostrils. It's easy to see."

"For you," she said softly.

"They come here every Turn and they haven't once tried to attack anybody. They are just as much a part of the Festival as the hooroop, the stinging jellies, the burbs and the poplings."

"Not everyone can trust nature the way you do, Danay. Not everyone is as charmed."

"I'm not charmed," I grumbled.

"Whatever you want to call it. Lucky, observant, intuitive — whatever. Like I said, you are my good luck charm."

I rolled my eyes and gave up.

A hoorup cried and my gaze was drawn back to the Deeps.

"You can feel it, right? It's almost time for..." I heard the smile in her voice.

"It's close." My heart fluttered in my chest. "Very close." My breath caught as I glimpsed the dotted horizon. My lips curled into a smile of their own. I was about to laugh, but I held it in. No one else had seen them yet.

Chapter Two

The Popling Festival

Beyond the crowd, a horn sounded. It was followed by an announcement, the exact same one we heard every Turn; urging everyone to move to a safe place — the burbs had been spotted and they were on their way.

"You kids shouldn't be there. Get behind the protective railings!" Mz. Fow'Ler, our teacher, scolded.

It wasn't even a school day and she was still telling us what to do.

"You won't be safe there."

I shook my head and looked away. Kit ignored her.

"You are going to get burrowed."

Every Turn Mz. Fowler threatened this. Neither of us had ever been harmed.

After shouting a few more warnings, she shut the opening to the observation dock. People all around her helped draw up the protective curtain that kept the burbs out.

The water below me buzzed with energy. It evaporated into the air so I could taste it. It made me want to dive into the water … and I hated getting wet.

"I can see them," Kit said in a hushed voice. She wasn't the only one who had become quiet. Everyone around had stopped talking; many were holding their breath.

The thrumming of a million or more pebble-sized creatures bouncing across the water's surface sounded like a whispered hum; millions of tiny voices, building in volume with every passing moment.

I could hardly stand to wait for their arrival.

The Popling Festival was why Nan'Dah had moved us to Tem. It was the only place on Uma'Three that the burbs migrated to.

My excitement was mirrored by the creatures around me. The shark gave an impatient flick of its tail. The hooroop flocked in a tight-knit pattern. And the stinging jellies bobbed to the water's surface making the water look as if it were boiling.

A thin cloud of burbs drew closer; each one half the size of my pinky nail and a beautiful golden brown. As they approached, all together, they looked like a fog — then more like a solid wall.

"Ah, maybe we should have gone onto the safe dock." Beads of sweat dewed on Kit's brow. Trickle lines ran down her cheeks. She wiped them away with the sleeve of her wet'skn.

"These burbs have lived on the ocean floor for three Turns now," I said trying to calm her. "They are finally mature enough for their next phase. That's why they're drawn to Tem. It's the only place where it's hot enough for them to transform." As if to confirm my statement, some of the burbs skipped across the surface of the water and into the air, trying to get warmer, trying to pop.

On the safe dock people cheered.

Kit looked from the dock back to the burbs, "They can also pop if they burrow into you." She moved away from the water.

"Relax. Remember: nothing bad happens to you when I'm around."

"That is true." She smiled and after a moment went back to enjoying the show. Everyone loved watching the burbs transform. It was a magical sight.

Of course not all of the burbs would pop. Those that didn't would become food for the hooroop. And if the transformed ones got too wet or drowned, they would make a nice meal for the stinging jellies.

Although I rejoiced for the new poplings, and everything else that was about to happen, I also needed to shut out the overwhelming excitement of it all — to hold on to the dock and prevent myself from leaping into the water.

Kit's hand pressed down on my shoulder, "Open your eyes. You'll miss the best part."

"Can you feel it?"

"Mz. Fow'Ler asked for a report on what we see — not feel."

Reluctantly I opened my eyes. "Mz. Fow'Ler doesn't have an imagination."

"Of course not, she believes in Science."

"I think you should be able to acknowledge the Magic even if you worship Science."

"I think she would disagree with you."

I knew Kit was right.

"Fine, I'm watching now."

She didn't let go of me. It was probably the only thing that kept me from giving in to my insane desire to go swimming.

People on the safe dock oohed and awed as an overanxious hoorup dove into the fray of approaching burbs but never surfaced. I knew a lucky shark had been rewarded with an early lunch.

Kit's hand pinched the muscle in my shoulder. She squeezed tighter and tighter but I didn't pull away. My eyes were trained on the tiny brown burbs, skipping across the water, bouncing into the air. Then, just as they started to overtake the docks, they exploded into pure white poplings.

"Amazing," Kit gasped as more and more of the burbs exploded. In their place were small, soft, round creatures made from wisps of pure white feathers. They rose up on the wind; flying about us until the air was a swirling white haze.

I couldn't see the people on the dock, couldn't see the hooroop in the sky, or even the water for that matter.

The burbs continued to arrive in droves. A few landed on the dock near where we sat, but before they got too close to us they popped. Then one landed on the leg of my wet'skn. I was not happy about the water it brought with it — as if that was the most harm it could do to me.

I'd been told that a burrowing burb hurts. I wouldn't know. Unlike most citizens of Tem I haven't had one yet. Kit had. I was away that day but she told me about how it felt as the burb burrowed deeper and deeper into the heel of her foot. They had to extract it with a vacuum needle. She limped for a week after.

I carefully picked the creature up between my thumb and finger. I held it up to my face. "Do you need a little help?" I asked. I wasn't crazy; I didn't expect it to reply. But I knew that's exactly what it needed.

I put my lips together and gently blew on it — like blowing it a kiss. I knew it would pop once I heated it enough. Every Turn I tried to see the moment it went from being a burb to a popling. Every Turn I missed it.

Just like that, the tiny, hard creature had disappeared and I felt something soft between my fingers. I let go before I squished it. It was whiter than the rest with a golden tint to the edges of its delicate feathers. I watched as it rose up on the current of my breath and joined the myriad of others around us.

The winds had picked up, clearing away most of the poplings. They would use their feathers like rudders to travel the currents until they reached their nesting grounds.

As the air cleared, I stopped watching the burbs and the poplings and started watching Kit. She really was the most beautiful girl in our village. I could see why she had admirers lining up to show their interest. When her fifteenth Royal Year came, she would be paired up fast.

Her hair was so long it fell beyond her waist. It was dark and thick with luscious curls. Her eyes were deep burb brown with the color of spindly seaweed interlaced through them. She had a huge barrel chest that protected her double lungs and was further protected by a layer of blubber that made her excellent at floating. Her hands had the perfect amount of webbing, coming all the way up to her middle knuckles. And her feet were completely webbed — the way they should be. She was the picture of an ideal Uma'Threeite girl.

A hoorup swooped down within three paces of us to collect a drowning popling. With its meal in its beak, it quickly started to rise. That's when a gray shark rose from the water to snatch the bird in its jaws.

It made Kit jump.

I laughed and was delivered a scowl.

"Why doesn't that upset you?" she asked.

"Why would it?"

"The poor hoorup."

"If no hooroop were eaten then it would be the poor sharks. They'd starve and die."

"That wouldn't be so bad."

I crossed my arms. "You don't understand. Sharks are just as important as the hooroop."

"I'm sorry, I just don't like sharks," Kit said.

"Well I do." I turned away to watch the last of the burbs arrive. Most of them were doomed. I could feel how the temperature had started to drop. They had lost their opportunity to pop and would wind up in the shallow pools near the docks where they would be ground up by a machine. That made my jaw clench. *That* wasn't right.

"The celebrations are about to start. You wanna walk around, scope out somewhere to get lunch?"

I think, for Kit, that was the best part of the festival. Every Turn, chefs from all over Uma'Three came to our docks to share their creations. It was tradition for them to try their newest recipes here first. I wasn't that hungry.

"I know what you really want to do." She bumped my shoulder with hers.

"Yeah, what's that?" I asked watching the villagers cautiously leaving the safe dock. Most would do as Kit had suggested. Food was the biggest part of the celebration for a lot of people.

"You want to visit the shallow pools," Kit was smiling smugly.

She knew me well. "You wanna come with me?" I asked. I was going to go either way.

"Okay," she said, "only, you have to do something for me first."

Of course, what she wanted from me was to open her present.

I brought the satchel out of my pocket and turned it over in my hand, pressing on it, trying to feel what was inside.

"You'll never guess." Kit's eyes sparkled.

I stuck out my tongue and continued to feel it. The material was popling cloth. It had a tight weave that was worn smooth.

It must have been made from pre-used cloth. Inside it was a lump. No bigger than a burb. It was hard like a burb too, and almost the same shape. I knew it wasn't a burb. But I couldn't think of what it *could* be.

"Just open it!" Kit was nearly vibrating.

For fun, I took a little longer than needed untying the strings and turning the pouch upside down. Finally I shook it, making her gift slide on to the palm of my hand.

"Do you like it?"

My breath caught. I was holding a handcrafted doll. It was so small it wasn't even half the length of my thumb. The doll's body was made from strands of hair. Kit said it was her hair. The doll's head was made from a common silver pearl.

"It's…" I didn't know how to thank her. "Wait a sec." I was looking at the doll charm, "Is this supposed to be you?"

She nodded, her cheeks blushing.

It was a very accurate replica of Kit, complete with a large round body, and chubby arms. "How long did it take you to make?"

"A while." She shrugged.

I closed my fist around it, slipped the empty satchel into my pocket, and looked into her eyes.

"A few Seasons," she gave a shy smile.

A few Seasons — try a full Royal Year. She must have started working on it just after my fourteenth birthday. "I can't believe you did this for me."

"Does that mean you like it?"

Like didn't cover it. "I love it."

She nodded. "Good." Then she turned so I couldn't see her face. "This way you'll still have a bit of me with you even when I'm gone away."

She was talking about next Turn. She had been chosen to apprentice in Marine Biology. I hadn't been chosen for anything. I would be staying in Tem while everyone from my grade went off to learn skills for their future. My Nan'Dah had tried to comfort me. Just last night she'd said, "*Danay, my par'mida, you are important. One day you will see this too. Just give it some time; all things will work themselves out*" I didn't believe her then… it was even harder to believe now.

As I continued to hold the doll, I swore I could feel Kit's warmth coming from it.

"I hope you don't mind that I gave you a pearl," she said.

I opened my hand to look at it again. The surface was not perfectly round, no pearls were, but it was smooth. As I ran my fingers over it, I got a quick flash of the cloudy pink clam it came from.

"I wanted to be sure you got at least one pearl." Kit paused. "You deserve more. And better. I would have gotten you a Royal Pearl if I could have afforded it."

I pressed my lips together. Royal Pearls were really rare and really-really expensive. Even this common pearl was too much. But she was right. It would probably be the only one I would get. Traditionally a pearl was given by a male suitor to the girl of his interest after her fifteenth birthday.

"So, is this your way of saying you want to start dating me?" I was trying to tease. After all, she was only trying to be nice, yet somehow her gesture made my lack of suitors feel more obvious.

"Um..." she blushed, "Well, as much as I like you, and I do like you, I just don't *like* you like that."

I knew she'd only given it as a friendly gesture. I ran my fingers over the doll again. She hadn't really given me a pearl; she'd given me a charm. I held it up. The pearl gleamed in the light of the three suns. How I wished this wouldn't be the only one I'd get.

"Want me to tie it onto your CoaB?"

The Coming of age Bracelet was usually made for a girl by her mother. Nan'Dah had given me mine last night. Nan'Dah wasn't really my mother — but she was the closest I had. She'd raised me after my parents died nearly fifteen Royal Years ago.

A CoaB could be made from anything, from simple sea twine to the finest of popling cloth. The quality of material usually pointed to the girl's social standing. We weren't rich. Quite the contrary. Nan'Dah had probably spent more on mine because she knew as well as I that mine would stay empty.

It really didn't need a pearl. It was lovely all on its own. It was made with nine strands of sea twine of varying shades of green. They were braided into an intricate pattern that only my

Nan'Dah knew how to do. She called it *Royal knotting*. She had also interlaced the braids with finely spun golden popling silk. It spelled out the word *par'mida* in ancient text. She'd taught me that par'mida meant precious one. I guess she wanted me to always remember that I was special to her.

After Kit added her charm, the bracelet felt warmer. I smiled.

"Kit'Una... Da'Nay..." It was Mz. Fow'Ler yelling again. And despite her being our teacher for over ten Turns, she never pronounced my name right. She refused to say it all together like it was spelt. Instead she put what she called the *proper* sconce in it. The way she said it would mean my first name was Da.

"You two should be off experiencing the festival." She was an average sized woman with three rolls of fat around her midsection. Her face was thinner so it looked like her skin was melting off her cheeks. She stood with her hands on her hips. "I expect at least an eight sheet report about today's events, due tomorrow. Understand?"

"Eight sheets?" Kit grumbled under her breath as we walked away, "Yesterday she told us six."

I suspected that we would be the only ones expected to write the extra two sheets. And even if Kit didn't, she wouldn't get in trouble for it. But I didn't say anything.

We turned down the docks heading away from the safe docks. Away from Mz. Fow'Ler, whose eyes I could feel on my back.

The shallow pools were on the other side of the temporary festival docks. We meandered through the crowds walking past several booths offering delicious smelling foods. Kit stopped to try every free sample along the way.

"Oh, that was the best. We'll have to come back to that one," she said as she ate something that had a deep, spicy smell.

"Forget that," she corrected herself after we'd stopped briefly at a place whose food smelled sweeter than anything else around. "This," she was downing the sample that was a vibrant orange color, "this is the place to come back to." She might have been right; there was already a lineup that was twice as long as any other.

Leaving the food docks, we moved through a large group of tourists who were coming down from the observation tower. The crowd started to press in around us. Suddenly there were too many sights and smells and sounds. People were happy, anxious, excited, impatient, angry, tired... their emotions cascaded over me like waves on an ocean threatening to drown me.

Finally we turned down a deserted dock. I could breathe again.

"It's not getting any better, is it?" Kit asked, following me.

"Nope." *If anything it was getting worse.* I took a deep breath and focused on the sky: cloudless, a magnificent turquoise hue, with the three suns pulling away from each other — creating an almost perfect triangle. This was the only time they did that.

Under the dock, the stinging jellies were bobbing along next to the shallow pools. Their long tendrils stretched over a lip of sand; searching for trapped burbs. There weren't too many within their reach.

"We have to hurry," I said, stepping from the dock into the sand that surrounded the shallow pools. The pools had been created Turns earlier as a safe place for children to play. The brown sand was heavier than most of the sand which lay below the water's surface, and it gave off a faint odor that only I seemed to notice. It was made from burbs that hadn't been consumed by hooroop or jellies. The jellies couldn't make it into the pools because of the surrounding dunes and the hooroop just stayed away. I only ever visited the pools once a Turn, even when I was young.

Hopping through the toe deep pools I made it to the farthest point. The ugly grinding machine had started to do its job, scooping up burbs and dumping their remains out its back end, like an endless stream of dakkah.

I was angry. It burned in my chest. I glared at the machine wishing it would break.

Kit waved from the dock for me to hurry up. It was dangerous, what I was doing. Any burb caught in the pools could burrow into me. But aside from that, during the festival this area was supposed to be monitored by security guards. If one were to come and find me in the water, I'd have a lot of explaining to do — and I had no real way of explaining this.

I saved as many burbs as I could find. Scooping them from the water, shaking them dry, and blowing on them until they popped and floated away. I was quick, but not quick enough.

I was only a pace away from Kit when she quietly said, "Danay?"

I wanted to keep going; I only had two more pools to search. But her tone stopped me.

I looked over: someone was approaching. Thankfully too far away to see what I was doing.

Quickly, I moved next to Kit and sat on the dock's edge. Whoever it was stopped a few paces behind us.

I sucked in my breath and held it, waiting.

Kit turned her head. She let out a soft "Oh," and turned her face back to me. Her eyes were bright.

"Okay, you caught us. Get on with it," I said.

"Get on with what?" a familiar voice asked.

Even though I hadn't heard his voice for most of a season, and despite the fact that he'd never used it to talk to me before, I would've recognized it anywhere.

Chapter Three

The Only Boy I Ever Liked

"Phillip?" I jumped to my feet and spun to face him.

He hadn't changed. His hair was still light blond — though not as light as mine — and so short and straight it seemed to stick out in spikes around his head. His eyes were bright blue; like the water surrounding Tem. His features were sharp, with high cheekbones and a pointed chin. He stood four finger widths taller than me, but he stooped so we were level.

"Kit... Danay..." he nodded his head to her then to me.

I tried to ignore the thrill I got from hearing him say my name. It was the first time he'd ever said it.

"What are you two doing here?"

"We could ask you the same thing." Kit stood. She craned her neck to glare at him.

"I came here because I saw the two of you. You know it's not safe here on a festival day."

"But what are you doing back in Tem?" I asked, taking a step towards him.

He took an equal step back.

That hurt. Did he think I was going to bite?

"Hey Phillip," Kit said looking from me to him, "Did you know it was Danay's coming of age birthday today?"

"Today?" He looked at me like he was seeing me for the first time. "Really?"

"Yup, this very day," Kit said taking my elbow and pushing me towards him.

"Wow," Phillip smiled. He didn't back up. He looked from the scant space between us to Kit and, finally, back at me. He held his hand out, "Congrats."

I knew he didn't mean anything by it. He was only being polite. Still, my pulse picked up a beat. I allowed him to take my hand, imagining that I felt a spark race between us.

He gave the back of my hand the softest of kisses. "Shame I didn't know earlier," he said, not quite looking at me. He straightened and said to Kit, "I would have gotten her something."

He had to be joking.

"Something?" Kit asked. I could tell where her thoughts had taken her. I was trying hard not to follow them.

"Yeah," he shrugged, "something. Tell me, where were you planning to have lunch?" He was still looking at Kit, *and still holding my hand*. "The least I could do is buy lunch."

He finally let my hand drop and started moving towards the crowded docks. Kit followed him until she realized I hadn't budged. She turned and stared at me — I knew she wouldn't understand. It didn't make any sense to me either. I wanted to go with them but I wanted to rescue the burbs still trapped beside the dock. If I didn't save them I knew they would be ground into sand — *I couldn't leave them*.

"What's the hold up?" Phillip turned to Kit.

"Why don't you two go ahead? I'll meet you there," I implored Kit with my eyes to agree, "At the stand serving the sweet orange stuff."

"O…k…ay," she looked toward Phillip and then back to me. Her expression implied that she thought I might be crazy, "we'll save you a place in line." She turned away, "Come on Phillip; let's hurry up before they run out of food." She caught his arm and started to pull him along.

He let her.

This was probably what he'd wanted all along. To be alone with Kit. I'd caught him checking her out more than a couple of times when he'd been at our school.

"What about Danay?" he asked.

I couldn't understand why he was protesting. It wasn't like he cared about me. I watched as Kit continued to haul Phillip to the top of the dock. "Don't worry about her. She'll be fine. She's not a fan of big crowds. It's a Danay thing. She'll join us once she feels better."

A Danay thing. I chuckled. That was as good an explanation as any for my quirks. There had been a time when we'd thought it was something to do with being the daughter of an off-worlder. After Phillip showed up, we couldn't say that any more. It was just me — *a Danay thing.*

I tried to put it out of my mind as I lay on my stomach to collect the burbs. I held them out to the suns, whispering encouragement while I blew on them. Then I stuck my free hand in the sand, up to my wrist, searching for any that I might have missed.

Even though I wasn't watching, I felt Phillip come back to the top of the dock.

"No one should be alone on their birthday," he was saying to Kit.

"Phillip, she'll be fine. Leave her." Kit's footfalls reverberated through the dock as she ran to catch up to him. My fingers found the last few burbs beneath the sand. I could hear the sound of his footsteps as he began running towards me.

"Danay! What are you doing?"

Before I could do anything, Phillip grabbed me by the shoulders. I made a fist around the burbs as he lifted me onto my feet. I slowly turned to face him; keeping my hand behind my back.

His face was livid, "What were you doing?"

"I was just watching the machine." I tried to make my voice sound casual. It didn't work.

He grabbed my empty hand, "With your hand in the water! Are you insane?" He held my hand up to the suns. It was still wet. The water dripped down my arm sliding under the sleeve of my wet'skn. Beads of water pushed up around the cuff as it drew the water out.

Phillip tried to grab my other hand but I fought him.

"What's your problem!" I yelled.

"My problem?" He flipped my empty hand from side to side. "I'm not the one caught with their hand in the water during the ban." His eyes found mine and narrowed, "What were you doing with your hand in the water?"

"I was," I was stumped for an answer, "I was just..." still nothing came.

Kit finally made it to us. She held her side wincing. "She was probably trying to attract a jellie. She likes looking at them," she said breathlessly.

Phillip wasn't letting me go. His fingers started biting into my wrist. "You *are* insane." His hands shook, "Don't you know how dangerous it is? What if you'd been stung? Or worse — burrowed?"

I tried to pull out of his grip. "You're hurting me. Let go!"

His hands immediately fell to his side. "Sorry." He looked down at them and quickly back to me.

I could feel the burbs in my closed hand. They were dry and warm, and ready to pop. I let them go — silently wishing them farewell.

"What the..." Phillip pushed me aside as his eyes trained on the poplings that had appeared behind me. "Poplings! Where'd they come from?" He spun in a circle looking down at the dock. "Careful, there could be burbs." He pushed me behind him and continued to look around.

I slipped the one burb that hadn't popped into my pocket; next to the satchel Kit had given me. Then I glanced at her.

"Wow, that was close." She looked just as afraid as she did relieved.

"Too close." Phillip looked directly at Kit, "Let's get you..." his gaze slid over to me, "both of you, out of here before anything bad happens." He didn't look away.

It was strange having Phillip's eyes on me so intently. I felt unnerved.

"Yes, let's," Kit said, drawing Phillip's attention away from me for only a moment.

"Let's," I said. He didn't say anything, he just stood there like he was waiting for... for *me*. I gave an awkward shrug and started walking.

"Thank goodness." Kit sighed as she fell into step beside me. "I'm so hungry I could eat a mammoth stingray." Her stomach gave a growl as if to punctuate her statement.

Phillip came to walk on the other side of me. I turned slightly to watch him. His eyes darted all about like he expected a wall of burbs to rise up out of the shallows and burrow us. I thought for sure when we got to the more populated area, he'd relax. He didn't. Yet every time I caught him staring at me he'd frown and shift his gaze to Kit. I turned away and tried not to look at him again.

We made it back to the wider dock where it was still crowded, noisy, and filled with conflicting smells. I hesitated, pulling a clump of my hair off my face.

Suddenly Phillip grabbed my hand, and held it up.

I froze.

"Who gave you your CoaB?" his hand was firm, but soft this time, as he held my arm out.

"My…" my breath caught, "…my Nan'Dah."

He angled my wrist, squinting at the letters. "Do you know the word that's written here?"

"Yes." I nodded.

His eyes stayed intent on me, "You can read the ancient language?"

"Well—" His hand felt like it was warming up against my skin. It was making it harder to think. "—not really, but my Nan'Dah taught me about this word."

"Yeah?" His finger traced the word. It made my mind numb to everything else. "What does it mean?"

"Pr—precious one."

His brow wrinkled, "Precious one." His fingers tightened against my wrist. "But," his eyes clouded and he gave his head a funny shake. "Precious one?"

I nodded. He hadn't let me go. As his eyes rose to my face my breath caught again and this time I couldn't seem to get it back.

"So I guess your Nan'Dah thinks you're special?" Phillip said.

Breath found. "I guess." I pulled my hand from his.

"Don't be mad." He quickly captured my wrist again. "It's just that…" his thumb ran over the word on my bracelet again. "This is excellent craftsmanship. These knots…" he smiled as if he was amused.

I couldn't help but smile in return.

"So, your Nan'Dah, she's your aunt, right? Is she an off-worlder?"

Of course she wasn't. Why was he even asking that?

Kit saved me the trouble of answering. "Her aunt is a true Uma'Threeite. Why?"

His thumb kept rubbing my bracelet as he looked to Kit, "Because not many people know how to do a Royal knot. Especially not on Uma'Three... and this material," he pulled my arm closer. "This material is rare. So rare it would cost the average worker three Turns of pay."

Kit whistled. "Are you sure?"

"Positive. This would have come from a queen popling's nest." His fingers traced over the letters that spelt par'mida. "There hasn't been a queen for eighteen Turns."

I closed my eyes as he explained how rare queen poplings were. I already knew everything he was saying but I loved the sound of his voice. It didn't matter if he was only talking to Kit now. I didn't want him to stop. I could listen to him forever.

But he did stop. "How did *your* Nan'Dah get this?" The suns reflection flashed in his eyes. "How could she afford it?

I pulled away with a shrug. I knew my Nan'Dah had spent more than we could afford — more than I was worth.

Phillip didn't try and grab me again. "Sorry," he muttered. "You must think I'm being rude. It's just..." He shook his head, his blond hair bounced with the movement, "I was just curious."

I felt cheated. All those Seasons when he hadn't shown me any interest. Now he finally was, but only to be suspicious.

He was still staring at me. His lips coming together to form a straight line.

"My Nan'Dah must have bought it when I was a baby."

"She would have had to have bought it before you were born," he said. His eyes searched my face, clearly disappointed.

I shrugged, "Maybe she did."

"I bet that's exactly what she did." Kit nodded in agreement. "She would have bought it as soon as she found out your mother was expecting — you."

Both Phillip and I turned to look at her.

"It would make sense, wouldn't it? She would have wanted to get you something special. She's always saying how you were a miracle. How your mom wasn't supposed to be able to get pregnant. She must have bought the queen cloth to celebrate. And I couldn't think of a better use for it than to make it into a CoaB for you."

"So…" Phillip looked from me to Kit and back again, "How is Nan'Dah your aunt?"

"What do you mean how?" Kit shook her head at the silliness of the question. "She's Danay's aunt in the normal way how."

"That would mean she was your mother's sister? Or your father's?"

"Right," I said with a nod.

"Which is it?" He was looking at me but Kit answered.

"Her mother's sister."

He fell quiet. I didn't like the way he was staring. Like he was judging me. I took Kit's arm and started towards the food stands; the crowds pressed in around us.

"Hold up," Phillip caught my free hand and used it to slow me down. Only, once we were walking at the same speed he didn't let go. "That must mean that your mother was from Uma'Three and your father was an off-worlder?"

I nodded numbly. *Why was he holding my hand?* It made me so nervous I tripped. He caught and steadied me but didn't let go.

Why was he still *holding my hand*?

Then the answer came, he probably wanted to hold Kit's hand, not mine, but it was improper for him to take her hand so he was settling for mine.

As the crowds got thicker, Kit took my other hand. We moved like an eel through the sea of people.

Kit stopped at every stand that had samples.

"Where was your father from?" Phillip asked.

I couldn't understand why he'd want to know this about me but with his hand clasped around mine he could have asked for all my teeth and I would have given them to him. "My father was from Unarrah."

He nodded. "And what did he do here? Was he some kind of official to the Royals?"

"No." *Why would he think that?* "No. He was a silt worker."

"A common silt worker?"

My hand flexed against Phillip's, "There was nothing common about him."

"I didn't mean… I'm sorry. I wasn't trying to say your father was common, just that being a silt worker is a common job. Surely he didn't come all the way to Uma'Three just to become a silt worker."

My hand twitched again. I was offended but I didn't want to pull away. "Why not? Intra-planetary travel hadn't been banned yet. He could have gone anywhere and done anything he wanted."

Phillip frowned, "Yeah, he could have, so why did he come here?"

This time I pulled my hand from his. "Why not here?"

He leaned towards me and brought his hand up to cup my ear then spoke softly. His breath tickled. "I'm not sure if you've heard this but Uma'Three is considered one of the least ideal places to live in all of Quista. No one *chooses* to come here."

I pulled away, "Then why are you here?"

His face paled. "Because my father's been looking for the queen… popling." He looked around like he was afraid someone would hear us. Not even Kit was paying attention — she was too busy eating another sample.

"Makes sense." I shrugged. With all Phillip was going on about the poplings it made total sense.

Phillip glanced at Kit. I couldn't be sure, but he looked disappointed.

"Okay," Kit said with a wide grin. "Let's go get some lunch."

Her stomach had stopped growling a while ago, but that didn't mean she was full. She never got full. I was the only one who got full — just one more thing that was different about me.

We followed Kit all the way back to the stand with the orange food.

"Trust me, this is the place to eat," Kit said to Phillip as we lined up.

Phillip was distracted; staring at my CoaB again.

I pulled it behind my back.

He looked up at me but turned quickly to Kit, "What did you say?"

"I was saying that now that I've tasted everyone's food, twice to be sure, I'm certain this is the best place to eat."

"Oh, really? Well then, it's time for me to buy your lunch. Danay, what do you want?" I felt his hand brush mine.

"I'm too full. If I have anything else I'll burst." Food was the last thing on my mind. I regretted pulling my hand away from Phillip and wondered if there was anything I could do to get him to hold it again. *What would he do if I took his hand?* I didn't dare try. I couldn't bear the thought of being rejected. I knew he wanted Kit, not me.

Phillip laughed. Kit was nodding.

I looked away. They were getting along so well. *I was the one who didn't fit.*

"Danay?" Phillip's voice broke into my thoughts. "Are you sure I can't buy you something?"

I turned back. Kit was about to order.

I shook my head, "I really am too full."

"One double meal," Kit said to the man behind the counter. "And a child sized plate for my friend."

The man at the window was an extra-large man. He had three chins and a sculpted moustache. He eyed Phillip suspiciously.

Phillip shifted so he blocked my view of the man.

"Are you sure you are still hungry for a full meal?" the man said in a low and rough voice.

"Yes, I am quite hungry." Kit said with a forced smile.

For a moment the man didn't say anything. Even though I couldn't see him I knew he was looking at Phillip. "It would be a shame to waste food."

"You want me to spend my money somewhere else?" Kit held her arms over her chest.

"Two to go, Jen'Ein," the man called back to the cook.

While Kit waited, I moved away from the stand.

Phillip followed me.

I watched as more and more people seemed to notice us. Not just notice, but openly stare at us. At me! I hated it. Because of the festival, people were visiting from other villages — villages where off-worlder's didn't live. Their staring made me feel exposed. Vulnerable. Ugly. Soon I was dizzy from trying to avoid everyone's eyes. It was even tougher to avoid the thoughts I imagined them having: *What are they doing here? They don't belong. They should go back to their own world…*

Phillip caught me as I fell.

"What's wrong?" Kit asked from behind us. "Danay? What's wrong?"

"I need…" I squeezed my eyes shut. My head was spinning.

"I think she needs to go somewhere quieter." As Phillip talked, I listened to his voice through his chest. It was soothing. I tried to concentrate on his breathing while my heart raced like a fish caught in a net.

"You should take her to the docks near the rafts," Kit said. "I'll get our food and catch up with you there."

Phillip kept me close as he guided me.

"What are you doing? You're going the wrong way." I said as he turned down the wrong dock. "Turn around. The rafts are the other way."

"Right," he said sounding frustrated.

The rafts had been a good idea. The line-up wasn't long and there weren't as many people around. Most of those who were there were from the city. City folk were less eager to stare at a couple of off-worlders.

Phillip found a bench and sat down with me.

I rested my head against his shoulder and shut my eyes. He smelled nice, like nothing I could describe.

After a while he tried to shift away.

I didn't want to let him go. *What was I thinking?* I sat up feeling my cheeks burn.

"Are you okay?"

No, there was definitely something wrong… "I think so."

"Any idea of why you fainted?"

I shook my head. I couldn't look at him.

"Are you sick?"

Maybe I was, "I have an appointment to see the Doctor tomorrow evening to get my next set of allergy shots."

"Allergy shots?" He laughed. "What are you allergic to?"

I was embarrassed, "Didn't you know?" I spread my hands out for dramatic effect, "I'm allergic to water."

"Really?" He sounded like he didn't believe me.

"Why would I lie about that?"

"Not lie," his eyebrows came together, "I would never accuse you of being a liar. It's just..." he shook his head, "I don't understand."

"What's to understand? If I'm wet for too long I get sick."

"But," he shook his head again, "how?"

"Well..." Wasn't it obvious? "Sometimes I faint."

"But you," He glanced around almost like he expected to see someone, "You haven't been in the water all day."

We were mostly alone.

"Are you sure it's the water?" he asked his eyes now intently on me.

"What else could it be?" He didn't have an answer. "Usually it just makes me itchy and the worst that'll happen is my skin will start to crack." I complained.

"Sure," he was looking around the empty dock again, "Same thing happens to me."

Of course today had to be worse. How embarrassing. I pulled myself from Phillip's arms and crossed mine over my chest. When he didn't say anything else I turned away to look out over the Deeps. The waters were quiet now. No sharks. No jellies. Even the hoorup had gone away.

"So, these shots." Phillip looked like he was trying to figure out what to say. "Do they hurt?"

"Well," I didn't want to sound like a weakling, "the shots don't hurt, but afterwards I feel kind of—" I couldn't think of the right word. If I was being honest, I felt sicker. Sicker and like it took longer to think, like I had a nest of poplings living in my skull. "—weird," I finished, "After the shots I don't feel like myself for a week or two."

He frowned and asked, "Who do you feel like?"

"Who?"

"Yeah, after these shots, do you feel more like you belong on Uma'Three or less."

I shrugged, that was a strange question. I didn't know where to look as he continued to watch me. I stared at the dock opposite us. A couple of boys I recognized from school were standing in line for the observation wheel. I noticed them because they looked like they were talking about me.

Phillip noticed them too. "Friends of yours?"

"Friends?" I scoffed then stared down at my lap. "No one likes me… just Kit."

Phillip hooked his finger under my chin and pulled my face up. He looked like he wanted to say something. But he didn't say anything for a long time. He continued to hold me. Finally he asked, "Ready to get a raft now?" and let my chin drop.

Chapter Four

Disappointed

"You two want a single raft?" The woman asked as we reached her booth. She spoke with a tone that implied I was less important and didn't deserve the effort. I was used to this.

Phillip gave a forced smile then turned to me, "We'll need a double, at least, so Kit'Una can join us… unless it's just the two of us?"

"Pardon?" *Had he just asked me to go on a raft with him alone*? Was he serious? I couldn't tell.

"What size raft do you want?" the woman asked impatiently.

"We'll take a raft for three."

The woman's lip curled and her eyes narrowed but she handed Phillip a popling-sized ball that would inflate into a raft large enough for three Uma'Threeites. "Payment please," she kept her hand out.

Phillip looked at me, his eyes apologetic. "I gave Kit all my money."

The woman frowned.

"It's okay. I got it." I said fishing into my pocket.

As I tugged on my coin case, the satchel Kit had given me slipped out. Before I could bend down to pick it up, the person waiting behind us yelled, "Burb!"

Panic rippled through the crowd. Everyone scattered, including the woman taking payment. Everyone but me.

"Run!" Phillip grabbed my arm.

"Wait. I…" I tried to pull against him but he had an amazingly strong hold.

"No p-please it's not safe."

As he ran, I had no other option but to follow. We ran towards the opposite end of the dock, past two uniformed officers who were running towards the booth.

As we got to the end of the dock Phillip turned to keep going but I yelled at him to stop.

He did, stumbling to his knees. He rubbed them as he stood up.

"What happened? Why did you run?"

He looked everywhere but at me.

"Phillip?"

"I'm sorry." He rubbed his knees again. "It was… ah, never mind."

He didn't move. Neither did I. When he glanced at me it felt like he was waiting for me to say something more.

"We should go back." I didn't know what else to say.

"We should," he said, but he didn't move.

I stared down the dock, watching the officers collect the burb I'd dropped and check for others. Finally they left and everyone returned to what they'd been doing.

"Ok, let's go." I went to take a step but it sounded like Phillip said, Dakkah under his breath.

"What's that?"

He shook his head, "Nothing." He turned to look up at the suns. Was he upset with me?

"I'm sure Kit will be getting here soon." I wondered if he was worried about her? She should have been here by now … maybe the dock had been closed off while the officers had worked.

"Okay." He said under his breath. But he still didn't move.

I rolled my eyes and started past him, "Coming?"

He nodded and as he took his first step his knees buckled slightly making it look as if he'd tried to bow.

Maybe Phillip wasn't upset, maybe his knees hurt from falling.

Kit arrived at the rafts as we did. Phillip seemed happier after he saw her. My satchel and the burb were gone.

~ ~ ~

Phillip stayed with us for the rest of the afternoon. After the raft ride, where he asked Kit all sorts of questions about her apprenticeship, he bought her her first, second and third dessert. We'd walked aimlessly around for the last hour ending up back by the shallow pools where Phillip had first found us.

That's where we were when the all clear signal blared.

"Thank the maker!" Kit exclaimed jumping from the dock into the shallows.

She wasn't the only one. Everyone was doing it. Most were sighing or exclaiming like Kit had.

I stood on the dock watching a procession of visitors head for the boats that were waiting to take them back to the city or to other villages.

Phillip had jumped into the water with Kit. He stared up at me—.

It was the first time he'd looked at me all afternoon.

—He held his hand out, "Danay?"

I knew I had to get off the dock, the tear down crew wouldn't waste any time clearing them away. They were only put up once every Turn for the festival.

I sighed and took his hand.

He didn't let go until I was safely in the calf deep water. "That's weird. That thing is in the same spot it was this morning." His eyes were on the burb destroying machine. He shook his head. "Anyways...." he looked at me again.

My stupid pulse started to race.

"I guess this is goodnight." He pulled my hand up to kiss it.

I yanked my hand from his. "I guess."

"Okay." He nodded his head.

"Good night." Kit said looking between us with a funny expression.

He bowed then finally started to walk away. After a few steps he turned back, "I guess I'll see you tomorrow."

When Kit looked at me, "We have school."

He looked from me to Kit, "Yeah, I'll see you there."

"But, you don't go there anymore," I said. "You moved away."

He nodded, keeping his eyes on Kit. "I'm still enrolled." He turned to leave but at the last second his eyes lingered on me. They shone in the light of the first setting sun.

It felt like he'd asked me a question and was waiting for my reply.

"What?" I said.

He looked down at my wrist. A soft smile played on his lips. "Happy Birthday," his eyes shot back up to my face. It took a few moments before he said, "Danay."

He bowed again and left.

Once he was far enough away not to hear, Kit said, "So it's true, all off-worlders are hoorup ass crazy."

I laughed, "It would certainly seem that way."

"I think he likes you."

"Doubt it," I said, "he was probably being nice to me so *you'd* like him."

She made a face like that was unlikely to happen. It made me feel better.

We walked around the village, keeping to the areas that weren't more than knee deep. With the setting of the second sun, the air temperature started to drop. We took a route that went through hip deep waters to keep warm. As we made our way home, music could be heard echoing between the buildings in the village.

"Hey, you wanna come over for dinner?" Kit said as we neared our complex.

We lived in a dwelling shaped like a pie — the only kind we had in Tem. The outside was rounded to create a strong surface that resisted the ocean's waves. Each slice belonged to a different family. The wealthier villagers had fewer neighbors — the wealthiest had a whole building to themselves. Our building was divided into sixteen units.

"I'm sure my mom's cooked something special in honor of the festival," Kit said. "Well, that and since Jef's home."

"Jef's home? How come you didn't tell me? Why haven't I seen him?" Even though Jef was her brother, it was like he was my brother too.

"Slow down," Kit laughed. "He's been off with his friends since he got here. But he promised he'd be home for dinner. So, you wanna come over?"

Now I did. It had been four Seasons since I'd seen him. "I don't think I can, I'm sure my Nan'Dah wants to spend tonight with me."

"Oh, yeah, silly me." She stopped staring at the opening to our stairway. It was a small cove with cheap silt'ment stairs that stretched from her wall to mine. "I forgot, today's your birthday." She winked.

"It's easy to do." I smiled back.

"See you tomorrow," she giggled and ran up to the landing. She was out of breath by the time she reached the top.

Feeling like I had someone's eyes on me, I looked over my shoulder. Of course no one was there.

"Happy Birthday, Danay," Kit stuck out her tongue then disappeared into her apartment.

I ran up the stairs and slid our front door open. The lights were out. Nan'Dah wasn't home. She probably hadn't been home for most of the day. This wasn't uncommon. She was the only midwife in the village. Her job called her away at odd hours for undetermined amounts of time.

I smiled at the thought of her being at a birthing. My Nan'Dah's words replayed themselves in my head, "To have a birthday on a Popling Festival day — that child is someone special."

Still smiling, I went about fixing myself a snack. I didn't fail to notice the fresh food she'd bought for our evening meal. I couldn't resist taking a small handful of lu'umon berries. They weren't in season; someone would've had to dive very deep to get them. These were an extra special treat, but I knew she'd understand my snacking. I'd never been able to resist lu'umon berries.

I sat on a large overturned container made from mussel shells. It was normally used to filter the water in the room. We had no water, but every room was still equipped with one of these pots. For my freakishly small frame the pot was the most comfortable place to sit. I kinda felt bad, because Mr.'Una had made a sofa special for me — having to form the silt himself in a workshop instead of the factory where silt'ment furniture was usually made. And Mz.'Una had made me extra fine sand pillows, too.

I settled in to wait and decided to work on Mz. Fow'Ler's assignment before it got too late and I ran out of time.

~ ~ ~

My school paper was on my lap — blank. I had no idea how to start. Or how to write eight pages worth.

Scratch that, I did know how. I could have written a small book on the Popling Festival. I just knew that what I wanted to say wasn't what Mz. Fow'Ler wanted to hear.

I debated not doing the project and receiving a fail. It would be my first, but what was the worst they could do? I already had another Turn of schooling. No one had picked me to be their apprentice so I was doomed to repeat the final grade.

As the last sun was beginning to set, I finished writing up slightly more than eight pages of the boring things I had noticed.

My Nan'Dah had not yet returned. Things must have gone poorly for her to be gone so long — especially without sending word.

Tears sprang to my eyes. Whenever I thought about there being complications I felt like I should be doing something to help. *I wish I knew where Nan'Dah was*.

I bit my lip while I debated trying to find her. She'd always told me to stay away but tonight I felt bold.

Only, when I tried to open the front door it got stuck. This was typical. With our dry apartment the water in the door track evaporated and the coating of lu'umon paste, which made the door float, would dry out. But today that wasn't the cause.

As I peered out the door I found the problem — something was attached to the door handle.

It was Kit's satchel. After dropping it by the rafts, I thought it had been lost forever. Who would know to return it to me?

Taking it off the door, I realized it wasn't the satchel Kit had given me — though it looked the same: same color, same size, same drawstring — this one was also hand stitched but it was clearly done by a tradesman. And the cloth wasn't worn, it was new.

I looked down the stairway as if I expected to catch the person who had left it for me standing there. I didn't, but I felt like I was being watched. After checking the stairway a second time, I went back inside.

There was something in the satchel and for one moment I thought it might be a burb. *But who would have given me a burb… and why?*

I leaned against the door as I realized the only other thing a burb sized lump could be was a *pearl*. It certainly was the right shape and size. My hands felt numb as I shook it into my palm. *It was a pearl*. I had to turn it around several times before I believed it.

That's when I noticed three letters scratched into its surface: PDH, with a mark between the D and H that was either a hyphen or a dash, I couldn't tell.

I wish I knew Phillip's last name.

A three initial name was rare on Uma'Three…

Could Phillip actually have given me a Pearl?

The pearl slipped from my fingers and bounced under the sitting table. My knees buckled so that the door was the only thing keeping me upright.

It had to be from Phillip!

I slid myself to the floor and crawled to the table to retrieve it.

It was unlike any pearl I'd seen before. It was blue — a very light blue. It was also completely smooth and roundish like a squashed ball. Apart from where the initials had been scratched, it didn't have a single blemish. Pearls were never this perfect.

My heart sank — *what if it wasn't a pearl? … what if it wasn't really a gift*? But if it wasn't a gift then what was it? And why had it been left on *my* door? *Was it even left there for me*? Maybe someone had put it there for my Nan'Dah?

I held it up. It was fascinating, the way it glowed in the light from the moon. I didn't care if it was actually meant for me — I wanted it.

I attached it to my CoaB; placing it between the 'r' and the 'm' of the word par'mida. I would have admired it all night, if my stomach hadn't growled.

Absentmindedly, I ran my fingers over the pearl, imagining I could see Phillip standing between the two buildings across from mine — watching my front door.

Without another thought, I went to see if he was really there. As I stepped outside, a gust of chilly wind blew into the stairwell; reminding me that I wasn't dressed warmly enough for our cold nights. But I wasn't going to let something as trivial as the wind get in my way of looking for Phillip. Not even when my teeth started to chatter.

It was something else that stopped me.

Chapter Five

Jef'Una, Need I Say More

"Danny!" only Jef'Una was allowed to call me that. He stood across the landing from me, the door to his house open behind him.

I was bathed in light and warmth… and smells — delicious, inviting aromas.

"What are you doing going out at this hour?"

I glanced up to the sky, it was later than I'd realized.

I turned to face Jef head on…

Well, head on might not be the most accurate description, since Jef was not much taller than his sister. The tips of his hair only came up to my nose. Still, he was probably one of the tallest boys on all of Uma'Three — he was definitely the tallest boy in the village.

"Good evening." I smiled. "You startled me."

"I'll say. You look downright guilty." He grinned at me. Jef had similar features to his sister. Same dark curly hair; his shorter than Kit's. Same warm brown eyes. Same soft round face. His smile, however, was unique because his front teeth were slightly crooked, but I liked that about him.

"Guilty of what?" I asked, though if I were being honest I did feel guilty… *Of what?*

He leaned against his doorframe. "Of…" he stretched the word out into several syllables, "begging food from your kind hearted neighbor." He moved to the side so I could get past him.

"Is there any left?" I asked, not waiting for his reply before I stepped over the water lip.

"For you," he followed me in and slid the door shut behind us, "always."

I wasn't sure if he meant for me because I didn't eat nearly as much as anyone else in their home did or if he meant for me because they had expected me to show up so they set some aside. Either way it made me feel welcome.

Their apartment wasn't anything like mine. First off, it was filled with three finger widths of water. The front entrance blended into the living area with an eel-bone sofa on one side of the room and a silt'ment dining table on the other. The table was set for one and I knew it was meant for me because, under the table, was the stool I used to keep my feet out of the water.

~ ~ ~

"It's a shame your Nan'Dah got called away today," Mz.'Una said as she piled more food onto my clamshell plate. "I saw her leave around noon." Her lips turned down in worry, "I sure hope everything's okay."

"I'm sure it will be Ma," Jef said. "It's Nan'Dah you're talking about. Even if something does go wrong she'll have a fix for it."

Mz.'Una tsk'd at her son as he tried to steal some food from my plate. "Jef, you leave her be. I'm sure she's starved. She hasn't had any dinner yet, unlike you who have had three plates worth."

"I can't help it if I'm hungry again!" He pulled away from her slap, holding a bunch of ebbin leaves, which he quickly popped into his mouth.

"It's okay," I said, "I can't eat all of this. Besides, I don't like the taste of ebbin so much."

She smiled at me. "Never you mind dear. You are far too kind. And the ebbin is the best part. It will put some fat on your bones."

I'd been eating ebbin my whole life and it hadn't made me any fatter.

When she left the room to get something for me to drink, I pushed the plate over towards Jef.

He took all of the ebbins and downed them in one gulp. Then he leaned close to me and asked, in a teasing voice, "So, I guess you noticed that my bones need fattening up?"

I hadn't, but his comment had me checking. He looked thinner — but not just thin — more muscular.

"Looks like your job agrees with you."

"Not really." He straightened up, "My boss is worried. I'm the only one of his workers to develop this condition."

Muscles didn't seem like a *condition* to me, but on Uma'Three, fat meant you had better water retention — the more water someone retained, the better suited they were for living here. That's why I stuck out like a white shark.

Jef put more space between us as his mom returned. She set a cup down in front of me then sat herself across from us.

"Are you sure I can't wake Kit?" I asked.

She shook her head. After a few moments of silence she said, "That's a lovely CoaB."

"Thanks," I held my hand up so she could admire it.

Jef looked over, "Right, today you've Come of Age." Jef grabbed my arm. "That's... that's..." he was turning my wrist this way and that. "Where'd you get a blue pearl from?"

"A friend," I said as his mother said, "There's no such thing as a blue pearl."

"What friend?" Jef asked, "I didn't know you had any friends?" He let my hand drop and successfully ducked another slap from his mother.

"Jef, you be nice."

"I'll be nice!" He raised his hands in a surrendering gesture. "I'll be nice."

His mother was scowling as if she didn't believe it.

He took my hand in his and looked into my eyes, "It is only fitting that such an amazing jewel be put on such an amazing CoaB. And you Danay..."

"Yes, both the pearl and the CoaB are amazing." Mz.'Una was glaring at Jef's hand. This time he wasn't quick enough to avoid her smack. "I know I've taught you better than to manhandle our guests."

"Guest," he scoffed while rubbing the back of his hand, "She practically lives here. She's like one of the family."

"And don't you forget it." Mz.'Una's eyes narrowed.

Jef looked away.

~ ~ ~

Nan'Dah hadn't returned by the morning. I felt grumpy as I rooted around the fridge for something quick to eat — I'd slept in. But after I finished off the rest of the lu'umon berries, guilt crept in. If Nan'Dah wasn't home to wake me on time and make me breakfast that meant there was someone else who needed her more.

"How can you be so selfish?" I scolded myself. Then I looked at the suns, "And late!"

I slid the front door open, prepared to rush out. Only I couldn't. Kit was in the way.

"I heard you had a late night snack at my place." She took up all the space in the doorframe. "Why didn't you wake me up?"

I couldn't quite meet her eye, "Your mother wouldn't let me and, with Jef there, I wasn't able to sneak into your room."

"Yeah, I figured... still..." She didn't move.

"Let's go, we'll to be late for school." I tried to push past her.

Kit blocked me. "We're going to *have* to be late." She peered into the apartment. "Has your Nan'Dah come home yet?"

"Nope."

I tried to get around her again. "Kit, you probably won't be in trouble if we're late but I..."

"Sorry," she said pushing me backwards. "Sorry," she said again sounding more genuine when I fell with a thud.

"What's your problem?" I asked rubbing my sore bottom. *Was she that mad about last night*?

"Eels." She shuddered at the word.

Not all eels were zapping eels. Only zapping eels were dangerous. But most people didn't bother sticking around to see what type of eel they had encountered.

I let her help me up then dashed past her, "Where are they?"

She followed me onto the landing and put her hand out to restrain me, "They're under the stairs. There's a whole nest of them!"

"A *whole* nest?" I pushed against her arm but she didn't let me pass. "I just want to look." I knelt down to peek under the steps.

It looked like there were six eels altogether. They were squirming around each other in a huge angry clump. Sparks were racing between them creating waves in the water.

"Something's wrong." I could feel it. "I'm going to try and get closer to see what it is." I ducked and made it past Kit's arm.

"You aren't going to touch them, are you?" Her voice was high with panic. I'm sure if she could reach me she would have pulled me back again. But I was already too far away and she was too scared to move.

I crouched on the lowest step I could without touching the water and watched. Sparks continued to race between the eels. Four were a dark orange with a crisscross pattern and two were a bright orange with a funny squiggle on their backs. Eels didn't mate outside of their color pattern; that was probably why they were so agitated.

"I wonder what brought them here." I tried to look under the stairwell.

Kit grabbed at my sleeve, "Don't."

She caught me just as I was about to step into the water.

"Fine." I only stopped because she looked in danger of having a heart attack. "Have you called animal control?" I asked hoping to distract her.

She nodded.

Darn. "When?"

"Just before I came to get you."

"So five minutes ago. Okay, that means they should get here some time," I mocked looking up at the sky, "around the last sundown."

Her grip tightened. "You can't know that. They might come sooner."

I doubted it. If anything, I suspected they'd be later. I kept my thoughts to myself as I used Kit's hold on me to lean out further.

"Why would the eels come *here* to hide? They should have known they wouldn't be safe from the suns under here." Our stairs were made without backs so these kinds of creatures wouldn't think of them as hiding places. "Where do you think they came from?"

"Danay! You're slipping."

I straightened for Kit's sake. Then before she could stop me, I slipped my foot into the water.

"What are you…!"

"Hush! Don't do anything to upset them." I had my finger over my lips. Kit was biting down on hers — hard.

"It'll be okay Kit. I'll move slowly." Even though I wasn't a local, I'd spent my whole life moving through the water without disrupting it.

"Be careful," she said, holding her hands like she was preparing herself to pull me back if the eels decided to zap.

"Kit'Una, put your hands down. You know how electricity travels. If I'm shocked the last thing that will help is giving the current a place to go. You should know this stuff."

"Sorry," she brought her hands together and held them to her mouth.

I took another step down and reached the smooth surface of hardened lava that created the Shallows. "I think it's safe." I waved for Kit to come.

She shook her head — she wasn't going to budge.

I looked to the left and right — no one was around. "Fine," I said and moved around our building, pushing through the water that deepened gradually to my thighs.

"Danay?" Kit called, "Where are you going?"

I knew there was a crack in the lava under our building. It was between the back neighbor's stairwells. Tem was built on cooled lava that had been formed during the splitting of Uma; the original planet. There were a lot of crevices and tunnels in the lava bed. The crack under our building was long and narrow. It led to an air pocket and under that was a tunnel that led to a larger cave. I'd found it a few seasons ago when a wounded quyii seal had been trapped there during a storm. Most of the tunnels and caves weren't safe for Uma'Threeites, so when the authorities found them, they would fill them. I wanted to check to be sure this one was still here.

With a quick breath, I dunked under the water and swam along the edge of the building until I found the crack between the silt'ment foundation and the lava bed. I pulled myself in. It felt like it had shrunk. My elbows brushed the smooth algae covered lava more than once and I had to work hard to keep my head from scraping along the silt'ment ceiling.

Finally I got myself to the air pocket created by a bubble in the silt'ment form. I checked to be sure the tunnel was still there then pulled myself up onto a short lava rock ledge. It was just how I remembered it — minus the seal. Judging from the direction I'd come, I was somewhere close to my side of the building. I could hear Kit as she called to me.

The eels could stay here but it would probably be too bright for their liking. The suns shone through a dozen burb sized holes in the wall opposite me. They'd probably keep going down to the real cave so long as I got them this far.

~ ~ ~

"I thought you'd gone off to school without me," Kit said when I returned.

"I should have," I said even though I would never do that to her.

"What are you doing?" Her voice rose in panic.

I was kneeling next to the stairs and had extended my hands under them. "I'm going to relocate the eels." Wasn't that obvious?

"Don't you know how dangerous that is?"

"Only if they zap me."

Kit stood on the landing, looking helpless as she watched. Her hands shook, "Danay?"

I could feel the eels just beyond my fingertips. They were creating a current that rippled past my hands. "Yeah?"

"Don't get zapped."

I smiled, "That's the plan."

However, that was all I'd planned. I didn't have a clue what I was doing. I knew that if I could just get the eels to come to me. I could move them into the tunnel. But how did one go about calling eels? I took a deep breath and tried to calm myself. This seemed to help. The eels stopped giving off electricity. It was probably the distraction of my hands — maybe they were curious creatures.

"Come on little ones," I spoke gently, "let me take you to a safer place."

I closed my eyes and imagined the eels wrapping themselves around my arms. Not that I expected it to be that easy. But then it was. First one eel, then the rest, coiled themselves around my fingers, hands, wrists, and all the way up to my elbows.

I started pulling them out.

"Well, you tried." Kit had made her way to the edge of the landing thinking I'd failed. As soon as she saw the eels coiled around my arms, she shrieked and fell back against the wall. None of this was done quietly.

I froze as all six eels tightened around me.

"Please don't do that," I said. The eels' grip loosened.

Kit's eyes bulged. "Doesn't that hurt?"

"It kinda tickles." I let out a soft giggle.

The eels were smooth and cool against my skin. They didn't feel much different than my CoaB, only tighter and constantly moving. With them coiled around my arms, I felt alert: aware of the breeze in the air, the currents in the water, the sound of the ripples lapping against the silt'ment stairs.

Getting them to the tunnel and releasing them took longer than I had hoped. By the time I got back to Kit, my feet were starting to itch. Looking at her, I could see her teeth were chattering.

I was too wet and Kit was too dry. At least one of those problems could be fixed. We would have to take the shortest route to school — going through shoulder deep waters most of the way. "Come on, it's safe now."

Kit stayed frozen.

"Come on, if we hurry we might get there in time for the second bell."

She moved slowly but when she was only halfway down the stairs, she stopped. In a shaky whisper she said, "Danay, don't move."

I looked down and saw the eels gliding past my legs.

"Well, that sucks." I put my hands on my hips. It didn't just suck — it was really weird. Eels didn't act like this. They should have at least stayed in the air pocket. But really they should have gone to the cave. Nothing should have driven them back outside — into the suns.

"Maybe they just like you?" Kit said. She was trying to be funny. The effect was lost with her shaky voice.

I climbed the stairs to the landing.

"Can we please wait for animal control now?" Kit asked.

I shook my head. I was taking their return personally — I was going to find a way to get both me and Kit to school if it was the last thing I did.

"What are you doing?" She followed me into my apartment.

"I'm going to see if there's something we can put them in."

"What do you mean *we*?"

"Did I say *we*?" I glared at her even though it was the eels I was angry with, "My mistake, I meant me. But just between you and me, I think those scouts picked the wrong girl when they chose you to become a biologist."

"That's what I told them." She didn't sound like she was kidding.

I was halfway through disconnecting one of our unused water filters when Kit asked, "Do you really think this will work?"

"It'll be perfect."

"It has a hole."

I looked at the bottom where the water pumped out. *I'd forgotten about that.* "I'm going to fix that."

"I don't think it's big enough for all six eels."

"We're not trying to set up a habitat. It will be fine for the day. Besides, if they wanted better they should have taken my first offer."

The mussel shell pot was heavier than I expected. I ended up needing Kit's help getting it out the door and down the stairs. Before I submersed it in the water, I stuffed one of my night-covers into the hole.

~ ~ ~

"Done, now let's go," I said as I watched the last eel sink to the bottom of the pot then loop about with the rest.

"Are you sure it's safe?" Kit stood on the step just above the water. "They can't shock us through the pot?"

I could feel the heat from the current they were putting off. It made the water warmer, but not painfully so. However, I felt sorry for whoever came to relocate them. "It's safe." I started wading towards school.

It didn't take long for Kit to catch up; her tiny ripples joining mine.

Chapter Six

And Then the Day Got Worse

Of course we were late — really late. I wasn't looking forward to what Mz. Fow'Ler would say to me. As much as Kit was sure we had a good excuse, I was sure our excuse would only vindicate Kit.

The school was actually five round buildings built tight against each other with a courtyard in the center. We cut through the waist deep water and headed straight for the door of our classroom.

"We're in luck," Kit said peering through a window. "Mz. Fow'Ler's not here." She slid the door open and sloshed in.

"You're late," Pal'Hon said, sitting at his desk in the front row.

"Thanks for stating the obvious. Where's the teacher?" Kit said leading the way to the back of the class.

"Not here," he answered.

"That's obvious." Kit rolled her eyes.

I kept my head down, staring at my feet as I walked through the three finger-widths of water. It had been a long time since someone had tripped me, but it was a habit I hadn't grown out of.

"Kit, Danay, what are…"

My heart gave an annoying flutter at the sound of Phillip's voice. I know he said he'd be here, but I hadn't really expected it. And now that I knew he was here I didn't know what to do. *Had he given me the pearl?* All my hopes were about to be confirmed — or denied. I took my time looking up…

Denied.

His eyes were narrowed and his lips turned down. Clearly he wasn't happy to see me. Obviously, he wasn't my secret admirer. Despite myself, I brought my hand up to touch my CoaB.

Phillip shifted his gaze from me to Kit, "Why so late?"

For her he could smile.

"Eels," she took her seat and turned sideways to face him.

I sat in my seat behind her and put my head down on the desk.

"Wow, that's gotta be a record. I've never heard of animal control being so quick."

"It wasn't animal control, it was Danay." I didn't listen as Kit launched into a full retelling.

To distract myself from the way Phillip was hanging on every word Kit said, I fidgeted with my CoaB.

Yesterday I thought it was unlikely I'd get even one pearl. Now I had two… though Kit's didn't really count. *Did this one also not count?* Had I been a fool for putting it on my CoaB?

As my fingers brushed the blue pearl again, a picture formed in my head of a cave. It was waterless and the walls were covered in these pearl things; all of them shone like stars in the sky.

The return of Mz. Fow'Ler pulled me out of my thoughts.

"Da'Nay! You are late!"

Of course she noticed me right away.

Before she could say anything else, the principal, Mr. Sr'Ros, entered the room. "Good, you're all here." He looked like he had run all the way from his office. He had water soaked up to his waist. "I have a very important message to give." His eyes swept the class lingering on me.

That was weird; I don't think he'd ever looked at me before.

"Can't it wait?" Mz. Fow'Ler's scowl deepened. "I was just about…"

"No, it can't." I'd never heard Mr. Sr'Ros speak so sternly. But under his sharp tone I heard fear.

The teacher looked daggers at me then nodded for him to continue.

"Good — good," Mr. Sr'Ros bounced nervously, giving off little splashes as he moved to the front of the class. "May I have your attention please," He didn't need to say this — everyone had been paying attention from the moment he'd entered.

His eyes swept the class, his fear even more obvious. "I just received notice that High Emperor Zigel—"

Something about hearing the Emperor's name made my lip curl. Despite my best efforts I wasn't able to stop it. I glanced about to make sure that no one had noticed. Phillip might have, I had the eerie feeling he'd been watching me. But when I looked, he was looking at the principal like the rest of the class.

"—has sent his officials to our planet. They will be visiting every school..."

"Every school?" Sal'Non asked. "Why schools?"

"When is he coming?" Mi'Lah asked.

"Not him," Pal'Hon corrected. "His *officials*."

"Silence!" Mr. Sr'Ros's voice rose, but not out of anger. "This is just the kind of behavior that can get you sentenced by the High Emperor."

I understood his fear. The Emperor had sent his officials to schools on other planets and when students had failed his tests, they had been taken away and never returned. But, I only know this because Mz. Kay'Lv told my Nan'Dah.

"It is of the utmost importance that you are ready for their tests," Mr. Sr'Ros said. "I want you all to do us proud. I don't want to hear that any of you were taken away to stand before High Emperor Zigel."

I flinched at the name again.

"I saw that," Phillip whispered across the aisle.

I cringed and tried to ignore him. *How come he only noticed me when I did something wrong?*

But he wasn't the only one to notice.

"Danay, what was that look?" Pel'Dob whispered from my other side.

"Nothing. I have a tick."

"You'd better watch that tick. It's just the kind of thing that could lose you your head." *Did he sound concerned for me*? I remembered Pel'Dob telling Kit once that his name used to be Pel'Hoo before his mother remarried.

I ducked my head. Pel watched me for a minute or two more. Phillip was watching Pel. Finally, they both turned away.

"...and they may ask to see some of you privately," Mr. Sr'Ros stopped to bounce a few more times as he studied his kelp paper. "Alright, I'm leaving Mz. Fow'Ler with the rest of the information you need to know. Listen to her and," his eyes swept the room one last time, again lingering on me, "do Tem proud."

Everyone stared as he bowed and left.

Mz. Fow'Ler frowned as she looked down at the thin piece of kelp paper the principle had handed her.

"Mz. Fow'Ler," Pal'Hon stood, "when are they coming?"

"Today." She looked up at him but her eyes slipped to me.

"Today?" Pal'Hon repeated.

She refocused on Pal'Hon, "Right now."

"But... but... we aren't ready for this," Sal'Non said without standing.

"No, we aren't." Mz. Fow'Ler leaned against her desk while she studied the kelp paper.

"What can we do?" Mi'Lah asked.

Mz. Fow'Ler rubbed her mouth as if trying to think of an answer. "Let's spend the rest of the morning reviewing our Royal history." She stopped as if expecting the usual complaints, when no one spoke she said, "Okay, clear your desks. Let's get comfortable. We are going to use every minute of our time making sure you are ready when the High Emperor's official's get here." She glanced at the door like she expected to see them already. No one was there.

Phillip dragged his desk closer to mine. It made my ink jar wobble. As I righted it he whispered, "Danay."

I hated how I was drawn to his voice — how my lips wanted to answer him. I shook my head.

"Danay, why do you hate Emperor Zigel?"

"I don't hate him!" I hissed but my face betrayed me.

"Why do you hate him?"

"Shut up. You're going to get me in trouble."

"You're already in trouble," he said back.

Before I got a chance to ask what he meant, the teacher asked her first question.

"How long has High Emperor Zigel ruled Quista?"

A sea of hands went up around me. I didn't bother. I was never picked to answer her questions.

"Da'Nay?"

I was so startled it took me a moment to get to my feet. I wasn't the only one. Most of the class watched me as if they didn't quite recognize me.

"Um, seventeen Royal Years." I knew the answer but the way I said it made me sound like I was asking, not telling.

"Correct. Don't sit. I have another question for you."

In the end it wasn't just one more, it was about a dozen. I stood, my feet in the water, answering them all.

She wanted me to explain why we needed the Royals.

"Only Royals have enough Magic to keep the planets from crashing into each other." They also were the only ones who could stop asteroids from breaking the planets apart… like what happened to Uma before the Royals were created.

"Correct." From there she asked me to explain where the Royals had come from.

"During the war between the Magic Weavers and the Scientists, Riel and Ursala were going to collide. If they had, it would have destroyed every world in Quista. The only way to save the planets was to find someone with great Magic abilities. But there wasn't anyone. So the Scientists agreed to use their knowledge to collect all the Magic from the Magic Weavers and put it into one person."

Mz. Fow'Ler nodded. For the first time ever I thought she might be impressed, her eyes sparkled. "Go on."

"Right, they found the Queen Empress for this. After she saved the worlds, she was crowned the ultimate Ruler and the Scientists were sworn to protect her."

"Quite right, Da'Nay, what happened next?"

I couldn't help but notice how every face was now turned towards me. Every pair of eyes staring, barely blinking. It made me feel a little breathless.

"Af—after that, even though she was beyond her Royal Years, she conceived and gave birth to triplets. A—and from then on Royals have always ruled in three."

"Very nice. However, High Emperor Zigel is our only Ruler. What happened to his siblings?"

The thought of High Emperor Zandr and Empress Zoe's death squeezed my chest. "Emperor—" I fought my desire to cringe, "Emperor Zi—" I felt my face bunching up. "E—Emperor Zigle's siblings died." I'd done it. It had taken everything in my power to do, but I'd avoided flinching.

Mz. Fow'Ler was looking at me like I was supposed to be saying something more.

I couldn't think of what it might be. Glancing at Kit she looked worried.

Mz. Fow'Ler coughed to draw my attention back, "How did *High* Emperor Zigel's brother and sister die?"

"How?" The thought made my face scrunch up — not in a flinch, but a wince. My eyes stung and my lungs felt crushed. "H..." I shook my head. I wanted to say High Emperor Zandr, but we weren't supposed to call him that since his brother took the throne.

"Louder."

I cleared my throat and began again. I tried to be louder, "Emperor Za..." I heard my voice break.

"Are you crying?" Sal'Non asked.

I wiped my face. It was wet.

"She's crying!"

"Answer the question." The teacher looked down at her sheet of kelp paper.

"Emperor Zandr and..." I couldn't make myself say the Empress's name. My legs were shaking. I grabbed my desk for support. It didn't help. I fell into my seat.

"Stand up," Mz. Fow'Ler said, her eyes hard on me. "These are simple questions. How will you pass High Emperor Zigel's tests if you can't even answer these questions?"

I couldn't stand up. I was trembling. I couldn't catch my breath. The room felt like it was tilting.

"Get up! Now!" Mz. Fow'Ler was walking towards me.

"Leave her alone!" Kit stood up in her way. "Can't you see how upset she is? Give her a break!"

"You foolish child, I will deal with you next. Now, Da'Nay, get up and..." Mz. Fow'Ler had tried to step around Kit.

Kit moved herself back in the teacher's way, "Mz. Fow'Ler you are nothing but a wicked-mean shark."

"That's enough from you." She shoved Kit against Phillip's desk. He caught Kit as Mz. Fow'Ler hauled me to my feet.

What happened next didn't make sense.

One moment I was being pulled upwards by Mz. Fow'Ler. Her grip was as strong as a strangling octopus. The next she had let go and was facing Kit. Then Kit hit the teacher.

I watched as Kit's slap rippled across Mz. Fow'Ler's fat cheeks.

I blinked and suddenly Mz. Fow'Ler had Kit by the arm, "Okay, fine, I will deal with you now." She left the room, pushing Kit in front of her.

Most of the kids ran to the door to watch them leave. The rest were gawking at me.

I couldn't believe I was still standing... then I realized I wasn't. Phillip was holding me up.

He brought his lips to my ear, "Now's our chance. We should leave."

"What did she do that for?" I asked. "Why...?"

"Come on, let's go."

I couldn't leave the class. I was already in trouble. If I left now it would only make things worse. I pulled away from Phillip and sat down.

He leaned over me, "Danay, we need to go."

I shook my head. *Where did he think we should go? And why was he saying we?*

"Danay, I... you... we..." his eyebrows came together as he ground his teeth. Finally he sat. He turned and stared at me.

I tried to ignore him by watching the rest of the class as they grouped up and started discussing what they'd just seen. It wasn't easy as he continued to glare at me.

Was he mad because Kit was in trouble for defending me? Why had she defended me?

When he finally spoke — leaning so close I could feel his warm breath on my neck — he said, "You need to get out of here. Let me take you somewhere safe."

There was a part of me that wanted to go, and an even bigger part of me that liked the idea of going with him. But where exactly would we be safe? I couldn't run away from this; if I left now I would be labeled a traitor and sent before the Emperor for sure.

"Danay," he whispered.

I turned to look at him — his nose was almost touching mine.

"You have to get out of here before the Emperor's official's take you for questioning."

"Why? I haven't done anything wrong. Have I?"

He looked around the room like he was hoping to see something. I looked about too. Most of the other students were talking quietly; a few were throwing me curious glances like they didn't know who I was.

Phillip sighed, "You need to leave because just the mention of the Emperor's name makes you look like a traitor."

I bit my lip — *that was a problem*. "But won't leaving now have the same effect? I'm not a traitor." I shook my head as Phillip continued to stare at me, his eyes wide. "I need to stay so I can convince them I'm not."

"You won't be able to." He looked sick.

"Why not?"

"Because—" he stopped and shook his head like he'd lost his thought, "Because—" his nostrils flared. "Just because."

If the only problem was cringing, I could control it... or at least I could explain it. Although the more I thought about it the more I realized I couldn't explain it. Maybe Phillip was right.

But running away would put Kit in danger. I'd be named a traitor and Kit, especially now, would be accused of being my accomplice. *What would they do to her for helping me*?

Phillip made fists then released them only to make fists again. "Tell me, Danay, how did High Emperor Zandr and Empress Zoe die? You didn't answer. Do you really think their deaths were an accident?"

My breath caught.

"Danay? You can't say it, can you? You can't say it because you know it's not true."

I didn't want to look at him. He was talking treason. I could get sentenced for just listening to this. I tried to pull away but his hand clung to my arm and — even after everything — I didn't want to pull away from his touch.

"What really happened? You know the truth." I could feel Phillip's eyes on me. I felt the heat of him warming me as he shifted closer. "You know it was *High* Emperor Zigel who — who prospered from it. Right?"

I bit my lip to keep it from trembling. I closed my eyes against fresh tears.

"You can feel the truth, can't you? *High* Emperor Zigel, he… well he didn't mourn his brother and sister's deaths." Phillip made a strange kind of choking sound, "Danay, you can't let his officials question you."

"Stop! Just, please stop." I rubbed my eyes with my fists, "You are talking treason. Aren't you terrified of losing your tongue?"

"No, I'm not scared of losing my tongue. There are far greater things I'm terrified of losing and I'd gladly give my tongue if it would save them."

I ducked my head, feeling his hand still gripping my arm, "You may not be afraid for your tongue, but I like mine where it is. I am not an Un-Loyalist."

"I am."

I gasped. Perhaps I shouldn't have been so surprised with everything he'd already said. Still, to confess it, out in the open — so boldly. I glanced around the room to be sure no one had overheard. Then I asked, "Are you serious?"

"I am." He leaned closer still. So close his lips touched my ear lobe. "My father was one of Empress Zoe's Loyalists."

His confession sent a shiver down my spine. Well, that and his lips as they brushed my cheek.

"*You* need to leave," I said. *It wasn't safe for* him *here*. What would they do to him if they found out?

His hand slid over to my CoaB. He ran his finger along the bracelet. "This is a very special CoaB. It has Royal knots and queen popling silk."

I wanted to tell him to get out. To run while he still had the chance. That he shouldn't worry about me. But all I could do was enjoy the thrill that raced up my arm from his touch.

"And this jewel…"

"It's a pearl," I automatically corrected him.

"That's no pearl. It's a very precious stone from Uma'Four."

"How would you know what a precious stone from Uma'Four looks like?" *Why wasn't he leaving*?

He let my wrist go and ducked his head to catch my eye, "I've been there, to the sacred cave where they grow."

"You've been there?" *He* had *given me the jewel!*

"Where do you think I was before I showed up here?"

"In one of the cities, or even another village. But…" My fingers brushed the jewel. *Why had he given it to me?*

"Danay, come with me. Come to my ship. Let me take you somewhere where you'll be safe."

Could he like me? Or… wait… "Why am I not safe here?" *He was the Un-Loyalist, not me.*

His face fell, "I can't — I can't explain that. Please, come with me. I promise I'll tell you everything the moment I can."

Chapter Seven

I'm Not a Traitor

Phillip was asking me to leave the world with him. I'd be leaving Kit and my Nan'Dah.

"Come with me p—please." He took hold of my CoaB hand in both of his. "Danay, please."

I couldn't leave them. Not like this. "No, I can't."

"Why not?" His hands tightened around mine.

"Because if I left I'd be labeled a traitor and Kit would be punished for being my friend." I couldn't even think about what they'd do to my Nan'Dah.

He looked like he wanted to say something more.

"What?"

He stared at me, his eyes pleading. He licked his lips, "It might already be too late for Kit'Una."

How could he say that!

"I won't leave Kit like that. I'm staying." I pulled my hand from his.

He nodded and licked his lips again, "Fine, then I stay too."

"No, *you* have to go."

"Not without you."

"Why? Why do you want me to come with you so badly? Why do you care?" My voice had attracted attention.

Phillip's voice stayed quiet enough that the students who were watching us wouldn't hear, "I'm here to… I want to… I'm only trying to help. And I'm… I'm not leaving here without you." He didn't say anything else. And he'd lost his opportunity to escape because just then Mz. Fow'Ler came back.

"Da'Nay," she said, her face lit up with a strange sort of smile, "you have been chosen to do a personal interview with the Emperor's officials. Get up, let's go."

It felt like a nightmare — a horrible, horrific nightmare. My knees were shaking as I got to my feet.

Then something wet oozed through my hair. I brought my hand up to check what it was.

"Phil'Lip! What are you doing?" The teacher's eyes were wide.

The palm of my hand was bright red. I twisted to see Phillip holding a bottle of ink. I could feel it dripping down my neck. Soaking into my wet'skn.

Mz. Fow'Ler started to walk closer, "I'm afraid it's a little late for that." She glanced back out the door like she was looking for someone. "Phil'Lip," she held her hand out drawing closer like she meant to grab him.

Phillip yanked the back of my wet'skn and pulled me behind him as the teacher came closer.

"You know, I always figured you for one," she was within reach of Phillip.

He lunged forward, keeping himself between us. He kept hold of me as he slammed into the teacher, swinging me past her and releasing me to stumble away from them.

"Run!" he yelled, and wrapped his arms around Mz. Fow'Ler so she couldn't reach me.

There was nothing left to do — I ran.

When I reached the hall, I froze. There was a man coming towards me. I didn't recognize him except for the official uniform he wore. I braced myself, sure I was about to be grabbed. But he didn't even look at me as he splashed passed and entered the classroom.

"The girl, Gil'So!" Mz. Fow'Ler yelled, "Find the girl!"

"What… Where?" He came back out.

I was heading to the front door.

I ran past several teachers, some students, and another official. Not one of them tried to stop me. As I got to the doors, I slowed. They were closed. Two off-worlder officials — one too tall and the other too skinny to be from Uma'Three — were posted outside. I was sure I couldn't get past them without being seen.

Then, one of the officials opened the main door and came in, "You stay here I'll see what she wants." He didn't even pause as he passed me.

I ducked to the side and ran out, not pausing as I passed the second official. I made it halfway home before I stopped. *I still wasn't being chased… Why wasn't I being chased?* I didn't know what to do.

I stood in an open space between three buildings. At the center was a tall rock that Kit and I often walked past on our way to school when we weren't in a hurry.

My heart thudded in my chest.

Kit — where was she? What was happening to her? What had I done? …What would they do to her now?

I had to sit. I leaned against the rock. What kind of trouble was I in?

…And what about my Nan'Dah?

My foot slipped and I slid down the rock so fast I couldn't catch myself. I came up sputtering. A red film ran off me as Phillip's ink dripped from my hair.

…Phillip!

I rubbed my eyes.

I should've gone with him when he asked.

"Hey! You!"

I looked up to see two of the officials from the school coming towards me.

I put my hand to my chest.

"Yes, you. Shouldn't you be in school?"

The shorter one said something I couldn't hear. Then the taller one called, "Is your name Danay?"

That couldn't be good.

I looked between the buildings, gauging whether I could outrun them. I could — but to where? I couldn't go home and I didn't know where Nan'Dah was. What if she was at home? What if they'd already gotten to her? Panic rose in my chest as well as a strong urge to vomit. The men continued to splash their way closer to me.

I knew I needed to run — but my legs had forgotten how to work.

"Danay Qwan." The shorter one called. When I didn't answer he said, "We have orders to bring you in for questioning."

This was it — I was going to be caught then I'd be boiled.

I stood up. The water was thigh deep. I might still outrun them... but swimming would be faster. I took a deep breath preparing to dive... then paused. There was a strange buzzing sound. It bounced off the rock; echoing around to me.

Both of the guards stopped too. They turned around as a jet scooter suddenly appeared from behind a building.

"Danay!" It was Phillip. He passed the guards; engulfing them in a wave of water. One fell backwards. Phillip wasn't slowing. He held his hand out to me as he neared, "Grab my arm."

He passed. I missed.

He swung the jet scooter around and came towards me again. "Danay!"

If I took his arm I wouldn't see my Nan'Dah again. I'd be leaving Tem... I'd be leaving Uma'Three. I'd be giving up my life in exchange for... for what? But what would happen to me if I stayed?

I didn't miss the second time.

Phillip pulled me onto the jet and swerved so it drenched the guards again.

They sloshed after us. "Traitors!" one yelled. The other pulled something out of his jacket. It flashed in the suns.

I held onto Phillip's sides and put my head against his back, shutting my eyes. Three loud cracks boomed above the engine whir, like someone had split a rock next to my ear. Phillip arced around the building and didn't slow. Water splashed my calves making them cold and numb. I gritted my teeth against the sting. I held tighter as Phillip took us around another building.

He kept going and I kept my eyes shut, clinging to him.

~ ~ ~

"Danay," The jet was stopped. "Danay, are you alright?" Phillip was in the water.

I blinked. We were in a narrow alley between two tall buildings. We had to be on the business side of the village. I could smell the pungent stench of raw silt'ment.

"Danay?" he turned and held my hands. "Say something."

I said the only thing that I could think of. "It's illegal to ride a jet scooter in the village."

He chuckled, "Yes it is." He laughed some more. "I'm sure if they catch us that will be our biggest worry."

He was making fun of me. I knew we had bigger problems. But I was trying hard not to think about the future and all of the people I'd doomed. "What now?" I asked.

"We have to get you to my ship." Phillip pushed the scooter, with me on it, through waist deep water toward the docks.

"Where's your ship?" I asked.

"It's hidden in the Deeps. But I've got a shuttle at the docks," his eyes darted all about, his head constantly moving. I could tell he was watching for trouble.

"Phillip?"

"Yeah," he didn't quite look at me.

I didn't care. "What did Mz. Fow'Ler mean by *she always thought you were one*?"

Now I had his full attention, "It figures that she's a Zigelite."

"A Ze—what?"

"A Commoner devoted to Emperor Zigel."

"Oh, and she figured out that you were an Un-Loyalist?"

He nodded, being watchful again.

"And now she probably thinks I'm one too?"

"Or worse."

"What do you mean worse?" When he didn't answer I grabbed his arm, "Phillip, what would be worse?"

He sighed, "We're almost there. We need to ditch the jet."

He moved his hand from the back of the jet scooter to my waist and pulled me into the water. My left knee buckled.

"What's wrong?" He held me up.

"My leg is stiff," I said trying to stretch the sting out.

His arm tightened around me as he stared into the water. "It's not stiff. You're bleeding." He cursed.

I looked down. Sure enough, a soft pink haze had formed around my left leg. "I must have scratched it." I tried to twist to see it better.

"That's not a scratch." His jaw tightened, "It's a bullet wound. They shot you." He cursed again.

I watched a surge of blood pulse out. "Oh. Ouch." Seeing it made it hurt even more.

"Hold on. As soon as we get you to my ship Sue will patch you up." He tightened his arm around me and pulled me through the water.

We reached the end of the building and he carefully peered around it. Then he cursed again. I felt every one of his muscles tense.

"What is it?" I pulled away, straining to see what he was seeing. There were officials swarming over the docks.

Phillip hit the wall with his fist, "Dakkah." Blood dewed on his knuckles. He shook it off in the water.

"We can't make it to the shuttle, can we?"

He shook his head.

"Is there another way back to your ship?"

He squeezed his eyes shut and shook his head again.

"Can you contact them?"

He continued to shake his head. "No one knows I'm here."

This was bad.

"And I can't send them a message without the Emperor's officials finding out." His eyes locked on me. His face darkened, "Dakkah. Dakkah. Dakkah." He banged the back of his head against the wall.

"Stop that." I flicked his forehead.

That seemed to snap him out of it.

"So, we need to hide." I smiled, "I've got the perfect place."

Chapter Eight

The Cave

Phillip insisted on wrapping my leg in seaweed before I took him to the cave. He wouldn't let me do anything for his knuckles — he wouldn't even let me see them.

"There's an air pocket a little ways in," I said as I dove under my building and squeezed through the gap between the silt'ment and the lava rock.

Phillip swam behind me and helped me onto the ledge when we got there. It was a tight fit.

"I hope this isn't it," he said, shifting so he could keep his eyes on the burb sized holes in the wall opposite us. The movement brought him next to me. I felt him exhale. "Though, it could be worse." He glanced at me, "Let me see your leg again."

"There's a larger cave further down the tunnel." With him so close in the dimly lit area, I felt more aware of myself than ever before. As I shifted my leg up it dragged along Phillip's body. "Sorry."

He unwrapped the seaweed. "It looks like the bleeding stopped." He continued to hold my leg. "I'd be happier if I could see it without your wet'skn on."

The thought of taking my wet'skn off made a strange feeling rise up in my chest. I jerked away. He reached out to take my leg again and I caught his arm, "Its fine, how's your hand?"

He made a fist and pulled away, "It's nothing."

After a moment of uncomfortable silence he said, "So, this cave, how big is it and how much farther down the tunnel do we have to go?"

"I'm not sure. Two Turns ago when I found this place, it was a bit of a swim, and I think..." I paused and sighed, "I know Tem sank a little since then. And... and there won't be anywhere in the cave to sit that's dry." I think I was most hesitant about that.

"Well, that's an easy fix." Phillip shifted and pulled something from his pocket.

The movement had him leaning against me. My heart raced and skipped a beat. I swallowed, hoping he couldn't feel it.

"I've got a raft." He held out his hand.

I took the popling-sized ball from him. It was a deflated raft just like the one we'd rented yesterday. "This is great."

From the corner of my eye I saw him grin, "I finally got something right."

"Okay, so now the only problem is making it to the cave before we run out of air." I was one of the best swimmers in the village because I didn't have blubber to slow me down. But I didn't have the double lungs that a naturally born Uma'Threeite did. "How are you at holding your breath?"

"Or," he held up his other hand, "we could use these."

He was holding two objects. They were oval and semi-flat like an ebbin leaf.

"Are those," I took one, "hum'gills?"

He nodded.

I'd never seen one before. They were really rare because they were made from a product found only on Uma'Four. Once trading was banned no more came. "Where'd you get them?"

"We had them on the ship. I thought they might come in handy." He grinned, "Two things right."

I rubbed the hum'gills, thinking about all the deep-sea workers who needed these. Kit'Una's father wouldn't have died if he'd had one when the mine had collapsed.

"Danay?" Phillip touched my cheek.

The movement brought me out of my thoughts. I blushed.

He pulled his hand back, "Here, let me show you how to put it on." He held his up. "First you place the oval over your mouth like this."

He puckered his lips like he was blowing a kiss then pinched the oval where it touched his cheeks. As he pulled, the disk stretched. Once he was happy with its length, he pressed it against his cheek. It stuck to him everywhere he pressed. He did the same on the top around his nose and bottom so that it folded over his chin. Lastly, he poked it into his mouth and each nostril.

"Now, when you go under you have to breathe in through your mouth and out your nose." He sounded like he was speaking with a plugged nose. He bent forward so his face was submerged and took a few deep breaths.

After I put mine on — Phillip double-checking that I had it firmly in place — I dipped my head into the water to test it.

When I leaned into the water, I intended to do it as smoothly as Phillip had. But once my head was submerged, all I could think about was how I couldn't breathe under water. I had had too many bad experiences of getting a lungful of ocean. So I sat, frozen, holding my breath.

Eventually I would run out of air. Eventually I would have to try to breath. *Eventually* took a really long time.

My first breath was in desperation. I gasped. The uncomfortable feeling of water rushing into my mouth didn't last long. I sat up coughing and gagging.

Phillip laughed, "You're supposed to breathe *in* through your mouth and *out* through your nose. Now you've got water in your hum'gil." He pulled it off my face and shook it so it returned to its original shape.

"Ready to try again?" he held it out to me.

I took it, not really wanting to. I put the hum'gil on, making sure it was snug. This time I pulled away when he tried to check it. "I got it."

"Fine." He nodded.

"Let's go." I fell to my right, sliding into the water. I sat, as best I could, on the floor completely submerged.

Phillip copied me.

Under the water Phillip's hair waved around in every direction.

If you knew what you were looking for, the opening to the tunnel was easy to find. If you didn't, you might mistake it for a misshaped part of the cave. I knew I had to follow the lip as it curved. I squiggled in.

The fit was tighter than I remembered, but I could cope. Feeling Phillip's hand brush against my foot every few strokes, I knew he was managing too. It grew dark. We were swimming away from Tem, away from my life. We were swimming towards... *towards what?*

My left leg was starting to sting again. I tried to use it as little as possible.

After thirty-seven strokes, the tunnel leveled out and widened. The water temperature dropped a few degrees. I continued to lead us forward.

I had planned on holding my breath the whole way but just before we reached the end, I felt the lightheaded panic of my brain telling me I wasn't getting enough oxygen. I pulled in a mouthful of water and reminded myself that the hum'gil would sieve air from water. I tried not to panic as it did its job.

Looking up, I could see that the surface of the water was lit by a soft glow.

The cave floor itself was a bed of cooled lava that had formed strange folds and pockets. It was littered with tunnel openings. Some led to dead ends; others back to the open ocean and still others to the volcano that lay deep below Tem. White sand had collected along a ledge of a particularly large hole.

I ripped the raft open and watched it shoot up to the surface. I knew I'd need to take another breath soon and hoped I could make it to the top before that happened.

Half way up something odd caught my eye. I'd only released one raft, but there were two shadows. It didn't take me long to figure out what the second shape was. Swimming towards me was a great white shark.

I gasped and the hum'gil drew air from the water. Below, Phillip emerged from the tunnel.

The great white continued to swim straight at me.

This was not the same one from Tem. First off, I could tell by the point of its snout that it was a male. It was also twice the size of my shark. I braced myself, ready to fight it off. But I didn't need to. It veered away, and began circling.

Phillip swam to where I was suspended half way between the bottom and the surface. He didn't understand what had stopped me.

I pointed towards the shark.

He let out a yelp. His hum'gil popped off and sunk in a swirl of bubbles. I looked down; preparing to go after it, but Phillip grabbed me around the waist and began to frantically kick towards the surface.

The moment he grabbed me; the great white changed its course and headed straight for us, picking up speed as we broke the surface of the water.

The whole cave was alight with the luminescent mi'lex that lived on the cave walls.

"Dakkah! Dakkah! Dakkah!" Phillip sputtered and scrambled onto the raft. He stood up and took my wrists trying to pull me from the water. The shark swam closer — barely a pace away. "Danay! What are you doing?"

The great white dipped under the surface before he reached me. He rubbed his side against my wounded calf. That's when I knew, beyond a doubt, that even though this was not the same white shark that had visited Tem, he was just as friendly.

Phillip managed to haul me up just as the shark made a second pass.

"Do you have a death wish!" he screamed. His hands were shaking.

I pulled off my hum'gil, I was offended. "No. Do you?"

"Me? What? No. I'm not the one who's trying to swim with the shark."

"But you are the one who lost your hum'gil. In case you hadn't noticed, our tunnel wasn't the only opening down there. If I don't get it now it could be lost forever."

"We can deal with that later," he said. He watched the great white, his eyes following it as it circled us. "Right now we have a bigger problem."

"No we don't." I swung my feet back into the water.

The splash made Phillip turn back, "What are you doing?"

"I'm going to find your hum'gil." I was putting mine back on.

"No you're not." He pulled me away from the edge of the raft by the back of my wet'skn.

"Don't!"

His fingers tightened around the top of my wet'skn and no matter how I twisted, I couldn't reach him to make him let go.

"Let me go," I demanded.

"I can't."

"Phillip!"

"Yes, par'mida?" He gasped. "*Par'mida*," he snickered. His grip loosened for a second. It redoubled when I tried to yank myself free.

"Please, let me go."

"I'm sorry, par'mida, I can't. You're bleeding. The shark's already had a taste of your blood. You can't go back in."

I crossed my arms. "Par'mida? Since when did I become *par'mida* to you?"

"Just now." His voice still had a laugh in it.

"Well quit it. And let me go." I watched the shark; it continued to circle our raft.

"I already told you, par'mida, I can't. It's not safe." The way he said *par'mida* didn't make me feel like I was *special* in the good way.

I gave up struggling and settled for crossing my arms, "Listen, Phillip, just because my bracelet says par'mida, it doesn't mean you should call me that. So, stop it."

He flinched, jerking me, "What's wrong with me calling you par'mida?"

"Because it's an endearment that only my Nan'Dah calls me." *What had I done to her? Was she safe? Was she worrying about me?*

"What if I was using it as an endearment too?" Phillip asked.

"Were you?" I tried to see his face. *Was he being serious*?

"I assure you that I only meant it as a compliment."

"A compliment? How?" The shark's pattern was bringing it into a tighter circle around the raft.

"Forget it." He sounded angry. "Until you tell me otherwise, I promise, I will call you nothing but Danay."

What a weird thing to say. "Good," I said. "Danay *is* my name. You shouldn't call me anything else."

His arm jerked again, "I said forget it."

The shark bumped the raft. Phillip fell, pulling me down onto his lap.

"Sorry." His face flushed but his hand stayed tight on my top.

I tried to get up. "Phillip, let go."

"Okay," he released me, "But please, Danay, don't go into the water."

I slid myself off his lap. "You need the hum'gil. Without it you can't get out of here." I stood up and started putting my hum'gil on.

"No!" He stood up and tried to grab me again.

This time I was ready. He didn't get me, but he managed to pull my hum'gil off. He slid it into his back pocket.

I rolled my eyes. I wouldn't need it anyways. The water wasn't that deep. I only wanted it for backup. I wondered, if I found his, could I put it on under water? Would it still work? I shifted closer to the edge of the raft.

"Danay," he took a step towards me.

The shark had backed off; returning to a wider circle the moment Phillip had let me go. That was all the proof I needed. So when Phillip lunged forward and caught me around the waist, I knew exactly what would be coming next, even without seeing the shark's fin.

Seeing it, however, helped me to prepare and compensate.

The great white slammed into our raft and sent both of us toppling over. Had the shark come at us from the opposite side, we would have both landed in the water, and I knew that right now, the water wasn't safe for Phillip. For a fleeting moment I was happy we were still in the raft. However, as I landed on top of Phillip again, that feeling was short lived.

When I tried to roll off him, he followed me. Now he was on top of me. He had a knee on either side of my hips and his hands held my arms down.

"Get off!" He had me pressed tight against the raft.

"I can't."

The shark slammed the raft again; moving us until we were against the wall. When the shark couldn't push any further, he backed off with a swish of his tail. Water rained over both Phillip and me. I got a mouthful that I spat out.

"You have to get off me."

"No Danay—" he said my name the same way he said *par'mida*, like I was the exact opposite of *special*. "—I can't."

"Listen," I craned my neck, tracking the shark. It had backed up all the way to the opposite wall. "You have to let me up."

"Why? So you can go swimming with a man-eating shark?"

"I promise I won't go swimming with a *man-eating* shark."

Phillip didn't let me go. The shark's fin disappeared and I knew I had less than a minute.

"If you don't let me go right now we will both be swimming with the shark." The shark was nowhere in sight. "It's going to flip the raft!"

Phillip looked up. His face changed. He raised his hands high in the air. The shark bumped the raft from below but he'd hit it too much in the center to make it flip.

I pushed Phillip and he rolled on to his back.

"Thank you." I scrambled to the edge of the raft. I was just in time.

The shark had swum to the bottom of the cave and was shooting up towards the raft like an arrow aimed at the heart of its prey. I waved my arms and it swerved, lunging out of the water next to me before sinking back under the surface. Its snout had come within a finger's width of my face. I put my hand out and touched it as it swam away.

Chapter Nine

Stung

"You promised you wouldn't swim with the shark," Phillip said as I bobbed to the surface with his hum'gil — which, I guess, was now mine, since he had pocketed the one I had before.

"I promised not to swim with a *man-eating* shark," I said.

Phillip laughed. "I was only trying to protect you," he added under his breath.

"Why?"

"Why what?"

I got the feeling he was only pretending not to understand the question. "Why are you trying to protect me?"

He sighed, "It's…" he studied his lap, "hard to explain."

"It shouldn't be." I clambered into the raft and sat next to him, pulling a rogue clump of hair out of my eyes. I tried to tuck it behind my ear but it didn't stay. I blew at it then looked up because my skin prickled like Phillip was watching me. I caught him.

He gave me a sad smile, "Can I see your leg again?"

"Can I see your hand?" I leaned forward to take it.

"After I look at your leg," he said dismissively.

"You've already seen my leg… twice. My turn."

He ground his teeth together when I didn't move. His eyes slid to the shark swimming on the outer side of the cave. "Danay, why do you have to be so stubborn?"

He was one to talk.

"My hand feels fine. I'm worried about you. You have a bullet in your leg."

I shook my head and rolled my eyes. "My leg will be fine. I put healing sand on it. I even brought some for your hand." I opened my fist to show him the sand I'd collected from the bottom of the cave. There hadn't been much and I'd used most of it on my leg. I hoped I had enough for Phillip.

"Healing sand?" He sounded like he'd never heard of such a thing. "Show me your leg."

"No Phillip. First you show me your hand."

He didn't move.

"Just give me your hand," I said.

He thrust his hand out, shut his eyes and sighed, "Fine."

I took it and twisted it to see it from every angle. His knuckles were skinned like he'd run them over a metal grate. "Does it hurt?" I asked as I spread the sand over his cuts.

He waited until I was done then jerked away, "Your turn."

I frowned and stood up facing away from him. He pulled the leg of my wet'skn up slowly. I hid my face in my hands as a blush started to warm my cheeks.

"I can see where the bullet went in but I can't see where it came out."

His fingers tickled in a strange way as he ran them over the spot again and again and…

"Wow, it's really healed but the bullet is still in there. Can you feel it?" He pushed on it.

I shook my head. *That was a lie*. I could feel it like a piece of shell in a sand pillow.

He bent my knee several times, twisting it back and forth. I had to concentrate to stay balanced. "Well, it doesn't seem to get in the way of your movement. I'll be happier after Sue's looked at it though."

He ran his hand over the back of my leg one last time. I hadn't expected that. My leg twitched and I fell. He caught me. Then he quickly shifted his position so I was beside him.

"The bullet's left a hole your wet'skn." He stared at my knee as I pulled the wet'skn back down. "By the way what is it made of? Because I don't think it works as well as mine does."

"It's the best we can get on Uma'Three." I pulled my knees to my chest. The left one felt like something was caught behind it. "Where's yours from?"

"Uma'Four."

"Right. That reminds me," I held up my CoaB, "this was from you." If I had any doubt left it was washed away by the look on his face. "Why'd you give it to me?

His ears pinked and he turned away, but he didn't answer.

"Phillip?"

He refused to look at me. Instead, he tracked the shark.

"Why did you give it to me?" *Was it a mistake?* "Did you mean to leave it on Kit's door?"

"N-no, I left it on yours… I just shouldn't have."

He had given it to me!… but now he regretted it? I felt my face fall, "Why?"

"I'm sorry." He turned to look at me then lowered his eyes. "I shouldn't have implied that I'm interested in you."

"You aren't interested in me?" *That really stung.*

He didn't say anything and he wouldn't look at me.

My teeth snapped together audibly. Now I was mad. "You gave me a jewel but you aren't interested in me?"

His mouth was turned down into a frown.

"Why, in all of Quista, did you give it to me then?" I wanted to pick the jewel off and throw it at him.

"Don't do that." He stood up his hands capturing mine. "Please, I want you to have it. The stone is sacred. It's even more precious than a Royal pearl."

"Then why did you give it to *me*?"

"Because," his hands squeezed mine, "Because, I want you to have it."

I wondered how he could say that and yet not be interested in me. I pulled away with a frustrated grunt and fell back into the raft to stare up at the ceiling. Phillip remained standing, tracking the shark, and glancing at me.

Finally he lay down beside me. "I am sorry," he whispered.

I wondered if he meant for me to hear him. I wanted to pull away, but I didn't. Eventually the feeling passed and we both slipped into an uncomfortable silence.

~ ~ ~

"They really are amazing." He was looking at the mi'lex.

"I can't believe you've never seen mi'lex before." Though I'm not sure these really counted. "These are some of the largest and most beautiful I've ever seen." They were as long as my forearm and as fat as my calf. Most mi'lex were a shiny brownish-black color. These were closer to silver with hints of pink and purple.

"So these aren't normal. That makes sense." He looked at me. "I was told that they are overgrown slugs."

"Slugs?"

Phillip smiled, "Right, you probably haven't seen a slug."

"I've seen illustrations, and I don't think mi'lex look anything at all like a slug.

"Do they all glow?" He was staring at the ceiling again.

"Most of them. Mainly the ones that eat eels."

Silence engulfed us once more.

I listened to the lapping of the water against our raft. Felt the strange waves the white shark created as he continued to swim about. And I watched the mi'lex move closer and closer together above our heads. The air was cooling. I could feel the dampness of my wet'skn clinging to my skin. It raised bumps along my arms. I shivered.

"Here," Phillip moved closer and put his hand under my neck. He was warm.

"Thanks," I curled into him, fighting off another shiver. "Is there any way to contact your ship?"

I felt him shrug. "Maybe I can use one of the tsunami warning beacons to send a message."

"Is that possible?"

"There's no guarantee. The ship's communication officer isn't expecting to hear from me, so it could take a while for him to figure it out. And my message will have to be encoded... so he may not even understand it."

It felt like there was something else he wanted to say but didn't. "If they don't figure it out, how will we get to your ship?"

"If they don't come for us in a day or two, we'll have to swim to them."

"Swim? How far into the Deeps is your ship?"

"Far." His bicep flexed under my ear.

"Can we make it that far?" I shivered.

He drew me closer. "We might have to try." He was quiet for a moment. "The hum'gils will give us air no matter how deep we go. The only thing we'll have to worry about is the water pressure... and fatigue."

I didn't like the sound of that.

"We should try and rest. We're going to need it."

"I don't think I can sleep." I was restless and nervous. No matter what, this felt like a doomed situation.

"Not tired?"

"No. It's just..." I really didn't like the idea of swimming around in the Deeps trying to find his ship.

"Well then how bout we talk." He shifted so he could look into my face.

"About what?" I asked.

"What do you want to talk about?"

Staring into his crystal blue eyes made my breath hitch. I blinked and thought for a moment. "Why don't you tell me why you didn't go back to your ship after the Popling Festival?"

His body went ridged, "I— I can't."

"Fine then," I said, but it didn't feel fine. "Why don't you explain why you, the Un-Loyalist are worried about me — a nobody — getting caught?"

"I— I..."

He gagged like he was in pain. Just hearing it made my throat itch.

"I..." He gagged again then shook his head.

"Fine," I closed my eyes, "why don't you just tell me about your ship."

He relaxed, "I'll be taking you to it soon enough. But," he tightened his arms around me, "okay."

~ ~ ~

Phillip's description of the ship launched me into a dream. I'd never really seen the inside of one — but after listening to him, I could imagine what it looked like. The dream was so vivid it felt like I was there.

I was in a brightly lit room. So bright that I wanted to hide my eyes, but my arms were like dead eels hanging at my side. I was on my back. Someone was holding me. I could feel open air all around the impossibly large hands that had me.

"Here she is," someone said.

My ears felt plugged.

"Danay," a woman spoke my name.

I knew that voice. I wanted to turn towards it but I couldn't get my neck to cooperate. I struggled and cried like a baby.

"Take care of her," the voice said. She was sad. She sounded like she was crying. I still couldn't see her.

Suddenly I was shifted to standing but my feet didn't reach the floor. Those huge hands continued to hold me as cloth was wrapped around me. The cloth felt as soft as a popling's nest.

From my new angle, I could see through a door. Lights were flashing — bright red angry lights.

"Go. Quickly," the familiar voice said.

"Are you sure?" I recognized my Nan'Dah. She was so close her voice filled my ear.

"Yes, I'm sure." The first voice was low but firm.

"Isn't there any other way?" My Nan'Dah pleaded, "Surely…"

"Surely not. You must do as I've told you. Go!"

I was moved — swung. Now I could see the other person. *Mom*! I wanted to yell. I kicked and screamed and cried as her face shrank from my sight. I was being carried away. Taken farther and farther away from my mother.

"I'm sorry my little par'mida." I was moved again so I could see my Nan'Dah.

She was younger. Her hair was lighter. Her skin less tanned.

"This is no way to lose your mother, but I promised her. I swear to you that I will take care of you as if you were my own."

I felt movement even though Nan'Dah was sitting with me in her arms.

She continued to speak to me. Soft words. Soothing words. Above her the stars danced and spun.

"Uma'Three," Nan'Dah said looking to the stars. "We are almost home."

Suddenly everything flashed into whiteness. When I could see again, the stars were gone. Instead bits of large gray objects were floating past my view. A few were on fire.

I cried again and when I looked to Nan'Dah for comfort I cried even harder because she was staring at me with wide eyes full of tears. She muttered almost incoherently, "No. No. She can't be dead."

Things blurred.

It felt like my body was being pulled away from my stomach.

I couldn't catch my breath.

"Oh, Danay," my Nan'Dah cried, "It's okay... It's going to be okay."

My eyes felt heavy.

"No," Nan'Dah said, "No! Wake up!"

I couldn't find my breath.

"Wake up, Danay! Wake up!" I was being shaken. "Danay! It's okay! Wake up! Please, wake up!"

~ ~ ~

I opened my eyes to Phillip holding himself over me.

"Wha..." I tried to sit up but Phillip had his hands on my shoulders — holding me down.

"Lie still."

I blinked as I realized that our cave was brighter than it had been before. Only the light wasn't coming from the ceiling, it was in the water.

Something splashed to the right of our raft and Phillip shifted to shield me from the water that shot up.

"What..." I stared up. Almost all the mi'lex had disappeared from the ceiling, "Where are the mi'lex?"

Phillip stared down at me, "In the water."

As he said it, the last few mi'lex slipped from the ceiling and landed with a loud plunk into the water around us. Phillip moved again to shield me from the worst of the splashes.

"What's glowing?" I twisted my head. All I could see was the surface of the water. It was rolling and pitching like it was a pot of boiling water.

"Um, Phillip?" He continued to pin my shoulders to the raft.

His body was pressed against me. "Yeah?"

"They're gone."

He didn't understand.

I pointed up, "All the mi'lex are in the water." He didn't move. "Can you get off me, now, please?"

His face turned red, "Oh. Sorry."

I sat up. Peering over the edge of the raft, the water was alight with zapping eels. There were hundreds of them. They outnumbered the mi'lex three to one. But the mi'lex were flying through the water, chasing the eels and eating them. Both moved with amazing speed and grace giving an underwater light show like nothing I'd seen before. "This is beautiful."

"Careful," Phillip's hand closed around my shoulder and pulled me back as an eel, with a mi'lex in hot pursuit, zipped up towards us.

The eel tried to swim right out of the water. As it hit the air, it lost its momentum and fell back. The mi'lex opened its jaw and downed the eel in one bite. Within seconds, the mi'lex's shine tripled. "Amazing. Wasn't that amazing?"

"It's impressive." He looked around. His tone didn't match his words.

The mi'lex started to swim to the wall. Though it wasn't really swimming, it was more being pushed by the strange current. Once it reached the wall, it slowly climbed back up. More and more were doing the same. The glow in the water dimmed.

I sat up straighter, craning my neck as they gathered over our heads.

Phillip watched through narrowed eyes.

I hadn't realized I was leaning against him until he sighed and shifted.

"Sorry." I pulled away.

The water was calming. The surviving eels were swimming downwards into the tunnels and holes that lined the floor. There was still a charge in the air that made my skin tingle but it was fading.

Phillip kept throwing me nervous glances.

I pulled my knees up to my chin. "Can I ask you something?"

He nodded.

"When I woke up, you were on top of me?" The memory of it brought a blush to my cheeks. "Why?"

His ears were pink. He brought his hand up to his neck then quickly pulled it away. "Because those suckers sting when they touch you."

That's when I saw that it wasn't just his ears that were red. He had a red welt on his wrist, his neck, and one on his ankle. And I could tell from the way he moved that he had more hidden under his wet'skn. "You're hurt!"

"No," he pulled away from me as I tried to touch him. "No, Danay, I'm okay. You were hurt. You were… screaming."

When did I scream? "I'm fine." I bit my lip. Phillip's spots were welling up and getting darker. It had to be painful. "You don't have to play brave for me."

"But," he moved closer, his eyes intent on me, "you're hurt." He ran his hand over my legs then my arms.

"Phillip," I caught his hands before they reached my chest.

He looked too embarrassed to apologize.

"Don't worry." I let him go. "I'm okay."

"But… you were… screaming."

I nodded pressing my lips together. *I must have screamed in my sleep.*

"Why were you screaming?" His eyes were wide — frightened — as he continued to stare at me.

Now I was embarrassed. "It was just a bad dream."

"Oh," he sat back, wincing as he did.

The burns would be setting in. I wondered if I could find more healing sand. I got to my feet.

"What are you doing?"

"You need something for your welts."

"Don't you dare…"

It was too late; I was out of his reach. I jumped before he could think about grabbing me. All in all, it was one of my more talented entries into the water. I managed to turn around as I jumped so I could watch Phillip the whole time.

I wish I hadn't. He was livid.

Without a hum'gil I had to resurface before I could go looking for the sand. I made sure not to come too close to the raft.

"Danay, get back here!" He knelt on the edge, his face contorted with rage. But I knew he was also in agony. I knew all about mi'lex stings, they were a common occurrence in Tem.

"Phillip, I'm fine." I shook the water from my hum'gil.

"I don't understand how you can be." He folded his arms then quickly unfolded them. I saw his pain slip through his carefully composed face.

"Don't worry about me. Now wait here. I'll be right back."

"But the water is full of eels."

I shook my head and dove under. Most of the eels were gone and the water felt nice. It was comfortably warm. There was even a gentle current that made my skin tingle like I was getting a body rub. If I wasn't so worried about Phillip, I might have stayed under longer.

It wasn't just warmer; it was clearer. Like someone had put the water through a high-powered filter making it easier to see everything. I looked from the mussels and clams that were shut tight — safely locked into their protective shells — to the minnows which hadn't been as lucky. Even under the water, they'd been burnt to a charred mass. I collected a few for breakfast and left the rest for other ocean carnivores.

When I reached the bottom there was no more sand to be found. I cursed myself for using so much on my leg. Then I remembered the second best remedy for mi'lex stings.

Zapping eel's blood.

Locating an eel wasn't as hard as I thought it might be. I found a group of them hiding behind a nook in one of the deeper holes. They were small — not much longer than my hand and skinnier than my pinky. I collected up three to be sure I'd have enough blood for all of Phillip's welts.

Holding them tightly in one hand, I looked for some bigger clams or good sized mussels. The eels tried to defend themselves sending a few currents up my arm. But they were too small to do anything more than make my skin itch.

When I got back to the raft Phillip wasn't kneeling anymore. He sat rocking and muttering, "Have to keep her safe. She's all that matters."

"Phillip?" I tossed everything but the eels down. I touched his arm — he was burning up. "Phillip?" I knelt in front of him. His eyes were glassy as he stared at nothing.

"Par'mida?"

"Danay," I reminded him softly.

"But Danay," his words were slurred, "You... ow... ow... p—par— Ow..."

He leaned into my hand, pressing his burning forehead into my cool fingers; heating them up at an alarming rate.

"Wha—ss hap—ping?" His teeth started to chatter.

"Mi'lex," I sighed, "one burn would have been enough to make a normal Uma'Threeite start talking crazy. You have more than four here."

He nodded, or it just felt that way with all his shaking.

"You need to lie down."

He didn't argue.

"Par'mida? Why did they..." He was staring at the ceiling, though I couldn't be sure if he could really see it, his eyes were unfocused. "Why?"

"It was a feeding frenzy." I sighed. "It's rare. Mi'lex are very peaceful by nature." I wasn't sure if he was hearing me, but talking to him made me feel calmer. "They only eat once a month, and even then only a few should have come down. This was an anomaly."

"It's not safe." He continued to stare upwards.

"Quite the contrary," I patted his shoulder, "we are good and safe now. All the mi'lex have fed. They should stay up there for at least a few weeks."

His shaking was getting worse. He tried to say something else but it was just a jumble of sounds.

"Just hold on."

I cracked open three large clams, dug the meat out and set the shells down for bowls. I snapped the eels in two with a satisfying pop of electricity. I squished their blood into the bowls, listening to them sizzle. I was being sloppy in my haste. By the end, the raft and I were covered in blood. I managed to spill some on Phillip but he was beyond noticing the dull charge it gave off.

"If any of the mi'lex were still hungry this would attract them." I chuckled to myself. It wasn't that funny, I just felt like I needed to laugh a little. "That's called irony." I wasn't sure why I was still talking. "Phillip?"

"Par'mida... so cold." Phillip rolled onto his side, and knocked over one of the clamshell bowls. There was so much heat radiating off him, it felt like he'd burn right through the raft.

"Almost done." I was waiting for the eel blood to stop sparking. "Phillip? Did you hear me? Stay with me."

He was unconscious.

I found six welts on his exposed skin; the four I'd initially seen and two more. Then I took his wet'skn off. It wasn't easy. It clung to him. Every time I shifted it, he cried out in pain. I found eight more stings on his back and down his legs.

I lathered as much blood on as I could. With each one, there was an improvement. Finally, his teeth stopped chattering and his delirium was replaced with sleep as the fever broke.

I had to leave him in his under garment; there was no way I could have squeezed him back into his wet'skn. The swelling from his stings made it impossible. For a moment I was glad he wasn't one of those boys who wore tight trunks… or was I? As I checked him over one last time to be sure I'd gotten everything, I noticed the hard lines on his chest. So unlike anyone else's on Uma'Three. I left him and moved to the other side of the raft.

The aftereffect of the frenzy was that the whole cave had heated up. It got so hot that steam started to fill the air. Tendrils of fog wrapped about me as sweat dewed on my forehead and behind my neck. I lay down to get under the steam and tried to sleep. Hearing Phillip's soft snores a pace away didn't help. I was overheating. I wasn't comfortable in my wet'skn. It seemed to be catching and holding the moisture, making me itchy everywhere. There was nothing for it. I stripped to my chest wrap and bathing bottoms, hoping when we woke it would still be foggy.

It wasn't.

Chapter Ten

Split Decision

"Your shark is back," Phillip said when I opened my eyes.

"Wha...?" I rolled until my hand dipped in the water. The great white slid past, brushing my fingers. "Mmmm," I yawned, "morning."

"I think it's closer to the afternoon."

"Afternoon?" I looked up at the mi'lex. They had spread themselves out over the entire ceiling.

"The warmer it is outside the further apart they get. The colder, the closer." Phillip smiled clearly proud of his theory.

"You look like you've recovered."

He was still in his swim trunks, sitting as far from me as possible.

"I have." He looked like he was trying not to look at me, but his eyes kept traveling back. "Did... did I do anything inappropriate last night?" His cheeks were red.

When he looked my way, I shook my head. *What could he possibly be thinking he'd done inappropriately?*

"Good." He rubbed his face. "I had some very strange, freaky, wrong, hallucinations." He wouldn't meet my eyes. "Then I woke up covered in blood... well, I'll just say I'm glad you slept through that part."

I sat up and ran my fingers through my hair to get the worst of it smoothed down.

He chuckled, "You know, when I first woke up I thought I'd killed you. All the splatters of blood, and the pool of it under me, and then I looked at you." His eyes flitted my way and away again.

I looked down. I was covered in blood too. "I should probably clean this off."

He wasn't looking, but he nodded.

"You need to, too."

Another nod.

I went for a swim with our wet'skns to clean them. Phillip refused to leave the raft. So I found him a clump of sea spindling to scrub the blood off. Once he was clean, he went to work on wiping down the raft. As he cleaned, he went from looking at me to the shark as if constantly checking the distance between us. After I was clean, I dove under the water to collect some fresh clams and mussels. I even found an eel. I snapped its neck and brought everything to the surface with me.

"Here," I was treading water holding his wet'skn out to him. He couldn't stay in his swim trunks — *it was too distracting*.

"You should wear mine." He refused to take it.

"Why?" I put his wet'skn next to mine, which was half draped in the water.

"Because mine is not a wet'skn, it's a *dry'*suit. It's made to keep you dry even in the water."

"And if I wear your dry'suit, what would you wear?" I had a thought of him staying in his swim trunks and ducked my head trying to hide my blush.

"I'll wear your wet'skn."

"Then you'll be wet." I tried to hand him his dry'suit again.

He refused it with a shake of his head. "It's okay. I'm not allergic."

"But you told me you have the same problem."

"Right—no. I don't get sick."

I glared at him and he glared back.

Finally I pulled myself from the water to stand next to him, "You're being stubborn. You wear your dry'suit and I'll wear my wet'skn."

"No Danay, it's you who's being stubborn." He bent and picked up my wet'skn. Before I could make another protest, he put both his legs in and pulled it to his waist. He stopped there, leaving his chest bare. "Now let's eat. I'm starved."

I couldn't take my eyes off him while he collected up the pieces of minnow I had gathered the night before. I really liked the contours of his chest. All the boys' chests on Uma'Three jiggled as they moved. Phillip's chest was firm — solid. The girls in Tem never liked that about him. They complained about it when he played during the lunch period game. I, on the other hand, had always enjoyed those times.

However, it was one thing to watch from a distance, and an entirely different thing having him so close. I found it hard to resist my urge to reach out and touch him — just once to see how it felt.

"Danay!" He stood up next to me.

"What?" I checked to be sure I hadn't actually touched him.

"Would you please put on my dry'suit."

I looked down where it was on the raft. *His dry'suit.* That would be like having him touching me, *kinda*. The thought made my stomach flutter nervously.

He didn't wait for me to do it. He bent, picked up his dry'suit and held it out for me to step into. When I didn't, he took my legs, first one then the other, and guided them into the leg holes. As he pulled the dry'suit up, I had to put my hand on his shoulder for balance. When he stood, I got my wish, my hand slipped to his chest. I kept it there as he continued to dress me. I could feel his heart beat. I admired how soft his skin was yet how strong his muscles felt.

I stared at his lips wondering how they'd feel. What would it be like to have them next to mine? I slid my hand to his neck without thinking… then I pulled him closer.

"Danay!" Phillip pushed my shoulder back and stepped away. His face was red, jaw tight.

"Sorry," I sat on the raft. *What had I been thinking?* I stared out at the shark. *What would my Nan'Dah say about the way I'd behaved?*

Phillip didn't say anything and I didn't know what to say.

After a while, he came over and dropped some minnows in my lap. I didn't touch them. I wasn't hungry. *Where was my Nan'Dah? Was she okay?*

"You should eat something," Phillip said, sitting behind me. "I think we should leave soon…" his voice faltered as he tried to sound casual, "as soon as you're done."

Leave? *He wanted to leave now.* Panic welled up in my chest. *I couldn't leave… not without making sure my Nan'Dah was okay.*

I didn't stop to think, I just dove into the water.

"Danay?" Phillip sprang to the end of the raft, his toes curled around the edge. But the great white swam past and he stepped back. "Danay? What are you doing?"

"I have to find my Nan'Dah. I need to make sure she's okay."

"You…" I could see panic in his eyes as he contemplated jumping in after me. "Don't go."

Was he afraid I wouldn't come back? "Don't worry. I'm not leaving you. I'll come back so we can swim to your ship together. I just need to say good bye."

"Danay, Please. What if they find you?"

"I'll be careful." I promised. "Besides, you're the Un-Loyalist. They won't be looking for me."

"But what if they are? What if…" he brought his hand to his mouth then cursed. His eyes locked on mine, "Please, Danay, stay with me. We'll swim to my ship. Once we're there we can send someone to find your Nan'Dah."

"No." It could take another day or two to get to his ship, depending on how deep it is… *and if we could even locate it…* I had to see her now.

He looked at the shark then back at me. "Danay, don't go home."

"I'm not going home." I was offended. "I'm not *that* stupid. I was going… I'll just go to…" but I wasn't sure what I planned on doing. "I'll find Mz. Kal'Lv and see if she knows where my Nan'Dah is."

"That's not a good idea." He fell to his knees and brought his hands together like he was begging. "Don't go."

"I won't be long." I stretched the hum'gil out.

"Danay," his eyes bulged like he wanted to say something more. "Don't get caught."

"That's my plan." I nodded then dove under the water before he could say anything else.

Just before I made it to the tunnel, the shark swam past. The water current spun me. When I turned myself back around, I found the shark lying across my exit. I put my hands on my hips and glared at him. He didn't budge. I shook my finger at him and pointed for him to move. He didn't. I swam up and gave him my best push. Nothing.

Fine, I thought, *that's not the only tunnel that leads out.* I swam away in search of another exit. The shark stayed where he was.

After finding several tunnels that led to dead ends, I decided to explore a small hole on the bottom of the cavern. I was a little nervous about the water pressure the further down I went. But I figured if it got to be too much I could always turn around and head back. I was becoming an expert at that.

It was tough going because this tunnel seemed darker. They had all been dark once I was away from the main cave with the mi'lex glow, but this one was completely devoid of light. After a while, I lost my sense of direction. *Was I going down — or up? Or sideways?*

I traveled a long way. Past any point where I could find air if my hum'gil failed… The thought scared me. I had to put a hand on either side of the tunnel and breathe deeply to calm myself. I knew I had all the air I needed. But I was suddenly terrified that the hum'gil would fall off the way I'd seen Phillip's do.

I strained my eyes for any sign of how much further this tunnel would go. It was no use, I was as blind as furi'mole. Then, suddenly, I could see a soft glow. For a panicked second I thought it might be a lava flow. But the water would be warmer if it was lava. I relaxed.

The glow faded.

I unlocked my grip from the sidewalls and swam towards the receding light. It was coming from outside the tunnel. I swam right out without thinking.

Looking around I could see a gathering of jellies swimming away. I tried to figure out where I was before their light faded. I was on the side of a cliff. Far above I could see a soft hue. The suns called to me like an old friend who I couldn't wait to see again.

I swam up.

The closer I got to the light the more I could see. The cliff was pocked with varying sized cracks and holes. All sorts of sea creatures had moved in, claiming the space for their own. They cautiously watched me as I passed.

Once I was within a pace of the surface, I stopped and waited. Above was Tem — my village. My home. Yet, I was now a traitor. *This was a really bad idea.* But I couldn't turn back now — there was no way I would find the right tunnel to get back.

Breaking the surface and taking my first breath of unfiltered air was euphoric. The feeling left me just as quickly as it came.

I was by the docks where Phillip had said his shuttle was. A floating dock jutted off to my right. I moved closer to it and kept my head low. Where I swam it seemed quiet, but on the other side of the inlet there was a lot of commotion. The Emperor's ship was docked there. People were coming and going from it. Some locals, a lot not — all wearing official uniforms.

I swam in the opposite direction. Away from the ship. Away from the route Phillip and I had taken to get to my house. Away from the market where Mz. Kal'Lv worked — I would have to find another way to get to her.

~ ~ ~

The market was located in an opening between several buildings. It was unusually quiet. There were only ten shoppers and three stands open. I walked over to the plump old lady who Nan'Dah had told me was her friend.

"Good morning Mz. Kal'Lv," I said as I looked about.

"Danay! What are you doing here?" Her eyes darted around the nearly empty square.

"I'm here to buy some food," I said trying to casually look the produce over.

She seemed distracted as she gathered up all the items I pointed to.

As she put them into a bag I leaned closer and lowered my voice, "I also need a favor."

"You need to hide yourself." She unfastened her cloak. "Put this on." She handed it to me.

I took it. The owner of another stand was eyeing me strangely.

"Quickly child," she said. Her eyes focused on the market's entry way. "Cover your head."

I obeyed.

"It's going to be a cold night." She rubbed her hands together, "I can feel it in my bones."

Two people had entered the market. By the splashes they made I knew they were off-worlders. I drew the cloak tighter around myself. *I shouldn't have come here. Phillip was right — I shouldn't have come back.* "I'm sorry, I need to go."

"Wait," she caught my arm, "you need lu'umon berries." She pulled up a bundle from behind the cart. Her eyes followed the slow progress of the officials as they made their way across the square.

I looked over my shoulder and sighed with relief as they left. With the men gone I felt more comfortable to ask, "Have you seen my Nan'Dah?"

She shook her head.

"Can you give her a message from me when you do?" I blinked back the tears that started to collect at the corners of my eyes. I couldn't believe this was how I was going to say good-bye to the only mother I'd ever had.

Mz. Kal'Lv's voice was sharp, "Child, fear not for your Nan'Dah. She will understand. Now go."

"Please… I just… I need you to tell her…" *Tell her what? That I was leaving her? That I'd never see her again? That I'd become a traitor?* "That I love her."

"Danay, par'mida," Mz. Kal'Lv twisted my wrist so the word on my CoaB was faced up, "Your Nan'Dah knows everything you want to tell her. Now get yourself to safety."

"Tell my Nan'Dah that I have to leave Uma'Three," I said.

"Yes, yes, child. You must leave the world. And be quick." She pushed the lu'umon berries into the bag with the rest of the produce and handed it to me. "Now, Go."

When I didn't leave she said, "Quickly child. No more dawdling." She looked frightened. I guess she had every right to be. I was a traitor: she would be in trouble just for talking to me — worse for helping me.

I took the bag and headed for the exit. As I got there, two new officials entered the square. They looked at me as if they were confused. But the longer their eyes stayed on me the less confused they seemed.

"Down with the false Emperor!" Mz. Kal'Lv shouted. I turned to see her throw several items of produce towards us.

The officials turned away from me and started towards her.

I wanted to stop them. I wanted to help her. *Why would she do that? How could she say that? She'd be beaten for it. She'd be killed.* I turned away before I saw what came next. Still, I heard it. The sickening sound of fists hitting fragile skin. The horrible sound of a body splashing into the water.

I bolted into a narrow alleyway. The business district had many corridors to get lost in. I walked as quickly as I could. I felt like I was being followed. I kept looking over my shoulder, expecting to see officials behind me. As I looked back yet again, someone pulled me into a large fissure in the building's wall. They clasped their hands about me tightly — one hand coming up to cover my mouth.

But these were familiar hands. I wasn't panicked. I hugged myself to them as tears spilled over my face. "Phillip, has everyone gone mad?"

"Phillip?" Jef asked. "You're with Phillip?" Before I could worry about what I'd said Jef continued, "Thank the planets and their maker." He continued to hold on to me, "Captain Dis'Hyroo will be so relieved to hear this."

"Who's Captain Dis'Hyroo?" I tried to pull away to look at him.

He held me firmly. "Phillip's father."

"You know Phillip's father?" My life didn't feel like my life. "How?"

"He contacted me shortly after…" Jef stopped and held me out, looking into my face.

I wanted to ask *after what* but I heard what had stopped him. Someone was coming up the ally where I'd come from.

Jef spun me so I was against the wall; he fixed the hood on Mz. Kal'Lv's cloak then leaned in, bringing his face close enough to kiss me. He froze there, "Don't move."

I couldn't even if I wanted to — this didn't feel real.

Whoever was approaching didn't sound local. I couldn't be sure but it sounded like two people. Probably more officials. I held my breath.

As we waited for them to pass I wondered if they were the same ones who'd passed me in the square, or the ones who'd beaten Mz. Kal'Lv, or an entirely new couple. *How many of the Emperor's officials were walking about Tem*?

Jef stayed in front of me the entire time. His frame was tense, the muscles in his forearm bulged like he was preparing to fight.

When we couldn't hear the people walking, and no one else came, Jef relaxed and said, "Danay, we..." his eyes searched my face, "We have to get back to Phillip. Where is he?"

"There's a cave under our complex. We've been hiding there."

"Under our building." He shook his head. "That's unfortunate. The Emperor has that part of Tem heavily patrolled. Is there another way to get to it?"

I nodded. "There is," I bit my lip, "but I don't think I can find it again." And, in any case, I only had one hum'gil. "Jef?"

His face was scrunched up like he was thinking. "Yeah?"

"How do you know Phillip's father?"

He didn't look happy, "I am..." his brow scrunched up further, "I serve the Empress."

"But she's dead."

He nodded, his eyes not leaving my face, "Yes, yes she is. But some of us believe in her spirit. We serve the spirit of her."

A spirit, not even a Royal one, couldn't move planets to keep them from colliding. I wondered if he'd told his parents he believed this — his father would have set him straight. "Did you tell your father about this?"

Jef's lips curled up at the edges, "He's the one who taught me." His voice dropped as we heard two more sets of feet passing in the lane. This time I could tell that they were locals by the sound — or lack of — they made while walking. But there was no way to know if they were officials.

Jef put his face next to mine again, like he was preparing to kiss me, perhaps if we were seen that's what it was supposed to look like. Once the people left, Jef took my hand and started to pull me along. "Come on, we can't stay out here."

My palm stung like he'd scratched me.

"I guess there's nothing for it—" he was saying "—we'll just have to go back to our complex and find a way around the patrols. Maybe..."

He continued talking as he pulled me along. I nodded like I was hearing him when in reality I couldn't quite follow his words and get my feet to work at the same time. My mouth felt dry and Mz. Kal'Lv's cloak started to feel heavy.

Jef stopped talking. That was good. I couldn't hear him over the ringing in my ears. I knew he was still holding me, but I couldn't feel it, my hands had gone cold.

"...Danny, how do we get to the cave?" He stood in front of me holding both my shoulders. He might have shaken me.

The alley felt like it was closing in on us. I kept blinking trying to clear my eyes. Everything was blurring.

"Danay?"

Everything went black.

Chapter Eleven

Great Escape

I opened my eyes to see that we were on a set of spiral stairs. I knew this place. It was the stairwell to the tsunami warning tower. The walls were worn smooth from all the waves that flooded them during the storms. I liked to hang out here because I could feel if a storm was coming by the way the waves moved against the outside of the tower. Today the waters were calm.

Jef was holding me in his arms. I was practically sitting on his lap.

"It's okay Danay, I've got you. Everything is going to be okay."

How could he think anything was okay? I bit my lip, "You know they took Kit?"

He nodded, then bowed his head to rest it on my shoulder. His voice was rough when he spoke, "She's been sent to the Emperor."

"What? No!" I pushed him away and stood up. I'm not sure what I intended to do but I wanted to do something.

"Danny, sit down."

"But we have to… we have to… We have to save her!"

"And we will." He pulled me down next to him and gave my hand a squeeze. "Danay, we will. But first we have to get you to Phillip's ship."

I pulled my hand away. "Did Kit know what you and your father were?" *What would the Emperor do to her if he knew this?*

Jef shook his head looking sick. "I wasn't supposed to tell her until…" his eyes searched my face, "until she came of age."

I closed my eyes. I had been so worried that *my* being a traitor would get her into trouble. This was so much worse! "Did my Nan'Dah know?"

I didn't open my eyes. I felt him nod.

His voice was soft, "She's the one who converted my father."

Now my eyes were open.

"Danay…" Bad news was written so clearly on Jef's face, "About your Nan'Dah…" He brought his arm around my shoulders — giving me no comfort at all. "She was caught last night. They were taking her to their ship when she tried to escape." He took a deep breath. "They shot her."

I slumped against Jef pressing my head into his shoulder.

"She loved you very much." Jef said.

I felt the tears rolling down my cheeks. Tasted them in my mouth. They stung as they slid down the back of my throat.

"…Danay?" Jef was saying something.

I couldn't hear him. *I didn't care.*

"Danay."

Jef moved so he was on the step in front of me. He took my hand, tugging it until I looked at him.

I blinked a few times and stared into his eyes — his golden green-brown eyes, "What?"

"We need to get to Phillip. I'm going to create a distraction." He squeezed my hand making it sting again, then he let it drop and pulled Mz. Kal'lv's cloak hood over my head. "Stay here."

I nodded and shut my eyes, resting my head on the smooth walls.

My Nan'Dah was dead and Kit didn't have long before she would be too. What was left for me? My life was unraveling and I felt like I was being taken apart with it.

I wasn't sure when I slipped into sleep.

~ ~ ~

"Danay? Danay? Danny," Jef pulled strands of my wet hair away from my face. "Come on, now's our chance. We have to go."

"Okay," I sat up but then fell back against the wall. My head was swimming.

He helped me to my feet and down the stairs into the bright suns. His eyes darted back and forth as he pulled me through the calf deep water. "We have to hurry. We only have a couple of minutes before they'll be back."

I nodded, "Okay," but I didn't have any strength. I tripped. He steadied me.

His eyes softened as he stared at me, "Danay, you can do this."

I shook my head, "You should go without me."

"I can't," he said continuing to hold me tight to himself.

"Why? I'm useless. Just leave me…"

Before I understood what was happening, Jef had leaned so close our lips were touching. He was kissing me! We were kissing.

Like a jolt from a zapping eel, I felt more alert.

"Okay?" he pulled away.

I nodded. I was standing without his help.

"Good." He looked over his shoulder, "Listen, if I don't make it, just keep going. Get back to Phillip, he'll know what to do." Jef pulled something out of his pocket. It was a satchel the same size as the one Kit had given me. He pressed it into my hand. "Take this. It's full of burbs. Use them if you get into trouble."

"Use them how?" Jef was pulling me around the edge of our neighbor's building. "Jef?"

We were coming up on the front of our place. Jef kept us close to the wall, craning his neck to look all around, "Good, they aren't back yet."

"Hey!" someone yelled from between the buildings across from us.

"That's them! That's the traitors!" a second person yelled.

"Run!" Jef pushed me forward.

He splashed next to me, pushing me towards our stairwell. The two people were closing the gap as we neared the center of the open space.

"Keep going," Jef said, giving me one final push.

I ran. I made it to the bottom of our stairs when two men wearing the Emperor's uniforms came out of my apartment.

I skidded to a halt and turned back.

Jef wasn't with me.

He was in the middle of the open space fighting with the first two.

"Danny, run!" he called looking back at me.

I scrambled backwards three paces, tripping over the mussel shell pot. The eels were still trapped inside — but not for long. One slid past my ankle.

I barely had time to get to my feet before the two officials from my apartment reached the bottom of the stairs. They splashed into the water with triumphant expressions on their faces.

Their looks quickly turned to shock and pain as an eel zapped them.

I stumbled back a few more paces, watching as one, and then both men contorted with the jolt. They fell onto my stairs.

I turned to look at Jef just as he was hit in the jaw and knocked into the water. One of the men picked him up while the other started making his way towards me. "Stop in the name of High Emper…"

I had the hum'gil out of my pocket and in place within seconds. I dove into the shallow water. Just as I slid under, I heard the distinct sound of someone new screaming out in pain. He'd been zapped too.

I wondered if I should feel bad for enjoying that sound so much.

I swam around to the back of my building. Reaching the tunnel, I slipped into it, hoping no one had seen me. I continued along it, not bothering to stop at the air pocket.

By the time I made it to the cave floor, my energy was fading again. My arms shook. My legs felt like a jellie's tendrils. I wouldn't have made it to the surface if the great white hadn't been waiting for me.

He swam over to me and I took a hold of his fin.

Phillip was ready as soon as we broke the surface of the water.

"Thank the maker and all his planets." Phillip took a hold of me and pulled me onto the raft, "Danay? What's wrong?"

"Too much," my lips quivered, "too much…" *This was all just too much.*

"Okay. Okay." He knelt down next to me. "What do you need? What can I do?"

I felt Mz. Kal'Lv's pack biting into my shoulder. I tried to pull it off. Phillip had to help me. The cloak she'd made me put on was soaked. It clung to me. I tried to lift it over my head but got lost in it. Phillip found me.

"Danay, what's wrong."

I shook my head. I was just too tired. I couldn't even remember how to lie down. I was going to pass out — I could feel it.

"How can I help?"

My eyes felt heavy as I tried to lift them to look at him, "Hold… me."

The last thing I felt was his arms around me.

~ ~ ~

Judging from the mi'lex spacing on the ceiling it was either mid-morning or early evening. Phillip was under me, his arms locked together around me. I lay for a few minutes feeling the rise and fall of his chest. I didn't want to move. I didn't want to wake him. I didn't want him to let me go.

Then my stomach growled reminding me that it had been too long since I'd last eaten. *Was it a day? Longer?* I squeezed my eyes shut trying to ignore it.

Suddenly a shower of water rained down on me. I jumped and Phillip bolted upright, still clinging to me.

"What?" he asked blinking and looking around as if expecting to see someone attacking.

"How'd… where'd all the water come from?" I asked. There was a pool of it in the raft under us.

Phillip looked down at me then, as if just realizing he was holding me, his hands dropped. "The water," he grumbled glaring out at the shark. "You can thank him for that. He's been showering us all night with it."

I glanced at the shark, *that didn't make any sense*. "Weird."

"I'll say. The thing made it absolutely impossible to keep you dry."

I shifted, pulling Mz. Kal'Lv's pack closer. My stomach continued to contract painfully like it was attempting to eat itself.

"Danay," Phillip was staring at me, "what happened yesterday? In the village?"

I didn't want to think about it. I couldn't think about it. "Have you ever tried these?" I held up the bundle of lu'umon berries.

"No." He was clearly annoyed that I'd avoided his question, but he didn't say anything about it. "I don't even know what they are."

"It's a kind of fruit that grows on the floor of the sea. When they're in season they float up to the surface." I picked a few to munch on, "These are my favorite. Every Turn, no matter what season my birthday falls in, my Nan'Dah gets..." It took all my strength to swallow. I didn't bother to stop the tears or even wipe at my running nose.

"You heard something about your Nan'Dah?" Phillip moved closer. He used Mz. Kal'Lv's cloak to wipe my face.

"Worse."

I told him everything.

He stayed quiet for a long time after I stopped talking. Until my stomach gave another growl.

"You need to eat." He picked up Mz. Kal'Lv bag. "Once you're done we'll leave for the ship." He took out the vegetables one at a time, offering each to me. I took one of everything. He took some things too.

"So, Kit'Una has a brother?" He asked. His voice sounded strained.

"Yeah, Jef. You didn't know?"

Phillip shook his head.

"Because he knows who you are. He's even talked with your father."

"First I've heard of it." Phillip scowled.

Was he upset that he hadn't known? I was upset. I hadn't known about any of this. I folded my arms.

"Danay, what's wrong."

"How could Jef be a traitor all these Turns?" I stared at Phillip until he shrugged. "And how could my Nan'Dah be one?" More tears stung the corners of my eyes. "How could... why didn't..." I rubbed my tears away. "I can't..."

"Shhh. Shhh." Phillip shifted closer and pulled me against his chest. "It's okay. It's going to be okay."

"How can you say that?" I pushed him away. "It's not okay." *Everything was wrong.* The tears blurred my vision. It made me angry.

"Danay?" Phillip reached for me.

I knocked his hand, "No. It's not okay and don't tell me it will be." I took another handful of lu'umon berries, and shoved them into my mouth.

A strange silence settled between us. I didn't care. I was just finishing off the last of the lu'umon berries when he spoke again.

"You know, there still might be hope for Kit'Una."

I understood why Jef wanted to believe that. I couldn't understand why Phillip would... unless he did like her...

"We can fight the Emperor," he said.

"Do you really think that's a good idea?"

"What wouldn't be good about it? The Emperor is... well he's not the best ruler. Everything he touches he turns ugly. Don't you think it would be better to have someone else on the throne?"

I shook my head, "Phillip, without his Magic all of Quista will be doomed."

Phillip sat forward; his eyes alight with excitement, "What if I told you we found another source of Magic."

"Do you mean the Empress's spirit?"

He nodded.

This idea scared me to the core. "But a spirit can't perform Magic? How are you going to keep the planets in their place the next time they have a close pass?

"We have a theory..."

"And you're willing to risk all the planets, and the lives of everyone who lives on them, on a theory?" *On a bad theory*, I didn't add.

"But I've seen it work. And it's not a spirit so much as..." he flinched, "um... we've found," he flinched again and brought his hand up to his mouth.

"What have you found?"

Phillip struggled for a few moments. He looked like he was trying to think of what to say. He opened his mouth then shook his head. He opened his mouth again then made a gagging sound. Finally he looked down into his lap and muttered, "Sorry."

I frowned. I wanted to demand he say something but as I shifted forward something dug into my hip. I pulled the bulge from my pocket and looked at it.

"What's that?" Phillip asked.

"Jef gave it to me." I turned the satchel over in my hands. "He told me it was full of burbs. He told me I should use them if I needed to."

Phillip's eyes were wide. He moved back a fingers width.

"What do you think Jef meant by *use them if I need to*?"

Phillip shrugged. "It couldn't hurt to keep them in your pocket though, just in case." His eyes stayed on me, making me feel like he knew something that he wasn't telling me.

"*How* am I supposed to use them?" I dumped the contents out onto the palm of my hand.

Phillip scrambled back, and then leaned forward. "Those aren't just burbs, there's a…" He reached out but stopped himself. "That's a pearl." His voice carried a tone of outrage. "You never said Jef was a suitor."

"He's not a suitor. He's Kit's brother." I shifted my hand so I could see the pearl better. "He's practically *my* brother."

"Then why did he give you a pearl?"

I couldn't think of a logical answer. I picked the pearl up and held it higher to see it better in the florescent glow of the mi'lex. It was slightly bigger than my thumbnail, lighter than the other pearl, and had an iridescent purple color. It also had a strange hole running through it, not like a professionally set one, but like some kind of weevil had bored its way right through it.

"Maybe he meant it just as a friend? Like when you gave me the jewel."

"Maybe," Phillip said between his teeth then he turned away and mumbled something to himself.

Jef had given me a pearl. Did that mean Jef liked me? *He'd never acted like he liked me…* But as I thought about it, I started to see our visits differently. The way Jef stared at me when he didn't think I was looking. The way he was overly friendly, even when Kit wasn't there — especially when Kit wasn't there. And, yesterday, he'd kissed me and I'd felt something. Something that was more than just being friends.

Had Jef wanted to be my suitor?

I looked up. Phillip was staring at me. His hand stretched towards me. "Give me the pearl." He almost demanded.

Why did he want it? What was he going to do?

"Come on, I'll put it on your CoaB for you."

I hesitated, and then handed it to him, "Thanks."

For a second he held it, rolling it between his fingers. He was frowning. I pocketed the burbs and held my wrist out to him. Phillip sighed as he slid the pearl onto the same string where Kit'Una's charm hung.

I held my arm up to admire it. It was one of the biggest Royal pearls I'd ever seen. *How had Jef afforded it*? Would he really have given me this if he only wanted to be my friend?

The shark bumped the raft and I looked up in time to see Phillip reach out. I thought he was catching me, but instead he pushed me into the water.

"Get her out of here!" he yelled. He was looking at the shark.

I looked past the shark. Several people were swimming up towards us. They wore official uniforms, diver's masks, and some of them held machines that pulled them through the water — fast. At least five had come through our tunnel and more were arriving behind them.

"Danay! Go!" He threw me Mz. Kal'Lv's shoulder bag with the rest of the food.

I hooked the pack through my arm, "What about you?" He was still standing on the raft.

"Just go."

I didn't want to leave without him.

I opened my mouth to argue but the shark gave an impatient flick of his tail, showering water over my head. Then he rolled towards me — handing me his fin. I took it.

"Stay with the shark. Someone will come to—"

The shark pulled me under the water.

I didn't have enough time to put my hum'gil on. The shark swam straight for the group of officials, mouth open, teeth bared. I got the hum'gil on just as the officials scattered like a school of tuna.

As we reached the biggest tunnel on the cavern floor, something whizzed past my ear. Then we were past the tunnel mouth and all too quickly we were enveloped by the dark. The shark was swimming so fast it took all my strength to keep my hold on his fin. The waters cooled several degrees with each moment. I worried about the pressure — we were descending fast. Suddenly the shark stopped.

Chapter Twelve

The Deep

All was dark. I couldn't see a thing but I sensed that we'd come to the end of our tunnel. I imagined an opening like a great mouth about to swallow us whole.

The shark was waiting for something. I took a moment to pop my ears and check my hum'gil. Then I adjusted my grip on the shark's fin and gave him a gentle squeeze. *I was ready.*

He took off.

Between the water that rushed past us and the pressure I could feel in my head, my breaths were shallow. My vision swam. Not that I could see anything in the dark — I just knew that if I could, I'd be seeing double. Yet, the dark wasn't quite as black as the tunnel had been.

I didn't dare try to pop my ears again, fearing that I would lose the hum'gil. Every shallow breath I took, I was relieved it didn't fall off. We were so far down I'd be dead without it.

Something flashed up ahead. Another quick red pulse flared as we neared it, passed it, and one last time over our heads as we continued to plummet further down. I wondered whose beacon it was.

Still the shark swam down, though I had no sense of direction. Hours passed, or minutes that felt like hours. Finally I was able to make out something, a very faint glow. We were heading straight for it. I wondered if it was the other side of the ocean and the shark was drawing me back up to the surface. Though, logically, I knew it couldn't be.

The closer we came, the more I could make out. I stifled a gasp when I realized it was lava. At first I worried, but the shark swam parallel to it, so I relaxed. Molten rock warmed the water around me. My fingers started to thaw. As the heat settled through me, I began to shiver, and as I shivered, the shark shuddered.

He was slowing, his movement choppy. He'd changed his course. My hair pulled at the back of my head instead of trying to rise above it. The lava flow snaked below us like a river and by its light I could see nothing in the murk of the water.

When the lava flow ran out, I was engulfed in the dark again. I wasn't sure how much more I could take. That's when I noticed a black shape looming ahead of us. The shark banked right and traveled along it.

I put my hand out to brush the shape. It was soft like fresh cloth — *could this be where the silk eels lived*?

The shark stopped. Below us a round spot glowed and gave off heat. It wasn't nearly as warm as the lava flow but it was warmer than the water around us. The shark swished its tail and my hand slid off. I drifted towards the light colored ground and my feet sank into it.

It was sand. White healing sand that glowed. I wiggled my toes, feeling the grains slip between them. It warmed me all the way up to my knees. I bent and thrust my hands into it, trying not to sigh my hum'gil off as relief flooded me. I could feel my fingertips again.

Healing sand. Mi'lex would be close by. They needed air — real air. There was real air somewhere nearby.

I blinked into the gloom that surrounded me. I looked up at the shark, swimming back and forth against the cliff. Then I looked at the cliff. *Of course*, there had to be a cave. As I looked for the opening, I realized that I was looking straight at it.

A patch of sand had gathered in a zigzagging shape up the wall. I tried to touch it. It wasn't the sand that was an odd shape, it was a crack. A crack big enough for me to fit through. The shark must have brought me here on purpose. I looked up to where he swam, now just a few paces above my head. For a moment, I deliberated, not wanting to leave my protector — *my friend*.

He swam down, nudging me towards the crevice. As he passed, I saw a gash running along his entire flank. He'd been shot and split open. Blood spiraled off him with each flick of his tail. I knew it was going to attract predators. I'd be safer in the cave.

I rubbed his snout as he made one final pass. Then I left him to his fate.

Navigating the crack was tricky; it was a tight fit. Once inside, I couldn't swim, I had to walk. There was a gentle incline. The path was lined in calf deep healing sand. The warmth from the sand transferred to the waters. It felt like being in the shallows around Tem. It heated my bones; drawing out the bits of chill that had clung to them.

My way was illuminated by the glow of the sand. After I ducked through a low part in the tunnel I could see, through the surface of water, cavern walls aglow with mi'lex. As my head broke the surface I gave a shout of joy which popped off my hum'gil. My voice echoed back to me and I fished my hum'gil out of the water to pocket it.

Walking to the shoreline, I saw that the cavern was as tall as my complex and almost as round. There were a good twenty paces of dry sand. The walls and ceiling were lined with mi'lex of a size I'd never seen before. These were a typical brownish-copper. Their glow wasn't as bright as the glow of the mi'lex under my complex but there were twice as many.

I thought about the mi'lex in the other cave, wondering if these mi'lex ever left the ceiling like the others had. Suddenly one of the creatures fell and landed on the sand a couple of paces away. I went to investigate. It was dead; its edges had already turned white. In a few days, the entire creature would crumble apart and become part of the healing sand.

Looking up, I didn't get the impression I was unsafe here.

There was nothing more for me to do, I chose a spot about half way between the water and the wall, lay down and covered myself with loose sand. Lying still, feeling heated from all sides, I let exhaustion take me.

I woke up a few times and ate a portion of the food I still had from Mz. Kal'Lv's pack. And I checked the mi'lex — they hadn't moved.

I wondered what it might be like to live down here if Phillip's people never found me. He was caught, so how would they know to look for me? And why would they — I was no one. They were better off without me. They could fight their battle with the Empress's spirit and leave me out of it.

I was almost happy about the thought. I could stay safe on Uma'Three. I'd never know if they'd been successful. On the other hand if they failed I might figure it out, as Uma'Three perished along with the eleven other planets in our solar system. For just a brief moment my heart felt heavy for everyone who would die. But I couldn't do anything about it.

The last time I buried myself in the healing sands they didn't sooth me. My food had run out. Next time I woke up, I'd have to do something about it. I was going to have to leave the safety of my cave. I dreaded waking up.

~ ~ ~

I awoke with a start, my mind telling me I wasn't alone. I froze. I was still buried in the sand. I opened my eyes and looked past the strands of hair that covered my face.

The water rippled like it had been disturbed but I couldn't hear anything else — then a boy said, "Check further in. I bet my dessert that she's here."

I blinked and strained my eyes as far as they would go without moving my head. Looking past my nose I could see someone. I blinked a few more times to bring him into focus and saw Phillip.

He smiled, his lips parting like he was about to say something.

I started to sit up.

"Remember, Phillip, we have our orders." The other boy said. "We are to take her back to the ship. No more talking about it — it has to be done so we can get off this wretched world."

Phillip tuned to look at the other boy, "How do you intend to make her go?"

"Tom gave me the stunner to use."

Panic cut off my air. *What was a stunner? Whatever, it didn't sound friendly.*

Phillip was blocking me from seeing the other boy. He was also blocking the boy from seeing me. "Collin, is that really necessary?"

"Yes." Collin said, but his voice wobbled. "We don't have any more time for this," he said, sure of himself. "She needs to come to the ship."

Phillip turned back to look right at me. "It looks like she might have been here earlier," he said. "But I don't see her now." He turned away. "Collin, why don't you double check further down the cliff? See if there are any caves that way."

"You don't see her? Well, crap," I heard him kick the sand, "I was looking forward to dessert. Rom is making chocolate cake."

"I guess it's doubles for me. Maybe she's in the silk nests." Phillip walked towards Collin — away from me.

I didn't want Phillip to go.

"Really? The silk nests? Why would she go there?" Collin said." It's cold out there. Let's just stay here. If she was here earlier then she'll be back."

"Collin, you should at least check it out."

"No Phillip, you go check. I'm staying here."

They were silent for a few breaths.

"Why don't I stay here?" Phillip said. "And you go back to the ship to give an update?"

"I don't want to. It's freezing out there," Collin said with a whine. "No, she's gotta be here. Where else would she go? That great beast of a shark is right outside. He died guarding *this* spot." He started walking closer.

I held my breath. His feet were headed my way — pretty soon he'd be stepping on me.

"Collin, stop!" Phillip said as I sat up.

Two paces from me stood a tall green-skinned boy. At first he looked surprised but as his gaze met mine his eyes narrowed.

"Get up," he said slipping his hand into his pocket. "It's time to go."

I looked at Phillip.

"Collin, can't you see how scared she is?"

Collin's face softened for a fraction of a second, "Hey, there's no need to be afraid. Okay? We're the good guys." He pulled something shiny from his pocket.

I shifted making sand fall loose. "Then why are you going to shoot me?"

"I'm not going to shoot you." His hand tightened around the object.

It was hard to believe him.

"Listen," Collin stepped closer, "*we* don't want to hurt you but other people do. You need to come with us." He pointed the silver thing at me. "Now."

"Some good guys we are," Phillip muttered. *But he wasn't stopping Collin.*

I looked at Collin. His eyes narrowed. His grip on the object was so tight his hand shook. But he continued to point it towards me. *How could I trust him… how could I trust either of them.* "Why? Why should I trust you? Why do other people want to hurt me? Why…"

"No more questions." Collin lunged at me.

I scurried back out of his reach.

"Collin, don't!" Phillip said. But he hadn't moved from where he stood.

Collin clenched his jaw. He looked sideways at Phillip, "Phillip, help me! She needs to come with us!"

Phillip closed his eyes, shaking his head, "Not like this."

"Fine, don't help. But you can be sure I will tell Tom about this." Collin turned to me and lunged again.

"Stop!" I put my hands up.

He stopped, holding the weapon a finger's width from me. Phillip had frozen too. He looked like he was reaching out to grab Collin.

I tried to sound brave as my heart thumped against my chest, "I'm not going anywhere until someone can tell me why…" I looked from Phillip to Collin. "Why do I need to come to your ship?"

Collin opened his mouth but nothing came out. He opened it wider then closed it, swallowed, and opened it again. His eyes bulged. He gulped like it was hard to swallow. He looked more like a tuna out of water than someone trying to speak.

I looked to Phillip. He just shook his head. I looked back at Collin, "I'm not going to your ship and you can't make me."

He took the tiniest of steps back then stopped himself. "No. You have to come with us." His words were closer to pleading than angry. His face, however, was closer to anger than pleading. His next words were said through clenched teeth, "I do this for you." He jabbed the silver object at me.

I ducked out of his reach.

Phillip grabbed Collin and pulled him away from me just as the sand in front of me exploded with jumping burbs.

"What the…" Collin scrambled back, tripping over Phillip. They both fell to the ground.

Phillip was the first to stand. He took Collin by his shoulders and threw him away from me. "Get out of here!"

Collin stumbled all the way to the water. "Phillip, remember what Tom said."

Phillip shook his head, "I don't care. I'm staying." He looked down at me then his gaze traveled to the hopping burbs and he slid back two finger widths. He looked at me again his lips pressed together.

"They aren't going to like this." Collin had his feet in the water. He pulled a hum'gil out of his pocket. "You should've let me stun her." He started to fix the hum'gil to his face.

I wanted the green-skinned boy to go and never come back. I narrowed my eyes to glare at him.

Collin yelped like he'd been bitten. He fell into the water and didn't surface.

Phillip stood looking away from me — watching the water where Collin had disappeared. "I'm sorry, Danay, Collin should never have…" his words died as he turned to face me.

"Phillip," I looked up at him as the burbs continued to bounce between us. "Why is it so important that I go to the ship?"

"Because you aren't safe here."

"Why do you care if I'm safe?" I didn't understand; he had given me the jewel, but he'd also said he didn't like me like that.

"Because…" He took a small step in my direction. The burbs were hopping so fast it was as if they were keeping time with my racing heart. "Because I don't want anything bad to happen to you." *So, I guess in some way he did care about me…*

I slid myself closer to the burbs — closer to Phillip. Suddenly I wished the burbs weren't in the way. I wanted to go to him… *no, I wanted him to come to me.*

Phillip stayed just far enough away that the burbs couldn't land on him. He was watching me: wearily… concerned… carefully… I could see that he cared. And it was because he cared that he wanted me to go to his ship. It made sense… *but why did Collin want me to go*? Why was Collin willing to stun me to take me to their ship?

Suddenly the burbs were hopping faster.

Phillip looked like he wanted to move back but he stayed where he was.

"Phillip, why do other people want to hurt me? Or was Collin lying?"

"Collin wasn't lying," Phillip said softly looking down at the sand.

"Then why do other people want to hurt me?"

Phillip ran his hand through his hair, "I… I can't explain it."

I was getting tired of this. "You have to tell me something!"

"All I can tell you is that I am Phillip Dis'Hyroo. Son of Gredd and Donna Dis'Hyroo, Un-loyalists to *High* Emperor Zigel of Quista. And I'm willing to fight him to put the rightful heir on the throne."

"But all the Royals are dead. High Emperor Zigel—" I gagged, "—is the only one left. He is the rightful heir."

Phillip took a huge breath and slowly released it. "That's not…" He frowned, "There's…" He shook his head.

"That's not… what?" I was so frustrated I made fists, "There's… what?"

He brought his hands up to his face rubbing until his skin was red. When he spoke, it was with a shaky voice, "I can't tell you."

I jumped to me feet, "Why not? Don't you trust me?"

"I trust you. That's not it. It's just that…" His voice cracked. "I *can't*."

My nails were biting into the palms of my hands, "Why not?"

"Please, Danay, please believe me — I want to tell you..." Before he was able to say *I can't* one more time, a burb landed on his foot and started to burrow. He howled and hopped backwards on his good foot. For just a moment I was glad he was in pain. Then the moment was over. The burbs seemed to follow him. They overtook him and he went down. Flat on his face. He rolled to his back and pulled his hands and legs inwards, away from the burb littered sand. But it didn't help. He had two burrowing tracks in one arm and five in the other.

The burbs continued to burrow deeper and deeper. His wails bounced off the walls and back at me from every angle. Blood was dripping out of the burrow holes leaving red tracks on his white skin. It poured off him making the sand sizzle under him.

"I'm sorry Danay," he choked. "I'm so sorry. Please — please forgive me."

His words sounded like a dying man's last wish.

"No." I fell to my knees flicking at a burb that had landed on his dry'suit. My swat caused it to fly paces away where it hit the sand and exploded into a popling. More burbs were landing on him.

Phillip convulsed as he drew himself in a tighter ball. Then his face paled and he started to moan.

"No! No! No!" I kept swatting until every burb was gone.

His limbs fell loose and his breathing became labored.

I leaned over Phillip, tears blurring my vision. "Phillip?" My voice wobbled, "Phillip?" He shuddered under me but didn't respond. "Phillip! You can't die."

I had to get the burbs out. *But how*? For everything I knew — I'd never been taught this.

Phillip reached a shaking hand up to my face. He tried to brush at my tears. The blood from his fingers mixed with them. I tasted copper and salt as they slid past my lips.

I caught his hand and held it. I could see the burrow hole just above his wrist. "I—" I looked down at Phillip. "I don't know what to do."

He stared up at me; a mixture of agony and awe on his face.

"I need to get the burbs out," I said through quivering lips. "But I… I don't know how." My shoulders fell as a sob wracked through me. I pulled his arm to my chest hugging it.

"Don't cry," his voice was soft, "talk," his eyes fluttered like unconsciousness wasn't far, "talk to them."

His eyes rolled into his head.

Chapter Thirteen

No Matter What, My Life Felt Doomed

"Phillip!" I shook his arm.

He winced but his eyes stayed closed.

"Talk to them?" *That sounded too easy* — after all, I'd been talking to burbs my whole life.

I held his wrist up to my mouth and gave it a gentle kiss. Kisses had always made me feel better when I was hurt as a child. His fingers twitched.

"Okay," I tried to imagine the burb. "This is not where you want to be." I said to it. My voice gained in strength with each word. "Come out and I promise I will help you pop."

At first nothing happened. I was disappointed, though I couldn't say I expected it to work. Then Phillip gasped, his back arching, while the blood from the wound gushed quicker. For just a second I worried that the burb had popped, but as I watched, I saw it tracking back up his arm.

As it exited, I caught it between my finger and thumb.

"That's a good burb," I said and blew on it until it popped.

It floated up to the ceiling; it's outer down tinged pink by Phillip's blood. Once it reached the top of the cave it hovered there where it was swallowed up by one of the mi'lex.

Phillip contorted in pain each time I coaxed one of the burbs from his body. That part didn't get any easier and my kisses, both before and after, grew in number.

By the time I released the last burb, which had burrowed near his collarbone, I must have kissed him twenty times.

Then I covered his wounds with healing sand that sizzled as the wounds knit shut.

As if he knew I was done he sighed and rolled to his side. I sat by him at first, but as the hours drew on I got restless. I paced the cave over and over, exploring every finger width of its outer walls. The only way in, or out, was through the water.

I half expected Collin to return. I spent a lot of time wondering what I'd do if he did — and what I'd do if he tried to stun me again. Then I wondered if he was waiting outside the cave. I didn't want to find out, but eventually I realized I had to: I had to leave the cave to find something to eat; my stomach was so empty it hurt.

When I went out, there was no one there. I was all alone.

Through the gloom I could see the remains of the great white — my protector. Tufts of skin hung from his bones; swaying in the subtle current. Jellies ghosted about, their tendrils collecting all the shark meat they could find.

I sat in the sand that had poured from the tunnel. I had to make a decision.

As I saw it I had two choices: Go with Phillip to his ship; where Collin would be with the stunner — where everyone was an Un-Loyalist — where they intended to use the Empress' spirit to wage a war on the Emperor. Or, I could leave now. Find another hiding spot somewhere on the ocean floor: without company, or food — alone. I would still be considered a traitor. I couldn't return to Tem. I wouldn't find out what happened to Kit, never see Jef, and definitely never see Phillip again.

I guess I had my answer, because no matter what, my life felt doomed — but I didn't want to face it without Phillip.

I took my time getting up to return to the cave.

I collected a few ribbons of the shark's fleshy meat for a last meal. Then my foot caught a patch of seaweed and dislodged a tumble bush thick with ripe lu'umon berries.

"Thank the planets and their maker!" Phillip's face brightened when he saw me. He was sitting at the edge of the water. He watched, unmoving, as I wrung out my hair and walked past him onto the sand.

I dropped the lu'umon bush and sat. For just a moment I admired Phillip's profile. He was staring at the water. His head was held high. His neck was slim and long. In his stillness he looked strong. "Phillip?"

He turned stiffly and winced.

"Still hurts?" I found that just a little satisfying — *I shouldn't have.*

"A bit." He crawled over to me sitting half a pace away. He plucked a single lu'umon off the bush and rolled it back and forth between his finger and thumb. "I told the cook about this fruit. He said they're poisonous."

"I eat them all the time. It hasn't killed me." I sat with the shark meat on my knees and started to pick off the bits of skin. "Just because most people don't like them doesn't mean they're poisonous."

"Don't most people use them to make floating paste?" He kept rolling the berry between his fingers.

"Yeah, that's all most people think they're good for. But they are delicious to eat."

Phillip looked skeptical.

"You should try it." I pushed his hand towards his face.

His eyes narrowed.

"Phillip, just eat it."

He put it in his mouth. I watched as his teeth broke through the tough skin and the thick sour juices hit his tongue. His face was priceless.

"Keep chewing. Don't swallow yet. Trust me, it gets better."

He looked like he wanted to spit it out.

"After everything I've trusted you with, the least you can do is listen to me about this." I raised my eyebrow at him.

His eyes watered as he labored to keep his jaw moving. Finally his face cleared. He'd worked past the sour taste to the sweetness, it took a while but it was well worth the effort.

"Oh my." He swallowed, and smiled, then took a huge handful and put the lot into his mouth. "These are better than any chocolate cake Rom could make."

I frowned.

"What is it?" he asked past the greatest sour shudder I'd ever seen.

"How long until Collin or someone else from your ship comes for us?"

He continued to chew and only after he'd swallowed said, "I was hoping to convince you to come to the ship on your own before that happens."

Perhaps I should have told him I'd already decided. Instead I asked, "And how are you planning on doing that?"

"I'm going to help you understand what's going on."

"Oh, yeah?" I crossed my arms. "How are you going to do that when you can't *tell* me anything?"

He shrugged, "I'm not sure yet. But I promise, you don't have to leave this cave until you want to."

I wondered what he could say that would make me *want* to.

He said nothing.

I plucked at the lu'umon bush.

Phillip watched me — still saying nothing. After an eternity of silence I wondered if he regretted making the promise.

"Here, try this," I said handing him some shark meat.

"I can't eat that!" He pulled away.

"Why not? It's good."

"It's… it's *your* shark."

"Yeah? So?"

"So!" His eyes grew wide like he couldn't believe he had to explain this to me. "That creature gave his life to protect you."

"He did." I smiled sadly thinking about it.

"How can you eat him after what he did?"

I frowned, "It would be disrespectful to let his sacrifice go to waste." I put a piece in my mouth letting the smoky taste tickle my tongue. After I swallowed, I held out a new piece to Phillip.

"But…"

"Quit arguing and eat it. It'll be good for you."

He took the shark meat and put a small bit into his mouth. He looked like he wanted to be sick. I turned away and ignored him.

He did eat it all, only slowly. Once he was done I went over to the farthest corner of the cave to toss the uneaten shark skins at the walls for the mi'lex. I watched them glide over to where the skins had stuck.

"Danay, I…" Phillip stood behind me.

I turned when he didn't continue. He was staring at me, looking the way Collin had: his mouth opening and closing without anything coming out. He shut it with a frown and scratched at his wrist.

All that was left from where the burb had burrowed was a soft pink scar. I resisted reaching out to touch it while I thought of how I'd kissed him there earlier.

"Danay you…"

I looked up at him.

He shut his mouth and dropped his wrist. His eyes were narrowed. He seemed to be chewing on his tongue.

"You don't have to tell me anything." I looked down at his toes. "It's okay. You can take me to your ship now."

"Uh-uh," his hand cupped my chin and pulled my face up to see him, "not until you *want* to come. I promised you that."

I pulled away from his touch, "But maybe someone there can tell me what you can't."

"That's the thing," his voice rose, "no one on the ship will be able to tell you this either."

"Fine!" I kicked out at the sand and started to walk away.

"Danay," he caught me by the shoulder, "listen."

"Listen!" I glared at him. I was so frustrated my eyes stung. "How can I listen when you aren't saying anything?"

"I'm trying," he growled.

"Well, don't let me stop you!" I folded my hands over my chest.

He laughed. It wasn't a short kind of laugh. It went on and on. By the end he sounded almost maniacal. Eventually the sound died in his chest. He rubbed his neck looking apologetic, "I'm sorry, but that *was* funny."

"Was it?"

He nodded trying not to laugh again.

I rolled my eyes and sat down, leaning into the cool cave wall.

He sat in front of me, "How about I start with some history."

"History? How's a history lesson going to help?"

"Because… because I can tell you this." He smiled at me, "Alright?"

My brow creased as a flash of Mz. Fow'Ler's questions ran though my memory. "I don't particularly like history."

He grimaced, "Maybe you'll like it better the way I tell it."

I shrugged. None of this really mattered. I'd already decided I'd go with him.

"Danay, how much do you know about Duncan and his two wives?"

"Duncan, Dorris, and Dezarah. They were the ones who found Quista." I knew this story well.

"That's right." Phillip nodded. "They came here looking for a new world because their solar system had died."

"I heard it was destroyed by the Scientists there."

He winced. "It's not quite that simple."

I'd forgotten he was a Loyalist. Loyalists were descendants of Scientists.

"There's two sides to that story," he said shaking his head, "but I wanted to tell you about Quista, not Earth."

"Sorry," I meant for insulting the Scientists. "You know, my Nan'Dah loved telling me this story."

"I think she told you a lot of things that are not so popular to talk about these days." He smiled. His blue eyes shone in the glow from the mi'lex. "But even though you've heard this already I need you to listen and really hear what I'm saying. Okay?"

I passed my fingers over my lips and nodded.

"Okay, so Duncan and his wives weren't the only people to come. They brought a whole shipload of people with them. And," he shook his head while grinning, "you're right — they were escaping a dying solar system that had been ruined by mankind's knowledge of science and their belief that through this knowledge they could control the worlds. But instead their ignorance and arrogance destroyed it. That's what drew Duncan here, he was looking for something better than Science and he found Magic."

I closed my eyes letting the story play out as Phillip described it. The whole crew had lived on the ship for over half their lives. They were tired and running out of hope. Then Duncan found it — a solar system with something more. Quista. Like a bright beacon of hope. I'm not sure how Duncan could tell it had Magic. No one understood that. But he did and he brought his wives and crew here to find it.

"When they'd left Earth, Duncan was only married to Dorris." Phillip said.

I opened my eyes. "But in the story he has two wives."

"Well, when they left Earth he only had one," Phillip said, "But after all those Royal Years on the ship Duncan fell in love with Dezarah, Dorris's little sister."

"His first wife's sister?" *How horrible for Dorris!* "I couldn't imagine having to share my husband with someone else, let alone a sister."

Phillip smiled, "Well, it happened before the law was passed banning duo marriages." He paused then continued, "Anyways, Dorris had four children with Duncan, but Dezarah didn't have any."

Somehow, that made me feel better.

"Did you know that when they found Quista there was only one planet they could live on?"

I nodded, "Uma."

He leaned down to draw a small circle in the sand. "Uma," he said writing the name on it.

Uma had gone from being the only good planet in the whole system to the least desirable—

He looked up, "That was before she was split into four."

—and of course I had to live on the least desirable of the four. Even Uma'Four was more popular. I smiled feeling Phillip's eyes on me. He was quiet. He started talking again when I looked at him.

"After Duncan landed, most of the people were just glad to be off the ship. They went about trying to live on this new strange world. But Duncan was determined to find the Magic he knew was hidden here."

Phillip continued to tell me the story: Duncan found the Magic and was surprised by it.

"Why?" I had to ask.

Phillip leaned back and took the last lu'umon berry from the bush. "I'm not sure," he said through his sour shudder, "The story just says he was surprised by what he found it in."

I nodded. That's all my Nan'Dah had ever said when I asked her.

Phillip continued telling me the story.

Duncan had discovered the Magic and raced home to tell his beloved wife: Dezarah. That's how it was said — *his beloved wife*. Only Dezarah wasn't home, Dorris was. Dorris could tell that her husband was happy and, I figured, she knew the only thing that would have made him that happy was if he had found what he'd been looking for — Magic. Dorris begged him to tell her where it was. She even got mad when he wouldn't. Finally she insisted that he didn't love her and that he had never loved her. When he argued with her, she said the only way to prove that he ever loved her was to tell her where the Magic was.

"You know Duncan called it the heart of the world?"

I nodded.

I also knew that Duncan never got a chance to give the Magic to Dezarah. When he went to show her, it was gone. Dorris had taken it. This was the part of the story that had always bugged me. Though, knowing what I knew now, about what Dezarah had done to Dorris, I understood — kinda.

"She consumed it and it turned her into the first Magic Weaver." Phillip said.

"Her, and all her kids," I added.

Phillip was watching me. "Did you know that Dorris consumed all the Magic? She didn't give any to her kids."

"Oh?" I hadn't known that. "Then how did *they* become Magic Weavers?"

He smiled like he was happy I'd asked, "They became Magic Weavers because they stayed close to Dorris. In fact, anyone who stayed close to her became Magical, it infected them. That included her children's spouses and all their children. It even infected the friends who went with Dorris when she ran away."

I frowned, Magic was everywhere in Quista. To be a part of it would be an honor, a blessing. "I wouldn't consider being Magical an infection."

"No?" he chuckled then shook his head. "Anyways after taking the Magic, Dorris changed. At least that's how the story goes. I'm not sure she changed that much." He shook his head again, "I think becoming a Magic Weaver gave her the ability to do everything she had wanted to do before, but couldn't."

Phillip shifted to his knees. "She took herself and her children far away from everyone else."

I'd always thought it was because of selfishness and spite that Dorris ran so far away. Now I realized it was more because of a broken heart. She was running away from the man who didn't love her anymore and Dezarah, *her sister*, whom he did love.

"Moving to the other side of Uma wasn't far enough." Phillip said.

How far would be far enough to mend that kind of hurt.

Phillip took his finger, starting from where he'd drawn Uma, and traced a larger circle around himself. "Dorris and her children used their powers to pull another planet into the same orbit as Uma, then they teleported themselves over to it."

"That was the Royal planet," I said and I knew I was right.

"Yes, and I'm sure you also know what happened from there."

I quickly rattled it off. *Over the course of the next hundred Royal Years, Dorris's descendants pulled a total of five planets into the same orbit.* Phillip drew out what I was saying in the sand around him. *However, the power needed to keep six planets in the same orbit was using up all the Magic Weaver's Magic. They fixed this by changing the orbit of three of them. But then the sun wasn't powerful enough to heat them all, so the Magic Weaver's made a second sun. But the two suns had too much gravitational pull on each other so they had to make a third sun which balanced everything out.*

The drawing had gotten more complex as I went on.

Phillip made three fist marks for the suns, "Then what?"

"Six planets weren't enough." I said, "Dorris' descendants had grown too numerous and they weren't good at sharing,"

He chuckled, "Well, that isn't quite the whole truth."

"No?" I bit my lip. No, it wasn't. Dorris and her descendants weren't trying to take the Magic away — *they* were trying to *get* away.

"How much do you know about Dezarah's story, after Dorris left? What do you know about Dezarah and Duncan?"

I shrugged. Nan'Dah never said much about them, apart from them being mad at Dorris and wanting the Magic back.

Dezarah thought she could get it back if she killed Dorris and anyone who had Magic in them.

"Okay, so, first Duncan was miserable that Dorris had taken the gift he'd promised to give his more cherished wife. Dorris had taken all the Magic and left his second wife with nothing. She'd even taken the children who were just as much Dezarah's as they were Dorris's. Some say even more so. Duncan had hoped that the Magic would allow Dezarah to have children. But without the Magic Duncan decided to teach Dezarah everything he knew about Science. It was through Science that Dezarah was able to have a dozen children."

"Sure. I mean that only makes sense." No one had told me this — but it did make sense.

"Dezarah was the first Scientist on Quista. But Science isn't like Magic. Dezarah's kids weren't Scientists just by being around her. She had to teach them — which she did. Dezarah made sure all her kids learned it. She had over a dozen in the end. And before she died, she made all of them promise they'd keep fighting until they got the Magic back."

I stared down at Phillip's rough drawing in the sand. Dezarah had made her kids promise to kill their half-brothers and half-sisters all because she was angry at Dorris for taking her Magic. But Dorris had taken the Magic because Dezarah had taken her husband.

What a mess.

And this war didn't stop after Dezerah and Dorris died. It went on, generation after generation. All the Magic Weavers and Scientists ever knew was how to hate each other and fight one another. What a waste. So many lives lost. So much spilled blood. So much Magic misused.

I wondered if they'd still be fighting today if Uma hadn't cracked.

"My Nan'Dah told me that Uma was the mother planet of Quista and she broke into four because her heart had finally broken." I knew it wasn't that romantic, in reality it had been a comet that had crashed into Uma making it break apart.

Phillip looked sad, "My mom believed the same thing."

"Was she a Loyalist?" It was a strange thing for a Loyalist to believe.

"The most loyal," he looked away, "Dad says anyways. I don't remember her. She died when I was just a baby."

I wondered what it would be like growing up without a mom. I'd always felt like Nan'Dah was my mom, but I missed having a dad. Would it be the same for him, only reversed?

He kept talking, "Everyone on Uma would have died if the Magic Weavers hadn't saved them. And because only Commoners and Scientists lived on Uma, everyone agreed that the Magic Weavers weren't as bad as they thought. After that, a fragile peace was formed. The remaining Magic Weavers were allowed to create three new worlds for themselves where they would be left alone to live." Phillip drew the outer planets: Zog, Zaffa, and Zoni.

He had to shuffle away to create the long orbits of each of them. They had made their orbits extreme so they would be harder to get to. They were still scared of the Scientists. However, the isolation also kept the Magic from affecting, or infecting, anyone new.

"With the Magic Weavers split up, their powers dwindled." Phillip said, "That's something they didn't expect…" He spoke more slowly, "But the Scientists had predicted it."

My breath caught. "The scientists knew?" I frowned. "Did they know that when it came time for Zaffa to pass the suns, the Magic Weavers wouldn't be able to get it close enough to warm it?" That without enough warmth, the planet would freeze during its long Turns away. I held my hand to my chest. *How could they know that and still let it happen?*

Phillip stared down at the small circle that represented Zaffa. "The frozen world." He drew an X on it then ran his finger down the second outer path "And Zog…"

I put my hand up for him to stop.

I knew what happened to them too; worried that they would have the same problem as Zaffa, the Magic Weavers on Zog overcompensated and pulled themselves too close to the suns. Instead of freezing, they fried. The thought made me ill.

"Danay, I'm sorry, it was a dirty rotten thing…"

"It wasn't your fault." I wiped away my tears and drew my knees up to my chin. Resting it there, I stared at Phillip's crude drawing of the Quista system. "Why are you telling me this?"

He rubbed his neck. “Because, because…” he shifted. “I’m a descendant of Dezarah. As is my father, and Collin, and almost everyone on the ship. Like you said in class, after the Royals were made, all the Scientists were turned into Loyalists.”

Although I knew about what had happened, the realization that Phillip was a descendant of Dezarah and a Loyalist made me feel slightly uncomfortable.

He sighed, “But we didn’t choose it. The Magic made it so we have to be loyal to the Royals — probably because we deserved it.” He smiled. “Dorris might have been greedy to take all the Magic. But I don’t think she meant to. She was just trying to save herself. She and all her descendants were never killers. During the wars, they did everything they could without killing Dezarah’s descendants or the Commoners. The same can’t be said about the Scientists. I think being turned into Loyalists was our penance.”

Somehow that made me feel less uncomfortable. “Okay, that was generations and generations ago. You descended from the Scientists and now you are a Loyalist… well, Un-Loyalist because you are choosing not to follow the only remaining Emperor. But what does this have to do with here and now?”

Chapter Fourteen

You've Got the Wrong Girl

Phillip turned his head, staring down at his drawings in the sand. "You remember how I said that everyone around Dorris was infected with her Magic."

I nodded and when I realized he wasn't looking I added, "Yeah."

"Well after the Scientists bound the Magic in The Royal Mother it wasn't contagious anymore."

"So?"

He looked up at me sharply, "So…" more teeth grinding. I watched his shoulders rise up. "So, this part is really important…" but he didn't say anything else.

"Don't worry." I went to touch Phillip's knee.

"No," he pulled it away. "No," he sighed. "I want to tell you. Just give me a sec."

I watched as he pulled in a few deep breaths.

When he remained silent, I asked, "Before, you said that Science had to be learned. Do you still have to be taught it?"

He stared at me.

A strand of my hair had dried in a clump in front of my eyes. I caught it and tucked it behind my ear.

"No," he finally said. "Well, yes and no. A lot of the things we just know now. Some things we still have to be taught."

"Like this? Like the stories of Dorris and Dezarah?"

He smiled and reached out to flick the strand of my hair that had come loose again, "How Quista was formed is only taught to Loyalists and the Royals." He smiled at me.

"I wonder how my Nan'Dah knew this then? Do you think she was a Loyalist?"

"She would have been," Phillip said then put his hand over his mouth like he'd bit himself.

"If she was a Loyalist does that mean my parents were too?"

Phillip didn't say anything. He looked like he was chewing on his tongue.

"Phillip, am I a Loyalist?"

He dropped his hand. "No Danay, you are something else. You are more special than that."

I scoffed, "There's never been anything special about me."

"You're wrong. Danay, you are the most special person I've ever met." He rubbed his forehead. "And because you are so special I'm going to tell you something..."

He trailed off so I didn't expect him to tell me anything.

"Even though the Royal's Magic isn't contagious it still radiates through them so that Common people will feel uncomfortable if they spend too much time around them."

When I didn't say anything he asked, "Do you understand what this would mean?"

"Sure, Commoners wouldn't want to hang out with a Royal. But they don't. The only people who spend any time with Royals are Loyalists. What does it do for you? Are you uncomfortable around the Magic?"

"No, Loyalists are made for it. In fact, we are attracted to it."

"So you feel it then?"

He nodded shifting forward.

"What does it feel like to be around a Royal?" I asked, then remembered he never had been around one. I frowned at myself. "Sorry, I guess you can't answer that."

He pressed his lips together as he stared at me.

"How old were you when they died?" I said. "What did that feel like?"

"I was just an infant when High Emperor Zandr died. So I don't remember what that was like. But my dad said I cried for days after he was gone. All the Loyal children did."

I closed my eyes then felt his hand on my cheek as he wiped the tears off. I leaned into his hand. It was warm and soft against my skin.

"What happened when the Empress…" I couldn't say it.

"When Empress Zoe died I was still young. Just a toddler. I know I felt it. Just like you do when you think about it." He waited for me to look at him. "But her Magic didn't leave. When she died her Magic stayed."

"Is that what Jef meant by the Spirit of the Empress?" I asked.

Phillip pulled his hand away almost like it was wrong to touch me. "Something like that. You know we came to Uma'Three because we've been sensing Magic growing here?"

"Do you think the Empress's Spirit is here?"

"We know it is. It's in someone here."

I looked into his face. *Was he serious?* "Her Spirit is *in* someone?" I smiled. "Well, that's a relief. I was afraid that you'd try and keep all the planets in their place with a spirit. Spirits can't do that." Spirits weren't able to do anything physical. "But with a real person… a real person can keep the planets in their places. A real person can care for the people and their needs. A real person can sit on the throne to rule Quista. A real person can fight the Emperor." While I talked, Phillip's face went from happy to worried.

"So, have you figured out who this person is?"

Phillip's eyes didn't leave mine.

"Have you?"

He nodded.

"Well," I rose up on my knees, "who is it?"

He shook his head, "If you can't figure it out I can't tell you."

Was I supposed to know the person? How was I supposed to know? I looked away and said the only person I could think of, "Kit?"

From the corner of my eye, I saw him shake his head.

"It couldn't have been my Nan'Dah." If she were still alive, I might have thought it was her. *Too bad, she would have been perfect.*

"It wasn't her." When I didn't guess again he said, "Come on, Danay, you can get this."

I turned to stare at him, "How am I supposed to get this?" There wasn't anyone else I could think of.

His eyes stayed on me. He was staring at me — into *me*.

"Well, it can't be me," I scoffed.

"Why not?" He leaned forward.

I shoved him away and stood up. "It just can't."

He was kneeling in front of me, staring up. His eyes were misty like I was someone special. Like I was this person he was looking for. This special person who had the spirit of the Empress in her… my stomach did an uncomfortable flip. I had to turn away. "You're crazy."

"Am I?" he stood. Even though he didn't touch me, I could feel him move closer. "How many other people do you know that have sharks as guardians or can talk to burbs?"

Well… no one… "But if I was this Magical Spirit person wouldn't my life be easier? Wouldn't I fit in better? Wouldn't I at least not be allergic to the water!" I turned to face him. "If I was Magical don't you think I would have done that!"

Phillip balled his hands into fists, "Yes," his jaw was tight, "Yes. I do believe you would have done all that — and more — if you could have."

"Well if I'm this Magical Empress Spirit person then why couldn't I?"

"Because," he ground his teeth, "you were being poisoned."

"How?"

His eyes were dark, "By your doctor."

I stepped back, "How was my doctor poisoning me?" *And why?*

"You said it yourself; after you get the shots you don't feel like yourself."

"That's because my doctor was giving me medicine to help me."

Phillip shook his head. "It wasn't helping you; it was taking away your Magic."

I put my hand to my mouth. I'm not sure what frightened me more; the idea of being this Magical person, or if I was, that I had been drugged and lied to my whole life.

"Danay…"

I held up my hand. He fell silent.

There was no way Phillip was right. He must have made a mistake. I couldn't be who he was looking for. I… couldn't… could I? "Okay, say I'm Magical…"

"You *are* Magical."

"I'm only *saying*," I fought off a shiver, "but even if I was — then how? How did I get this way?"

"You would have been born this way."

"But…" my hands shook, "But how?"

"Before the Empress died she gave her powers to you."

My lips trembled, my voice was barely a whisper, "Why me?"

"Because Danay, you are her daughter."

My knees were threatening to buckle. "I can't be her daughter. She didn't have any kids."

"Well…"

"No!" I put my hand up. "She didn't. She couldn't have. If she did everyone would have known."

Phillip shuffled closer on his knees, "She had to keep it a secret from everyone, to keep it a secret from *High* Emperor Zigel."

I stepped back. I could see in his eyes — this is what Phillip believed. "Fine," I shook my head, "fine. But even if the Empress did get pregnant. And even if she had been able to keep it secret and even if she did have a child, why in all of Quista would you think it was me?"

"Her spirit is here," he shuffled closer still. "How many people on Uma'Three do you know who can pop burbs and swim with zapping eels?"

"I…" I wanted to argue. I wanted to keep denying it. All I could do was stand there, trembling and stuttering. "I…" *I was the only one*. Kit had called it a Danay thing… what if it was more than that? What if it was a Royal thing?

Phillip caught me before I hit the sand. He held me close as every muscle in my body shook. "I know it's hard for you to believe. But you really are…"

"Don't say it." I put my hand to his mouth. *It was too much*. I stayed in his arms feeling his breath on the tips of my fingers.

He didn't say anything. He stared at me. His eyes alight with his belief.

"Phillip…"

He nodded.

"I'm not a real Royal though, am I?"

"Why not?" His arms squeezed me.

"I'm not a real Royal because I'm not a triplet. Or… or was I?" If I had been, then where were my siblings? What happened to them? I cringed at the thought.

"You're right. You aren't a triplet. Empress Zoe only had you. But she made you a real Royal by giving you her powers before she died." His face darkened, "Tom can explain it better."

His words rattled around in my head: *I was Empress Zoe's daughter… I was a Royal… She'd given her powers to me*. Had the Empress died because she'd given her powers to me? *Had making me a Royal killed her*? How could I be the Empress's daughter! "It's not possible," I sat up, pushing him away. "It can't be possible."

"Why not?"

"Because," I had a million reasons why it wasn't possible, they just escaped me at that moment, "because it's never happened before."

"Just because something has never happened before doesn't mean it can't happen. Magic is strange that way."

I crossed my arms. "You've got the wrong girl."

Phillip laughed, his eyes dancing, "I didn't think it could be you either — all those Seasons in the same class, sitting in the desk next to you. If someone had told me you were who we'd been looking for I would have thought they'd been stung by a mi'lex and gone crazy. You are the exact opposite of what a Royal would be. You have so much off-worlder in you. Someone with Royal powers would have blended in better." He chuckled, "Actually, that's not true they would have stood out because they would have been perfect."

It was silly to be offended by this — but I was. I pulled my arms tighter to myself. It hurt, even if he was only confirming what I was saying.

He laughed again. "You are so out of place here on Uma'Three. Like a fish out of water. I passed you over in one glance." He pulled the clump of hair away from my eyes again. "I was sure it was Kit'Una. She's so much closer to what we figured the princess would be. But, Danay, I couldn't stop thinking about you — there was something about you. I couldn't keep my eyes off you."

"Really?" I sat up a little. "I didn't think you even noticed me."

"Well, I did." His neck went pink. "But I couldn't let you know it. After all, I am an Un-Loyalist in hiding. When we got the orders to move on I had to move on." His eyes stayed on me, "Only I almost couldn't leave you."

"But you did." I slumped back down.

"Those were the orders." He sighed then smiled. "You know, I actually counted off the days to the Popling Festival. I knew I'd get to come back to Tem — and I'd be able to see you again." He blinked and looked down, "You see Tem is always buzzing with Magic on festival day. This year we were seeing spikes that were off the charts. Mitch, Sam, and I were sent to find the source.

He chuckled, "I was ordered to stay away from you. Only we saw you with that shark, outside the safe area, and Pal'Hon went on and on about how you always did that. *Every year*, he said. Like he thought you were some kind of show off. Then you went and touched that shark as if it was your pet. After that both Sam and Mitch were sure we needed to follow you. That's what we were doing when I caught you down at the shallow pools collecting and popping burbs. That's when I was sure... or at least I thought I was."

He shook his head, "You must have had an Ignorance Spell put on you. Because it was hard for me to keep the thought in my head. And then I was sure because when I was holding your arm you told me to let go and I did. Only *I* didn't want to let go — you made me. You told me to and I had to listen because you'd commanded it."

I wanted to shake my head but my neck wouldn't cooperate.

"That's not the only time you commanded me. It was just the first. You see, because I'm born into the service of the Royals when a Royal commands me to do something I have to do it. Even if it were *High* Emperor Zigel. The Magic has programmed me — all Loyalists — that way. So when you told me to let go, I had to obey. It happened again at the rafts, when we were running to the end of the docks. Remember?"

"Sorry," I said thinking about how he'd fallen to his knees when I told him to stop.

"I'm not. I knew who you were, even if I couldn't remember I knew. It still felt good to be doing what I was made for."

And there it was, his real feelings for me. He didn't love me — it was the Magic. The Magic made him loyal, faithful — it made him feel responsible for me.

"Do you believe me now?" he asked.

I shrugged. I wasn't sure... Actually, I didn't want to be sure because I *was* sure I didn't want that kind of power. Nor did I want that responsibility. And I really didn't want a bunch of people trying to serve me, especially not Phillip.

"Either you do or you don't."

"What if I don't?"

He rolled his eyes, "This will only work if you do."

"So, if I did, what would I have to do?"

"All you have to do is say it out loud."

"Say what? Say that I'm the daughter of Empress Zoe?" *The words sounded crazy to me.*

"For starters," he stared pointedly down at my CoaB.

I held it up, running my fingers over the word my Nan'Dah had braided into it. "Par'mida?" I asked. "That just means my Nan'Dah thought I was special."

He chuckled but the sound carried no amusement, "Did you know that the actual translation of par'mida is princess?"

I looked down at my CoaB again. "No, my Nan'Dah said it means precious one." I bit my lip as my stomach did a somersault.

"Your Nan'Dah told you what she needed you to know at the time. But in the end she couldn't stop herself from being completely honest about who you are."

I looked at the word: par'mida — princess. My eyes rose to Phillip again. "That — I'm — a — princess?"

Phillip's grin doubled. "That you are *the* Princess. Daughter of a Royal. Danay," his voice had a laugh in it, "I've spent the last five days doing everything I can to protect you and keep you hidden because you are the daughter of Empress Zoe. You, Danay, are Princess of Quista." He bowed.

"What just happened?"

He jumped up and took my hands in his, "You just broke the Information Ban. Anyone who tried to say that you are the princess couldn't. Like the words got stuck in their throat... and that's only if the thought didn't disappear right out of their heads from the Ignorance Spell."

I listened impassively as Phillip explained everything. The bottom line was that even if someone figured out who I was they wouldn't be able to say it out loud because of the Information Ban. I remembered all the times Phillip seemed to choke on his words or bite his tongue. But most people would never even suspect I was the Princess because of the Ignorance Spell. That was why so many people seemed to take such little notice of me. The spell made me practically invisible. And the reason anyone who did notice me seemed to find being around me uncomfortable was because they were Commoners — they weren't designed to be around pure Royal Magic.

"So you see, Danay, it wasn't you." Phillip said.

"It wasn't me." I repeated. "It was a spell my aunt put on me so no one would like me." *That made my Nan'Dah sound bad.*

"She did it to keep you safe." Phillip rubbed his neck, "You know, your Nan'Dah wasn't your *real* aunt. She was your protector, probably one of the Empress Zoe's most trusted Loyalists. Sue might be able to help you figure out who she really was. But even then it might not be that easy."

"Why?"

"Because, Nan'Dah would have borrowed your Magic to change her appearance so she looked like an Uma'Threeite."

"Nan'Dah was able to use my Magic?"

Phillip nodded, "It was so she could do her job until you came of age. As your protector she would have been given the right to use it."

My life really hadn't been my life. I felt numb. But numb wasn't the best description of what I felt: I was hyperaware.

As much as I tried to listen to everything Phillip was saying — and now that his tongue was untied he was saying a lot — I was also aware of the mi'lex that slid along the cave ceiling. They were gathered over me, moving as I did. *Had they always done that*? I could also sense the jellies outside the cave entrance. They'd abandoned the shark bones and were waiting for me. *For me to what*?

In another part of my mind I was thinking about my Nan'Dah. Where was her body? *And if she could use my Magic — why hadn't she used it to escape? Why hadn't she escaped and found me and told me all this herself*? And what about Jef? Did he know who I was? Is that why he tried to protect me? Is that why he'd given me the Royal pearl? What had happened to him after he was caught? If I had known who I was could I have saved him? Could I have commanded the Emperor's officials to leave me alone? To leave all of us alone?

And what about Kit? Jef said she'd been taken to see the Emperor — could I really save her?

And what would happen now that my identity had been revealed? Did the Emperor know about me? Had he heard? What would he do when he found me? *How was I supposed to fight him*? Surely I'd lose. *But what if I didn't*? Then I would have to be the ruler of Quista. I'd have to keep the planets in orbit... How could *I* do that? I might be Empress Zoe's daughter, but I wasn't a triplet, I wasn't a true Royal.

Phillip had stopped talking. He was looking at me with concern, "Princess?"

I had one hand on my stomach and the other covering my mouth, "Don't call me that." I stopped and swallowed down bile. "You promised to only call me Danay."

He bowed his head, "Danay." He said it with the exact same inflection. I tried to ignore it along with the sick feeling that was creeping its way back up my throat.

"Are you ready to come to the ship now? Are you ready to meet *your* Loyalists?"

When he put it that way — NO, but I nodded, numbly-hyperaware, and followed him to the water. I followed him through the fissure, out the side of the cliff, past the shark bones, and all the way to the ship.

Phillip and I weren't alone, a group of jellies swam above while brightly colored zapping eels swam just under us and a school of tuna surrounded us on all sides.

As we neared the ship, I saw it by the glow of the jellies. It was a huge gray thing similar in shape to a clam but far more smooth.

I followed Phillip into an opening just big enough for us to take turns climbing in. He went first. I hesitated for a moment before I followed. The opening spiralled closed behind us and there was a rush of current as the water drained somewhere near our feet. Phillip started to laugh as soon as the water level had cleared his face, "Oh sure you aren't the Princess," he pocketed his hum'gil. "I dare you to try and argue with me now."

I wanted to but I couldn't find my voice.

As the water drained, Phillip seemed to slip into a quieter state. Finally, all the water was gone. With a loud click and metallic whirring, the doors before us opened. Phillip stood up straighter.

Chapter Fifteen

Inside the Ship

Six people stood on the other side of the doors. The man standing in front was unmistakably Phillip's father. They had the same blond hair, the same bright blue eyes, and the same pointed chin.

"Princess," he bowed low then quickly stood, "I assume you know who you are now?"

I nodded.

"Good, good." He looked over at Phillip. "Can I assume this was your doing?"

Phillip nodded stiffly.

"Well, I guess that will excuse the report I got from Collin." He frowned at Phillip. Looking at me he smiled and bowed again, "Princess, please forgive our primitive accommodations." He gestured at the room we were in, "This is a spacecraft, which is not that well equipped for deep sea adventures." He stood and fell silent as if waiting for me to say something.

I glanced at the other people, trying to figure out what I was supposed to do. The one woman in the greeting party was tall and had long wavy hair the color of dirty sand. Her eyes were as black as a hoorup's skin and her chin was split down the middle. The rest of the party was an odd mixture of men. One of them reminded me of Collin, he had the same light green sheen to his skin, same eyes and hair color too. Another, who was as short as an Uma'Threeite, had a bald head and skin that looked like an over baked tuna. The others were just a little taller than Phillip, both had large white teeth.

I had an uneasy feeling they were waiting for me to say something. I swallowed.

"Alright then," the man who was unmistakably Phillip's father said with a frown. "My name is Gredd Dis'Hyroo, I am the captain of this ship. On behalf of myself and everyone aboard, let me be the first to tell you what an honor it is to have you here." He bowed low again. The other five mirrored him.

"Are you well? Is there anything you need?"

I shrugged. To be honest the only thing I wanted was to ask him to stop bowing.

"Good — good. Let me introduce you to my most trusted companions," he stood to the side and gestured towards the person on the far left, "This is Fred, our ship's mechanic."

Fred bowed. His teeth were really white, and they looked twice the size they should. His nose and eyes were also oversized for his head.

Gredd gestured towards the woman, "Sue, is our healer."

She bowed too.

He pointed at the man I was sure was Collin's dad, "Morris."

"At your service, Princess." His brown eyes shone as he bowed.

"Rom." Gredd continued down the line.

Rom bowed, revealing a patch on his head where hair didn't grow. His skin there was just as charred looking as the rest of him.

"I'm the cook." He beamed.

"And lastly, meet the ship's pilot, Erik."

Erik's teeth were as white as Fred's, but his nose and eyes were well proportioned. However, his fingers were extremely long and thin.

It was strange not to tower over everyone in the room. All my life I'd stood apart from everyone else because I was either too tall or too skinny and most times I was both. Looking around I could almost feel normal. Being bowed to by everyone dispelled that feeling.

"Please, Princess, let us show you to your suites," Gredd said.

~ ~ ~

As I was escorted into the inner chambers of the spaceship, I got the impression that everyone was in a rush. We passed door after door, connected by shiny metal walls, smooth floors, and brightly lit hallways; and they seemed identical from one turn to the next.

Finally we walked into a large room with tables and a small raised platform.

"This is where we will be serving the banquet," Rom said softly. I knew he was talking to me even though he didn't look at me. The few people who had been seated at various tables stood up and bowed as we entered. They stayed bowed the entire time.

I was guided out and through another maze of smooth, bright, shiny halls. I wondered, with all the turns we made, if we were going in circles.

Then we entered a room that looked like a jungle. My feet slowed. Uma'Three didn't have jungles. I wanted to see every leaf, tree branch, and blade of grass that grew beside the pathway.

"Please," Gredd turned to look at me, "follow me."

I didn't want to leave, but I listened to him.

Gredd eventually stopped before a set of double doors. They were made of the same smooth, shiny material as the rest of the ship, but depending on how you looked at them, they had a peculiar rainbow sheen.

"Your suites," he waved me forward.

Everyone was watching, waiting. I took a hesitant step towards the doors. They slid open with an almost inaudible sigh.

Gredd bowed, "Princess," he gestured for me to go in.

I looked to Phillip and then to his father and finally to the rest of the group, "Are you coming with me?"

"No. Oh no, we have things to attend to," Gredd said. "Please, make yourself at home. We will keep you safe now."

Alone? "I…" Panic rose in my chest.

"Is there something wrong?" Gredd asked. "Don't you want to rest and freshen up?"

Resting sounded fine, freshening up just as nice, but not alone. I took a shaky step towards the open doors that for some odd reason began to feel like a very shiny prison. "Stay with me." I said looking at Phillip.

He stepped out from behind his father. "I'll stay with you." He stared at the ground.

Morris made a sound in his throat. "Phillip…"

Gredd cut him off with a quick flick of his hand. "He can stay with you today, Princess." Turning to his son, he said, "Just for the afternoon, understand. Tonight you need to be somewhere that's not here. That is an order."

Phillip nodded and turned — waiting for me.

It was easier to enter the suites knowing Phillip would be with me. It didn't even bother me when I heard the doors click shut and were locked behind us.

"Wow." Phillip wasn't looking at me. He was staring, mouth open, at the huge room we'd entered.

"Wow," I agreed. The ceiling was double high, reminding me of the cave where we had escaped from the uniformed officers. My feet squeaked as I made my way across the polished floor to an open archway. Beyond it was a living room filled with soft looking furniture, sofas, cushions and plush chairs — all covered in a material that was beyond what I could have imagined; perhaps silk, but not from Uma'Three. A magnificent carpet covered the floor in the center of the room.

At the far end was another archway. Through it, a dining room fit for a king or, I guess, a princess. The table could easily have seated fifty people. It had an intricate pattern chiseled into every part of its surface and it was surrounded by high backed chairs that were carved with a similar design. The table took up less than a quarter of the room.

A door on one side of the room led to a *mini* kitchen, at least that's what Phillip called it. It was seven times the size of the one I had grown up with. Another door led to a smaller room with a second version of the huge table — only this one was plain, no intricate carvings, no candles dressed it, no silk runners to cover it and the room it was in was smaller. Phillip called it my meeting room.

The last door led to a sitting room which was similar to, but cozier than the living room. The walls were dressed with quilts. The sofas and chairs arranged closer together around a beautiful low table.

At the end of the room there was a set of double doors. And beyond the doors, an enormous bedroom, the bed was draped in a sheer material, and surrounded by so much open space it made me feel dizzy.

To the side of my grand bed was a huge bathroom. Phillip stood at the center of the bedroom his mouth gaping.

"This is all for me?" I had to close my own mouth.

He nodded then lifted his face to the ceiling and whispered, "Wow."

"Wha..." I copied him. The entire ceiling was painted a mosaic of scenes. One I recognized as the suns setting on Tem during a festival day. The others, I suspected, were scenes from the other planets which made up Quista.

"Is this all for me?" I repeated because it was unbelievable. I was standing next to the bed. Four posts, double my height, held up the frame. At the top were rods hung with curtains. I reached for the nearest post and got a handful of silky cloth.

"Queen popling silk." Phillip moved closer to me.

I hadn't recognized it. Neither did I know what had made the violet sheet on the bed. It wasn't as sheer as the curtains, but it felt like a hug as I pulled it against myself.

"Silk from Ursala." Phillip reached out to touch it too, but pulled his hand back before he did. "The sand worms spin this deep under the planet's surface. If you need to rest I could go wait in your sitting room."

I shook my head. I was tired, but I didn't want him to go.

"May we enter?" Someone asked from the doorway.

I looked up. There was a girl who I assumed was my age, with hair like it was on fire. The rest of her was hard to see behind a bundle of fabric. A boy stood on either side of her. The one on the right I didn't recognize. The one on her left, who was standing back from the group, was Collin.

"May we come in?" The girl repeated.

Phillip stood up taller and moved away from me. "Danay," he swept his hand out towards the three, "These are my friends, Mitch, Samantha, and you've already met Collin." Mitch was tall. He looked very similar to Collin only with pale spotted skin. I knew about freckles but no one from Uma'Three had them.

Collin stepped further back when Phillip said his name.

"May we — come in?" Samantha asked, adjusting the load in her arms.

"Yes," I said realizing they were all waiting for *me* to answer. *I wasn't sure I'd get used to that.*

"Thank you," she curtseyed and hurried to a panel along the sidewall of my room. She pressed a button and it opened to reveal a closet big enough to be a bedroom. She pressed more buttons and opened up a set of drawers.

Mitch followed Samantha halfway across the room, then turned towards me and stopped two paces away. He gave a shallow bow, "Princess."

After he straightened, he looked over at Phillip and fought for a few seconds with a grin. The grin won. "How'd you do it? Everyone is dying to know? How did you break the Information Ban?"

"Actually, it was easy, I simply stopped trying to tell her who she was and, instead, focused on telling her the truths she needed to know."

"Well, I'm super impressed. But if anyone could do it, I knew it would be you. Now, Collin owes me a week's worth of desserts." Mitch grinned, afraid to look my way.

"Collin is going to lose a few pounds if he keeps gambling away his desserts like that." Phillip laughed.

Collin hadn't moved from the doorway. I could feel him watching me, wearily, like he didn't trust me.

Phillip followed my gaze. "Collin, something wrong?"

"No," he stood up taller.

"Then come in."

"Thanks," I saw his feet slide further apart, "I'm fine here."

"But she told you to come in." Phillip was clearly offended.

"She didn't *tell* me to come in. She said I could. I don't have to."

"Collin you're being silly and rude." Samantha had finished putting everything from her arms into the hidden cupboards.

Collin folded his arms over his chest, "I'm fine here."

"He's afraid." Mitch whispered to Phillip.

"Afraid?" I turned slightly to look at Mitch, "Of what?"

Mitch blinked; clearly he hadn't meant me to hear that. "Of..." he looked around the room at the other three, "Of you." Then before I could ask why, he leaned closer to Phillip and said, "does she have like some magically enhanced hearing?"

Phillip mock whispered back, "Nope, idiot. Your voice carries."

Mitch turned a little green, "Sorry Princess," he lowered his head like a scolded child. "Maybe I should go stand with Collin." He didn't wait for my response.

Before I could feel too bad about that, Samantha spoke up, "That's a perfect idea. In fact, Phillip, you should go with them. I need some time alone with the Princess to get her ready for this evening."

Collin and Mitch were quick to disappear. Phillip hesitated.

"Shoo." Samantha pushed him.

"Sam," he let her push him all the way to the doors but turned back before she could shut them. His eyes slid towards me.

"What?" she said impatiently.

"Just remember that the Princess is a *person* too."

"Whatever." She gave him an extra shove and closed the door behind. "Okay," she turned to face me. Samantha was my height. Her red hair wasn't that much longer than mine but it was straighter. Bits of it fanned away from her face like it had been made to do that. Her eyes were as bright green as spindly seaweed and set perfectly between them was a cute button nose. Her hands were small but her fingers were long. It was weird looking at them — they had absolutely no webbing between them.

"What are we going to wear tonight?" She asked.

I didn't know how to answer her. Really, all I wanted to wear was Phillip's dry'suit.

Samantha walked over to me then took my arm guiding me to where she'd put the clothes away. She pressed a button to open my closet, "Pick something."

I stared up at the clothes... *My clothes* — that was a strange concept. The closet housed enough outfits to dress every girl in my school, and they were all for me — but nothing looked familiar.

"Anything catch your eye?" She hadn't let go of my arm. I felt trapped by her grip.

How was I supposed to choose? All I'd ever worn was a plain inside-out wet'skn. I tried to explain this to her. For some reason my voice wouldn't come out anything louder than a whisper.

"Well, then I guess anything with a skirt is out." She smiled at me, gazing from my clumpy dried hair to my bare toes. She turned back to the closet.

I stared at my clothes. All I could see was a sea of colors and foreign material.

"Princess?" Samantha's voice broke into my thoughts.

"What? Yes?"

"I was asking about your favorite color? I think purple will look good with your complexion, but Uma'Three is known for its blues." She looked up into the closet then back at me, "You don't care that much about this do you?"

I shrugged.

"Do you mind if I just pick an outfit for you?"

I nodded, happy to look away.

"Well, that will make my job easier." She took down something dark purple and, holding it in one hand, she used the other to guide me into the bathroom. Once there she let go, ordered me to undress, and turned to fiddle with the taps on the tub.

When she turned back, she frowned. I was still completely dressed. But she didn't scold me like her expression made me think she wanted to. Instead she came over to me and, without a word, started undressing me herself.

"Wait," I said, "wait."

She had been quick and I'd been slow. Somehow I was already in nothing but my undergarments. "Samantha, stop."

She stopped, jerking upright. She stood blinking at me, "Princess," her head was slightly bowed.

"I can bathe myself, you know. I've been doing it since I was six."

She nodded but her expression implied she wanted to say something more.

"What's wrong?"

She didn't answer and kept her eyes averted.

"Samantha, tell me what's wrong."

"It is my job to care for you." She cupped her hand over her mouth.

"Yes? And?" I coaxed when her pause grew.

"If you don't look good I will be held responsible."

"That hardly seems fair. How would it be your fault?"

"Because," she glanced at me then looked down, "You are the Princess — you have greater things to be thinking about than what to wear. That's why you've been given me; to take care of the lesser things for you."

"What *greater* things should I be thinking about?" I worried that I was already failing at my job.

"Surely you must be concerned for the safety of Quista, the planets, the moons, the people, and all the creatures too," she answered.

How I wished there was something closer for me to grab and hold on to. I had been worried that I wasn't a good enough Princess. I'd been dreading having everyone watching me — knowing that I was bound to trip, or slip and was most likely going to spill something on myself tonight. I'd been wondering if I'd ever have friends, and worried for the only friend I had. But *all of Quista*? Twelve planets and fifty-six moons, with billions upon billions of people and so many more animals — and me being responsible for them all. *That had not been on my mind — until now.*

I swallowed down my nausea.

"It's okay." Samantha reached forward. I thought she was going to try and comfort me, but she just went back to undressing me.

I didn't protest. I let her strip me naked and guide me to the tub. I was mildly aware that the water didn't feel like it was from Uma'Three, it was silkier against my skin. Samantha washed every inch of me, from my scalp to under my toenails.

When I was out and wrapped in a towel, she went to work on my hair, adding something that held the strands in place. After that she applied color to my face. Once that was done, she showed me something called a bra that worked better than my chest wrap. Finally she helped me dress in a smooth shimmery suit.

It wasn't a suit like my inside-out wet'skn, or Phillip's dry'suit. This one had fabric that didn't cling. It flowed around me causing little breezes to circulate in areas that had never felt breezes before. It made me feel even more self-conscious about walking, and to add to that, Samantha put me into things she called sandals. *Apparently everyone wore them*... and liked them.

All this took a very long time. Once we were done, Samantha led me from my bathroom, through my bedroom, and into the sitting room where Phillip, Mitch, and Collin sat waiting. As I entered, all three of them rose to their feet. They stared, mouths open.

I looked at Phillip, trying to find comfort with everyone's eyes heavy on me. He seemed to be frozen. Finally, he cleared his throat.

"I was given something for you," he pulled out a thin silver band from behind his back and handed it to Samantha, "I'm told it will complete her wardrobe."

Samantha took it and placed it on my head. It had looked light but once it was on my head it felt heavy.

Mitch was the first to bow, dropping to one knee and holding his hands over his chest. Then Collin did the same and Phillip too. When I turned to Samantha, I saw that she held her hands the same, and was lowered in a curtsy.

"What now?" I asked hoping this would encourage them to stop bowing.

All four stood.

"We have a banquet to take you to." Mitch said. "Are you ready?"

I didn't think I'd ever be, but I nodded.

As if they'd spent months practicing the move, the four of them surrounded me. Mitch stood in front, Samantha to my left, Phillip on my right, and Collin took the rear. They walked in unison with me. If I slowed down, they automatically followed — same if I sped up.

We made it to the outer doors of my suites.

"Morris should be along soon," Collin said when the doors didn't open.

I turned around. Everyone was still copying me. "I don't…" I waved for them to leave me, "I don't need an escort to go sit on the sofa," I said.

"Okay," Mitch bowed again.

I huffed and went back to my formal living room. Phillip joined me a few moments later.

"What's wrong?" he asked quietly.

"I don't think I can do this." I said glaring at where the other three were standing away from us.

"What can't you do?"

"Be your Princess." I stared around the room. The pink walls made me feel like I was shut into a clamshell. A really big clamshell. The room was so large; there was too much spare space. *What did anyone need with so much open space.* The rug in the center of the room had a strange pattern; it had to be Royal knotting. On it sat two silver sofas, both long enough for four people from Uma'Three to sit together. They faced each other with a table made completely of glass between them. The table was so clear it almost didn't look like it was there. Along the outer wall were three chairs lined up, waiting for use.

Finally I looked at Phillip.

He gave a sad smile, "I don't think you get a choice."

"But what if I'm no good at it?" My voice rose.

"Why would you say that?" He asked.

"Because I can't lead anyone," I said, "And how in all of Quista am I supposed to take care of everyone… in all of Quista!" I rubbed my face and caught Samantha scowling at me. "And… and how am *I* supposed to beat the Emperor?"

Phillip glanced over at his friends, rubbing the back of his neck. "We're not… That's not… You shouldn't be thinking about that tonight. That's not…" He sighed. "Maybe you shouldn't try to be everything at once. Maybe you should just focus on what you can do."

"What's that?"

"Well, for starters, you can have dinner with *your* Loyalists."

"But what if I don't say the right things… or I end up saying all the wrong things? What if…"

"Don't worry about that," Phillip said, then leaned closer, "*You* are exactly what we've been looking for. You are the Princess. Nothing you say or do can be wrong."

The way Collin, Mitch, and Samantha were carefully watching us said otherwise.

Phillip continued, "After the whole sea escorted you to the ship, no one should doubt who you are." He reached out as if he was about to take my hand. He didn't. "Listen, the fact that you stand *here* right now is another confirmation."

I didn't understand.

Clearly he saw this because he continued, "Danay, do you know who these chambers used to belong to?"

He didn't give me a chance to answer, "Empress Zoe. And her mother before her and her aunt before that. But when Empress Zoe died they were sealed shut. No one, no matter how much we tried, could open them. And then today, you arrive and, well…" he held his arms wide, "You see? They opened because you *are* the Princess. And because you are the Princess, you are exactly what we want." This time he reached out and took my wrist. His fingers pressing against my CoaB. "Trust me." He let me go as he turned back to look at the others.

It was hard to trust him when I saw the lines of disappointment etched so clearly on, not only Collin's face, but also Samantha's and Mitch's too.

It didn't matter. Morris had come to escort us to the banquet.

Chapter Sixteen

Banquet

We entered the banquet hall and someone said, "All hail Princess Danay." Everyone genuflected; placing a fist to their chest and reciting in unison "Hail Princess Danay."

I flinched. Phillip's fingers briefly fluttered against mine, "See," he whispered so only I could hear, "we all love you."

They all *loved me.* I shivered.

I really hadn't realized how lucky I was when no one had noticed me. I never had to worry about how many ways I might disappoint everyone.

Gredd stood next to a table on a raised platform, waiting. Phillip, Mitch, Collin, and Samantha stood next to their seats at the table, backs rigid, heads held high and eyes ever shifting as they stared out at the crowd.

It made me feel like the room was dangerous.

There were two doors on either end of the room; the one we'd come through and another directly across from it. The ceiling was as white as a common pearl. There were long lighting shafts hanging from it, placed at even intervals. The walls were the same color as the ceiling with lights in the shape of water drops arranged like stairs going up and down all around the room but never leading anywhere.

The floor might have been made of polished silt'ment. I longed to take my sandals off to feel if it was as hard and cold as it looked.

I took my place at the table and everyone sat.

There must have been over a hundred people in the room. Some were conversing in hushed voices. Most were waiting for dinner to be served. These people were all so different from the people I'd see in Tem, even on a festival day. A few were shorter than your average Uma'Threeite. Most were tall, like me.

Collin wasn't the only one with a green sheen to his complexion. There were at least five other men in the room including Morris who had walked with us to the hall. Some of the women had a violet hue to their complexions.

I'd never realized how diverse the people of Quista could be, or how beautiful. Each person was unique in his or her own way. The Emperor had taken away this diversity when he'd ordered everyone to return to their planet of origin. I scowled and looked toward Gredd.

He grinned and said in a loud voice, "Princess may I be the first to let you know how wonderful it is to be in the company of a Royal again." He threw a gesture towards the room. "Having you here makes us all hopeful for our future."

All their hopes were tied to me. *What if I let them down?*

"Dad," Phillip leaned forward.

Gredd's eyes flashed towards Phillip, but his smile stayed fixed in place. "Son?"

Phillip shook his head and sat up again. Collin shifted his chair a few finger widths away from Phillip as if afraid of being associated with him.

"Princess," Gredd said. I turned to look at him. "Just having you aboard this ship has filled everyone here with an indescribable joy. And that joy will spread once the other Un-Loyalists hear that we have found you."

"There are more of you?"

"Plenty more." Gredd was pleased about this. "At least enough to fill your palace on the Royal planet."

My palace? I suddenly wished this was a dream — one I would hopefully wake up from soon. I pressed the palm of my hand against the table. A table made of wood. I'd never seen one before, let alone felt it… I couldn't dream something like this up — *this wasn't a dream*.

"When *High* Empror Zegil took the throne," Gredd was saying, "we went into hiding, waiting for the Magic to make things right."

"The Magic?" I frowned. "How can the Magic fix things? Magic isn't alive."

Gredd leaned forward. I expected him to scold me. "That is where you are mistaken, Princess. The Magic is very much alive. And although it has chosen to be used through the Royals, that doesn't mean it isn't in everyone and everything in Quista. But I shouldn't have to tell you this — surely you have felt it."

I nodded, I *had* felt it. But I never thought of it as alive.

He smiled.

Several people entered the hall with trays of food. Sue brought us ours.

I looked into her black eyes and felt nervous though there was nothing about her that was all that frightening. After she served us, she bowed and left. We sat in silence. No one ate. Finally I picked up my fork and tentatively poked at the green things on my plate. As if that's what they'd been waiting for Gredd, Phillip, Mitch, Collin and Samantha started eating.

It was hard to eat when I knew everyone was watching me. They weren't staring, and they were smiling, but it was clear I was the focus of everyone's attention. My chest felt tight. Sue didn't say anything as she bowed low, again, and removed my barely touched plate only to replace it with a new one.

How many times had she done that? Five? Six?

Rom, the cook, brought my next dish. He bowed.

I stared at the patch of blackened skin in the middle of all his brown hair. It looked like an island in a stormy sea. He sat, his eyes were sad.

"Is the meal not to your liking?"

"I'm…" I didn't want to say anything that might hurt his feelings. Clearly he'd gone to a lot of trouble to make this meal. "I'm not hungry."

"Perhaps tomorrow I can make something you are more familiar with." He smiled. His lips were deep red, the color of blood next to his baked skin. "Tell me, what are some of your favorite dishes?"

I told him.

He picked up my untouched plate.

Phillip, Samantha and Mitch hadn't eaten all the food on their plates either. Somehow this made me feel better. Collin had licked his clean.

"The food was excellent," Gredd said as Rom took his plate — which was empty, "You've outdone yourself tonight."

Rom tipped his head towards Gredd and hurried away.

This time when Sue came she had an extra bowl which she kept for herself.

"What's this?" I asked as I pressed my spoon into the hard looking white liquid.

"Dessert," she said. She smiled as she ate it.

I glanced at Collin, he'd already eaten most of his. Mitch was glaring at him.

"I don't know if you remember me?" Sue said after she'd had a few bites. "I'm the ship's healer. Phillip told me that you used to see a doctor once a month for check-ups?"

Thinking about my doctor made my stomach ache. I recounted what Phillip had told me about him, "Didn't he medicate my Magic away every month?"

Sue frowned. "Yes, well, it's unfortunate you had to find out like that." Her eyes rose to Phillip.

He met her gaze. His hands were folded in front of him on the table. He hadn't touched his dessert.

"What do you want to know about my doctor?" I asked. I didn't like the way she was looking at Phillip.

Sue turned back to me, her eyes glancing at Gredd on the way. "Ah, well, I was hoping you'd know where we could find him?"

"No." I said pushing my bowl away. The contents had become more of a runny liquid. "Why, is he missing?"

"Yes, he is." Sue said with a frown.

I crossed my arms over my chest. I didn't like thinking about the doctor who'd been lying to me my whole life... He and my Nan'Dah. "I can't believe my Nan'Dah never told me the truth about — *me*."

"Yes," Gredd looked apologetic or worried — I couldn't tell. "That was unfortunate. But my guess is the plan would have been to tell you after your Coming of Age. Only that's the night the Emperor's officials arrived."

Now I felt worse. My Nan'Dah had died protecting me. *Had the doctor done the same*?

"Why do you need to find my doctor?"

Sue looked at Gredd who was looking at his hands. He sighed and put his spoon down then levelled his eyes with mine, "He's... needed... to help us... get off the planet." Gredd was carefully choosing his words. It made me wonder what he wasn't saying.

"Why?"

"Because..."

Phillip shifted like he was going to say something. I looked at him; he was glaring at his dad. When he spoke his voice was low so it wouldn't travel. "She doesn't need to take any more of his *poison*."

Collin slid his chair further away from Phillip.

I turned back to Gredd. He was glaring at his son, his lips pressed into a thin white line. "This is not the time, nor the place to discuss this."

"Is that why you need to find the doctor? So you can give me more medicine?" The thought made me shiver.

Gredd's eyes softened. "That is not..." Gredd stopped and shook his head. "In order to make your medicine the doctor would have to understand your Magic. We need him to...to help *us* understand."

Again I felt like there was something Gredd wasn't telling me.

"I don't want to see my doctor." I said. If my medicine really was poison I didn't want to take it ever again.

"Please Princess," Gredd reached out like he meant to touch me. He stopped when I flinched away. "Princess, no one here is trying to hurt you."

I was not sure I believed him. "I don't want to see my doctor ever again. Do you hear me? Don't ever make me see him again!"

Gredd's mouth snapped shut. A muscle in his cheek bulged. "Fine, you will not have to see your doctor again. But we still need to find him to get off this world."

I pushed my chair out and looked at the room. More people seemed to be watching us now — no, watching me. Their curious eyes felt heavy on me. Were they all just curious or were some unhappy? ...disappointed? Resentful?

"I want to go back to my suites now." What I really wanted was to go home, but I was sickeningly aware that that wasn't possible.

"As you wish," Gredd said, getting to his feet.

Everyone bowed as I stood up and was escorted out. At the door Gredd turned to me and bent low, "Princess, may your sleep be deep and may you awake refreshed."

His words gave my heart a painful ache. Those were the exact same words Nan'Dah had used to tuck me into bed every night right up to our last night together — the night before she had died to protect me.

I followed Mitch. He was walking stiffly in front of me. Phillip was beside me. I wanted to reach out to him; to feel him. To reassure myself he was still there. To know he hadn't been taken from me too. Everything familiar to me was gone. Everyone I loved was missing or in danger... or dead. I needed Phillip — he was all I had left.

But I resisted.

All too soon we stood at the open doors to my suites.

"Good night, Princess," Samantha said. She, Mitch, Collin, and Phillip bowed.

"I don't want to be alone," I said.

I'd been speaking to Phillip but Samantha answered. "I'll stay with you."

I didn't want her. I looked at Phillip but he wouldn't meet my eyes. "Can't you stay?"

His head shake was jerky, "My father has some things he wants me to do."

"Can you come back when you're done?"

He didn't answer.

"Please?"

"I'm not sure I'll be done tonight." Still he wouldn't look at me.

"What if... What if I need you?" I looked at Samantha, she was glaring at Phillip.

"You…" he was staring at his feet, "You shouldn't need me." He quickly looked up, then away.

I didn't know what to say. *I did need him.*

"Come, Princess, let's get you ready for bed." Samantha took my hand and started guiding me into my suites. Phillip still wouldn't look at me. The last thing I saw before the doors shut was Collin and Mitch glaring at him.

I endured another humiliating experience of Samantha changing me like I was a life-sized doll. I didn't complain. I didn't want to be alone. My chambers felt even more like a prison now. At least with Samantha here I wasn't the only one locked in.

However, all too soon she was done.

I followed her to the front doors, wanting desperately to tell her to stay but the words got stuck.

"Princess, go lie down. I promise sleep will come swiftly if you just allow it." She turned and stepped into the hall. For a moment she stood perfectly framed by the double doors. I blinked as the doors slid shut — leaving me alone.

"No," I stepped forward and pushed on the doors — gently at first, but eventually with all my strength — they didn't budge. My knees buckled and I slid to the floor resting my forehead on the cool polished floor.

"Phillip," I moaned.

~ ~ ~

That's where he found me. I'm not sure if it had been seconds or hours, but he came. As the doors opened, I stood and fell onto his arms. He gathered me up and carried me to my bed. At first I thought it was a dream. But when he set me down I caught his hand and could feel how real he was.

"Don't ever leave me again," I said squeezing his fingers.

"Okay," he said but pulled himself free. "You're good here. You'll be good here." He looked away towards the door, "I'm going to go stay in the sitting room. Okay? I'm not leaving you." He quickly added, "I'll be close enough to hear you if you call for me."

I caught his hand again before he could leave. I pulled it to my chest hugging it. "Stay here." I choked.

"Okay," he said staring down at me, "What if I were to lie down here on your floor. I'll be where you can see me. And I promise I'm not going anywhere."

I shook my head. It wasn't good enough. I needed to feel him. I wouldn't be able to relax unless I felt him next to me. I'd stay awake all night just to be sure he didn't sneak off.

He closed his eyes and sighed in defeat when I told him this.

"Danay, I don't want..."

"Stop," I said. I didn't want to hear what he didn't want. *I* wanted it — I *needed* it. And that's when I remembered something that made me smile.

"Danay?" his tone implied worry, "What are you thinking?"

"What if I commanded it?" I shifted forward.

He stiffened, his arm going rigid against my clinging fingers, "Please don't."

"If I command it then you have to obey." I knew this was cruel — I knew he didn't like me like that. But tonight wasn't about that. *Not really*. I was all alone and Phillip was the only person left from my life before I became a *princess*. I just needed to feel like I had some part of my old life left.

"I'll stay." Phillip pushed the curtains aside and sat on the bed next to me. "I'm staying, see. You don't need to command me."

But if I didn't command him he would be able to steal away as soon as I was asleep. I didn't want to wake up and find him gone. "Phillip, I order you to stay the night, in my bed, next to me."

His face was a mask of pain as he lay back.

I knew it was wrong, but I couldn't feel miserable — as much as I knew I should. I only felt relief knowing he would stay with me all the way through the night. Knowing he'd be there when I woke up in the morning.

I didn't look at him as I lay on my back next to him. I took a deep breath then rolled so I could rest my head on his chest. He brought his arms around me and sighed.

Samantha had been right, sleep found me swiftly once I allowed it.

~ ~ ~

I woke up when Phillip shifted out from under me.

What I'd done the night before came flooding back. *I'd commanded him to stay with me… in my bed.* That had been so wrong. *I needed to apologize.* I stretched out to find him.

He'd moved too far away. He was probably angry.

"Wait, let me explain." Phillip whispered urgently.

My eyes snapped open. We weren't alone.

Through the sheer curtains, I saw Gredd and two men I didn't recognize. The men were holding Phillip between them.

"Please father—" Phillip struggled to break free.

Gredd held his hand up. He had the same silver object Collin had tried to attack me with in the cave. *The stunner.*

"—you're making a mistake," Phillip said struggling harder.

Gredd touched the object to Phillip's temple. Phillip looked at me and I saw fear. He fell limp. *Was he afraid for himself, or for me?*

Gredd turned. His eyes locked on me and he said something that I suspected was a curse. "Get him out of here!" He ordered the two men. He took a step towards me, "Princess…"

"Don't!" I scrambled to the other end of the bed.

"Princess," his hand reached out to my bed curtains.

"No! Stay where you are." I wanted to sound braver than I felt.

Gredd stopped. He still held the stunner like he meant to use it — on me.

"Princess," his voice was low.

"Leave— leave me alone!"

He bowed, stiffly, and walked out of my room.

I waited, trembling, afraid he'd come back.

What had I done? I'd ordered Phillip to say in my bed! *There had to be some rule against that.* I felt my face heat up the more I thought about it.

I should have let him sleep in the other room. They wouldn't have needed to take him away if he'd slept in the other room… And I bet they wouldn't have tried to attack me if I'd let Phillip sleep on my floor. *This was my fault.*

Tears spilled from the corners of my eyes. I pressed the heels of my hands into my eyelids trying to stop them. *I shouldn't have made him stay*... but I had wanted him. And now I was missing him.

I missed my Nan'Dah too. More tears fell. *She'd know how to comfort me*... even if she would be mad about what I'd done.

I missed Kit. I knew she'd understand and she'd probably even try to make a joke so I'd laugh. Only for the life of me I couldn't figure out what the joke would be. The tears fell faster.

I rolled to my side hugging my arms around myself. Finally the tears slowed and eventually stopped.

I realized how alone I was.

I missed Phillip.

I squeezed my eyes shut fending off fresh tears.

~ ~ ~

When I opened them I wasn't in my bedroom anymore. I was in a new room. The walls were white and bare. The room had a single light fixed to the middle of the ceiling. There was a square table and two chairs, one on either side of it, in the middle of the room. Nothing else would fit. But I was exactly where I wanted to be because Phillip was there.

I started to reach out to him then stopped. His hands were bound around the back of his chair.

"What's happening?"

He didn't turn. He continued to keep his head to the side, watching the door as if he hadn't heard me. I tried to take hold of his shoulder. When my hands went through him, he shivered and looked around. His eyes slid past me as if I wasn't there.

What was happening!

Before the panic could consume me, the door opened.

Gredd walked in and I backed up to the wall.

His eyes traveled the room... and clearly he couldn't see me either.

As the door slid shut behind him Gredd touched his hand to his forehead. "Can you imagine my horror this morning when I'd been told that you hadn't returned to your room last night?" Gredd asked still covering his eyes.

Phillip's face pinked.

Gredd raised his voice, "And the even worse humiliation of finding you not only with the Princess — where I distinctly ordered you *not* to be — but in *her bed*!"

Phillip slumped, pulling against the handcuffs.

"Phillip?" Gredd dropped his hand, "In her bed! What do you have to say for yourself?"

"It was wrong." Phillip stared down at the table.

"You're right it was wrong. And you know better." He crossed his arms. "So, why did you do it?"

"Danay—"

"The *Princess*," Gredd corrected.

"—she asked me to stay."

"That's not good enough," Gredd walked over to the table and leaned on it. "She asks and you say no."

Phillip looked up, "But dad she's all alone and scared."

"So? *You* don't stay! You have Sue or Samantha stay with her. Either of them would have been acceptable."

"They're strangers to her," Phillip said softly, "Everything is changing for her. I'm the only person she feels safe with. I couldn't leave her."

"The Princess has many challenges ahead of her, the least of which is learning to sleep in a new bed."

"But dad, can't we show her just a little compassion?"

Gredd hit the table. Both Phillip and I jumped. "Your feelings are not driven by compassion alone! I can see that — everyone can see it. Your feelings are clouding the way you see things."

Phillip didn't say anything.

Gredd took a long deep breath, "But despite that, I know you would have not done this all on your own accord." Gredd narrowed his eyes. A muscle in his jaw twitched. "What did the Princess say to you that made you stay?"

Phillip looked down.

"Either you tell me or Tom will make you tell him."

I didn't like the sound of that. "I commanded him to stay," I said.

Gredd's gaze hadn't left Phillip, "Son? Last chance."

Even though it was clear neither could hear me, I turned to Phillip, "You should tell him I commanded it."

With a sag in his shoulders Phillip said, "She commanded me to stay next to her, in her bed, just for the night."

"I suspected as much." Gredd nodded.

Phillip kept his eyes down. Every breath he took made him strain against his binding. It had to be painful. He winced and looked to the door with his next breath.

Gredd was watching him too. His eyes becoming even more narrowed, "And what else did she say to you that I need to know about?"

Phillip kept his eyes on the door; his lips pressed together.

"Phillip?" Gredd's voice rose.

"She said," he looked at his father with a frown. "She said I was never to leave her again."

"Of all the…" Gredd took a deep breath. "You understand what this means, don't you?"

Phillip nodded.

But I didn't. I looked from Phillip to Gredd and asked, "What?" not expecting an answer.

"I have to stay…" Phillip didn't get to finish. Someone came in.

I recognized the person from when I'd first come aboard the ship. His face glistened as he mopped at his forehead.

"Fred, what is it?"

"Sir, you told me to inform you the moment I detected an increase in activity."

"Yes, yes."

"Well, it has… increased."

"How much?"

"Tripled in the last half hour. If this remains steady for any length of time, we will not be able to mask it. Our shields are already working at full capacity."

"Any word about the doctor?"

"No word yet. But we found the boy and we're working on a plan."

"Good, carry on. Meanwhile I'll see if Sue knows of anything that could help."

"I have an idea," Phillip said.

"I don't want to hear anything more from you," Gredd snapped. "Fred, tell Tom I need him to find a way…" Gredd's eyes softened as he continued to stare at his son, "to break him."

I gasped and the room, along with everyone in it — including Phillip — disappeared. I was back in my suites.

I jumped from my bed and ran towards the main doors. I wasn't sure what I intended to do. I wasn't sure what I could do. I slowed… I wasn't even sure of what I'd seen.

"Ready to get dressed?" Samantha said, as she entered the room.

The main doors quietly slid shut behind her.

Chapter Seventeen

Pledged

I stood, staring at the doors. *Had I really seen what I thought I had seen?* ...or had it just been a dream.

Samantha called from the front sitting room, "Coming?"

I moved to see her better, "Where's Phillip?"

"Busy." She smiled.

I scrutinized every line on her face. Would she look so calm if Phillip was off somewhere being *broken*? *It had to have been a dream.*

"Well, come on," she said turning to walk further into my suites.

I followed her.

What a crazy dream... But it had felt so real.

Samantha washed me and dressed me again. She stayed quiet until I talked.

"Did you see Phillip today?" I asked.

She shifted her gaze from me so quickly it felt like she was avoiding me. "No." She slowly dipped a tiny brush into a glob of thick black liquid. It reminded me of squid ink. Finally she looked up. Her expression was soft — kind. "But I did talk to him." She smiled, "He said I should tell you to have a good day."

That made it sound like he wasn't planning on seeing me... *or he couldn't*!

I pulled back from the strange brush Samantha held up to my eyes — it had deposited the ink onto my lashes. They stuck as I blinked. "Won't..." I blinked a few more times. "Won't he be able to tell me that himself?"

She was staring down at the brush and ink again, her lips pursed. "I don't know. He might... he might be tied up."

Before I could ask if she was being serious someone called, "Breakfast."

Collin and Mitch were standing in the entrance to my room. Neither smiled. But then, I'd never really seen either of them smile at me.

"Where would you like to take it?" Mitch asked. I couldn't be sure but it felt like his eyes narrowed slightly as I met his gaze.

I turned to Samantha intending to ask about Phillip again.

"How about in the meeting room?" She nodded still smiling, "It's cozy there."

I turned back to the boys. They were starting to leave.

"Where's Phillip!" I blurted.

Both stopped. Neither looked happy. But all they'd tell me was that Phillip was busy. When I repeated what Samantha had said, about him being tied up, she laughed it off. Mitch laughed a little too. Collin shrugged and looked away, scowling.

"Where I come from that's just a saying," Samantha said once she'd stopped giggling — mostly.

"It's a saying on my world too." I grumbled feeling like Uma'Three was being picked on.

"Okay," she patted my arm. Her face grew more serious, "You seem tired. Did you get enough sleep?"

I was starting to wonder if I had.

Samantha sent the boys along to set up breakfast. Then she had me change into something called a *dress*.

I didn't like it.

It left too much of my skin exposed to the harsh dry air. But Samantha said it was a more appropriate outfit for a princess to wear than a wet'skn.

I quickly realized I'd have to adjust the way I walked to keep the skirt from flipping up and exposing my *underwear*, a thinner and more see-through version of my bathing bottoms. I blushed at the thought. I'd also have to keep my knees together when I sat for the same reason.

Samantha also wanted me to wear something called *shoes*. They were upgraded versions of the sandals she'd made me wear the night before. Clearly, by the way she went on about them, they were something she felt were very important.

I didn't agree. "You can't make me wear them." I said after she'd made it clear I couldn't walk around barefoot everywhere. "I'll just wear sandals."

"As you wish." She said with a bow.

~ ~ ~

I'd forgotten how big my meeting room was. Even though it was smaller than my dining room, it still had a table that would easily sit twenty people.

Collin and Mitch stood side by side. Despite their complexions, Collin being green and Mitch closer to my coloring, they looked nearly the same. At least, they both wore the same expression: cautious, leery, and unsure.

"Princess," both Collin and Mitch said, bowing.

I really hoped this wasn't how they were going to behave around me all the time. "You know you don't have to do that," I said.

Mitch moved to hold a chair out from the table for me.

"Yes we do," he said as he came around to sit one seat away.

"Not for me."

"Yes we do — for you." Mitch looked at me and gave a forced smile. It was the first time I'd seen him even attempt to look happy for me.

I frowned, "Well I don't like it."

"What don't you like about it?" Samantha asked. Her smile was genuine. She sat between Mitch and me. Colin sat to my right. He stared down at the smooth surface of the table, his lips held in permanent disapproval.

"It's weird to have everyone make such a big deal over me." I sat back in my seat reminding myself to keep my knees together.

"But you *are* a big deal," Mitch nodded with each word.

"I didn't used to be," I said under my breath.

"You were a big deal then too," Mitch said. "It's just that with the Information Ban and Ignorance Spell, no one knew how to express it."

I thought about the people in my life: my teacher who always seemed angry with me; my classmates who found it so easy to forget about me; all the strangers who would completely ignore me. Then I thought about Mr.'Una and how he went out of his way to show me affection, and Mz.'Una who had been like a second mother. Then Jef, he'd risked his life for me, and Kit…

I sighed.

"What's wrong?" Samantha reached out to put her hand on my arm.

Her skin was soft, soothing. I sighed again, "I'm worried about my friend."

"Which friend?" Mitch asked.

I wanted to laugh. "My only friend. Kit'Una." Then I thought again about Jef. "And her brother."

Collin looked up from the table. His light brown eyes seemed conflicted. "Seriously? Only one friend? Ever?"

Even after I nodded, I could tell he didn't believe me. I tried to explain what it had been like. Remembering it all was hard. All the times I'd been tripped, and ignored, and glared at. "No one liked me. Even Kit;" my voice faltered, "even she wouldn't have been my friend if her father hadn't told her to be."

Collin's eyebrows were pulled together, his forehead creased, his green sheen darkened. "Well that… that…" He stared at me for a few uncomfortable moments then his eyes softened. "That must have been rotten."

"But needed," Mitch said. His eyes had narrowed on Collin.

Collin shook his head, "No. She is the Princess. She should have… Someone should have…" He continued to shake his head then used the same foreign word Gredd had. "Everyone should have adored her."

"Remember, Collin," Mitch's voice sounded a little angry, "we are living in dangerous times. Using an Ignorance Spell was perfect. She couldn't be found if people didn't notice her."

"It was a rotten price to pay for her safety." Collin crossed his arms.

"But can you imagine what would have happened if someone had recognized her?" Mitch sat forward. "Can you imagine how much worse things would have been for her if she had been discovered by the wrong person? Ignorance was best."

Collin and Mitch sat glaring at each other. Then Samantha laughed.

They both turned to look at her. Clearly they couldn't understand why she was laughing… I couldn't either.

She covered her mouth but kept giggling, "The spell was so good that even Phillip didn't recognize her — and he was looking for her."

The mention of Phillip made me slump in the chair. *Where was he? What was he doing? Had I really seen him cuffed to a chair*?

Collin turned to look at me, "I'm sorry you had to grow up that way, Princess."

I shrugged, I was used to it. Actually, I missed it. I didn't like being bowed to every time I moved. I wasn't sure I liked being called *Princess* either, but even more I hated what it all meant. Right now I was only worried about a few people: Phillip, Kit'Una, Jef… soon it would be my job to worry about *everyone*. Everyone! Everywhere! *How was I supposed to do that when I couldn't even keep the people I cared about safe?*

"…Princess?" Collin was looking at me like he'd said something.

"Pardon?"

"I said we do have news about your neighbor, the 'Una boy. Jef'Una I think is his name."

"What about Jef?" I made a fist around the pearl he'd given me, hoping it wouldn't be more bad news.

"This morning Gredd sent out a rescue party. He should be arriving soon."

The idea of seeing Jef again made my chest feel lighter. I sat up, "And what about his sister? Kit?"

At first no one would meet my eyes. *This was bad!* "Is she… Did the Emperor…" my voice broke.

Samantha took my arm again, "She's alive… for now." She went on to explain that Kit had been chosen as the Emperor's newest bride, a position that had been filled several times before by girls from almost every planet in Quist. However, none of them had survived.

This was really, really bad!

"Why," my lips quivered, "why aren't they surviving?"

Again no one wanted to answer. I looked at Collin first. His eyes were turned down to the table again. When I looked at Samantha she ducked her head but answered.

"The Emperor's trying to create... some kind of... special child. It's supposed to... secure his throne — forever... somehow."

And he was going to do this with Kit! I brought my hand up to cover my eyes, "She's as good as — dead." My lips trembled.

"Not necessarily." Samantha said.

When I looked up I caught Mitch glaring at her.

Samantha ignored him and continued to explain, "*High* Emperor Zigel is using dark Magic to create this child. It's the Magic the girls can't — survive. But your friend, Kit, she's more tolerant — because she'd built up an immunity — from being around you — all the time."

I felt sick.

I'd doomed her!

Samantha squeezed my arm, "It'll be okay Princess."

There was no way this could be okay. I shook my head.

Samantha nodded, "But *you* can save her."

"How?" Anger coursed through me. *How was I supposed to save her*! Everyone thought I had all this Magic, but I'd never *done* anything Magical!

Samantha pulled her hand away from me with a gasp. When Mitch looked at her, she shook her head. "It's okay," she said softly, "You'll learn."

What if I couldn't?

Before I could say this Samantha sat a little taller and asked, "Didn't you guys bring food?"

"Lunch." Mitch stood up slowly.

"Dessert," Collin jumped to his feet. I noticed that he seemed to move a little slower favoring his right foot. Had he always had that limp? Was he limping like that when he took me to the banquet last night? I couldn't remember, but I might not have noticed.

"We can't start with dessert," Samantha said holding her stomach.

Collin's green complexion deepened, "Who says we can't? There's no one here to stop us." He started dishing something dark brown onto a plate. Once it was full, he brought it to me, "Besides, she didn't eat any last night. So, it's not like she's starting lunch with it, she's just finishing her dinner, after a really long pause."

"Collin I don't think…" Samantha's hand balled into a fist.

"But it's not up to you." He moved the plate closer to me. "It's up to the Princess." He passed me a fork.

I wasn't hungry and besides the plate looked as if it was piled up with dakkah.

"Just try it." Collin smiled at me.

It was the first time he'd smiled at me. I took the desert.

Collin kept watching — hopeful.

I smelt it. It didn't smell like hoorup droppings.

"It's cake," he said.

Mitch set a second plate of food next to my elbow. "Just in case you want something else."

The cake tasted sweeter than I expected.

"You like it!" Collin said wearing the biggest grin I'd seen on him yet. "You know if you wanted you could make a command that every meal starts with a desert."

"Collin!" Mitch scolded. "That would be a rotten command!"

"Not for me," Collin grumbled, his lips turning down.

To be honest the cake was almost too sweet for me. "I'll tell you what," I smiled at Collin, "I won't make it a command, but I won't mind if you want to start with desert when it's just us."

Collin's grin reappeared, "Thanks Princess." He consumed three helpings before he went on to have two plates of the other food. Mitch had a plate of lunch before he ate a piece of the cake.

I politely sampled all the dishes the cook had prepared. He had *tried* to make more local food. Unfortunately, everything came out a little too salty. I ended up eating a whole bush of lu'umon berries instead.

"What was this again?" Mitch held up most of his unfinished food.

"Tuna."

"Huh, it sure doesn't look anything like the tuna on Riel."

"Doesn't taste like it either." Collin tried to spit his mouthful discreetly into his napkin. It would have worked better if he hadn't made such a face.

"It was a little overcooked." I popped the last of the lu'umon berries in my mouth.

"Those are supposed to be poisonous, you know?" Mitch said.

"I think you've been misinformed."

"They are," Collin said. "But you're the Princess, that's why you can eat them."

I pushed my plate away and leaned back into my chair. I did not bother telling them that Phillip had eaten a whole bunch and he hadn't died. I stared down at my hands. Where was Phillip? *Were they doing* anything to him? Would I able to see him soon?

Samantha jumped to her feet, her hand over her mouth, "I—" she started running. I didn't catch the rest of what she said. When she didn't come back Mitch went to find her.

Being alone with Collin made me feel uncomfortable. But when I looked at him he smiled and asked, "Is there anything I can do for you?"

I shook my head. I didn't want to slip back into a strained silence. "Why do you limp?" I said.

He ducked his head, looking like he didn't want to say, "It's from the burb — the one that got me in the cave..." His words trailed off.

"Oh," Now I felt bad, *again* — I had wished that to happen to him. "Sorry."

He looked up and shrugged. "It's okay. I don't think you knew what you were doing."

"I— didn't." I stared at him. *Had my wishing for it made it happen*? I wanted to apologize — again... No, I wanted to take it back. I wished the burb had never gotten him. "Can I see it?"

He looked like he wanted to say no.

"Please."

He hesitated then pulled his shoe off and extended his foot to me.

I could see the nasty red scar just under his ankle. I slid forward and ran my finger over it. His skin was still warm near the spot where it had burrowed, but I could tell they'd gotten the burb out before it had popped. Still, it had to have been very painful. "I'm so sorry."

He shivered and pulled his foot away.

"Does it still hurt?" I asked.

"No, not anymore." He put his shoe back on then glanced at me with a strange expression.

Mitch came back in. "Samantha's sick," he was mostly talking to Collin, "I called for Sue to come get her. Oh, and Tom's on his way."

"Tom?" I stiffened at the name. *He's the one who was supposed to break Phillip*… I looked from Mitch to Collin. *Or had I just dreamed that*? "Why is Tom coming here?"

"To see you." Mitch said. "Tom's our…" he frowned. "Well, he's kind of our local teacher."

I wondered if he would be as angry with me as Mz. Fow'Ler had always been… or worse? *Surely he was coming here to talk to me about what I'd done to Phillip*. Suddenly the air felt harder to breathe? *I'd ordered Phillip to stay in my bed*… No matter what, I knew that had been wrong. Would it be un-princess-like to hide under the table? I was sure it would, but it didn't stop me from wanting to do just that.

Collin stood. His face was a deeper shade of green. "Princess Danay," he said moving in front of me and dropping to one knee.

Mitch stepped forward. His expression was hard to understand, "Collin?"

Collin shook his head keeping his eyes on me.

"What are you doing?" My voice rose. Whatever it was made me feel nervous.

His color deepened into a solid green. "I'm about to pledge myself to you."

"Pledge yourself… what…?"

"Collin, are you — sure?" Mitch asked. His voice was tight.

Collin turned to glare at Mitch, "Positive. Aren't you?"

"No." Mitch crossed his arms.

"Huh." Collin shook his head then turned back to me, "Well, like I said, I am."

Panic tightened my chest, "Why…?"

"Because you're the Princess."

I took a deep breath balling my hands into fists. I glanced under the table, *that's really where I wanted to be*. "Do you — do you have to do this now?"

"He doesn't *have* to," Mitch said keeping his eyes on Collin. "Think about it. We only get to make this choice once."

"Yeah, and now I've made it." Collin hadn't looked away from me, "Please, Princess, I *want* to do this. Let me do this. If I don't then I'm bound to serve every Royal equally, including *High* Emperor Zigel."

I flinched. "But how can you know I won't turn out as bad as him? How can you be sure you won't want to change your mind?" After all, Collin had a permanent limp because of me. And Phillip had to be stunned and dragged away because of what I'd done. "M-maybe you should wait a while. Just to be sure."

"I *am* sure," he said, and he didn't give me a chance to say anything more.

"Princess Danay, I, Collin Meer, pledge my life, my love, my devotion to you. I swear to protect you in every way I know. From this moment on, I live for you and if need be, I will die for you."

I could feel it like silt'ment hardening into its form. He was pledged to me. There was no going back. Whatever I said — he would be bound to do — and yet, somehow, I felt like I was now indebted to him.

"Good afternoon." A tall, older man with silver-gray hair stood in the doorway to the meeting room. His face had deep lines that were set in his loose skin. His eyes were keen and alert as he surveyed the room. They stopped on Collin, still kneeling, before they finally lit on me.

Yup, he looked about as mad at me as Mz. Fow'Ler would be.

I shivered and pulled myself into my chair.

Collin stood up and turned to face Tom, partially blocking my view. I got the impression that he meant to do this, like he was trying to shield me.

Mitch turned. His arms still crossed over his chest. "Tom," he bowed his head.

"At ease," Tom said casually. "You know I mean no harm."

Mitch shifted into a more relaxed stance. Collin didn't budge.

"Princess," Tom said. His voice was strong—commanding.

I looked cautiously around Collin.

Tom's eyes were cold and hard. "There are some things we need to clear up," his lips turned down. "When you're ready I'll be waiting in the front sitting room." He gave a single nod and left.

I stood.

"You know you don't have to go," Collin said.

"It would be better if she did." Mitch made a face as he studied Collin then added, "But no one can make you, Princess."

Chapter Eighteen

Royal Lessons

Tom was sitting on the long silver sofa. He seemed comfortable — no, superior. Like he belonged, like he was a Royal, and I was nothing more than a Commoner.

As I approached he stood; tall, upright, and formal. *So this is how everyone in Tem felt when I stood near them... dwarfed.*

"Princess," he held out his hand. His voice was not loud or demanding but I got the distinct impression that he was a man who was listened to when he spoke.

His skin was cold as he gripped my small hand. It reminded me of when the eels had been wrapped around my arm, only the eels had felt friendly. He gave the smallest of bows, rolling his shoulders forward a fraction before he let my hand drop.

I moved to sit on the sofa across from him. He sat down on the silver sofa. Mitch and Collin stood on either side of me. There was no mistaking that they were guarding me. I didn't feel protected.

My stomach turned waiting for Tom to speak.

"I knew your mother," he said after a while. He crossed his legs and sat back. "I had the privilege of being one of her teachers." It seemed like his eyes were searching my face — looking for something.

Was he comparing me to her? Was I anything like her? … or was I nothing like her at all?

The pause stretched. Finally Tom looked away, "I must say, she was a pleasure to teach." When he turned back, his eyes looked dark. "At least I enjoyed my lessons with your mother far more than those with either of her brothers."

He'd taught them all. I wondered if this was supposed to make me feel better. If he'd taught all of them, then he knew all of them. *He knew my family better than I did* — that thought was unnerving.

"Your mother, Empress Zoe, had a mind for history. She was a wonderful student." He paused. "Of course, your uncle, High Emperor Zandr, was also a great student. A little too great." He chuckled to himself, then shook his head. "His mind was quick and sharp. He often understood a lesson before I was finished teaching it. But he liked to play pranks." Tom pressed his lips together and shook his head again. "I did not like the pranks he liked to play."

I tried to picture it. Tom, the man before me, teaching the last Royals. Was he as frightening to my mother or my uncles as he was to me? Probably not, Tom most likely never had to order any of them to be stunned... and they probably wouldn't have commanded a Loyalist to spend the night in their bed. I folded my nervous hands together and squeezed them tight.

Tom was talking about the rest of the Royal family, "The Ancient Royals; Avery, Amanella and High Empress Affie had focused on advancing Quista while they'd been in power. The Great Royals; Corinna, Cara and High Empress Connie continued in their parents' footsteps. But when the Elder Royals; Erikah, Elanna and High Emperor Emin were ruling, there was an inquiry from the Commoners. Many were dissatisfied with the advancements that had been made.

"By the time your mother and uncles were ready to take the throne, the Commoners had become discontented. Your mother took the Third throne — Empress to the people," he added thinking I didn't know that. "And, of course, your uncle Zandr was called to the High throne. They were quite successful attending to the Commoner's concerns and reuniting them. That was until..." Tom sighed. "Well, until all the ugliness happened." He pressed his lips together as if he'd said too much — as if he wouldn't say any more.

He folded his hands and stared at me. His eyes traveled from the crown of my head down to my feet. He frowned then looked into my face.

"I know you are overwhelmed to learn of the greatness from which you came. But we have little time to spare." He rubbed his mouth. His dark eyes clouded. "There are things you need to know. Things you must be taught. And things you will have to learn."

He stopped. I'm not sure if he expected me to protest or ask him to continue. When I did neither he looked from Collin to Mitch and back to me.

"And things we must prepare you for." His voice faltered for the first time. "As you must know by now we need you to take the throne from Emper— Emperor," he covered his mouth, wiped and started again, "*High* Emperor Zigel."

I cringed.

"This will not be an easy task. Especially since you are — so — underprepared." Again he looked me over, clearly unimpressed with what he saw. "We have far to go. We might not even have enough time to train you properly before…" He looked away from me and sighed, "Then ready or not, we will have to fight."

For a brief moment I thought I might be ill.

"Now, before we get started," Tom sat up straighter. "Princess, you should know that your little stunt last night has had devastating results."

I covered my face as it heated up. *Ordering Phillip to stay in my bed had been wrong.* "I'm sorry." I kept my face covered so I couldn't see everyone's eyes on me. But, I could still feel them.

No one spoke.

"I-I shouldn't have given that rotten command." I confessed.

"It was *rotten*." Tom agreed.

I nodded, keeping my face covered waiting for Tom to tell me what my consequences would be.

When he didn't I glanced up.

He regarded me with one eyebrow arched. "Exactly what command are you talking about?"

I couldn't believe he was going to make me say it out loud. "Or-ordering Phillip to stay," my cheeks burned. I bit my lip. "To stay in my bed."

I couldn't even imagine what my Nan'Dah would have said about what I'd done. Princess or not it was very un-Danay like.

"That, my dear," Tom's voice cut through me, "is not the problem here."

When I looked up his eyes narrowed.

"Oh, do not get me wrong. That was extremely inappropriate. But had that been your only command last night Phillip would not have to be locked up."

I covered my mouth. *He was locked up*!

Tom continued, "You, Princess, need to learn to watch your words."

"My words?"

Tom's voice rose as he explained that when I told Phillip he was never to leave me again, Phillip had taken it to be literal — as if it was a command.

I felt winded, "I-I didn't mean it like that! It was just... just a saying!"

"Yes," Tom leaned forward, his voice going quiet, "and every word that comes out of your mouth can be taken as a command."

I cringed away.

He paused to take a breath sitting back again. "That is why you need to think about what you intend to say before you say it."

I pressed my hand tighter to my mouth. My Nan'Dah had always told me how dangerous words could be. I suddenly understood what she had been trying to teach me. I nodded solemnly, "Okay, I promise. I will. Now can you please let Phillip go?"

"No." Tom said curtly. When I looked up he said, "No. It's not possible," only this time he spoke more softly.

"Why not?"

"Can you imagine what would happen if Phillip were allowed out of his room?" Tom scrutinized my face again. "You have commanded him never to leave you. He would be compelled to find you and stay by your side."

On first thought I liked that idea. If he never left me again I'd never be alone. He'd go wherever I went… everywhere I went. Suddenly I pictured Samantha trying to give me a bath — it was already bad enough with her there but Phillip… The idea made me blush again. I pressed my lips together.

"You don't want that," Tom said, though it sounded much closer to a question.

"I don't want that." I agreed. *I didn't want it… not really. Not like that.* "So I'll just *un*-command him."

Tom shook his head slowly, "Commands, once given, are very hard to *un*-do." When I didn't say anything he continued, "That is why you must learn to choose your words carefully before you use them."

I nodded — I'd promised I would, and I would keep the promise.

"Because of you Phillip may have to live under lock and key for the rest of his life." Tom's eyes stayed hard on me.

I nodded again. "I understand."

"He can never see you again."

I wanted to shake my head. I fought the urge. The idea of never seeing Phillip again made me want to cry. To scream. To demand he be brought to me right away. I bit my lip and nodded. "O-okay," I said keeping everything else I wanted to say inside.

"He will be a prisoner until the day he dies." Tom hadn't looked away.

"Enough!" Collin said stepping closer to me. "Enough," he said again more quietly going a deep shade of green.

"Enough?" Tom's eyes pierced into Collin. "You think our lessons should be done for the day?"

Collin's hands balled into fists. "I think the Princess understands what she's done."

From the corner of my eye I saw Mitch shaking his head. When he caught me watching he stopped and glared back.

"But it *was* a mistake," Collin continued. He shifted even closer to me. "She didn't know what she was doing. She said she's sorry. So, just lay off her."

"Do you think she will learn what she needs to know all on her own?" Tom asked. "Perhaps we should just feed her cake and hope that she never *accidentally* condemns anyone else to a life in prison."

"It was an accident." I slid forward. *Did Tom really think I could do that to someone on purpose*? Could he really believe I'd do that to Phillip on purpose? I thought of Phillip, in that room, handcuffed to the chair. "I will find a way for Phillip to be free of my command." I said.

Tom regarded me with his eyebrow arched — skeptical.

"I will." I bit my lip. "Just-just take the handcuffs off. He doesn't need to be in handcuffs."

Tom leaned back a finger width. "Who said anything about handcuffs?" He looked from Collin to Mitch. Both shook their heads.

"You said he was under lock and key." I said quickly realizing that I had seen what I'd seen and also that no one knew I'd seen it. And without fully understanding why, I didn't want them to. "A-and Samantha told me he was tied up."

Tom's brows bunched to almost touching. He regarded me for a long moment. Finally his face relaxed, "All right."

He shifted and reached beside the sofa to pick up a large cloth sack. As it moved, I could hear clinking sounds.

Tom placed the sack on the floor between his knees and pulled out three yellow spheres. He placed them on the glass table between us. "Now, lift these into the air."

I leaned forward to pick them up.

"Use your Magic." Tom instructed.

I pulled my hand back. *Use my Magic*? How was I supposed to know how to do that? I fought the desire to reach out again. Instead I looked at the spheres.

They were each about the size of my fist. Perfectly round. All yellow, though each had a different hue... I wondered how much they weighed. Were they light or heavy? Would they feel warm or cold? Soft or smooth? Would any of that make a difference?

"Princess?" Tom's eyebrow was raised again.

"How— how am I supposed to lift them with my Magic?"

He crossed his arms, "It is simple, really, all you need to do is tell them what you want them to do."

As I started to open my mouth Tom snapped at me again. "Use your Magic!"

I shut my mouth. I looked at the spheres, thinking about how cool it would be if they rose up off the table, spinning around in the air, maybe buzzing past Tom's head so he'd have to duck.

But as much as I wanted that to happen the spheres did not move.

I tried, over and over again. For—a—really—long—time.

"Princess," Tom said shifting closer.

My eyes rose to his, "I," I glanced at the spheres again, "I can't."

"You aren't trying hard enough."

I looked back at the spheres.

"It is a simple task; even a child should be able to do it."

Collin crossed his arms. "If it's so simple they why don't you do it?"

"Come now!" Tom snapped, "You know that only Royals have Magic."

What if I really wasn't a Royal? I slouched back, "Maybe I'm not true Royal. I wasn't a triplet. I only have the Magic my mother gave me. What if that isn't enough."

"You are Magical enough." Both Collin and Tom said at the same time.

I'm pretty sure they didn't mean to do that.

Tom laced his fingers together, "I assure you, Princess, you are Magical enough to do this."

I didn't like the way he said 'I assure you'. I didn't feel at all *assured* when he said it.

"Maybe all those Turns of being drugged by her doctor made her Magic go away." Collin said.

How did Collin know about that?

Tom kept his gaze on me and answered, "Your medicine has nothing to do with this."

"Are you sure?" I asked expecting him to *assure* me again.

He didn't. His eyes wandered to the spheres he'd put on the table. After a moment it was clear he didn't intend to answer me.

"Tom? Are you sure?"

"I'm..." he paused like he needed to choose his words carefully.

"Don't lie to me!" I snapped, "Don't ever lie to me!" I crossed my arms over my chest. Then, too late, I realized I'd just given Tom a command.

He levelled his eyes with mine and nodded, "Yes, I am sure that when you are ready, you will be able to do this."

Great, now it would be my fault if I couldn't do it.

He leaned forward and took two of the spheres away, "How about trying it with one?"

And now I was a total loser.

I glared at the single sphere. Nothing happened. I stared at it until my eyes watered. Nothing happened. I blinked and stared some more. Still, nothing. The stupid yellow sphere — such a warm color, and yet my feelings towards it were growing quite cold — stayed exactly where Tom had put it.

I wanted to throw it across the room. I wanted to watch it hit the wall and smash into a million tiny pieces. None of those thoughts helped.

Finally I stood up, picked up the sphere, and held it over my head, "Done."

Collin laughed.

"Very funny Princess, but I don't think you understand the gravity of the situation."

"Oh? I don't!" I dropped the sphere hearing a very gratifying clunk as it hit the glass table. "What don't you think I understand? That I need to learn to do this so *I* can control the planets; all twelve of them, plus their fifty-six moons and the three suns." If I couldn't even get a tiny sphere the size of my hand to levitate off the table how was I going to keep the worlds safe? And if I couldn't do that how was I going to defeat my uncle? And if I couldn't defeat my uncle then Kit would die.

"Princess, calm down." Tom sat up so tall he was almost the same height as me standing.

I kicked the table. "No! I don't know how you expect me to do this." I shook my head. "I mean how am I supposed to defeat my uncle when he's had his whole life to practice his Magic? He is the *high* Emperor. Children don't take the throne, it's supposed to be given to them. And I'm not even old enough! I'm not eighteen Royal Years! I can't…"

"That is enough." Tom stood. His eyes were hard. "That is quite enough for today." He looked down at the single sphere. "We will try again tomorrow. However, I expect you to practice tonight." He rolled his shoulders slightly forward then he straightened and left.

I glared at the sphere. I didn't need to practice failing — I had that down.

~ ~ ~

I dismissed Collin and Mitch. Mitch seemed relieved. Collin was worried about me missing dinner. I told him he could go enjoy it for both of us. With them gone I made my way back to my bedroom where I fell onto the covers and buried my head in the pillows.

Sleep came even more swiftly than the night before, but it was filled with frightening images and terrifying thoughts.

I dreamed about Emperor Zigel — even though I didn't know what he looked like, I knew it was him. He knelt in a cave filled with the flickering flames of a hundred dark candles that looked like they were bleeding instead of melting.

He was chanting words I didn't recognize. But I didn't need to know the words to know what he was saying was meant for harm. And I could tell by the curl of his lip and the set of his brows, that the idea of them brought him great pleasure.

He smiled; it wasn't a nice look. It made me want to shrink from him. His chanting increased, his smile deepened, the smoke grew thick and then someone screamed.

I sat bolt up in my bed. *It hadn't been just someone who screamed. It had been Kit.*

Chapter Nineteen

Night Visit

I sunk back into my pillows. Dread filled my stomach. More than ever, I needed to see Phillip.

It happened again, the same as it had the first time. Suddenly, without leaving my suites, I was in a new room. Phillip was there. He sat on a cot pushed up against the wall. His hands still bound behind his back.

"Phillip!" This time when I moved, he looked up. *He could see me*! "Phillip?" I knelt next to him being careful not to touch anything — for fear of falling right through.

His eyes tracked my movement.

"You can see me, right? And hear me too?"

He nodded slowly.

"Is something wrong? Why aren't you talking?"

In response, he glared past me. I turned around to see Collin sitting in a chair, next to a desk, against the opposite wall.

"Anyways," Collin said, "you were right, she *is* amazing."

"Yes, she is." Phillip's eyes flickered to my face and back to Collin.

Collin had missed it, "I get it now, how easy it was for you to get drawn in by her."

"Yes," he said lowering his head. "That was easy too. But enough about me. How were her lessons with Tom?"

Collin launched into a rather long-winded explanation. I summed it up in two words, "They sucked."

Phillip grinned at my response, then turned back to Collin, waiting for him to finish. Surprisingly, Collin sounded impressed with me... I couldn't see why, I hadn't done anything. I couldn't even get one sphere to levitate off the table.

"...I could see how hard she was trying. I don't know why she couldn't get it."

"She probably just needs to practice."

"That's what Tom said." Collin frowned.

Phillip's brow wrinkled, "Is Tom coming back to teach her again tomorrow?"

"Yeah," Collin's brows came together, "But maybe she needs better instructions than just *do it*."

"Is that all Tom told her? Just *do it?*" The edges of Phillip's mouth were hard. "That's not much to go on. Maybe tomorrow you could ask him how High Emperor Zandr described it. Or even how one of the Greats or the Elders did it?"

Collin nodded, "That's a good idea, I'll ask. But Phil, what if she's not ready for this? What if... what if she's not ready even when she needs to be?"

I turned to look at Collin. *What if I wasn't?* What would happen to Kit... or Collin, or Phillip, or even Samantha if I wasn't ready when I needed to be? Fear washed over me like waves on the sea.

"Don't you worry," Phillip said. He was looking at me. He switched his gaze to Collin, "She will be. Like you said before, you can see how good she is. She'll be ready when she needs to be."

"She is good." Collin beamed. "I mean really, really good. She's amazing. She's..." Collin sat forward, "I pledged myself to her."

"You did?" For the first time Collin had Phillip's undivided attention, "How'd that go?"

"It was way easier than I thought it would be. Uncle Morris was right. I felt it," he put his hand on his chest. "I was moved and I just knew it was the right thing to do."

Phillip glanced at me, "And what did Danay think about that?"

"Well," Collin laughed a deep laugh, "she was kinda freaked out. But she was already totally freaked out about Tom coming, so I'm not sure what upset her more. She started trembling at the mention of his name. Do you think she knows?"

"Probably," Phillip said. He bowed so I couldn't see his face.

"Anyways, I saw how terrified she was. She needed someone who was — you know — on her side, like what you've been doing. I totally get it now. And now that it's done, I gotta say, wow. I feel so much better. That's how you felt after you pledged yourself to her, right?"

Collin didn't wait for his answer. "I just can't believe how much freer I feel. It's right, you know, as Loyalists, it's what we are meant to do. Fighting it seems so silly now."

"What does Mitch think about this?" Phillip asked.

Collin shook his head, "He doesn't get it. But he'll come around. I know he will."

Phillip's lips pressed together.

"Anyways," Collin stood and started towards Phillip.

I tried to step out of his way so he wouldn't walk through me. I wasn't quick enough. I shuddered and turned to see him clap Phillip on the shoulder. *How long had they kept Phillip like this? Hadn't I told them to take the cuffs off?*

"Don't worry about the Princess," Collin said. "I'll take care of her until — until all of this gets sorted out." Collin went to the door and banged on it three times, "I'm done here." The door slid open and he left.

"Danay?" Phillip's voice was just a breath.

"Yes?"

His forehead wrinkled, "Are you really here?"

I nodded.

"How?"

I didn't get a chance to give an answer. *Not that I had one.* The door hadn't closed behind Collin. Someone was standing there.

Phillip looked beyond me, startled, "Tom."

Tom's keen eyes searched the entire room twice, like he was looking for something. *Like he was looking for me.* Finally he stepped in. He had a tray of food. He brought it to where Phillip sat and set it down beside him. Then he undid Phillip's cuffs.

Phillip rotated, shook, and massaged his arms for several minutes. He was careful not to look at the spot where I stood. Tom seemed to be watching him, suspicion clear on his face.

"Any word when we might be leaving this planet?" Phillip asked as he started to pick at the food — not bothering with the utensils.

"Now that we have the doctor," Tom's tone was guarded, "it shouldn't be too long."

Phillip made a face, "And you still plan to…" he was cut off.

"You are not in any position to be discussing our plans."

Phillip dipped his head, "Of course." When he looked up again his eyes flitted to me — just briefly.

Tom spun to look at the spot where I stood. He glared through narrowed eyes. After a few moments, he turned back. "Is there…"

"Done." Phillip pushed the tray away. He'd barely eaten anything. With a deep breath, he held his hands out.

"No, you are free of the cuffs for now."

"Really? That's kind of you."

"It wasn't me." Tom said, "You can thank the Princess for that."

"No I can't." Phillip said but he shot me a quick glance.

Tom sat on the cot next to Phillip and exhaled, "Maybe you can thank her in your dreams."

"I'm not ti—" he looked down at the empty cup in his hand. Then his hand went slack and the cup fell. "You…" He blinked a few times like he couldn't focus his eyes. "Why'd you do that" He slumped against the wall.

Tom caught his head and guided his body to the cot. "Because I know how compelling a rotten command can be." He moved Phillip to his side and took off his shoes.

After he'd straightened he turned as if expecting to see me.

I'm not sure if he did. I gasped and blinked and suddenly I was back in my room again. I shrieked in frustration and fell into my pillows.

"Danay?"

I straightened at the sound of Phillip's voice.

He was standing at the edge of the bed, just outside the curtains. His chest heaved like he'd been running and couldn't catch his breath.

"How'd you get here?" I said crawling over to him, "I just saw…"

"I don't know," his eyes were wide.

I pushed the curtains aside and tried to grab his arm but my hand went right through him. We both jumped. The curtains fell back into place. "What's going on?"

He shrugged looking white and pasty. "I'm not sure. It must be something you did." He stared at me for a while. "You must have brought me here. Well, at least you brought part of me here." He waved his hand through the curtains that separated us without disrupting them at all. He looked... unhappy.

"Are you okay?" I asked drawing my knees to my chin. *Was I hurting him more*?

He gave a tiny nod and answered in the same overly breathy tone, "It'll be fine."

I was glad to have Phillip with me, but it wasn't fair to him if he didn't want to be here. I took a moment to look into his light blue eyes. "It's not fair. You shouldn't have to stay if you don't want to."

He shrugged, "I can stay."

"Sure, you *can*," I drew my arms tighter around my legs. "That's not really the problem is it?"

Phillip laughed. It was a nice sound.

I told him how I wanted to un-do my command. I also told him about how Tom said it wouldn't be easy. "I'm really, really, really sorry." I said feeling miserable.

"I know." He tried to pat my knee but his hand went through it. "Danay, I know. You didn't mean it. You didn't know what you were doing."

"It still doesn't feel fair." I wiped at my tears wondering what I could say to free him from my command. "What if I just command you to stop following my commands?"

"Don't." Phillip held his hand up to my face. "Don't," his gaze bore into me. "Don't ever. That is a forbidden command."

"Why? Why can't I just..."

"Because I'm a Loyalist, bound to serve Royals. It would not be natural. Please do not command me to be something I'm not."

"But..."

"No Danay— just... no. It would not be good for anyone, especially not for me."

I wanted to argue that if he didn't have to follow my commands then he could choose to be with me — I didn't. He could also choose not to be with me. I bit my lip.

"Danay?"

"What if I commanded you that it's *your* choice when you come and go?"

Phillip stepped back bringing his hand to his chin, "Maybe… I think it — you could try." He said with a shrug.

That wasn't very convincing. I tried anyway. "Phillip Dis'Hyroo, I command that you can come and go as you desire." I waited.

He didn't speak. He didn't move, but his eyes darted back and forth like he was thinking.

"Did it work?"

He smiled at me, "I guess we'll know when I want to leave."

Did he really just say he *wanted* to stay?

"Now," he stepped back, "where are these balls Tom wants you to levitate."

~ ~ ~

The spheres were exactly where Tom had left them — in the bag. Except the solitary yellow one that sat on the table. I steadied my gaze on it and glared.

Still nothing happened.

Phillip was looking at it thoughtfully. "You know, that looks like one of the suns in our teaching model of Quista. I wonder…" He bent down then cursed as his hand went through the bag. "Danay, can you pick that up for me."

I picked it up and held it open.

He frowned, "I can't see if all the planets are in there."

"Only one way to find out," I said. Then I dumped the contents of the bag onto the table.

The clanging of each sphere as it tumbled out, sounding close to breaking, was slightly nerve wracking. And as more and more colored spheres rolled off the edges of the table and across the carpet the sheer number of them was enough to make me feel overwhelmed. Soon I'd be expected to make all of them float in the air… and eventually I'd have to do the same thing with the planets they represented.

"There's too many." I said sinking to my knees.

"No." Phillip knelt next to me, "No. Don't think like that. Don't worry about all of them, just..." He craned his neck looking around. "Just worry about one." He stood up and moved to the edge of the carpet where a smaller blue sphere had come to rest.

He waved his socked foot through it, "Danay, this one. Just worry about this one."

I picked it up. As soon as I touched it I felt a sense of familiarity.

"That's Uma'Three," Phillip said peering over my shoulder. "And if you turn it a quarter turn to the right you'll see — Tem."

"It's..." I looked at my home village. My vision blurred as tears sprang to my eyes. "It's beautiful."

I could hear the smile in Phillip's voice, "This is my favorite world in all of Quista. See the dark blues of the Deeps and the light blues of the Shallows. I didn't know such contrast existed in just one color until I saw Uma'Three. This orb doesn't do her justice."

I turned the sphere around, looking at it from every angle. The more familiar it became the lighter it felt.

"Before we moved to Tem," Phillip continued, "we stayed in Mocc." Phillip helped me find the city. He told me about how it was built on a dying coral reef. But they were restoring it. Now it housed humans and a vast array of animal life too. He also pointed out a few of the other cities and villages where he'd visited. "You know I had the privilege of reading Great Empress Connie's journal a few turns ago."

I was barely paying attention to him but I nodded like I was.

"She said that when she learned to move the planets she didn't feel like *she* had to control them. All she had to do was allow the Magic to work through her."

Suddenly, I realized the sphere was spinning. And it wasn't being moved by my fingers. They weren't even touching it. I took my hands away and the sphere stayed where I'd left it; slowly spinning at shoulder height in front of me.

"That's my Danay," Phillip said softly. I felt it as his hand tried to brush aside my rogue clump of hair. He gave a frustrated sigh as his fingers went through it.

I pushed my hair out of my face then looked down to the other spheres.

"What are you looking for?"

"Uma'Four."

Uma'Four was a much deeper and more consistent blue. I tried to get it to levitate but it fell to the floor as soon as I removed my hand.

I tried to levitate Uma'One, the only Uma planet that wasn't almost entirely water. It had tall mountains between great expanses of water. I could feel them like dull spikes as I pressed my hand around it. I rotated it trying to become familiar with every detail of its strange surface. I knew there were long docks that connected all the mountains. I wondered if they used lu'umon paste to make them float or if they'd found another way.... Or were the docks rooted to the ground beneath them like some of Tem's permanent docks.

As I attempted to levitate each sphere, Phillip asked me questions about my life. What was my favorite part about living in Tem: the Popling Festival, though a jellie hatching came in as a close second. If I'd been good at any particular subject: swimming. And what had my Nan'Dah been like.

"She was a midwife." I told Phillip when he'd asked what her job was.

"I bet she was good at it," he grinned. "You know she would have been your mother's midwife, right? She would have," he blushed a little, "You know, midwifed you."

I hadn't thought about who Nan'Dah was before she was my Nan'Dah but I guess that made sense. "She was the best."

Uma'One was nearly four finger widths above my palm. It floated almost half way up to where Uma'Three was still rotating.

"When we moved to Tem there were two other midwives there." Phillip seemed to be hanging on my every word. "But within a year one moved away and the other quit; no one wanted the others once Nan'Dah started working."

"Cool." His smile grew. "Did she ever take you with her? I mean, were you ever able to watch her work."

"No." I said a little too grumpily. As I did Uma'One gave a strange shudder and seemed to jump to the floor — going right through Phillip's foot.

"My mistake," he said as I bent to pick up the sphere.

"Your mistake?" I got Uma'One to lift a finger's width off my palm but it didn't seem to want to move higher.

"Yeah, of course you wouldn't be able to go with her." When I didn't understand, he looked pointedly at Uma'One and 'Three. "Your Magic, though mostly medicated out of you…" he pressed his teeth together until they squeaked. Then he shook his head, "Anyways, Commoners aren't meant to be around it. Can you imagine how it would have changed a baby if you were there when it was being born?"

This reminded me of Kit. I'd changed her. I bit my lip wondering how I was going to save her. If I'd be able… *or if I'd be too late.*

I stooped down to pick up Uma'Two. The world had islands like Uma'One but they weren't mountains; instead they were small regions of beaches. It made the sphere spotty. I'd been told that its sand was smoother then the finest sand on Uma'Three. When I pressed on the golden spots they did feel silkier.

"When do you think we'll be able to leave?" I asked. When he didn't answer I added, "I heard they found the doctor. So what are we waiting for now?"

Phillip rubbed the back of his neck, "Jef…"

I turned to look at him, "Have they found him? Are they…?" I didn't want to hope for too much. The last I'd seen of him he'd been knocked unconscious and taken away.

"They've found him. He's on his way."

My heart jumped. I felt my cheeks lift. Uma'Two and 'One floated above my hand like they were chasing each other. "So once he's on the ship, are we going to go?"

"Maybe. My dad wants…" but he didn't finish his thought.

"What does your father want?" I picked up Uma'Four again but it wasn't lifting off my hand. I prodded it with a free finger.

"He wants the doctor to make you more medicine."

The thought of it made me flinch. "Why?"

Uma'Three sunk to my hand settling next to Uma'Four.

"Well, your Magic is kinda out of control. It's all over the place. Right now we're using the ship's shields to keep it hidden, but with the power it's taking there's no way we can get off the world." Phillip stopped. He must have seen the horror on my face.

I couldn't let the ship be found. If it was, it wouldn't just be me they'd find! What would happen to everyone on the ship — all the Un-Loyalists — if we were caught? *I couldn't believe what I was about to say,* "Okay then, I'll take my medicine."

I felt Uma'Two fall into my palm.

"No!" Phillip tried to grab me. His hands sunk right through my arms.

"But we need to get off the world." I said. Uma'One dropped.

None of the spheres were levitated any more.

"Getting off the world isn't the biggest problem. Whether we're off world or on it, until your Magic is under control we will always be at risk of being found."

"Then maybe I need to keep taking my medicine all the time." Bile rose up my throat making me choke a little.

"No!" Phillip was shaking his head... actually, *he* was shaking. "Listen, your medicine wasn't made to take only a little of your Magic away. It takes it all. Danay, you need your Magic. And even worse every time you take your medicine it makes it that much harder for you to find your Magic again."

The four spheres felt heavier in my hand. My arm ached. I had to put them down.

Phillip took three long breaths then spoke again, "What you really need to do is learn to control your Magic yourself. And Tom needs to," he ground his teeth, "teach you. I mean, he hasn't really done anything!" Phillip started pacing, "What's all this business of *just do it*. Do what! How are you supposed to know how to do something you've never done before! He's the teacher. He should know how to explain it to you. He should be *teaching* you!" He continued to pace, grumbling incoherent words.

"Okay, *you* don't want me to take my medicine."

Phillip continued to pace.

I stood in the way so Phillip had to stop — or go through me.

He stopped.

"I get it. You don't want me to take it. But I do." He looked like he wanted to argue. "No, losing you or Collin or Samantha…"

Phillip flinched at Samantha's name.

I realized I hadn't seen her since breakfast. "Is something wrong with Samantha?"

It took a lot of coaxing to get him to tell me Samantha was in the medical ward. She'd gotten sick when she was with me and though Phillip didn't say so, I was pretty sure it was because of me — because of my Magic. I remembered how she'd jumped when I'd gotten angry, like my anger had somehow hurt her.

It was like I was an eel sending off Magic that zapped everyone around me.

"I have to go see her!" I said running to my front doors.

They didn't open when I got there.

Phillip arrived behind me, "They're made to lock you in." He shook his head. "Dad's afraid that if you get out you might end up wandering around the ship giving commands to everyone. He didn't think that would be safe."

Not just commands, I thought, *but also zapping people with my Magic.* I could only imagine how many more people would be in the medical ward if I'd been wandering around the ship. *No one was safe with me around.*

"For you Danay," Phillip said as if he knew what I was thinking. "He didn't think it would be safe *for* you. We all want *you* to be safe, even though he may not do it the way I think he should."

"Oh?" I didn't know what to say. I turned back to the door and started pounding on it; screaming to be let out. I needed to see Samantha. I needed to undo what I'd done to her!

The doors never opened.

I slid to the floor, but I wasn't giving up. *There was a way I could leave my suites — and they couldn't stop me.* I crossed my legs and let my hands drop to my lap.

Phillip knelt next to me. "What are you doing?"

I looked at him. "You need to go back to your body."

"But I…" he closed his mouth and shook his head, "I don't want to leave you alone."

I nodded. He was being Loyal. “Thank you. But I'm ordering you to go back to your body now.”

His face turned down. “No, you commanded that it was my choice to come and go.”

I had. I scowled. “But, I meant your body, not your spirit. Now leave me and don't come back until all of you can be here.”

He shook his head but I blinked and he was gone.

Chapter Twenty

Healing

Leaving my body was harder to do now that I knew what I was trying to do. I was only able to manage it by thinking about Samantha.

When I opened my eyes all I could make out were bright lights. For a moment I panicked because my Nan'Dah had told me once that after you died you would go to a warm bright place. I thought maybe I'd followed Samantha there.

I blinked again and things came into better focus.

The room was long and narrow with eight beds, four along either side of it. Beside each bed was a small machine that looked as if it could be connected to a person by two red wires. Only one of the beds was occupied.

Samantha lay on her back, eyes closed, her chest barely rising with each breath. The number on the machine next to her bed was slowly blinking red.

"Go get some rest." Sue stood next to Samantha's bed. She was facing Mitch. "I promise if anything changes I will send for you."

Mitch's jaw flexed, "I don't..."

"You need to lie down. That is an order."

"Fine." Mitch scowled then did an about face and walked right through me. I shuddered.

"Mitch," I heard Gredd's voice and spun.

Gredd was standing just inside the door.

"Captain." Mitch bowed. He straightened up and looked at Gredd as if he expected him to say more. That's when I saw that Mitch's eyes were red and puffy like he'd been crying.

When Gredd didn't say anything Mitch bowed again, "Evening," he turned and left.

Gredd watched him go then came over to Sue.

This time I was able to avoid being walked through.

"I see the shaking has stopped," Gredd said, sounding hopeful.

Sue had been holding Samantha's hand. She tucked it under the covers with a frown. "Yes, but I'm not so sure it's a good thing, Sir."

Gredd shut his eyes.

"Sir, are you sure there's no way to get word to her parents? If she were my child I'd want to know."

"They are on Suvityd. It's too far to reach by com and a pod would be intercepted. I'm afraid that, for now, we can't even send a message to the surface."

"Does that mean you've lost communication with the rescue party for the 'Una boy?"

I put my hand over my mouth and looked at Gredd.

"Yes," Gredd shifted and straightened, "but I'm sure they are fine. Last I heard they'd made it out of Tem."

"Good." Sue stretched, fighting a yawn.

"Keep me informed of any changes." Gredd gave a nod and left.

"I will Sir." Sue watched him leave then sat down next to Samantha's bed again. "Sam, if you can hear me, I would like it very much if you didn't die tonight."

Samantha didn't stir. She was so pale she already looked dead.

Sue bowed her head, resting it next to Samantha. She started to sob quietly.

I stepped closer to Samantha's bed.

She wasn't like the girls on Uma'Three. All the girls there had a dark complexion and round faces. Samantha's coloring was closer to a common pearl like mine. Her lips were a deep pink and her nose was more pointed than I was used to, but she was still pretty. In sleep she looked younger. I'd thought she was close to my age, now I wondered if she'd reached her coming of age. She didn't wear a CoaB, but I think I'd read somewhere that the Coming of age Bracelet was only practiced on the Uma worlds.

Sue's sobs had been replaced with soft snores.

I tried to imagine what it would have been like if I weren't the Princess and Samantha had been my friend... That was foolish. I was the Princess. But regardless, Samantha was still kinda my friend.

I had to save her. But— how? The answer came before I'd finished asking the question: *my Magic.* Only how was I supposed to use my Magic?

I bit my lip... *Was I really biting my lip if I wasn't in my body*? ...If I wasn't in my body could I still use my Magic? ... But I had to do something — anything! I tried to take hold of Samantha's shoulders. My hands slid right through her.

She arched her back and gave a gasp. I pulled my hands away.

Sue stirred.

I bit down harder on my lip, waiting for Sue to fall back asleep.

"I'm going to fix you," I said holding my hands above Samantha's stomach. Then I slowly lowered them until I could feel her all around me. She felt warm, like healing sand. How I wished I had some healing sand right now, it could probably heal her better than I could.

Samantha started shaking.

"I have to heal you," I told her. "I don't want you to die."

She started to thrash. An orange light on the machine flashed. Then it beeped.

I pulled my hands away. "Please," I said. "If you die it'll be my fault. It will be like I killed you." My legs wanted to buckle. As I sagged, I tried to use the bed to hold myself up — but my hands passed through it. "You're not allowed to die." I held my hands to my knees bent so far down I couldn't see Samantha any more. I righted myself. "You hear me? You have to get better!"

The machine fell silent. Samantha was still again. Then her eyes snapped open with a gasp. She turned her head left and right. The room was filled with a loud whistling sound.

Sue was on her feet before she was really awake. "It's okay. It's okay," she held Samantha down.

"The Princess," Samantha choked.

"Relax, we need you to get better before you can worry about her."

Samantha's eyes found me. She stopped fighting and lay back, her gaze staying on me.

Sue held a small machine against Samantha's belly. It had a screen that Sue was watching. At one point I saw a beating heart.

"Princess," Samantha murmured.

I nodded, "How do you feel?" I asked. Sue asked the same thing a second after me.

"I'm better," Samantha said. She looked from me to Sue and back. "Did you do this?"

"I'm not quite sure," Sue's voice was thick with disbelief. "Perhaps my prayers worked."

"Are you sure you are *all* better?" I asked stepping closer to Samantha's head.

She nodded, "Completely." She tried to sit up but Sue held her down.

"Not yet. I need you to stay put. The bed cannot monitor you if you do not lie still."

Samantha's hand worked its way out from under the sheets; she reached out and through me, "Thank you."

"Thank the maker and be still girl," Sue snapped with more of a chuckle than displeasure.

"Okay," I said feeling as relieved as Sue sounded. I turned to go then looked back. "Don't ever get sick again," I said.

Samantha nodded solemnly, "I promise."

Sue tsked her and put a hand on her head. "Patience child. We're almost done."

I left the room through the side wall, intent on exploring the ship, but instead walked in on Gredd, Tom and Morris — who I walked right through.

I shivered and Morris's green sheen darkened.

I could see how I'd mistaken Morris for Collin's dad. Their features were so similar.

Tom looked at Morris his eyes narrowing, "Everything alright?"

"Fine, I guess." His color returned to its normal tone.

"You don't agree with the plan?"

Morris shook his head, "No I wasn't..." He stopped shaking his head, "I felt a—" his eyes looked around the small room.

This room was the same one I'd first seen Phillip in. The small square table separated the three men. Each sat along their own side. I slid into the empty space.

"—a chill," Morris finished. "I'm fine. And the plan is... fine too."

Tom's sharp eyes passed over me at least twice as he looked around the room. Finally they returned to Morris, "Good, then it is unanimous."

Gredd brought his hand up to the back of his neck the way I'd seen Phillip do, "*I'm* not so sure anymore."

Tom closed his eyes taking a long deep breath. "Why not?"

"Phillip." Gredd said.

Tom pounded the table, "That boy of yours..."

Gredd slammed both his hands onto the table and leaned forward, "That boy of mine might just have a point."

They stared at each other for a few moments.

"He didn't try to escape." Gredd finally said leaning back.

Tom put his elbow to the table and held his chin in his hands. "He didn't."

"Because the Princess commanded him in his dream," Morris said also leaning forward but sounding doubtful.

"And that is why I say we need to continue with the plan." Tom said.

Morris nodded. Both looked to Gredd.

"Fine," he said, pushing his chair out to stand. "Fine. But if this doesn't work..."

"Then we will come up with another plan." Tom said, as he stood and moved towards me.

I jumped back.

~ ~ ~

I was back in my suites lying on the floor. I got up stiffly and made my way to my bed where I slipped into a restless sleep.

I was following the Emperor down a narrow hallway. If he turned around I had nowhere to hide. I didn't want him to see me. I couldn't fight him. But I *had* to see where he was going. It was important. I had to know what he was doing.

He made it to the end of the hall and stopped at a door. The door was ordinary looking but by the way he put his hand against it I knew it was special.

I moved closer.

"You think I would let you see all my secrets that easily?" he said. His voice was as smooth as queen popling silk. He shook his head. From the part of his face that I could see he was smiling.

Then he started to turn.

He was a very handsome man. Long sleek neck. Nicely defined chin. Not at all what I expected him to be. His eyes were just about to find me.

I sat up out of my dream, sweaty, my heart racing. I pulled my arms around my legs and waited for the feeling of impending doom to pass. It took a while.

How was I supposed to fight the Emperor?

I needed to figure out my Magic. But first I needed to have a bath and change my clothes.

~ ~ ~

The bath was a disaster. I couldn't get the water temperature right. I also made it too slippery with the soap I used. I slipped right under when I tried to get out.

Sitting up, sputtering the sour tasting water out of my mouth and nose, I wondered if Samantha would be allowed to come back and help me today. Standing in front of my closet I realized how much I needed her.

I ended up re-wearing the dress Samantha had put me in the day before.

Cleaned. Dressed. I started towards the front sitting room with the intent to practice with the spheres again.

"Morning Princess," Collin said as I entered my smaller sitting room. "We've brought breakfast."

We've? I thought, expecting to see Samantha. *We* was Collin and Mitch. I tried not to look as disappointed as I felt.

"Should we set it up here?" Mitch smiled but it didn't look right. He took my silence as assent.

I slowly came closer. "Where's Samantha?"

Was it me or did Mitch clench his jaw?

"She was sick, but she's recovering."

It wasn't me.

"Didn't you wear that yesterday?" Collin was looking at me with his finger to his lips.

Both Mitch and I turned to stare at him. *What did it matter*? I thought. Mitch said it aloud.

"Come on, she can't wear the same thing two days in a row. What will people think?"

I wondered what people Collin thought I'd be seeing today who'd be noticing my clothes. The first name to come to mind was Phillip, but I didn't want to be too hopeful. Then I thought about Jef. "Any news on Jef?"

"They expect him to arrive soon," Mitch said with scowl.

"Come, you should change." Collin started towards my bedroom.

Both Mitch and I were staring at him again.

"Come," he turned back to me.

"Um..." Mitch said. His face was pale, "Collin, what do you think you're doing?"

"I'm helping the Princess find a new outfit." Collin rolled his eyes.

"I'm not sure," Mitch looked from Collin to me, "that's really appropriate."

"I'm only helping her pick it out. I'm sure she can get dressed herself."

Collin took me to my closet. He whistled when he saw everything I could choose from. "Remind me to compliment Samantha on the job she does next time I see her," he said. For a moment I thought he might give up like I had. But he didn't.

It took a while to find something. Collin wasn't adverse to taking things out and holding them up to me. He joked about one outfit that was nothing more than eight paces of cloth, one pace wide. "Perhaps," he said, "you lie on the floor and roll into it."

We both laughed.

Mitch watched at the doorway for a while. Collin invited him in to join the 'fun' as he called it — I guess the way he was going about things it was fun. Mitch declined and moved away to where we couldn't see him.

"He doesn't like me very much." I said.

"He doesn't trust you." Collin answered frowning at one of the outfits.

"I guess that makes sense." I thought about what I'd done to Samantha. Even though I'd fixed it, not that they knew it was me. And besides, I couldn't take back the fact that I'd hurt her — that I'd nearly killed her.

"It's not just that." Collin put the strange outfit back on the hanger and pulled a new one down. "His mom," he looked at the doorway to make sure Mitch hadn't returned, "His mom was a Commoner. It's rare, Loyalists don't usually marry Commoners, but it happens sometimes. His dad was stationed on Phossin so it wasn't too bad. But one day *High* Emperor Zigel came to visit the moon and suddenly she was pledged to him. She wasn't the only one."

When I asked how that was possible he said it shouldn't have been. But High Emperor Zigel found a way.

No wonder Mitch hated me. And, if that wasn't enough, Collin went on to explain that when his father fled from the Royal planet he'd left Mitch's mother and his twin sister behind. Everyone assumed they'd been killed.

Mitch returned to the doorway. His frown was so long I was sure he'd heard what we'd been talking about.

"Sue's here to see you," he said not quite meeting my eyes.

I nodded.

"Wear this." Collin said handing me the outfit he'd just pulled out of the closet. "It'll look nice."

I didn't really want to; it was a dress with an even shorter skirt than the one Samantha had put me in the day before. But I did because Collin had picked it.

Chapter Twenty-One

Un-Loyalist

Sue stood next to the coffee table, a large rolling trunk next to her. Mitch stood close by, not quite looking at me.

I wanted to say something to him. To apologize for what I'd done to Samantha... To apologize for what my uncle had done to his family. But I didn't quite know how to say sorry for such horrible things.

"Princess," Sue gave a bow. "Do you remember me?"

I moved closer, nodding. *How could she think I'd forget her*? Then I remembered that she didn't know I'd seen her last night at Samantha's bedside. In fact, the last time she'd seen me was at the banquet where she'd been asking about my doctor.

I took a seat on the sofa across from her, remembering to keep my knees together—I even pulled at my skirt so it covered as much of my legs as it could. "You brought food to me at the banquet." I said. "And you wanted to know if I knew where my doctor was?"

She shifted uncomfortably. Collin clenched his jaw. Mitch frowned as he looked over at Collin. *Or had he been frowning at me*?

"Yes, actually that's why I'm here." Sue undid the snaps to the trunk, "We found the doctor. He's on the ship."

"No medicine!" Collin jumped in front of me.

I pushed Collin out of my way so I could look at Sue, "It's okay..."

"No!" He stood in front of me again.

"I'm not here to give her medicine." Sue's voice was soft, innocent — almost too innocent.

I pushed Collin off to the side again. Mitch was definitely glaring at him... *or me... or both of us*.

I looked at the chest Sue was reaching into, "That's an awfully big trunk for just one small needle," I said to Collin.

"Oh." He seemed to relax a little.

Sue opened the lid to reveal several familiar looking machines. "I was going to say that your doctor needs me to give you a few tests." She pulled out the machine that tested my lungs. "May I?" She held up two tubes like limp eels but I got the impression she was concentrating on them so she wouldn't have to look at me.

"Why you?" I asked.

She still didn't look at me as she tried to attach the tubes to the box — backwards. "Well," she fumbled a few times before she turned them the right way around, "you kinda commanded that we weren't supposed to make you see him." She clicked the second hose into place.

Another command I'd given with my casual words.

"And after these tests we should be able to leave?" I asked.

Sue stared down at the machine as she answered, "Yes, once your doctor gets these results we should be good to go." Sue held the hose out for me to take. "Ready."

I wasn't, and I knew it. But we needed to get off the world.

I took the machine and started to blow into it. Sue administered each of my routine tests. Her ineptitude made every one of them take twice as long as it should have. Collin watched with suspicious eyes. I caught Mitch glaring a couple more times but I still couldn't tell if it was meant for me or Collin.

"Last test," Sue said as she passed me a familiar looking half-ball.

I sighed and took it. *I hated the balance machine.*

It was my job to stand on it for as long as I could. It wasn't that easy. Partly because I normally had terrible balance, but also because the machine would move like it was filled with burbs trying to pop. I always fell off at least once.

I bit my lip as I stepped onto the machine, wondering how hard the ground would feel as I fell onto it. I knew I'd have the answer soon enough.

Only, as I lost my balance, Sue caught me.

A spark raced between us like a zap from an eel.

"Ouch!" I gasped.

Sue let me go.

Mitch caught me. He looked just as surprised about it as me. He quickly lowered me to the sofa and let go.

Collin grabbed Sue and threw her to the ground. "What did you do?" he growled pushing his knee into her back.

"Get off me." Sue demanded. When Collin didn't budge she looked to Mitch, "Help me."

He took a step like he meant to help her then his eyes shifted to me and he stopped.

"What did you do?" Collin's voice shook. His fingers dug into her arms.

"Let go! You're hurting me." Sue squirmed but Collin had her pinned.

I stared down at Sue still feeling sore from where she had touched me. "What did you do?" I said.

Sue's face turned to me. "I didn't do anything," she snapped.

"Then what happened?"

"Collin, get off me!" She tried to push herself up and winced as Collin dug his knee deeper into her spine.

"Tell me what happened." I said rubbing at my sore arm.

Sue turned to me again. "I'm not sure." She exhaled. "I think..." she blinked a few times, "I think being pledged to *High* Emperor Zigel left a mark on me."

"You are pledged to my uncle?" I said. My stomach knotted painfully.

"Was." She winced as Collin's knee shifted.

"What do you mean *was*." Collin shook her. "You either pledged yourself to him. Or you didn't."

"I pledged myself to him. But I am no longer loyal to him," Sue said angrily.

"That's not possible!" Collin shouted.

"It is, and if you'd let me go I can explain it." Sue stopped struggling and stared at me.

Collin looked at me too.

My stomach continued to contract. If she was still loyal to my uncle then we were all doomed... but if she *was* loyal to my uncle then why hadn't she already given us up? I bit my lip.

Sue's dark eyes still scared me, but the compassion she had for Samantha made me hope that I could trust her. Regardless, I wanted to know what she'd say. "Collin, let her go."

He wasn't happy to, but he did. Sue pulled herself onto the sofa opposite me rubbing her arms where Collin's fingernails had left deep dents. Collin stood close, making it clear he was ready to pounce again if she even blinked wrong. This time when I caught Mitch glaring, it was unmistakably at Collin.

"Explain," I commanded.

Sue explained how she'd been looking forward to pledging herself to my mother for Turns. She was excited to reach her coming of age so she finally could. Only when the time came she was called to a special meeting with my uncle. When she got there she was tricked into pledging herself to him. Then she was forced to be loyal to him for many Royal Years.

She sounded genuine when she spoke.

Collin still didn't believe her. "You can't be forced to give your pledge! The Magic won't allow it."

"How is that any different than forcing a Commoner to Pledge?" I asked. Both shouldn't have been possible but my uncle had found a way. *How was I supposed to fight someone who knew how to do so many impossible things*?

Collin glanced at Mitch. Mitch's brows came together as he looked from Collin to me. "You..." he looked back at Collin. "You told her about my mom? Why?"

"She had a right to know."

"Why!"

Before Collin could answer I said, "Mitch I'm really sorr..."

"Don't even!" He held his hand up to me.

"Mitch!" Sue scolded.

"Ugh!" He threw his hands up in the air and stalked off towards the chairs against the wall. He slumped into one and crossed his arms glaring at the room. Or maybe at me but I tried to ignore him.

Sue picked up the balancing test and started to put it away.

"How did you get free of your pledge?" I asked Sue.

"I didn't get free," she said, her lips turned down. "I am a natural born Loyalist. I will always have to be loyal. However, High Emperor Zandr was able to reassign me to himself." Her frown deepened.

"Why aren't you happy about that?"

When Sue looked up she tried to smile, "I am happy." Her eyes betrayed her. "It's just..." She pressed her fingers to her lips for a moment, "It's just that I had wanted to be pledged to Empress Zoe." She sighed. "I never got the chance," her eyes brightened, "but it could have been worse. I could still be pledged to *High* Emperor Zigel. This is why it is important for you to take the throne. You need to continue the work High Emperor Zandr started and free all the Loyalists from false pledges."

Collin added quietly, "...and the Commoners."

As if taking the High Throne from my uncle wasn't going to be difficult enough; and ruling the worlds alone wasn't an impossible task, I'd also have to fix all the damage my uncle had done. I swallowed hard. So many lives depended on me.

"What's going on?" Samantha stood in the doorway to my sitting room.

"Samantha!" Mitch jumped off his chair and raced over to her. As he reached her he scooped her up in his arms pulling her tight to him. The hug felt so intimate I wondered if it was wrong to be watching.

"I'm okay. I'm okay," she said wriggling free of his arms. She turned and came directly over to me. Mitch trailed after her.

"You sure you're okay?" I asked.

"Better than." Her smile grew as she lowered herself to one knee and held her hands up to her heart, "Princess Danay..."

"No!" Mitch lunged towards her grabbing her arm to try and pull her up.

"Let go!"

He let go when she slapped his hand. "Sam, please... please think about..."

"I have. I've thought about it all morning. And I talked about it too. First I talked with Gredd, then Morris, and even Tom."

"You talked to my Dad?" Mitch looked unnaturally green. "What did he say?"

"That it's my choice." She turned to look at me. "And I've already made it. This," she glanced at Mitch and spread her hands out in front of her, "is just a formality. In my heart I'm already pledged."

"But why?" he choked.

"Because it's the right thing to do. When you're ready you'll see it too." Samantha turned back to me, "Princess Danay, I Samantha Wr'Ton pledge my life, my love, and my complete devotion to you. I swear to protect you in every way I know. From this moment on, I live for you, and if need be, I will gladly bleed for you."

Just like with Collin I felt Samantha's life silt'menting itself to me. But it was slightly different, I think, because when I'd healed her I'd already realized how important she was to me.

Before the silence could get too uncomfortable she stood up and asked, "So, what did I miss?"

Collin tried to fill her in as Sue put away all the machines she'd used. With the trunk packed she asked one final question. "Phillip mentioned you were shot? Can I see the wound?"

Being shot was news to Collin and Samantha and they seemed to make quite a bit of fuss over it — going between wanting to hunt down the shooter to offering to carry me around everywhere. Mitch rolled his eyes more than once. After they finally calmed down Sue was able to look at my calf.

The same painful jolt raced up my leg as she ran her fingers over my scar. "Sorry."

Collin looked like he was debating tackling her to the ground again. When I glanced at Samantha she looked like she was having the same thoughts.

"It's okay," I said more for them than Sue.

"I can't believe your wound healed so fast." Sue stood. "Have you always healed so quickly?"

"It wasn't really me. It was the healing sand."

"Healing sand!" Sue got so excited, her dark eyes almost sparkled. She'd heard of the healing sands, but they were only found on the Uma worlds, and even then they were rare. When she heard there was a cave full nearby she insisted on leaving my suites — to collect some for the ship.

Collin volunteered to take her. I'm not sure if he meant to help her or if he still didn't trust her. Either way, after they left it was just Samantha, Mitch and me.

Chapter Twenty-Two

Fresh Air

"Phillip and I were talking," Samantha said as she pulled me toward the front doors, "and we think you might feel your Magic better if you weren't locked in your suites."

"Where are you taking her?" Mitch asked pacing me on the right.

Samantha glanced over her shoulder, her eyes danced with excitement, "To get some fresh air."

"She can't leave the ship." Mitch said.

Samantha shook her head, "Actually she could if she really wanted to. But there's not really a ton of fresh air on the bottom of the sea." She continued to drag me past my front doors.

Two guards bowed as we came out. I expected them to try and stop us. They didn't, they just followed us as we continued away.

"Where is she going to get *fresh air* on the ship?" Mitch grumbled.

"You'll see."

Samantha brought me to the room where the forest grew. The moment I stepped in I breathed deeper.

"See, fresh air." Samantha laughed. The doors shut behind us leaving the guards on the outside.

"What the hell are we doing here?" Mitch asked folding his arms and leaning on the wall.

"I already told you," she copied his stance on the opposite side of the closed door.

I stood staring between the two not quite sure what I should do.

"Go on, explore." Samantha bobbed her head towards the path.

I took a few steps away.

Samantha and Mitch stayed where they were.

I quickly bent and undid my sandals which I walked out of. Then I moved further down the path until I was alone. *Trying to find my Magic...* I took another deep breath: the air was fresher. Warmer too. And filled with lovely and strange fragrances. I shut my eyes, swimming in the growing symphony of smells.

But my Magic isn't in the smells, I thought with a sneeze.

I left the path to explore deeper: the grass was cooler than I expected it to be. Each blade was smooth and prickly against the soles of my feet. It reminded me of my shark.

I wondered where my shark was? Would I ever see her again? My heart sagged a little. I missed her. I never got to say goodbye.

I leaned against a tree. Its trunk was as thick as me — no, thicker. Its bark was harder than I imagined it would be. Trees like this wouldn't survive on Uma'Three. I thought about the smooth rubbery trees where the poplings nested. They were so thin even I couldn't hide behind them.

Then I thought of the poplings. The air around their nests was always full of the fluffy creatures; white, bright, and soft when they brushed against you.

I moved deeper and deeper into the room examining the trees, the bushes and the varying types of plants. Magic was in everything. I could feel it. It had a deep slow moving kind of feel. But it wasn't my Magic.

I stopped moving. The room was quiet. There was no breeze, no other noise than my breath. Suddenly I felt very sad and alone.

I quickly returned to Samantha and Mitch. "I think I'm done."

"So soon?" Samantha asked. She looked disappointed. "Something wrong?"

"It's lovely, but I don't feel my Magic here more than in my suites."

"Oh," she scrunched up her nose.

I swung my foot over the prickly blades of grass. "Yeah, I would have expected some kind of animals to be here. Bugs at least."

Samantha reached out for my hand again. I expected her to take me back to my suites.

She didn't. "You want animals?" She led me deeper into the wooded area than I had traveled. When she stopped she was standing next to three trees that grew together in a strange spiral that created a kind of spindly ladder.

"Up there is an emergency escape hatch. You should see something through it."

The emergency hatch was just big enough for me to sit in. It made me feel like I was in a little air bubble at the bottom of the deeps. And I did see lots through it.

I'm sure the ship hadn't been here long enough, yet somehow it had been covered in what looked like a mature coral reef. Sea urchins, anemones and every variety of fish pressed tight to it as they would the living rock of a coral reef. Everything was lit up by several families of jellies.

I pressed my hand to the glass as an octopus swam past and disappeared around the edge of the ship. Two mammoth stingrays danced overhead. But I never felt my magic nor did I see my sharks.

What if I couldn't find my Magic? How long did Phillip think I could take? When would Tom initiate his plan? Surely we needed to leave already…

"Mitch!" Samantha's voice rose to me. I looked down but couldn't see them through the leaves. "Mitch, stop." Her voice was high and tight.

I climbed down a few paces.

"Why?" Mitch's voice was so low, it was almost a growl.

I climbed down a few more.

"The Princess," Samantha said.

I froze.

"What? Just because you've pledged yourself to the Princess we can't kiss now?"

Had they been kissing? I blushed at the idea.

"No," Samantha's tone was sharp, "but I will not kiss you here, while we are supposed to be on duty."

"Ugh!" Mitch growled, "I knew pledging yourself was going to change you."

"I haven't changed!"

"Uh… Yes you have."

They didn't speak. I waited a moment then started to make my way down again. I'd made it about halfway when Samantha said, "You know, if you'd just pledge yourself too…"

Mitch cut her off. "I told you, I am not going to pledge myself to *any* Royal, ever." He sounded like he was speaking through clenched teeth.

"Do you really think that's an option?" Samantha asked, "After all you are a Loyalist. You can't stay un-pledged *forever*."

"Oh, yeah? Watch me."

I squinted trying to see through the tree canopy but I was still too far away.

"You know," Samantha's voice was softer now. "I think you should at least tell the Princess about your family."

"Don't have to." Mitch grumbled. "Collin already did."

"Collin told her about your dad?"

"No!"

I'd made it to the top of the branches. If they looked up they'd see me. Neither looked up. Samantha stood close to the tree trunks. Mitch was back a pace. He held his arms by his side but I could see his hands balled into fists.

"I think she has a right to know about your father."

Mitch shook his head, "Of course you would."

"What's that supposed to mean?"

"Ever since you pledged yourself to the Princess you've gotten a little stupid. You and Collin both."

"Yeah, well, Mitch," Samantha's cheeks flushed, "you can be a *lot* stupid all on your own."

"I'm not," he brought his hands up to his face and rubbed it a few times. When he spoke again it was with a softer tone, "I wasn't saying that *you're* stupid. It's just… it's just when it comes to the Princess you can't think straight."

"I could say the same about you. Now that I've pledged myself I've realized how crooked your thinking is when it come to the Princess."

Mitch shook his head.

I climbed down another pace. I meant to clear my throat, or make the branches creak; to do something to let them know I was returning. But the branches stayed silent — and so did I.

"You used to feel the same way I did." Mitch took Samantha's hands in his. "Don't you remember? You promised me you'd never forget how rotten a Royal could get."

She pulled her hands away, "I remember and I haven't forgotten," she tilted her head to the side. "But I never realized how *good* a Royal could be either. You have to see it... can't you see it? The Princess *is* good."

Mitch crossed his arms. "There isn't enough goodness to make up for what High Emperor Zigel did to my father." His nostrils flared.

I knew what my uncle had done was terrible. Forcing Mitch's father to abandon his wife and daughter. I kept lowering myself. I wanted to make it to the ground so I could promise Mitch I would never do that — ever.

"The Princess is a different person. She didn't order your father to kill High Emperor Zandr."

I froze. *My uncle had ordered Mitch's father to kill the High Emperor*? My foot slipped. I grabbed for a branch and tried to find purchase with my feet. *Mitch's father had killed High Emperor Zandr*? My hands slipped and I fell to the ground.

I was lucky. The grass was soft. The air was only temporarily knocked out of me.

"Princess," Samantha jumped back.

Mitch glared, "You were spying on us!"

Samantha bent down to offer me her hand, "Are you alright?"

I wasn't. But it had nothing to do with the fall. I refused Samantha's hand, not really wanting to get up.

I knew my uncle had ordered the death of his whole family by the hands of their Loyalists... but I didn't think any of those Loyalists were on the ship. I didn't think any of them would want to be. But Samantha had said she'd talked to Mitch's father... so had Collin. That meant he was here. "Mitch," I asked, "who's your father?"

He stared at me, his jaw tight.

After a moment Samantha said, "Morris is his dad."

"Samantha!" Mitch hissed through his teeth. "That question wasn't for you to answer."

"You don't like me answering? Then answer yourself next time you're asked."

Mitch accused Samantha of being a brainwashed loyal. She said something about how he was an un-pledged moron.

I didn't pay attention. I was too busy thinking about Morris. He'd greeted me when I first came aboard the ship. He'd escorted me to the banquet. He'd smiled, and bowed, and called me Princess like everyone else… like he was happy to see me. *Was he happy to see me?*

I'm not sure how he could be. After what my uncle had commanded him to do. And after what he'd done! *He killed High Emperor Zandr.* Killed a Royal! And because of him, my uncle, Emperor Zigel was now the High Ruler! He'd done this… been forced to do this…

"He won't hurt you, you know." Samantha sat down next to me. "Morris," she said when I looked at her. "He's not… he can't take any more orders from *High* Emperor Zigel. Before High Emperor Zandr died he made sure of that." She gave my arm a squeeze. "So you don't have to be afraid of him. Him or… Tom"

"Samantha!" Mitch fell to his knees bringing his hand up like he meant to slap her.

"Don't," I said. No, I commanded it.

Mitch flinched like he'd been whipped. His hand was extended but I realized it wasn't meant for harm; it was held up in a stop gesture.

He dropped his hand to his side. "I would never hurt Samantha."

She looked between us, "Well, you certainly won't be able to now." She smiled.

I tried to smile.

Mitch continued to scowl, "Didn't Tom tell you not to give your commands so lightly?"

He had. But I hadn't given it lightly or by accident. I'd meant to command Mitch not to harm Samantha. And I wasn't sorry about it in the least. *I wondered what Tom would think about that*? Then I wondered why Samantha had told me I didn't need to be afraid of Tom.

The reason came to me quickly. "Who did Tom kill?" I asked dully. *How many people on this ship had murdered someone in my family?*

Samantha looked at Mitch again then answered, "He was commanded to kill your…"

"Sam!" Mitch's eyes bulged. "You don't have to tell her."

"Mitch. Shut up," she held her hand up to him like he'd done to her earlier, "the Princess has a right to know."

"But *you* don't have the right to tell her."

"Either you do or I will."

"Tom should." Mitch crossed his arms.

"Tom isn't here." Samantha copied his gesture. "Besides, *he* should have told her this yesterday."

"Fine!" Mitch narrowed his eyes, "I will tell her." He turned to me, "Tom killed…" he paused, his eyes softening, then started again, "Tom… he killed your… he was commanded to assassinate your mother."

For a second I felt like I was underwater without a hum'gil. Then I became outraged. He'd acted all superior. Like I wasn't good enough. Yet… "He killed my mother?"

"No!" Samantha seemed equally upset, "No he didn't. In the end he wasn't able to. He was sent to, but your father stopped him." Her face turned down. "But your father died protecting your mom."

"But," my voice sounded raw — I felt it in my throat. "I don't understand. If my father died, how did he stop Tom?"

"He fought with Tom long enough for Tom to come to his senses, I guess." Samantha's brow wrinkled.

This didn't make sense.

Samantha must have known this. "You know, my parents say that Tom was able to break free of the command because he had been pledged to High Emperor Erin. The High Emperor before Zandr was called to the throne. But Collin's dad thought it was because High Emperor Zigel wasn't really a true *High* Emperor since he took the throne by force. And Captain Dis'Hyroo says it could be something else." Samantha stopped to take a breath. "For whatever reason, Tom did stop. And it's a good thing otherwise you would have never been born."

I wondered if this was supposed to make me feel better about Tom.

"But the true hero was your father." Mitch said quietly. He looked away.

I wondered, like I had so many other times in my life: *who was my father*?

Every time I asked Nan'Dah about him she'd say either one of two things. One: he must have been an amazing man for my mother to fall in love with him. And two: he was the luckiest man in all of Quista to have the love of my mother.

This gave me the impression that Nan'Dah hadn't known him very well. Now I wondered if she knew him at all. I wondered if anyone had known him.

"Princess," Samantha touched my wet cheek.

I bit my lip, "Does anyone know who my father was?"

No one answered.

When I looked at Mitch he shook his head.

I looked at Samantha.

She frowned, "Your mom kept him a secret. Tom is the only one who ever met him and Captain Dis'Hyroo says he was commanded never to speak of him."

"Do you think…" there was a name on Uma'Three for children born to unmarried mothers. It wasn't a nice name. "It's unlikely they ever got married, isn't it?"

Samantha shrugged.

Mitch shook his head, "We don't really know."

Great, not only was I a single birth, but now I wasn't even sure if I was a legitimate child. *How could someone like me take the throne*?

"There you guys are." Collin said walking out from the trees. He stopped a pace away looking between us. His hair was wet, it shone when the light hit it. "Did it work?"

Samantha gave the tiniest of head shakes.

Right, I'd come here to find my Magic. I'd failed. At this rate we'd never get off the world!

"Take me back to my suites," I said. At least there I could practice with the spheres.

Chapter Twenty-Three

Bad Medicine

"Oh good, food! I'm starved." Collin rushed into my formal sitting room.

Sue was there, a large pot and several bowls were set up on the table.

"Mind your manners." Sue said. "The Princess is always served first." She ladled a glob of mushy, gray-looking, soup into the bowl and handed it to Mitch.

He took it with a frown.

"Porridge." Collin made a face.

"What's wrong with porridge?" Sue asked. "It's good."

"It's not good." Collin rolled his eyes. "It's supposed to be good *for* you."

I'd never had porridge before. Uma'Three didn't have any kind of facsimile. I wondered if it would be anything like cake… though Collin liked cake.

"It's not as bad as Collin makes it sound," Mitch said handing me the bowl. He'd thrown a handful of lu'umon berries into it.

Sue's eyes followed the bowl.

Collin took it before I could. "No, it's worse." He picked up a container of what looked like sea-lilly nectar and poured a healthy amount over it. Then he added more lu'umon berries. "But with this it should be tolerable." He handed me the bowl.

"You should be careful how you feed the Princess," Sue said.

"I'm not the family pet," I said staring into the bowl. Porridge did not look very appealing at all. The smell was even less inviting.

"No." Samantha sat beside me with a bowl of her own. "You are something far more important," she looked up at Sue, "and Collin feeds her just fine."

Sue looked like she wanted to disagree but she didn't say so.

I only picked at the top-most layer of lu'umon berries — the ones that hadn't touched the nectar or the porridge. I shuddered through my first mouthful.

Sue was watching me with a frown but when I turned to look at her she quickly replaced it with a smile, "I have news for you, the rescue party for your neighbor has returned."

"Jef," I shifted forward swallowing, "can I see him?" My heart raced at the idea.

She nodded, "As soon as the doctor gets him all suited up."

"Is he okay?" I thought about the last time I'd seen him.

"Just a couple of bruises." Sue watched me. "You should eat more."

I nodded taking another few untainted lu'umon berries onto my spoon.

Jef was here! On the ship! And soon he'd be here, in my suites! Then I realized he'd want to know about Kit — he'd want to go save her and I wasn't ready. I wasn't even close to ready... *What if she was killed before I could save her*?

Suddenly my stomach felt very uneasy. I put down the bowl and covered my mouth.

Samantha jumped to her feet, "What is it?"

"It's okay, Samantha, the Princess will be fine." Sue said leaning forward.

I wasn't so sure about that. "We..." I took a deep breath, "We need to get off the world... but..." I bit my lip. "But I'm not ready. I'm not ready to fight my uncle. And I'm really not ready to win. I can't even levitate more than three spheres yet and I'm... I've never been off world before."

I pressed my hand tighter to my mouth.

Samantha took my free hand. It was trembling. "Don't worry. You'll be ready when you need to be."

I pulled my hand away afraid I'd hurt her again as anger raced through my veins, "No! I *need* to be ready now — but I'm not! Kit is... she's with my uncle. He's... who knows what he's doing to her! We need to get off the world. We need to stop him! We need..." I didn't know what. I looked at Samantha, Collin, Mitch and Sue. I looked around the room. "I don't know what I need."

"You need to finish your porridge." Sue said, sitting back in her seat. The frown was on her face again. "It will help. It's full of good stuff for you."

"Vitamins and minerals," Mitch said, ladling himself a second bowl.

Collin had eaten three. He'd taken a fourth bowl but stopped when he realized there wasn't any nectar left. The bowl sat beside the pot. He looked at mine longingly.

"I'm not that hungry," I said, pushing the bowl further away. My stomach was full of jitters.

"You should eat anyway," Sue said, picking up the bowl and holding it out to me.

"What's going on?" Samantha looked from the bowl to Sue, to Mitch, to Collin and finally to me. Then she looked back at the bowl.

Collin's face looked as curious as Samantha's. However, both Mitch and Sue seemed nervous — hesitant.

"Please eat it," Sue said stretching so the bowl was closer to me.

"Why?" I asked. *Why was it so important that I eat the porridge?* When Sue didn't answer my question I commanded an answer.

Sue's frown doubled, "It— it has your medicine in it."

"Oh?" The idea of taking my medicine made my mouth go dry but I reached for the bowl anyway.

Collin knocked my hands away, "No!"

The bowl fell to the ground, spilling half the contents.

"Princess, you don't need your medicine!" Collin said, grinding the spilled porridge into the rug.

"She does need her medicine!" Sue said, picking up the half-filled bowl and scurrying out of Collin's reach.

Samantha pulled me to my feet. "Come." She tried towing me away.

I was able to stay rooted to my spot. "Stop," I said, but Samantha kept pulling on me.

Mitch grabbed Samantha's free hand, "Let go of the Princess," he said.

She pushed him away.

Sue was able to duck around Collin and ran towards me; the bowl held out. "Princess."

Samantha spun around and pushed me behind her; holding her arms out like a shield. Collin was behind Sue, but before he could tackle her she handed the bowl to Mitch. Mitch passed the bowl to me as Collin let Sue go and lunged at Mitch. Mitch ducked out of reach.

I held the bowl to my chest trying to decide if I should tip it up to my lips like a drink or scoop the porridge out with my hands. I had to swallow down an unfriendly taste as I thought about doing either.

Collin snatched the bowl from me.

"Give it back." I commanded.

"I will not allow you to poison yourself." Collin raised the bowl to his mouth and tipped it up. The porridge, nectar, berries, medicine were all gone in one mouthful.

"What are you doing?" I said pushing past Samantha.

"Idiot!" Mitch said.

"Spit it out!" Sue said.

"Foo ewww," he said through his mouthful, then swallowed it all.

"Why?" I screamed. "You could have just dumped it out!"

"No." It looked like Collin tried to shake his head, but then his whole body started shaking. "I couldn't dump it out. You wouldn't know how poisonous…" He made a funny choking sound as he fell to the floor.

I threw myself on the ground gathering him into my arms, "Collin."

He wasn't breathing.

"Here." Sue stood over me, Mitch beside her. "We have to get him to the doctor."

"No," I said pulling Collin closer to me. "No." He'd taken my medicine to prove to me how poisonous it was — but whether or not it was poisonous for me, I knew it was deadly for him. The medicine was made to stop my Magic. What would happen to him if he was taken away from my Magic? "No," I said again, "he stays with me."

Mitch fell to his knees beside me, "Please Princess he's not breathing! He needs to see the doctor."

"Not the doctor." I said. But Mitch was right, Collin needed to breathe. I leaned closer to Collin and whispered, "Breathe."

Collin's chest rose and fell. I watched it a few times to be sure it wasn't just a one-time thing.

"What the…" Mitch looked from Collin to me then leaned back onto his heals, "okay."

"I think you need to leave, Sue," Samantha said through her teeth.

"This is foolish!" She glanced from Mitch to Samantha and back. "You guys are being foolish. That boy needs medical help. And the Princess *needs* her medicine."

"Leave," Samantha said. I'd never heard her sound so angry.

Sue shook her head and stormed out.

"Are you going to do this every time someone tries to give me my medicine?" I asked sitting up straighter. Collin's head rested on my knee. I brushed my fingers through his sandy hair. *He was such a fool.*

"Yes." Samantha sat down on the floor beside me. She took one of Collin's limp hands in hers. "Every time."

I expected Mitch to object but he just sat down next to Samantha.

I bit my lip, "How come you didn't stop when I commanded you to?" I asked. It was confusing. I had to be careful what I said, because my casual words could be taken as a command — yet I'd given a command and…

"Crazy, isn't it." Samantha smiled a mischievous grin. "It's a little program we've got built into our Loyalty. If we think your safety is at risk we can disobey almost any command."

I thought about that for a moment. "How the hell did my uncle convince a bunch of Loyalists to kill the entire Royal family when you won't even let me take my medicine?"

"He used our protective nature against us," Mitch answered. "That's what dad said. Your uncle tricked him into thinking that killing the Emperor was the *only* way to keep the Emperor safe. It wasn't easy and I'm sure there were many dark sacrifices made. Tom assured us no one will be tricked that way again."

I thought again about the way Tom's assurances never made me feel assured.

"Princess," Gredd said from the doorway to my sitting room. Tom stood next to him. It was as if just thinking about him had conjured him forth. I cringed back jostling Collin as I did.

He moaned.

Tom looked over, his face completely unreadable. *Was he angry — again? Or disappointed? Or was he here to kill me?* But even as I thought it I couldn't believe it was true. Not really.

"May we come in?" Gredd asked.

"No!" Samantha was on her feet racing over to them. She held her hands out the same way she had when I was trying to get the porridge from Sue.

Gredd and Tom stayed in the doorway.

"Please Mz. Wr'Ton, we mean no harm." Gredd said.

"Prove it." Samantha put her hands on her hips.

Mitch made his way over to her. He stood parallel with her crossing his arms over his chest.

"How is Collin?" Tom asked but his eyes stayed on me.

"He'll live, no thanks to you," Samantha answered.

Tom shifted his gaze to her, "I assure you I had no part in this."

Samantha pressed her lips together. "Well I assure you that if you send any more medicine here I will be the next you will have to ask about."

Tom turned to Mitch, "What are your feelings on this matter?"

Mitch looked from Samantha to Tom with an expression like he was going to gag, "I would like very much not to have to worry about Samantha's safety."

Tom nodded, "...and what about yours?" When Mitch didn't answer he added, "Have you pledged yourself to the Princess yet?"

"I haven't." He glanced over to me, "And I won't. I still feel the same way about pledging. However," he looked my way again, "my feelings about the Princess *have* changed."

"I see." Tom's deep voice rumbled in his chest.

"Do you? Do you really? Can't you see how good she is?"

Samantha looked at Mitch quickly but turned back to Gredd and Tom and gave a hard nod. "She's better than good."

Tom's lips pressed together, "That is not where our problems stem from."

"Have you forgotten that everything we do is to protect the Princess?" Gredd said. He hadn't once looked at me since he'd come in.

I wondered if he'd also been one of my uncle's assassins. *Who would he have killed*? It could have been one of many Royals. I wasn't sure I liked having all the people who murdered my family now *protecting* me.

"But we will not be able to protect the Princess if the she is found." Tom added frowning down at Samantha.

Gredd sighed and held something out to her.

"What's this?" she asked taking it.

It was a vial of healing sand. *Why hadn't I thought about that*?

Suddenly there was a loud metallic noise that seemed to echo around the room. The ship shuddered. Samantha and Mitch fell to the ground.

"What's that?" I asked pulling Collin tighter to me. I'm not sure if it was fear that made my chest feel tight or something else.

Gredd had grabbed the doorframe as the ship shook. He let go, staring up with a thoughtful expression. Mitch got up quickly then offered Samantha a helping hand.

Tom hadn't needed the support but he too stared up. "Was that a hit?"

Gredd shook his head, "Not us." He turned back to Samantha, "Do you hear that?" I don't know why he was asking. I was sure everyone on the ship had. "That is the sound of our impending discovery. We need to get off the world now."

Samantha nodded, "Then you best be sending Phillip along so he can help the Princess learn what she needs to."

They didn't say they would as they left. They didn't say they wouldn't either. I tried hard not to get my hopes up. If Phillip didn't come then I'd have to find a way to get away from Samantha and Collin so I could take my medicine. Because Gredd was right. We needed to leave the world now!

I had Samantha mix the healing sand in a glass of water that I slowly poured down Collin's throat. He only choked once. By the end he was awake and sitting up.

~ ~ ~

I sat on my sofa trying to get just one sphere, Uma'Three, into the air. It felt heavier today.

Samantha had cleaned up. Mitch and Collin had helped. They were all sitting across from me. Watching. I kept glancing at the door.

I prodded Uma'Three again.

Nothing happened.

"So Morris is your uncle?" I asked Collin more to break the silence than anything else. And to try and focus on something other than the three of them watching me — fail.

He nodded, and before I could ask about his parents, he told me that when they'd gone on a mission to Ursala, they were caught and sent to stand before my uncle. No one had heard from them after that.

My wrist was beginning to hurt. "I'm sorry," I whispered as I put Uma'Three down and tried with one of the lighter moons.

Collin stopped staring at me and, instead, was watching his hands in his lap.

The silence got loud again.

I turned the moon in my fingers. I wondered if there was a way to tell which world it belonged to. Glancing at the pile of them they all looked pretty much the same. My eyes rose to Samantha. She looked so hopeful.

Mitch was beside her, his hand on the small of her back. Collin was still staring at his lap.

"Why is your skin green and Mitch's isn't?" I asked again to break the silence.

Mitch gave a small chuckle. "I'm lucky."

"Ha!" Collin laughed. It was so unexpected it made me jump. "He's not cool enough to pull off green," Collin said.

Mitch nodded grinning, "Yeah, I don't think that tone would go with my hair."

Mitch and Collin's hair were almost exactly the same color.

I put the moon down.

"What's wrong Princess?"

"I don't think I can do it."

The room fell into silence.

"*I* think you can." Phillip said.

Chapter Twenty-Four

Returned

Phillip stood framed by the entrance to my formal sitting room. Although it hadn't even been a full day since I'd last seen him, it felt like it had been so much longer. His golden hair bounced as he continued into the room.

"Phillip!" I knew I shouldn't. I knew he didn't feel about me the way I felt about him. I knew it wasn't very princess-like. But I couldn't stop myself. I ran to him and wrapped my arms around him.

"It's okay Danay. It's okay." His lips brushed my ear as he spoke. It made me shiver and hold him tight.

I wanted to tell him that he was never allowed to leave me again — I stopped myself.

He tried to pull away but I resisted. I couldn't let him go, not yet.

He sighed, picked me up and carried me to the sofa. I clung to him as he tried to sit down. I ended up on his lap. I didn't care.

He cleared his throat as he shifted me to the cushion next to him.

"I thought I'd never be able to see you again." I choked back my tears. Tears of joy that he was back. Tears of pain that he'd been gone in the first place.

"It's okay. I'm here, now." He tilted his head slightly to the side. "Um, Danay, may I please have my arm back?"

I let go and drew my legs up to my chest. I rested my forehead on my knees, hiding my face. *If I kept acting this way they'd never let him near me again.*

"Danay, we don't have a lot of time. You need to learn to control your Magic." He gave me a gentle squeeze.

I shook my head. "I've been trying. I — I *can't*... find it."

Phillip moved his hand to my knee. He ducked his head to catch my eye, "I have an idea."

"Going to the forest..."

"Didn't work," he said. "I know. And I think I know why."

When I asked him, he told me he thought my Magic was tied to animals.

"I saw animals, outside of the ship. I felt the Magic but it didn't feel like *my* Magic." I looked at his hand on my knee. The truth was none of the Magic I'd ever felt, felt like mine. What if I didn't have my own Magic? What if it was all my mom's and I'd never be able to control it. My worries came out in a hushed whisper.

Phillip hooked his finger under my chin to pull my face up where he could see it. "You can control it. I know you can."

I tried to shake my head but it was impossible with him still holding my chin.

"I've seen it," Phillip said.

Before I could ask *when* Samantha added, "So have I."

"Whe..." I bit my lip as I was cut off by Collin.

"I have too."

Mitch didn't say anything but he was nodding.

My teeth dug deeper into my lip.

"Please Danay," Phillip smiled as he released my chin, "will you at least try?"

I shut my eyes and took a deep breath, "Okay."

"Good," Phillip squeezed my knee. "Now keep your eyes shut."

I did.

"And relax."

I tried to ignore that I was responsible for Phillip, Samantha, Collin, and even Mitch's, lives. I tried not to think about what would happen to them if I failed and we were all caught. I tried not to think about anything at all. But Phillip's hand was still on my knee and I couldn't quite stop thinking about that, about how his grip was both strong and gentle at the same time; how his fingers hugged my knee.

Warmth radiated through his hand. It made my heart flutter. The more I thought about it the warmer it felt. Tingles raced up my leg and spine.

"Now, Danay, I want you to think about poplings."

My cheeks lifted of their own accord.

"Good," Phillip said, "now think about when a burb becomes a popling."

I'd never-ever been able to see that moment. I peeked through one eye to look at Phillip.

He was watching me so intently. His face filled with such hope. They all were. My heart started to sink. We needed to go. We needed to get away right now. We didn't have time for this.

"Relax," Phillip's voice was calm. He put his finger to my lips as I started to protest. "Close both of your eyes and just concentrate on your body."

It was easier to think about *his* body, but I tried to do what he asked. I could hardly concentrate with his finger against my lips and his hand on my knee. It felt like I was standing in water after a mi'lex feeding frenzy. Electric and yet soothing in the same moment.

"Now," he said, "think about what it feels like when you pop the burbs.

I never really paid attention to my body when I was talking to the burbs. And I certainly hadn't assumed it was *me* that made them pop. But as I thought about it now… It always made me feel alive. Like every molecule of me was its own burb trying to reconnect with ancestors. I wanted to laugh. Phillip was right; I made the burbs pop. *If I could do that, then, surely I could do this.*

I turned to look at Phillip, but not with my eyes, or my head. I was still sitting beside him, only it was like there was two of me. There was my physical self and my other self — the part of me that had gone to visit Phillip twice — my *spiritual* self.

I could see Phillip as clearly as if I was looking at him, but I could also *see* a bright colorful haze surrounding him… as if he was bathed by the light of suns.

I turned to look at Samantha and she too was bathed in a soft purple haze. It was soothing like the baths she made for me. Collin was surrounded by a vibrant orange light that reminded me of zapping eels. And Mitch's color was an even deeper orange, almost brown.

"Have you found your Magic yet?" Phillip asked.

In my spirit state, I saw Phillip's lips move but the words felt like they were traveling farther to get to me.

I shook my head slowly side to side. I watched myself do this. It was weird.

I studied myself. Trying to see my color but couldn't find it. I stepped back. It still wasn't there. That wasn't true. I could see I had a color but I couldn't see the end of it. I walked backwards until I reached the door to my outer room and I was still *in* my color. I walked halfway across the entrance room. I could see myself with Phillip and Samantha, Collin and Mitch, all leaning closer, watching me.

Surely my color was my Magic.

I'd made it to the outer doors and, just like in real life, they didn't open. I debated stepping through them when someone rang the buzzer.

"I'll get it." Samantha left the room and came straight towards me.

"Keep trying," Phillip said. He squeezed my knee.

I watched him do this. I heard him from far away and up close at the same time.

The doors opened behind me.

"Can I help you?" Samantha asked.

"My name is Jef…"

I didn't hear the rest. I'd turned to see him and suddenly, like a rubber band had snapped me back, I was in my body again. I opened my eyes and stood up. "Let him in Samantha," I called.

"Who?" Collin and Phillip asked. Mitch shifted to standing.

I ignored all three and stood frozen, watching the door. Finally Samantha brought him in.

Jef looked the same as when I'd last seen him. Same fancy seaweed and burb colored eyes, same dark curly hair, same round face, same firm, not quite Uma'Threcitish chest, and same crooked teeth.

"Jef!" I ran towards him.

He smiled and his pace quickened.

"Danny," he picked me up and spun me, "you are a sight for sore eyes."

He stopped and put me back on my feet.

"How sore is your eye?" I asked brushing it with the tips of my fingers.

"It's fine," he caught my hand then held it out, stepping back to look at me, "what are you wearing?"

"It's a dress." I twirled, "Do you like?"

"It's," he swallowed, "lovely." He took a moment more to stare at me. His smile doubled, "I see you found my gift." He shook my hand. His pearl bumped against his sister's charm.

"I love it. How on Uma'Three did you ever afford it?"

His eyes were fixated on my CoaB, "I found it a few Turns ago. It was torture having to wait so long before I could give it to you."

Phillip came to stand next to me putting his hand on my waist, "Danay, you were trying…"

"You must be Phillip." Jef let me go and thrust his hand out.

Phillip shook Jef's hand keeping a tight grip on me with the other.

"Tell me," Jef's fingers stayed clenched around Phillip's, "aren't you all bound by some code to call Danay *Princess*?"

"We are," Phillip also kept his hand firm around Jef's. Both their fingers were turning white.

"Then what makes you different? Isn't she *your* princess?"

"She's everyone's," Samantha said pushing her way between the two. They let go of each other and moved back a little.

Phillip reached out to take my waist again but Jef put his arm around me and started walking me to the sofa.

"Jef? How long have you known about me?" I allowed him to guide me. At the sofa, Jef sat in the middle and pulled me down next to him.

Phillip perched himself on the armrest on the other side. Jef glared at him.

"Jef. How long have you known?"

"Yes, Jef," Phillip said leaning past me, "how long have you known who Danay really was? How long have you been keeping that secret from her?"

I tried to put some space between Jef and me, which caused me to press against Phillip. Phillip put his hand on my shoulder.

"Danny," Jef said his face looking somber, "Princess," he flicked my rogue curl.

It's funny, everyone on the ship called me Princess and I hated it. But when Jef said it, it made me feel special. Like being the princess might not be a completely bad thing.

Jef cleared his throat, "I wasn't allowed to tell you. I was bound to secrecy."

"Bound to secrecy by whom?" I asked at the same time Phillip said, "And how long ago was that?"

Jef shifted, but he continued to look into my eyes, "By your Nan'Dah. I was commissioned by her right after my Coming of Age. I was told I could either join my father in his role as your secret protector or she would make me forget everything about you." He twisted his head, one of his dark curls flopped in front of his eyes.

His curls were almost as familiar to me as my own reflection. It was comforting having this small part of my life back.

"I didn't want to forget you," Jef said.

I smiled at him. He shifted closer and put his head down onto my shoulder like he used to do when he hung out with his sister and I. He hadn't done this since he'd… "Wait a sec."

"Yes?" he looked up at me.

"It was your job to protect me? How? You were always away."

He sat up. "Well," his grin spread ear to ear, "you see, it was my job to keep an eye on you." He paused. "You weren't supposed to know. So I had to stay hidden."

"For two Turns you've been following me around, watching me?" I was torn between feeling disturbed and impressed. I think I was leaning towards impressed. Never once had I suspected.

"You spent Turns peeping on her?" Phillip said. "Creepy." His hand tightened on my shoulder.

"Protecting her," Jef said. "And I wasn't always watching her; sometimes I had to check out other people. People who might be a threat to her. Like mysterious off-worlders who just happened to show up at her school one Turn before her Coming of Age." His eyes stayed hard on Phillip.

"What would you do if you thought they were a threat?" I asked.

Jef crossed his arms, "I'd tell the doc. He'd take care of that."

"How?" Collin asked.

I put my hand up. I didn't want to know. "Did Kit know — what I am?"

"No, she didn't. Your Nan'Dah was planning on letting you decide if you wanted to tell her after your Coming of Age."

"What about your mother?"

"She didn't know until very recently." Jef looked away. "She found out just after my father died."

I felt a twinge of guilt. His father had died on the job — his job was to protect me. *His father had died because of me*. "She must hate me."

"Are you kidding? Danay, she loves you." Jef's brown-green eyes looked sad.

"But it's my fault your father died. And— and I changed Kit, you know?" I closed my eyes against the tears. *They would have been better off never knowing me.*

"Yes, being around you changed my sister. But did you know that before you moved to Tem, Kit wasn't nearly the prettiest girl, or the smartest, and certainly not the most popular. Your Magic changed her into the best version of herself she could be. You made Kit better. Mom saw it. She was thankful for it."

"Sure she *was*, but how about now? Because of me, Kit has been chosen to..." I couldn't catch my breath just thinking about it: she'd be forced to marry my uncle and then forced — to have his child.

"She's still thankful. She believes in you." Jef put his hands on either side of my face. He stared into my eyes until I looked back, "Even if we hadn't known you, Kit might still have been picked. But we do know you and we know you can get her back."

I nodded, "I... I want to. I was..." I paused, looking at Phillip.

"Danay was learning to shield her Magic so we can leave." Phillip explained for me.

Jef let me go and shifted to glare at Phillip, "You are aware of what's going on outside this ship, aren't you?"

"Yes." I felt the muscles in Phillip's arm flex as he continued to hold my shoulder.

"And you still think we have time for this?"

"What's going on outside the ship?" I asked.

Jef blanched, "No one told her?" He glanced at everyone then turned to me. His face was hard, but it quickly softened as he talked, "High Emperor Zigel's officials know we are hiding down here. They've created a search grid. They are systematically getting closer by the minute."

Jef tried to take my hand.

Phillip bumped me as he stood up and knocked Jef's hand away.

"What's your damage?" Jef stood too.

"Listen, Danay doesn't need to be scared right now. She almost had it. If you hadn't interrupted..."

"Danny," Jef turned to me, holding his hand out again, "trust me."

I started to reach for him.

Phillip moved so quickly it took me a moment to realize what he was doing.

"Stop!" I said.

Phillip froze. He held Jef by the front of his wet'skn, his free hand drawn back.

"Phillip, let him go."

Phillip stared daggers at Jef. His hands shook.

"Phillip?"

He did.

"What a yeah-yeah." Jef said under his breath but not so quietly.

I ignored him and stood up so Phillip would have to look at me. "Why are you so angry? Jef isn't the enemy."

A muscle in Phillip's jaw bulged as he glared at Jef, "I'm not so sure about that. He's been helping the doctor poison you for Turns."

"What poison?" Jef asked over my shoulder. He glared back at Phillip, his nostrils flaring. "Do you mean her medicine? It's not poison. It helps her. It's what has kept her hidden up to now."

Phillip unclenched and re-clenched his fists, "You've been poisoning her for so long you can't see the damage it does."

"Listen you yeah-yeah," Jef leaned towards Phillip, "I'm the reason Danay wasn't caught on *your* watch."

Phillip backed up a finger-width, "On my… what?"

"When I found her in the village. When she was *supposed* to be safe with you!" Jef brought his hand around me taking my arm — I think he meant to turn me to look at him.

Phillip grabbed Jef, "Keep your hands off her, Fish-Boy."

"You are wasting time my sister doesn't have!" Jef said. His voice was hard but I heard the panic.

"You're the one wasting time." Phillip's teeth ground together. "Danay had it. She was doing it." He looked at me, his eyes softening, "It *was* working." He put his hands on my arms, "Please, sit. You had it."

"No, we don't have time for this!" Jef swung and clipped Phillip under the chin.

Samantha put herself between me and the fighting boys. I think Collin was trying to help. Even Mitch rushed forward.

Everyone stopped at my shout.

I put myself between Jef and Phillip again.

Phillip stood with both his hands balled into fists. "Danay…"

"No, Phillip. Just sit down and stay quiet." He did. I ignored the way he looked — like I'd ordered him.

"Now, Jef," I turned to look at him.

"Danay, you know I wouldn't do anything to hurt you." He caught my hand in his. "And you know how important it is to leave right away, right?"

I nodded. I wanted to tell him I agreed. But my tongue suddenly felt numb.

"The doctor made your medicine so we could hide you. He's very careful to test you every time so the measurements are just right. It's only supposed to help you stay safe."

I tried to nod again but my neck was too stiff.

"I know you're the princess and your Magic is strong. I know you can learn to control it. But we have to leave now."

I blinked and couldn't remember how to open my eyes again.

"Kit's life is in danger. You need to save her," Jef said. He squeezed my hand. It stung the same way it had when he'd scratched me before — back in the business district.

I tried to pull away but he held fast. And yet, somehow, I was falling.

Chapter Twenty-Five

Kit'Una

I was falling and even though someone caught me — I kept going. I fell into and through the floor, out of the ship and all the way down to the bottom of the ocean. And when I reached the ocean floor I kept going. I fell all the way through the middle of Uma'Three and out the other side. Out into space towards the stars that winked at me.

Before everything went black, I heard Phillip calling. His voice was telling me to come back, but I didn't know how. "What have you done?" I could hear him yelling.

Then I heard something that sounded similar to Kit slapping our teacher.

Kit's life was in danger. We had to leave Uma'Three… I had to save her.

When I was able to open my eyes again, I wasn't in my body.

I was in a dark room, filled with voices… in all sorts of accents.

From somewhere behind me I heard, "The one from Uma'Three." I moved towards it.

Although I couldn't see the speaker I did see — Kit. She was crouched in a tub only half-full of water. Her skin stood up in bumps all along her bare arms. Her teeth chattered like she was too dry.

"Good girl. Good strong girl." The thing that spoke walked in the shadows. Its voice dripped with decay. "Master will be proud."

Kit stayed quiet, tracking the creature with her eyes as it circled the tub.

"Ready soon… yes, yes, very soon. Master will be pleased. Master will reward." The speaker moved closer to the tub.

It hadn't been walking in the shadows — it was made of shadows. All I could make out was the outline of a blur — a tall, thin blur.

Then with a flash of movement, it dipped its finger into the water. *Not a finger.* It was a sleek, black, bony, tentacle that appeared out of the blur. When it touched the water, black sludge oozed from it.

Kit shifted backwards as the sludge encircled her. "Please don't," her voice trembled.

"Mmmm, we likes the pleases. Uma child afraid is so delicious. Just a little more." It dipped its tentacle into the water again.

More sludge seeped from it and where it touched Kit her skin turned gray. She screamed as the sludge started to climb up her arms. Then she went under the water like she'd been pulled down. As she gasped for air, the black water filled her mouth. Her head surfaced and she bent over the side of the tub gagging. Her hands clung to the edge. Her fingers were bone white.

"Please, don't," she pleaded. "No more. Please."

"More pleases," the creature hissed coming closer.

"P— please, no more." Her shaking got worse.

"Yes, yes, good play time." The creature returned to circling Kit's tub.

"Play time?" Kit's eyes flashed. "You're just toying with me?" Her face hardened. She let go of the tub and glared at the shadow creature. "Enough playtime. I won't give you anymore pleases."

"Too bad. Not your choice." The creature reached towards her.

I saw Kit's resolve in the set of her shoulders. "No. I won't be your play thing anymore."

"Yes, yes, yes, Master said so. We gets play time with Uma girl."

"No," Kit said crossing her arms.

"Yesssssssssssss." The creature lunged forward. Without the shadows to hide it, I saw its face. It was as black as its tentacle; it had a mouth, nose slits, and dozens of eyes that oozed a black substance like the tar from an inking squid.

I gasped.

It paused, "What's this?" The shadows surrounded it again but I could feel its eyes were focused on where I stood.

It had heard me. *Could it see me*?

I didn't talk. I didn't move. I didn't even breathe.

Kit was looking right through where I stood. She'd also heard me.

Finally the creature turned back to Kit, "One more pleases, we thinks." It jumped into the tub with her.

She screamed and writhed, her body thrashing as if she was being jolted by a zapping eel. Finally, in a choked gurgling wail she screamed, "Please stop, PLEASE!"

It stopped. The creature's laugh was cruel. It made my eyes sting and my ears ring. It left the tub bringing most of the water with it. I watched the wet marks it left on the floor as it exited the room.

"Good, sweet, play thing." Its voice trailed away leaving Kit alone in silence.

I waited to be sure it was gone.

Kit held the side of the tub panting and shivering. Finally she pulled herself upright, covered her face, and let out a soft moan.

"Kit?" My voice was shaking so hard even I didn't recognize it.

"Who's there?"

"It's me. It's Danay."

"Where are you…? How'd you…? You can't be here! You have to go!"

Why was she angry?

"Did you go?" she asked, looking left and right making it clear she still couldn't see me.

"I… I want to help you." I said.

"You want to help me? Then leave. Save yourself. If the Emperor catches you he'll…" she shook her head.

"But what about you?"

Her eyes got hard, her shoulders stiff, "It's too late for me."

"What…?" I stopped when I heard a new voice.

"She's ready?"

In comparison to the creature's voice, this new voice was like sunshine on an overcast day. Hearing it made me want to breathe deeper. Made me want to smile… to run to it with open arms and embrace whoever was talking.

"Well, then, maybe she *will* be the one."

"Yes, Master," the shadow creature hissed, "Uma girl very strong. Feeling her energy all the way here."

"I feel it too my pet." It was the kindness in his voice — the love for the vile creature — that frightened me most.

"Go!" Kit screamed. "Leave me!"

I left, though I wasn't sure how. Kit vanished. The room disappeared. The shadow creature and the person with the beautiful voice were both gone. I was back in me.

"I don't understand." Jef's voice was tight with worry. "Why did she pass out?"

"Why did she pass out?" Phillip's voice, in contrast, was loud with rage. "You — poisoned — her!" For a moment, he seemed unable to form coherent words. "*You*. She's passed out because of you!" He was shaking as he held me. His hands were trembling against my skin, "You drugged her. Why else would she pass out!"

"But I…" I heard the regret in Jef's voice. "But it wasn't supposed to hurt her. It was only supposed to…"

"To what?" Phillip cut him off. "Take her Magic away, right? Well you've succeeded. You've taken her Magic. This is Danay without her Magic."

"But," Jef's voice rose, "it wasn't supposed to hurt her!"

"I told you!" Phillip growled. "You've been poisoning her so long you can't see how much it was hurting her!" He shifted me, "Danay?"

I wanted to answer. I wanted to tell him I was okay — but I couldn't. I couldn't because I wasn't. I felt myself fading. The only thing that kept me from completely fading away was the feeling of Phillip's hands holding me.

"Danay?" Phillip touched my hair. "Danay? Can you hear me? Come on, come back."

I lay in his arms trapped in a frozen body.

"Here, I can help," Jef said.

Phillip went rigid, every muscle strained, "Touch her and I swear I will do more than deck you this time."

"I'm trying to help." Jef growled back. "I can help Danay."

"Oh yeah? The same way you *helped* her before?"

"No... no... not with medicine with..." Jef sighed loudly, "Just trust me, I can help."

"The only way you can help is to go find that doctor of yours. Whatever he did needs to be undone."

I didn't want Jef to leave. I tried to say this. My lips couldn't form the words. They cracked as I pushed air past them. My throat felt dry like a dying mi'lex.

"Listen, she doesn't need the doctor. I can give her what she needs."

"How?" For a second Phillip's grip loosened.

"I can... There's a thing..."

When Jef didn't continue Phillip roared, "Someone do something!" He pulled me tighter to his chest.

"I'll get Sue," Collin said from somewhere over my head.

"Healing sand!" Samantha called.

Phillip's hands brushed my face, "Danay, can you hear me?"

Jef's voice was closer, "Okay, just let me..."

"What?" I was moved, pulled away from Jef.

"I have to..." Jef's voice cracked, "she needs— someone— someone's energy. Here..." I was jerked away again.

"Tell me how. I'll do it," Phillip said.

"I don't think you can."

"Why not! What do you need to do?"

"I need to..." Jef cleared his throat. "Someone has to... kiss her."

Phillip's arms tightened around me like a wince. Something touched my forehead, it was smooth and hard — *his forehead*? His breath hit my face once, twice... He straightened up.

"See, you can't do it. Now let me..."

For a third time I was pulled back.

"I've done it before," Jef said.

Samantha gasped.

"Ouch!" Jef yelled, "Get off me girl!"

"When before?" Phillip demanded.

"In the village when we were trying to get back to you."

"And why did you have to kiss her then?" Samantha's voice was shrill.

"Ouch!" Jef called Samantha a rude name.

"Did you drug her in the village?" Phillip asked. His arms were taut around me. "You've drugged her before! Is that when?"

"Only a little dose." Jef had moved, his voice came from further away. "Stop hitting me! I only did it so the officials wouldn't know who she was. Ouch!"

"Idiot." Phillip swore. "When she got to me in the cave she passed out for a whole day. It's a miracle she didn't pass out underwater and drown."

Jef gasped, "She…" He was silent for a moment, "Listen, she needs… She needs *someone* to kiss her." Jef moved closer. His voice was quieter, "You can't, so..."

Phillip didn't pull me away. "Try it and it's the last thing you'll ever be able to do with your lips." Phillip's hand was hard against my cheek. It hurt.

"Listen you Loyal ya-ya," I could sense Jef just mere finger widths from me. "You can't do it. You aren't allowed to. But I can. I have."

I felt his breath on my forehead. *Did I really wrinkle my brow or only imagine it*?

"If she could talk she would tell you she wants it."

I thought about Jef's kiss. It had been my first. *I felt cheated*. But he was right — I needed it. However, he was also wrong — if I could talk, I would command Phillip to kiss me. My lips stayed dry and frozen.

"Phillip, Danay needs this. Your Princess needs this. Are you going to deny your Princess what she needs?" Jef's hand brushed my arm.

Phillip's hands relaxed, "No." He shifted me. He wasn't saying no to Jef — no was the answer. *He wouldn't deny me what I needed*.

Phillip was still next to me, but he let me go and twisted away. A chill swirled between us.

Jef pressed his lips to mine. They were colder than last time but gentle. How I wished they were Phillips. However, as I felt my strength returning, I didn't care. I was drawn to the kiss — hungry for it. I brought my hand up to Jef's hair, lacing my fingers through his curls. Finally I could open my eyes.

Jef was staring into them, "There's my Danny," he whispered against my lips.

I tried to pull back. Our lips parted for only a moment before he followed me — his lips chasing mine. As they connected again I could feel my strength growing. But at the same time I felt doubly cheated. *This wasn't real.* This wasn't how my first — or second — kiss was supposed to be.

I pulled back again. Before Jef could follow me I put my hand up to his mouth. I tried to push him away. *Where had all my strength gone?* I couldn't stop him from drawing closer.

"Stop," I croaked. The word hurt my throat as it came out.

Phillip turned around and drew me into his arms, "That's enough from you, Fish-Boy."

Jef press his lips together. His eyes narrowed. But he sat back.

Somewhere over my head, I heard Mitch snickering, "Fish-Boy, good one."

I wanted to tell them that name was rude, but I was too spent. My eyes felt too heavy. They started to droop.

"Danay, what do you need?" Phillip asked, brushing my hair off my face.

I tried to swallow. My throat felt scratchy like dried shark skin. I couldn't even get any sound to come out as I pushed the air past my lips.

"Sam, get her some water!"

I gave a small nod — *that's exactly what I needed.*

"Danay, I'm sorry; I didn't mean to hurt you." Jef's hand touched my shoulder.

I managed to pull away. I wasn't upset about him giving me my medicine; I was upset that he'd cheated me out of my first kiss — twice.

"No, means no," Phillip said holding me tighter to himself.

I closed my eyes; too tired to keep them open any longer.

A glass was pressed to my lips, "Drink Princess," Samantha coaxed.

I did. The action felt odd. The water was gone too soon. "Mo-ore." I begged, trying to open my eyes. I couldn't. They felt like they'd been silt'mented shut.

A second cup was given to me. I was so greedy for it that half of it spilled down my neck. Everywhere the water hit my skin I felt the first bits of relief — until it evaporated.

"More!" I cried when it ran out. "All over." I gasped against the pain.

"Sam, forget the cup, just bring the jug."

My hands were reaching, searching for the next glass. I brushed the edges of the water jug, too feeble to hold on.

"I got it," Phillip said. He poured it over me, starting on my neck, then all the way down my chest.

Samantha gasped, "What are you...?"

"Go run a bath," Phillip said.

"A bath?"

"Just do it!" His voice rose. "She's too dry." His chest heaved as if breathing was hard for him, "The drugs were made for her while she was on Uma'Three. *In water*. She needs water to get them out of her system."

Suddenly the other night in the cave with the shark made sense.

Samantha hadn't stayed for the explanation; I heard her footsteps run out of the room. I suspected that Phillip continued to talk for Jef's benefit. I felt myself being lifted up. I listened to the echo Phillip's steps made as he carried me through each room. Finally I heard a much better sound — running water.

"Faster," I choked. After Turns of hating the water, it was strange to discover just how much I'd needed it.

Phillip stopped and I wanted to cry. "You and your lips are not welcome here," Phillip said.

"I'm coming too." Jef said, "I've been caring about her longer than you have."

"With people like you, *caring about her*, she has no need for the enemies who are out to kill her."

"There was no way for me to know," Jef said.

"I told you," Phillip said.

"I know... I'm— I'm sorry." I got the impression Jef was saying that to me.

I wanted to tell him I forgave him but I felt like I was shriveling up like dried out seaweed.

Phillip hadn't moved. "Take one step into this room and I'll kill you." His voice echoed off the bathroom walls. "You have no business here."

I only heard one set of steps as Phillip carried me over to the tub.

"You shouldn't really be here either," Samantha said softly when Phillip got to her.

Phillip gave a tight bark of a laugh, "*You* can't make me leave. Besides, you need my help."

The water was splashing right next to me. I moaned. *Why wasn't I in it*?

"Just a few more minutes, Princess, then the tub will be re— Phillip, what are you doing?"

Phillip was moving me again. The splashing sound changed. I could feel the water under me, evaporating into the air. It caressed my dry, achy skin. And finally I was in it.

I sighed as the water caressed my tight skin. Soft currents tugged at my clothes. I tried to relax. Phillip was under me, holding me up, cushioning me against the tub. I didn't want him to go but he was keeping the water from reaching all of me.

"Is it working?" Jef called from the doorway.

No one answered him. I tried to wave towards him, to let him know I was okay.

"Don't you worry about him," Phillip whispered in my ear, catching my hand in his. "You just concentrate on making yourself better."

"I got Sue!" Collin's voice came from somewhere near where Jef was. He sounded winded.

"Phillip?" Sue said, her shoes clicking on my bathroom floor, "what are you doing in the tub with the Princess?"

"Just pour the sand into the water!" Phillip answered but his chin, which was resting against my cheek, felt warmer.

"There wasn't time to do anything else," Samantha explained.

"Your father isn't going to like this when he hears about it," Sue said.

The sand made a thrumming sound as it hit the water. The water warmed up. Where the sand touched me, I felt like a dried out jellie being brought back to life.

"Which part won't my father like?" Phillip asked. My head bobbed with each word. "That I got in the tub with the Princess, or that he nearly killed her with her medicine?"

Sue's huffed, "Well, I suspect both."

"Is it working?" Jef called again.

I smiled, feeling my lips crack. My bones felt like they were defrosting. I reached down to the bottom of the tub to scoop some sand up.

"Here," Phillip shifted.

I tried to open my eyes but it was as if they were frozen shut. "Don't go," I said letting the sand drop and clinging to his clothes.

"I'm... I won't." He picked up some sand and started rubbing it against my arms. "Relax, I'm just helping."

While he did that, I reached down and got some sand for my face. I pressed handful after handful to it until I was able to blink my eyes open.

Looking around the room, I saw Samantha sitting next to the tub just like every other time she'd given me a bath. Sue was standing over us. Phillip didn't seem bothered by Sue's impassive glare as he continued to bring sand up to rub along my arms, around my neck, over my bare shoulders. Jef was watching from the door with a scowl on his face. Behind him both Collin and Mitch stood facing away.

My legs were still numb. I shifted, trying to reach them, but my dress was in the way. I caught the bottom of the skirt and started to pull it up.

"Um, Princess..." Samantha said.

"I need it off." I struggled with it. It was clinging to me. "The sand has to touch my skin to work."

Samantha, along with Sue, helped me pull my dress over my head.

I leaned back into Phillip, letting Samantha brush sand along my legs. I worked on my stomach even shifting my bra so I could reach under it.

Phillip worked the sand through my hair.

Finally I could feel the last of the drugs being leached out of me.

Samantha smiled, "Your color is returning."

I closed my eyes and relaxed into Phillip.

His hands continued to work through my hair. He was rinsing it out… Dripping water over my skull and running his fingers through my hair until the grittiness of the sand was gone.

Even though I felt better, I stayed against Phillip, not wanting to move. I timed my breaths with the rise and fall of his chest. It was soothing, a sound that made me feel confident.

I was the Princess — I really was. Somehow hearing Jef say it was like the final proof I'd needed. *I was the Princess* — it was time for me to start acting like it.

"Princess?" Samantha asked.

I'd sat up.

"Is there something I can help you with?"

"I need to see Gredd."

Chapter Twenty-Six

Birthright

No one spoke as they escorted me from my suites.

I could feel everyone's energy around me; Phillip's yellow, Samantha's lavender, Collin's orange, Mitch's darker orange and Jef's green. Each color felt brighter, as if agitated. Sue, whose spirit was a sort of gold color, was the only one who didn't seem on edge.

Finally we made it to where Gredd was: the helm.

Sue urged me forward, "The doors won't open for me. But you are the Princess; if you command them to they will."

I was the Princess. I commanded it.

The helm wasn't what I expected. I thought it would have windows to the ocean. It was a closed room with several stations each with their own screens. There were nine people in the room. I recognized three: Gredd, Erik, and Fred. Everyone paused to look at me as I entered. Once they saw me they returned to their screens — though they continued to steal glances at me and my group.

The far wall was made of several monitors each displaying a different view — probably a different angle out of the ship. Every monitor was filled with life. Not only were there the animals I'd seen earlier, but more: a gathering of jellies feeding off the carcass of a mammoth stingray as well as groupings of animals that were never found together — octopi and eels, seals and burbs, tuna and rock fish.

They were here to protect me. Hiding the ship for me.

"Princess?" Gredd stood next to a control panel by the screens. "I didn't expect…"

I held up my hand and he stopped. "We need to talk."

He looked to Jef then Sue. "What happened?"

"I told you the medicine wouldn't work." Phillip pushed his way past me.

"Phillip?" Gredd frowned at his son then his look changed, "Why are you wet?"

Sue stepped forward, "He saved the Princess."

Gredd's brow wrinkled, "Saved the…" he turned to look at me again. "It really…" his eyes bulged as he seemed lost for words.

"Is there somewhere we can speak that's more private?" I asked.

"Yes," he pointed upwards, "we can speak in the observation gallery."

~ ~ ~

Nearly half the observation gallery was made of glass including part of the ceiling and half the floor. Eels lit the room from the ground up. A shadow of the remaining mammoth stingray glided overhead. A lone sentinel keeping watch. The dead mammoth ray and jellies were not visible but even unseen they weren't forgotten. Schools of every kind of fish took turns swimming close to the glass.

I was content to stay near the glass and stare into the Deeps. This was my home, my planet. I was going to miss it — even the water.

"Princess, I feel I must apologize again for what your medicine did to you," Gredd said softly coming to stand to my right.

He'd already apologized several times on the way up.

Morris and Tom sat silently at the long, oval table that stretched between the glassed and un-glassed parts of the room. Gredd had filled them in on what had happened to me when we'd gotten there. Neither seemed overly eager to talk to me. I wasn't really all that eager to talk to them either.

"You are forgiven, Captain Gredd Dis'Hyroo."

Gredd bowed but stayed by my side.

Through the glass the tuna suddenly scatter. In the open spot they created, a great white shark appeared. She looked identical to the one who had always visited me in the village.

I put my hand to the glass and could feel the cold of the ocean trying to press in.

The great white came up next to where my hand was as if she wanted me to pet her. “Hello my old friend.” I smiled. *It was my shark from Tem.*

“You know her?” Gredd asked.

I was impressed, not many people took the time to learn the gender of a shark. “This is the same shark that visited me in the village.” I pressed my nose to the glass. She kept her belly against the other side.

“She showed up the day after you did. She really is magnificent.”

My feelings for Gredd warmed. “I’ve always thought so.”

She finally pushed off the glass and started away. I gasped.

“What?” Gredd moved closer. Somehow having him this close didn’t feel as frightening as it had before.

“She’s been hurt.” I pointed at her fin as she looped back. It was healing, but there was a long gash down the one side of it like someone had tried to slice it off.

Gredd swore. “Who would…”

“Tons of people,” I said turning away from the glass. “No one understands sharks here.” I rubbed at the angry tears in my eyes.

“Do you think she’ll be alright?” He seemed genuinely concerned.

Yup, I definitely liked Gredd a lot more now. “Probably. As long as she stays away from people.” I didn’t look back as I made my way to the table, “I’m going to miss her.” I sat.

“Who knows?” Gredd took the seat next to me, “Maybe one day you’ll be able to come back and see her?”

“Maybe,” but for me this felt like as much of a good-bye as I’d get for her and the planet I’d called home all my life.

Tom and Morris both sat across from me. I looked at Morris.

“Princess,” he dipped his head and his eyes stayed on the table.

“You killed my uncle, High Emperor Zandr,” I said then I turned to look at Tom. “And you were sent to kill my mother.” I brought my hands to the table and laced my fingers together.

Tom nodded slowly his eyes narrow; filled with disapproval. "What would you have us do?" he asked. He brought his hands up from his lap and put them on the table. They were held in the same position as mine.

Do? I sat back surprised. "I would have you know that I know." I had hoped it would help Tom not always act so smug. But from his expression I was pretty sure that wasn't going to go away any time soon.

Tom leaned forward. "Then I would have you know, so I know you know, that it was *your* uncle's rotten command that put us here. Not our desires."

I sat back a little more. As much as I didn't feel like I could trust them, they probably didn't trust me. I was a Royal. I could just as easily give them a rotten command and they couldn't do anything to stop me.

"Okay," I bowed my head. I thought about how my Nan'Dah had always told me trust had to be earned. But here, it wasn't just them who needed to earn my trust, I needed to earn theirs. "Clearly we have all gotten off on the wrong foot. I think we need a fresh start."

Morris sighed, nodding. Tom stoically waited for me to say more.

Gredd smiled, "That would be nice. For us both." Then he apologized, but not about the medicine. This time it was for not trusting me enough to be completely honest about everything. They had been worried: worried about the commands I could make in ignorance — but worse, the ones I could make knowingly. If I was angry, or at all like my uncle: power hungry, vengeful, spiteful, I could hurt a lot of people.

I understood, kind of.

And of course, there was the problem of my out of control Magic.

"Did you know my medicine could be so dangerous for me?" I asked, looking first to Morris.

He paled, losing most of his green sheen. "No, Princess. And I am truly sorry that we were so adamant about forcing it on you."

I nodded. Tom looked away, his jaw muscle moving, like he was grinding his teeth together. Had he known? Was that his plan?

"Tom?"

He slowly turned back, his neck muscles moving as if he was fighting the action. "Princess?" he said through his teeth.

"Did you know that would happen?"

He glared at me, his nostrils flaring. His pause was so long that by the time he spoke, I wasn't the only one watching him. "No, my Princess, I had not known that would happen." His jaw bulged.

He couldn't lie… so why did I feel like there was something I was missing.

"Princess," Gredd shifted, "clearly there was a mistake in the measurements of your last batch of medicine. We will not use it on you again. However, unless you have figured out how to contain your Magic we are still stuck on this world." His gaze rose to the waters above. Through the school of minnow the mammoth ray could barely be seen. "We came close to being discovered once; I am not sure how many more times we will be so lucky."

I nodded. "Have the doctor make a new batch." I felt bile in my throat again at the thought of taking more medicine. I shuddered as I swallowed it down. "I guess there is no other way."

Gredd's brow furrowed, "Perhaps you will have mastered your Magic before it's done." He sounded hopeful.

I shruged, "Maybe…"

"I will personally oversee the doctor this time." Tom said, the muscle in his jaw was tight. "I assure you no harm will come to you with the next dose."

I nodded. Strangely his assurance worked this time.

~ ~ ~

Eyes closed, legs crossed, and sitting on the sofa in my suites, it was easy to see my Magic. It filled my suites, possibly the entire ship. But what I couldn't figure out was how I supposed to *hide* it. In this strange state I could feel things beyond the walls.

The people on board were worried. Their minds were filled with the fear of being discovered… and of the Emperor's officials discovering me. As if that was the worst thing that could happen to them; even worse than their own death.

...I wasn't so sure I could agree.

The animals outside the ship were nervous too. But their worries were more founded. Something was moving through the water and it didn't vibrate right. Suddenly the mammoth ray landed on the ship causing all the other animals to scatter as a submarine passed overhead.

Everyone in the room jumped at the sound... everyone in the ship, actually. Startled, I opened my eyes.

Tom was standing at the entrance to my room. *How come I hadn't sensed him coming in*? I couldn't tell; it almost looked like he'd been smiling. His cheeks fell as he saw my eyes open. "I have your..."

He held the needle in his hand, "Do you still require it?"

I hadn't learned to hide my Magic yet. I put my hand out and watched as he slowly came forward. He carefully placed it in the palm of my hand.

"Tell me something Tom," I wrapped my hand around the needle swallowing down the ugly taste that started to creep up my throat. "You're supposed to be my teacher so how come you can't teach me this."

After some deliberation Tom finally admitted that only Royals can teach another Royal how to control the Magic. "But I assure you, every Royal can conceal their Magic once they've learned how."

Before I could respond, my breath caught. I felt it as a family of quyii seals deliberately sacrificed themselves to cripple the submarine that had passed over us. My heart ached at the loss of innocent lives. Not the people in the submarine. They'd be fine. Fixing the ship wouldn't take that long then they'd be up and on the search again. It was the quyii seals, such unique animals. Silver-white in the suns with long whiskers and intelligent eyes. It had been a quyii seal I had saved in the cave two Turns back. Strangely I wondered if it was among the family.

Phillip wiped at my tears. "What's wrong?"

"We need to get off the world."

My hands shook as I took the cover off the needle. I glanced at Collin, Samantha and Phillip all bound by the command I'd given. Tom had explained that if my command was given before the situation became a problem then it would override the fear for my safety. So I'd told them that if they even thought about stopping me they should leave my suites.

They watched silently.

"Danay, don't do it," Jef said as I pressed the needle to my thigh the way Sue had said to. "It's too dangerous."

I had a feeling my whole life was going to be too dangerous. "I have to." I pressed the needle in. A prick stung through me making me want to pull the needle out before I emptied the medicine into myself.

"What if something goes wrong again?" His hands were balled into fists.

His weren't the only ones.

"If something goes wrong you have my permission to kiss me again," I said though I really hoped it wouldn't come to that.

He looked at me to be sure I was serious.

Phillip looked away and muttered *great*.

I nodded again and pressed the liquid into my leg. The reaction was instant. My leg started to sting. I jerked the needle out and held it up to Tom.

He bent to take it.

My fingers felt feeble as I dropped it into his outstretched palm. My eyes started to droop. I flopped back against the sofa.

"What do you need?" Samantha asked.

"Water?" Phillip asked.

"Healing sand?" Collin held up the rather large jar he had acquired — *just in case*.

"A kiss?" Jef leaned in close, positioning his lips next to my cheek.

I groaned. "Just get us off the world." I muttered then shut my eyes.

I heard Tom leave. And sometime after that, I felt the ship vibrate.

I tried to raise my head.

"It's okay," Phillip said patting my arm. "It's just the engines."

"Oh," I mumbled as my eyes fluttered open. Jef was sitting on one side of me, Phillip on the other.

Jef looked tense. I reached out and put my hand on his knee. He didn't joke about offering me another kiss — *maybe he was afraid of flying…* I kinda felt nervous about it too.

I thought of all the animals around the ship. Would they be safe? I could only hope so as the ship shuddered and started to move up to the surface of the ocean.

I buried my head in Phillip's chest as the ship rose out of the water and into the air.

Soon after — *or maybe it wasn't so soon after, and it only felt that way*? — Gredd came by to say that we'd made it. We were off world.

I nodded feeling the emptiness of space pulling on the ship from all sides. I closed my eyes again.

"It will be a few hours before we make it to Dustata," Gredd said as he turned to leave the room.

"You should get some rest, Princess" Samantha said. "Come on, we should go."

I hadn't opened my eyes but I could hear she'd stood. I was about to tell her to stay when Jef jerked next to me.

"Get off girl!"

Samantha was trying to pull him to his feet.

"Don't go," I said reaching out to Jef. I caught his hand but I could feel how feeble my grip was. I couldn't hold on to him.

"Stay." I locked eyes with Samantha.

She pursed her lips and sat back down.

Jef put my hand back on his knee and held it there. He shifted closer, "Just say the word and my lips are ready to serve."

Phillip let out a low groan.

Jef leaned closer, "Danny, did you say something? I couldn't hear you. Do you need me to kiss you yet?"

I tried to push his face away.

He didn't budge.

Phillip put his hand on mine and pushed Jef back for me, "Come on, we've been over this, Jef, no means no." Once Jef moved away, Phillip laced his fingers between mine, "I've got you Danay."

"You know, you never told me why you don't call her Princess," Jef said.

I felt Phillip flinch, "I promised her I wouldn't call her anything but Danay until she told me not to." Phillip was rubbing my Coming of Age bracelet. "She sort of commanded it before she understood that she had the power to command me."

"So it's true," Jef's hand tightened over my other hand, pressing it into his knee, "pretty much whatever she tells you to do — you have to do."

"Mostly."

"Mostly?" Jef snickered, "I'll take that as a solid yes."

No one said anything else.

~ ~ ~

My sleep was punctuated by moments of consciousness. Each time I woke, I was in a different position. The first time my head was on Phillip's shoulder. The next time my head was on Jef's chest. Another time Phillip had my feet on his lap, and was rubbing them while my head was in Jef's lap.

"Are you planning on staying awake?" Phillip asked as I shifted to sitting.

The next time I woke up my head was on Phillip's knees, my legs were on Jef's lap. Phillip was running his hand through my hair. When he saw I was awake he stopped.

"Good morning," Jef said offering me his hand.

"Is it morning?" I took it and he pulled me upright.

"Beats me. We aren't on Uma'Three anymore. So it could be any time of day… or night." Jef smiled.

I rubbed at the sleep that stuck in my eyes. "How far are we from Dustata?"

"We're about halfway there. If you're really awake, Tom has requested to see you," Samantha said.

I debated trying to go back to sleep.

"What about lunch?" Collin asked.

I stretched. "Is it lunch time?" I wasn't particularly hungry.

"That depends." Collin looked unusually green.

"On what?" I asked.

"On you." His stomach growled. "You see, we just left Tem where it is coming up on breakfast time and we are a few hours from Dustata on Turlyn, where it is dinnertime. So split the difference and it makes lunch, right?" Collin smiled like he meant for it to be a joke, but his stomach growled again.

"For you it's always lunchtime." Mitch rolled his eyes.

"Well it's always lunchtime somewhere," Collin agreed.

"Okay," I nodded, "just for you Collin, I'll say it is."

He grinned and bowed.

Chapter Twenty-Seven

Yeah-yeah's and Fish-Boy

When Tom arrived I was sitting on the sofa with Jef and Phillip beside me. Collin was on the chair closest to Phillip and Mitch was on the chair next to Jef. Samantha had cleared away our lunch dishes and was standing behind me.

Tom moved in to sit down across from me. He'd brought the bag with the spheres.

I'd been expecting this.

"Are you ready to do some practicing?"

"You can't expect Danay to do that now," Jef said shifting forward. "You've just medicated her. Can't you give her more time to..."

"Time is a commodity we don't have." Tom placed a single yellow sphere on the empty table in front of me. "Princess?" He raised an eyebrow at me.

Jef turned to look at me, "I can help. I can give you a..."

"No!" Phillip cut Jef off. "No. That's not necessary. Danay can do this." He looked at me, "You don't need help. You're strong enough all on your own."

I nodded even though I kinda agreed with Jef. The drugs were going to make this more difficult, if not impossible. I thought about accepting Jef's offer.

"Tom, hand me Uma'Three," Phillip said.

Tom reached into the bag and quickly found the orb.

Phillip pressed it into my palm. It was strange, the last time I'd held it I was still on the planet it represented. With it next to my skin, I realized that I was already missing my world.

"I'm here to help if you need me to," Jef whispered in my ear.

As I held the sphere, I wasn't as tempted. This was Uma'Three, I knew her.

I rolled the ball around in my hand until Tem was facing up. I thought about my white shark, the jellies, the eels, the mi'lex, the Deeps and the Shallows. Then I thought about the kids in my class, Pal'Hon, Sal'Non, Pel'Dob…

Samantha drew in her breath behind me and Jef twitched.

Phillip leaned close to my ear to whisper, "Told you so."

"Well done Princess," for just a moment a smile touched Tom's lips. It disappeared too quickly. "I told you all she needed was a little practice."

How come this felt like his victory not mine?

"Okay, now let's try it with more spheres," Tom said.

"I've only been able to do it with Uma'Three, Two and One." I took my hand out from under the sphere. It stayed afloat, slowly spinning, as if in some insane singular orbit. "But I couldn't get it with Uma'Four."

"Then let's start there." Tom reached into the bag. The balls clinked together as he moved his hand about. He pulled out Uma'Four's replica.

"How'd you do that without looking?" Samantha leaned over me to ask.

"Each sphere has a unique feel. They've been constructed with the material indigenous to their planets. Some are smoother, others are colder. I've also learned to recognize the land formations on each one." Tom handed me the ball. "Of course Uma'Four doesn't have any land masses but, unlike any of the suns it's cooler and it's softer than all the moons."

As I held it, I could sense the water of its surface.

"That's Shiprock," Jef said, "May I?"

I nodded.

He poked his finger into it. "Shiprock can only be found on Uma'Four. It's been illegal to take it off-world for generations, even before the trading ban." Jef pointed an accusing finger at Tom. "Where'd you get it?"

Tom's returning smile looked more like a warning, "These planetary replicas have been used by the Royals for at least thirteen generations."

"Oh," Jef pulled his finger back.

"How'd you know what Shiprock looks and feels like?" Samantha asked Jef.

"My..." his face flushed, "my Pop had some. Originally he was from Uma'Four. When the Emperor ordered everyone back to their home planet Dad chose to stay on Uma'Three, to be with Mom."

I squeezed Jef's hand.

"We were on Uma'Four, before we came to Uma'Three," Phillip said. "We visited the floating cities and even stayed with the mer-folk for a bit."

"Really?" Jef's eyebrows rose but he refused to look at Phillip. Instead he stared at Samantha. "What were they like? Were they as..." he blushed and cleared his throat, "As beautiful as the books say they are?"

"Absolutely," Samantha said sounding a little breathless.

At the same time, Collin said, "No." He looked at Jef for a moment, "Well, I suppose by Uma'Three's standards they would be. All the girls were *well* rounded."

"But the men..." Samantha said to no one in particular, "they had more of a muscular layer." She stopped abruptly and glanced towards Mitch. He wouldn't return her look.

"I'd love to go there one day," Jef said wistfully.

"You should," Phillip said, "If you'd like we could arrange to transport you there now."

"Phillip," I glared at him.

He sighed, "Sorry. Hey, Samantha, why don't you tell Danay about the city that we all visited. You know, Mes'Muna."

"Mes'Muna, oh," Samantha brought her hand to her mouth. "It was beautiful. It's one of the biggest cities on Uma'Four. Like all the cities there, it's made from Shiprock. But unlike the other cities, Mes'Muna is several pieces of Shiprock fused together by bridges and walkways..."

She went on to describe Shiprock. It was a type of coral. The coral itself was a community of creatures much like those in the forests on Zoni. When they died, huge chunks would break away from the rest and float to the ocean's surface. Each piece was about the size of Tem.

Of course I knew this from all the books my Nan'Dah had read to me. But from the look on Jef's face he didn't know.

"The whole place is made from Shiprock, from the ground right up to the sky. The streets, buildings, even the bridges and walkways." Samantha was still describing Mes'Muna. "See how the the Shiprock reflects light? Princess, hold it up a little. See how it looks brighter the closer it gets to the light? Well, at high noon, when the suns are directly overhead, the whole place glows white."

"You know the mer-folk..." she went on to explain how it was the mer-folk's job to care for Uma'Four. If they did their job well then there wasn't a lot of new Shiprock. A few generations back everyone on every world had wanted to use Shiprock on their own worlds. People from all over Quista had come to harvest it. If they had succeeded there would have been nothing left on Uma'Four. That was why the ban had been created.

My Nan'Dah had taught me about this. She told me that the Royals could have made it so that there was Shiprock on all the planets. Several Commoners had petitioned the Royals to do so. But the Royals decided not to. They said they wanted the people of Quista to learn to appreciate their own worlds the way they were. Nan'Dah had explained to me that if we kept changing the worlds for selfish reasons then nothing would be precious anymore.

I remembered thinking: *what a hard job it must be to be a Royal*. My opinion hadn't changed.

"Do you know how the mer-folk came to be?" Phillip asked his eyes intent on me.

"Sort of," I continued to turn the replica of Uma'Four in my hand. The longer I held it, the more it felt like being reacquainted with an old friend.

"Why don't you refresh our memories?" Tom said.

With every eye on me, I felt like I was being tested.

I looked away. "After Uma split into four, only three of the new planets were inhabitable. Uma'Four was always too hostile. That didn't stop people from trying. For generations many lives were lost on the never ending stormy seas of Uma'Four. High Empress Emma always liked the old-old legends about Earth and thought if Uma'Four had mer-folk instead of humans they'd have a better chance of surviving."

"Sounds logical," Jef said when I paused.

"Sure, logical," I said. "But she changed everyone on Uma'Four into mer-folk without their permission." I pressed my lips together.

I'm not sure he meant to but Jef moved just a fraction away.

I could feel everyone's eyes on me. I thought it was because of what I'd said but then I realized that I'd dropped my hand, and Uma'Four's sphere hung in the air.

It was floating over to where Uma'Three was. As the two neared, they moved into an identical rotation, spinning on an invisible axis as if they were playing chase with each other.

"I knew you could do it," Phillip said, leaning so close his eyelashes tickled my cheek and his breath heated my neck.

Jef patted my knee then left his hand there.

"Phillip you were right." Tom stood and bowed. "Now I must take my leave."

"You were right?" I asked, once Tom was out of earshot.

"I knew I was."

Jef snorted.

"But what were you right about?"

"You." That's all he said before he changed the subject. "Come on, Danay, don't stop now you're on a roll." He passed me Uma'Two.

It was easy to get Uma'Two and 'One into orbit with the rest. Watching all four planets circle around one another felt good. I wanted to try more but after a long time with barely any success, I had to give up from exhaustion.

~ ~ ~

Samantha woke me in the morning. We were on Turlyn. It was time for my training. She bathed me then helped me pick out something to wear, though neither of us knew how I should dress. *What does one wear while learning Magic?* She chose a long dress with soft material that reflected the lights around it.

When I came into my sitting room, Collin, Mitch, and Phillip were all waiting for me with breakfast.

"Where's Jef?" I asked as I sat. Collin brought me my plate. He apologized that it wasn't cake. I was just glad they hadn't tried to give me porridge again. I was also happily surprised that there were lu'umon berries. I'd thought that once we'd left Uma'Three I wouldn't see them again.

Phillip helped himself to some of the berries. When he caught Mitch staring he said, "They really are quite good."

Mitch shook his head, "Must be nice to be in the Princess' good favor."

"You could have some too." I offered him the bowl.

He shook his head again and looked away.

The door buzzer sounded and before Samantha could get to her feet, Mitch was out of the room with an, "I'll see who it is."

Phillip shifted to look at me. His plate abandoned, "Did you sleep well last night?"

I shrugged. *I'd slept well enough*. Though, if I were being honest, I missed the moisture in the air. I'd felt so dry I'd contemplated making myself a bath to sleep in.

Phillip laughed when I told him this.

Mitch wasn't back. Who was at my door? Why weren't they being welcomed in?

I reached out with my thoughts. I didn't even have to close my eyes to do it.

"Danay?" Phillip said.

I pushed my thoughts past Mitch's murky orange spirit to feel Jef's deep green aura. *Jef. Yes, Jef. Jef was here!* I hadn't realized how much I had missed him... but something was wrong. He wasn't moving. Why wasn't Mitch bringing him in?

"Danay?" Phillip asked as both Collin and Samantha said, "Princess?"

I jumped to my feet and walked as quickly as I could through the dining hall and formal sitting room just as Mitch said, "That's far enough Fish-Boy."

Mitch's hand was held straight out. "I've been ordered to keep you out."

"Did Danay give you that order? Or did it come from someone else?"

"You are a distraction the Princess would do better without right now." Mitch puffed his chest out.

"Oh yeah? Then what about…" Jef caught sight of me. "Danny," he tried to push past Mitch.

Mitch caught Jef's arm and spun him, twisting it around his back. Then he kicked the back of Jef's knee which sent Jef to the floor with the sickening sound of a belly flop on solid ground. Mitch landed on Jef, digging his knee into Jef's back, still holding tight to his arm.

"Hey!" I ran forward, "What do you think you're doing?" I fell to my knees next to Jef. His face was squished to the floor.

Mitch didn't budge. "Princess, I don't think Jef is…"

"Let him go," I ordered, "this instant."

Mitch gave a quick bow and released Jef. He took a small step aside, put his hands behind his back, and stood over us watching Jef like a hungry hoorup.

"Are you okay?" I touched Jef's face. His lip was bleeding.

He pulled away, wiping it on his sleeve, "It'll be fine."

"What was that about?" I asked looking up at Mitch.

For a moment, he tried to avoid my glare. Then with a sigh he said, "Tom…"

"Tom!" I was on my feet. "What about Tom?"

Mitch stared down at Jef who had to wipe his lip again. "Tom doesn't think Jef is a safe influence for you right now."

"And you believe him?" *What did Tom really know about me?*

Mitch looked from Jef to me then down at the ground. He gave a small shrug.

"But you chose to listen to him?"

Another shrug and a head nod.

I didn't see everyone else as much as I felt them. Phillip, Collin, and Samantha had come to stand in the doorway to my entrance room.

"Well, now you have another choice to make," I said to Mitch.

Mitch looked slightly green. "I won't pledge myself." His jaw snapped together. "And if you command me then…"

"I wasn't going to make you pledge yourself," it was my turn to feel sick. I stared down at Jef whose lip continued to bleed. "But you do have to decide who you are going to listen to." I stopped to take a breath. This was a command. I knew I had to be careful about how I said it. Luckily Tom had taught me something, finally: how to word tricky commands. I locked eyes with Mitch, "When it comes to what is best for me, either you are going to listen to Tom or you will listen to me. However, if you choose Tom then you are no longer welcome here. Choose."

Mitch looked past me to the others, who stayed in the entrance. For just a moment I thought he'd choose Tom. He shifted to stare at the floor, "I will listen to you, Princess." He looked up, his eyes meeting mine, "please, Princess, what is best for you?"

What *was* best for me?

I turned to look at everyone who stood in my doorway. I needed them. I needed Samantha. I needed Collin. I needed Phillip. I looked down at Jef, I needed him too. "I need Jef. He's my guest. I want him here — and none of you are to stop him from being with me." I said.

Samantha and Collin nodded immediately. Phillip took a moment then shut his eyes and bowed his head.

I turned back to Mitch, "Is that clear?"

Mitch bowed low, "Yes, Princess."

"Good," I held my hand out to Jef and helped him to his feet. Then I led him to my bedroom.

"Princess," Samantha started to protest.

I put my hand up. "I don't want to hear it."

Samantha curtseyed. "May I chaperone you?"

"No," I locked eyes with her. "I want to be alone with Jef."

Samantha pressed her lips together and nodded.

"Now, you've all done enough damage here. Go wait for me in my sitting room."

Samantha, Collin, and Mitch obeyed.

Phillip hesitated.

"I mean it. I want to be alone with Jef." I locked eyes with him. "Don't make me order you."

He bowed stiffly. "Danay," he said as he stood straight, "is there anything else you need?"

"You can get me some healing sand," I said, thinking about Jef's lip.

Jef was alternating between licking and wiping it trying to keep the bleeding under control.

"As you wish," he bowed and left.

Once alone Jef tried to grin. He winced.

"What?"

"They really are your *yeah-yeah's*."

I smacked Jef's arm. "I told you to be nice."

"Ouch, hey!"

As if I'd really hurt him. I started towards the bathroom. He followed.

"You know it's not just these yeah-yeah's—"

"They're called Loyalists."

"—who have it in for me." He followed me all the way into the bathroom and leaned into the counter to rub his face. When he brought his hands away, his eyes looked sad. "No one likes me here."

"That can't be true."

"It is."

I shook my head. "It's not. I like you."

He smiled briefly, "Thank you," he said staring at me for a moment, then chuckled darkly, "boy, have the tables turned." He stepped forward and took my hand. "I know how hard it was for you growing up — I saw it. But I never," his eyes shone, "I don't think I ever really understood. I'm sorry."

"It wasn't you," I said. It felt weird having him this close. His hand around mine felt different. Warmer, somehow.

Phillip knocked. I pulled my hand free and went to the door.

"Everything okay in there?" he asked while handing me the jar of sand.

I checked over my shoulder. Jef was wiping his lip again.

I shrugged but shut the door.

I didn't say anything as I applied the healing sand to Jef's swollen lip. He didn't say anything either.

As I set the jar down on the counter, Jef reached over and grabbed my wrist.

Holding me by the CoaB he stared at me. It felt like he was asking me a question that I didn't understand. Then his second hand came around my waist and he started to pull me closer.

I was caught off balance. I put my hand against his chest to stop myself from falling into him. His chest was squishy and made a strange wet sponge-like noise. I pushed myself back. "What… what are you wearing?"

He let go of my waist. "This?" he said, slapping his chest. "Check it out. Specialty made water-suit. The doctor designed it. It keeps me from drying out."

I admired the water-suit for a moment, feeling foolish. I'd forgotten that he wouldn't be able to survive out of the water. The water-suit was ingenious. But somewhere along the way I stopped looking at the water-suit and started to see the boy inside of it.

"Does it really work? You aren't suffering, are you?"

"Nope. Though it would be nice if all your yeah-yeah's would stop calling me Fish-Boy."

I ground my teeth. "They aren't yeah-yeah's—"

Jef let my arm go.

"—any more than you are a Fish-Boy! I mean, of all the mean spirited, stupid, rude—"

"Danay?" Jef waved his hand like he was trying to cool it off.

"—biased, narrow minded, idiotic things to call you. If you are Fish-Boy, then… then… then I'm their Fishy-Princess."

"Danay!" Jef's voice was sharp. He held his hand out. "You burned me."

"What? No!" I reached over to grab the jar of healing sands. "Here."

He pulled away.

Was he scared of me. "Jef, I'm sorry."

"I know." He was looking at me as if I was a different person, "But…" He didn't finish.

"Jef?" I took a pinch of sand between my fingers and tried to apply it to his arm.

"No," he stepped farther back, falling into the tub.

I turned to the mirror, "Do you want me to leave?"

"No. I'm okay. It's just…" His reflection was staring at me. "You're stronger… like really stronger."

"I'm still me." My voice was low. With everything that had happened, I didn't feel like myself.

"Yes, you are still you." He stood up and cautiously climbed out of the tub. "Only you are also the Princess." He extended his hand to me. "The healing sand will heal me," he licked his already healed lip, "but I'll wager you can heal me without it."

Chapter Twenty-Eight

Training on Turlyn

We returned to the sitting room where Tom was waiting to escort me to the Turlyn training area. I didn't miss the way he looked at Jef. I took Jef's hand in mine and glared, challenging him to say something.

His eyes stayed narrowed as he turned away.

Jef squeezed my hand while fidgeting with the collar of his water-suit with his free hand.

Tom held out a cloak that looked similar to the one Mz. Kal'Lv's had given me. "It's still chilly out," he said holding it open.

Morris and Tom walked ahead of me as we left the ship. Jef and Phillip were on my right, as well as a man I had only seen once before. Mitch, Collin, and another person I'd never seen were on my left. Samantha walked behind me, sandwiched between the two guards from outside my suites.

The cavern we'd landed in was so large I couldn't make out the ceiling. The walkway from the docking ramp stretched out into the gloom. The dim light from the lampposts made the walk to Dustata, the only city on Turlyn, feel dangerous.

In Dustata, the homes looked like floor to ceiling columns. They were no larger than five paces wide. Morris said that each floor was only one room and the floors were connected by a spiral staircase that ran through the center of each house. The bedrooms were nearer the bottom and the kitchens were at the top. I imagined anyone who lived there would have thick legs from climbing so many flights of stairs every day. But I hadn't seen anyone to know if my guess was right.

I was escorted past a deserted square. In the center was a lowered arena with crude benches carved into the rock bed. I wondered what sort of performance could be held there. The place felt important.

"Where is everyone?"

"It is still early here, Princess," Tom said. "Most are sleeping. Those who are up know that you are not to be disturbed."

We left Dustata. There were no more house columns and the air grew colder. About halfway across the huge empty cavern I could see the wall we were headed for. Drawing closer, I spied the entrance to a tunnel. "What are you going to teach me today?"

Tom's stride slowed, "I am not to be your teacher today." He stopped and bowed low. "This is as far as we may go." He stood straighter and looked longingly towards the tunnel. "You must make the rest of this journey on your own."

"I…" I glanced at the tunnel. The opening was less than twenty paces from where we stood. It was pitch black and forbidding. "I can't. Not alone. Can't you at least walk me to the opening?"

"I am sorry Princess," his eyes betrayed him, *he wasn't just sorry — he wanted to come too*. "Only Royals may enter. Commoners and Loyalists are forbidden. Any who have tried have never returned." Tom gave a nod and the four extra men shifted their packs off their shoulders.

"We will wait here for your return," Morris said looking greener than usual.

Why was he so nervous?

Morris glanced at the cave then looked away.

"Princess?" Tom's eyes bored into me.

I took a shaky step towards the tunnel. Jef, whose hand I was holding, stepped forward with me. He wasn't the only one, Phillip and Samantha did the same.

"It's forbidden," Morris said looking at Jef.

"I'll risk it," he said.

That made me braver. I took another few steps. Phillip and Samantha followed me.

"Samantha, Phillip, what shall I tell your parents when you don't return?" Tom asked sounding dead serious.

"Tell my parents that I served the Princess," Samantha answered without turning back.

"Phillip, what do you think your father will have to say when he hears of this foolhardy mission?" Morris's voice was tight.

"I suspect he'll say the same thing he always says when I do something he disapproves of." Phillip turned to look at both Tom and Morris, "But you can remind him that it was my foolhardiness that brought the Princess to us in the first place."

Jef and Phillip insisted on taking the lead. Jef's elbow knocked Phillip's. Phillip put his foot in front of Jef's. Jef managed to avoid tripping by grabbing Phillip's arm, and then he pushed him away.

It was time to enter the tunnel. Phillip went in first, Jef followed him, then it was my turn, and Samantha followed me.

"The air feels thick," Phillip whispered. "Can you feel it?"

I felt something. It made the hairs on my neck tingle. The tunnel was carved from the same silvery rock as the rest of the moon. But the path was worn smooth. I wasn't the first one to have walked here. I took comfort in that. However, the farther we went, the more I felt like the walls were watching me. Faces seemed to appear and disappear in the rough surface. I tried not to act as frightened as I felt.

"Sorry," I said as I walked right into the back of Phillip.

He smiled but it looked forced, "No, I'm sorry."

"For what?"

Phillip looked to Samantha and back, "I believe this is as far as we get to go."

"What do you mean?"

Samantha sighed, "We can't move forward."

"What?" I stepped past them and turned back, "I can. What's wrong with you two?"

"Three," Jef frowned. He put his hand out then drew it back quickly. "This is as far as I can go too."

"Go on," Phillip encouraged, "you can do this. We'll wait here for you."

I didn't want to leave them. I didn't want to go on alone.

"It's okay, Princess," Samantha said. Her smile was light, "we'll be fine."

Princess, Princess, Princess the word seemed to be echoed by a thousand murmurs through the tunnel. At first it sounded like a question but as it continued it felt more like a confirmation. *Princess.*

With a sigh — it was probably closer to a whimper — I continued on alone.

It felt darker without any company to drive the shadows away. My footing became unsteady as a feeling of uneasiness settled in. I felt like a trespasser, like an intruder. Like I was a child sneaking into her parents room when they weren't home to stop her.

Finally I saw a light ahead. In the light, the shadows were more defined. They were walking with me — escorting me. They stopped feeling dangerous and started to feel familiar — like I should know them.

When I got to the end of the tunnel I looked out and was so shocked I had to blink to be sure I was seeing right. It was the living room from my home before Nan'Dah moved us to Tem. It had the same smooth armchair where she always sat watching over me when I played on the dry floor. My blanket was spread out as if it were waiting for me. I spent a few minutes looking over all the familiar objects: the clamshell lamp, the barnacle table, even the mussel shell candy dish.

I jumped when I heard a soft clanking noise. I knew that noise. It was the sound my play disks made when they were knocked together. *But who had made the sound*? Carefully I peered around the chair. There, in the center of my blanket was a small boy. He couldn't have been much older than I was when I'd last played with my disks.

He looked up at me with the same blue eyes I'd seen in the mirror every day staring back at me from my own face. His hair, however, couldn't have been more different than mine. It was dark, thick, and curly; it kind of reminded me of Kit's. He was a healthy size, chubby, but also tall.

He smiled, "Will you come play with me?" He held up my childhood toys in his chubby hands.

"I think I'm in the wrong place. I'm supposed to be training."

His face fell, "Everyone is always too busy to play." His lower lip jutted out. Something about it reminded me of Jef, the shape or the color, or just the action.

I looked around the room. There was nowhere to go. No openings to be seen, not even the one I'd come through. I moved forward and debated where to sit — on the chair where my Nan'Dah would have sat, or the floor. I chose the floor.

The boy's face broke into a wide grin, "I saved these for you." He handed me my old metallic toys.

The feel of them in my hands brought back memories I'd long forgotten.

"Can you make them dance for me?" the boy asked.

I held them out between my two palms. They fit so much easier now that I was grown up. "How do I make them dance?"

The boy stood up placing one small hand on my shoulder, "Don't you remember when you used to dance them?"

I blinked… and I did. *I remembered it all!* I remembered how Nan'Dah had laughed with delight as I made my toys spin, twirl, and flip through the air. I had been so young — younger than the boy who stood beside me.

I put my old toys down. "What happened?" I'm not sure if I was asking him or myself. I ran my fingers over the smooth material of my blanket. Queen popling silk. I still had a part of this blanket with me —lovingly laced into my CoaB.

"Danay, you are a good girl," the boy said. That had been what my Nan'Dah said to me: *Danay, you are a good girl. One day you will become a great Princess. But not today. You are not ready yet. You must grow and get stronger. In order to do that you must forget yourself for a while.*

I had listened to her. I'd forgotten it all.

"Are you ready to remember now?" the boy asked, his grin was so much like Kit's when she was excited.

I nodded. I was ready.

~ ~ ~

Time lost meaning as the boy and I *played* with the toys in the room — first with my old ones, then with new strange ones that appeared out of thin air. Soon I was levitating, spinning, twirling, and making them fly about, with no thought at all.

"They're ready for you now." The boy looked up past me. An opening had appeared in the wall, where the kitchen would have been if this really was my old apartment.

I stood up and looked down to where the boy stayed, "Aren't you coming?"

"Oh. No, I don't get to run. That's only for you."

I nodded and looked at the entrance to the new tunnel. It didn't look scary, didn't feel scary either, I just didn't want to leave the boy.

"Go on, the others will show you what you need to see." He pushed a disk around the blanket making it spin between his fingers.

"Come child," a voice whispered from somewhere inside the tunnel. Looking, I thought I could see a shadow, a human shadow; it waved, beckoning me to step forward.

I tilted my head to the side.

Its waving became more insistent. Then the shadow grew and became two — the second also waved me forward.

I continued to stare. The shadows continued to multiply, taking up more and more space along the wall, over the floor, and across the ceiling.

"Come, Princess," they whispered.

My foot slid forward, on its own accord. Then my other foot stepped up and toward the opening. I was walking. The whispers increased in volume. They were happy, excited. I wanted to turn back to the boy, to see if he was okay, to see if he was still there, and to see if he was watching. But the entrance had already closed behind me.

My feet were moving faster and faster, picking up speed, each step taking me farther than the last. Soon the tunnel disappeared and I was on Uma'Three. I was home — or home was here…

I could see everything and everywhere, and I could smell and feel things that I knew and things that I did not know. I was in Tem, but I was also in Mocc, and Qorl, and Evsta. I experienced the Shallows and every nook and cranny of

Deeps. I lived through every Season from the Popling Festival to the Rainy Month. I breathed in the smell of the water, felt the electricity of the mi'lex feeding frenzy, the eel's hatching and the hides of sharks and rays and other sea creatures. I could feel the suns and taste the light from Uma'Three's moon. Every part of me tingled with excitement and I began to form an understanding of things both seen and unseen.

I ran faster and faster and the experiences came to me in waves.

I was seeing people now — a mother snuggling her child, a boy learning to swim, an old man waiting in an office. Everything came to me so quickly.

I slowed when I saw a popular girl from my old school talking to a group of my classmates.

"It's because she was friends with that traitor Danay, that's why Kit'Una was sentenced to death." The girl smirked. "Serves her right."

I stopped and the scene froze.

My heart pounded. I was livid. That was a lie. Kit'Una hadn't been sentenced to death. I was so angry at the girl for saying that. So angry I wanted to hurt her.

I took one step forward.

The girl fell into the water as if she'd been pushed.

Another step.

She didn't get up.

"Did I do that? Was it me?" I wondered.

There was no answer. There were no shadows to be seen. Or were there?

I spun in a quick circle trying to catch them. I looked at the water where the girl fell in. She didn't deserve that.

"I take it back. That shouldn't have happened."

I stepped backwards.

The girl was standing in front of her friends again.

"Much better," I said then stepped forward.

Nothing happened to her. She continued to say mean things about me and Kit. I didn't want to hurt her so I ran away, making new scenes unfold around me.

"Good child," a voice said. I continued to run until I couldn't see Uma'Three.

I ran all the way to Uma'One, then Uma'Two and finally to Uma'Four. There I saw the mer-folk; the beautiful and noble race of changed people. I saw the cities of Shiprock, some smaller than Tem, others bigger. I ran through Mes'Muna; Samantha's description hadn't done it justice.

After that I ran to Riel. Though it was a deep blue world, it wasn't all ocean like Uma'Four and there were no Shiprock cities. It had islands, but they were rooted to the ground and they were covered in vast forests. Riel's people resembled the land dwellers of Uma'Four's and they shared customs as well as dialects. I learned that Riel's people had very white teeth from a vegetable; calpodda. It made their bones grow strong causing all sorts of abnormalities. *This would be where Fred and Erik had originated from*.

From there I ran to Ruebyn with its spongy copper marshes and teal green vegetation. I ran through Unarrah where the men had green skin, and the women had purple skin. Something in the pigment converted the second sun's rays into a digestive enzyme that would break down the tough vegetation. It also made it so they digested food at double the rate of a normal skinned person.

"Why are the women so many different shades of purple while the men only have two shades of green?" I asked.

No one answered and before I could ask again I'd run to a new world.

Ursala was a harsh dry world with great mounds of sand that covered over two thirds of the planet's surface. It also had a race of changed people who had skin like a shark, but far more baked looking. They needed it to protect themselves against the raging winds. I ran through one of the windstorms. It whipped up so much sand that if I'd really been there it would have taken my skin off.

As the dust cleared, I found myself on Zaffa, the frozen world. It was completely devoid of life, yet it took a long time to run through. With no one there, it was eerily quiet, but it was filled with painful memories that screamed and echoed around me.

Running through Zoni I was surrounded by dense vegetation. So dense, that if I had physical form, I couldn't have pushed my way through. As I ran it was a blur of oranges, from rajah to tangelo, mixed with azure blue. I didn't see the people, as if they were hiding from me, but I did see the animals. There were so many, I lost count — all colorful, all strong. A pearl jungle cat tried to pounce on me. A Valque, I thought seeing its wings tucked neatly to its sides.

I ran and ran and ran some more. I didn't get tired. I didn't feel hungry. The more I ran the more I saw. I didn't want to stop. I needed to see everything but I didn't get to. I ran right out of the tunnel. It was so sudden I fell onto the floor of my old apartment. When I looked up the boy stood over me, his eyes aglow.

"What did you see?"

"Have you never gone in there?" I asked.

He shook his head, "It is only for the Princes and Princesses of Quista. I am neither."

My heart broke for him, to be so close and not be allowed in.

He touched my cheek, "Please, tell me what you saw."

"It was amazing," I said, then sighed because I felt bad for saying that. I sat up taller and patted the floor for him to join me. Once he was comfortable, I told him everything I could remember. "There was so much and all of it is so… so… well, just so amazing."

He nodded, "Its Quista. Of course it's amazing." He sounded beyond his Royal Years.

"But I didn't get to see everything." I frowned.

"Of course you couldn't." He laughed at me. "Even you shouldn't know everything." His nose wrinkled. "I'm hungry." His voice had returned to its original, childish tone.

"What are you hungry for?" I asked and when he told me, I made it appear for him. He wanted roasted sqa from Zoni, cooked ugil from Rubyn, fried ketswonus from Riel, and stewed pomus from Unarrah. I made a ripe bushel of lu'umons appear and held it out for him.

He smiled but pushed it away. "No, my Princess, those are special for you."

I didn't argue. I ate them all.

When my stomach was satisfied, I got up and realized there was nowhere to go, so I sat back down, only in the chair Nan'Dah had used.

The boy came to stand before me. I wasn't sure what he wanted but I opened my arms. He climbed into my lap and rested his head against my chest. His thumb slipped into his mouth. We sat quietly for a few moments.

"You really are my favorite, of them all, you know?" he said.

I nodded. There was something so familiar about this boy. Something so sweet, so special, I didn't want to let him go. "Do you want to play some more?" I asked.

He shook his head. His thick curls tickled my chin, "There's no more time for play." He sounded ageless again. "It's almost time for you to return to your friends."

My hands tightened reflexively about him.

"Why are you scared?" He pulled back to look at my face.

"I'm not ready," I said.

He blinked, his bright eyes felt like searchlights that could see right into me. "But you are."

I nodded even though I still didn't feel ready.

"Princess, you are." His soft hand touched my cheek, "You have to be. They need you," he turned to look at the wall I'd come through. The entrance re-appeared, "we all need you." He climbed off my lap and looked at me. His eyes made me feel like I was the child not him.

I stood. "When I leave where will you go?"

"Back to where I came from." He smiled, not looking at me. He ran over to the blanket and picked up my old toys and brought them to me.

"You keep them," I said.

He shook his head, "They are yours. You can give them to me another day."

I took them. He held the blanket to his cheek. I thought he was going to give it to me too, but he put his thumb into his mouth and turned to walk towards an opening at the far end of the room.

Before he disappeared into the dark, he turned back and said, "Goodbye Princess Danay. You really are my favorite."

"Goodbye... what's your name?"

He turned his head. I noticed there was a strip missing from the blanket, and it was fraying. "I will be Andrew."

"Goodbye Andrew. Will I see you again?"

His face brightened, "Oh, yes, you will, soon, very soon." He bowed then turned and ran. I watched his curls bounce against his head. His curls were really just like Jef's.

I stood up suddenly worried for Jef and the others.

Chapter Twenty-Nine

Proof

"Princess," Samantha smiled, "is everything alright?"

I walked slowly over to her. But something seemed wrong. Jef and Phillip were standing almost exactly where I'd left them. "My training is done."

"Done?" she asked.

"Great," Jef said. "That means we can go back to the ship now, right?" He nervously pulled at the collar of his water-suit.

"How was it?" Phillip asked.

I shrugged. I didn't know how to answer and there was a part of me that didn't want to share anything about what had happened.

"But you're done? That means we can leave?" Jef locked his eyes on me. I could see that he didn't want to be here.

I nodded but hesitated, there was something about this place, a connection I didn't want to leave.

"Ready to go?" Phillip held his hand out to me. He didn't feel comfortable here either.

Jef sneered at Phillip and extended his own hand, "Let's get out of here."

I was already reaching for Phillip. As his hand closed around mine, it felt like I'd chosen something more than just whose hand I would hold. I quickly took Jef's extended hand in my free one.

I let them escort me out of the tunnel even though I didn't really want to leave. I missed the voices and the shadows; they didn't follow me here. Even with Phillip and Jef and Samantha near me, I felt alone. If they hadn't been with me, encouraging me to leave, I would have stayed — forever.

~ ~ ~

"Done?" Tom looked surprised.

I looked around, the men hadn't even started to unpack. "I've been gone for hours."

"It was less than five minutes," Tom said.

"But it felt… longer."

"Perhaps you need to go back? Maybe you weren't done." Tom looked down his nose at me.

"No." *Had he meant to insult me*? "My training is done."

Tom looked skeptical.

I ground my teeth trying not to be angry. "I'm returning to the ship. Are you coming?" I started walking.

No one spoke as they took up their positions around me and we began the trek back.

As we walked, I could hear them talking about lunch, wondering what the cook would prepare and how happy they were to be off Uma'Three — where every dish tasted like the sea.

Only, it wasn't *they* who were talking. It was Collin, and he wasn't *talking* — I could hear him *thinking*.

Collin smiled when he caught me looking at him. I heard his stomach growl. It wasn't as loud as it could get, but it was loud enough for everyone to hear it.

So glad I didn't inherit that from my father. This was someone else's thoughts.

Mitch looked past me toward Samantha. *I wonder if she'd still like me if I did. I wonder if… wait, she's looking at me. No— she's glaring at me. Why is she glaring at me? Oh, yeah, right, I'm supposed to be watching for danger.* Mitch looked from side to side then forward. *The only danger here is that Fish-Boy. If I had my way…*

My hand flexed on Jef's. I didn't want to hear that. I didn't want him thinking that.

Jef sighed, then whispered, "When we get back I need to talk with the doctor."

I nodded, distracted. I had to concentrate to keep everyone else's thoughts out.

We passed a family as we neared Dustata. A father and mother stood up and bowed — clearly caught off guard. Their daughter, who looked about three-Royal-Years-old, curtseyed but she peeked up through her bangs at me. I waved. She gave me the prettiest of smiles.

My daughter was the same size the last time I saw her.

I looked around, trying to see whose thoughts I'd heard.

She and Mitch used to play together so well… I wonder what she looks like now? I peeked at Morris. He was staring straight ahead looking stoic. His face didn't reveal what he was thinking. I was impressed; his thoughts were laced with such longing.

I quickly looked over to Mitch. He was still trying not to look back at Samantha. He hadn't given the girl a second glance. I wondered if the girl really looked like Mitch's twin or if Morris was just seeing what he wanted to see in her.

The farther into the village we went the more people we passed. Rumors were traveling faster than we were. The more people we saw, the less shocked they seemed, and the quicker they were to bow.

As we approached another group of eager Loyalists, I noticed the arena we'd passed earlier. I stopped. Everyone who had been escorting me stopped and turned outwards to watch the gathering crowed, shielding me from the masses.

"I know what goes on here," I said to Tom. "I know what the people will want to see here."

"Yes, Princess?" His eyebrows lifted.

"Me." He didn't seem to understand. "This is where I am supposed to demonstrate what I've learned in the cave."

"Really?"

Now that I'd like to see. Morris's thoughts were loud.

"Yes," I looked back to Tom, "Will you set it up?"

~ ~ ~

By mid-afternoon, I was standing in the center of the stage with hundreds of people sitting on the benches. I felt confident. In my hands were my old toys. I figured if I started with them it would be easier. At my feet lay the bag of spheres.

I took a deep steadying breath and looked to where Phillip sat. Behind him was a young boy who looked like Andrew. At first I thought I might be seeing things then he waved. It *was* Andrew. He sat as tall as he could, to see over Phillip's head. He gave me a big smile and a thumbs-up.

I smiled back. Then, with very little effort, I made my toys dance and twirl, creating designs and patterns with them, and making them soar over everyone's heads.

Andrew nodded and clapped as the arena filled with cheers.

"Well done," Gredd called.

I hope she's learned more than that. I've seen Royal children half her age do that, Morris thought. His thoughts were so loud I could hear them all the way across the arena. He leaned over to Tom, his eyes on me, and whispered something.

I tried to block his thoughts out of my head while I put my old toys away. I emptied the bag of planets onto the ground and levitated the whole lot of them. They quickly formed into their proper orbit around the three suns. It was a perfect mini-Quista replica suspended high enough for everyone to see.

This got me more cheers.

And because I could, I made the suns glow.

Everyone cheered even louder.

"Well done Princess," Gredd called again.

That's more promising. Morris smiled.

Gredd stood. Everyone copied him.

"Wait," I said before anyone could start to leave. "I have one last thing to show you."

Most sat. A sense of barely contained excitement ran through the crowd.

"Something more?" Tom asked.

I held the bag open and levitated each planet into it. They did loops, zigzags and swirls. Then I grouped the moons together so they looked like a shark and animated it to look as if they *swam* into the bag.

I made the suns chase each other so fast they were nothing but a bright yellow blur.

Gredd walked to the platform. "Amazing," he said and , with a bow, took the bag and returned to his seat.

"Everyone in the front row should move up unless you don't mind getting wet," I said.

Some moved. Others didn't.

I closed my eyes and thought about my home. I thought about it until I tasted the salt in my mouth and smelled the moisture in the air.

All around the arena people were gasping.

I opened my eyes to see a few scrambling into higher seats. I'd filled the center of the arena with a deep pool of water from my world. In it were the animals I knew and loved — zapping eels slid past my ankles and stinging jellies bobbed up and down making the water look as if it were boiling. I reached down to scoop up a handful of burbs, then blew on them until they popped.

Mitch stood up clapping. Soon everyone was standing and clapping. They looked so happy, excited even. I was someone they could believe in. I'd given them hope. I was good.

As the applause began to quiet, Tom stood up and said, in a very loud voice, "Princess, is it only Uma'Three that you can create? Or are there other places you can conjure up?" *Was his challenge supposed to sound like an insult?*

"What would you like to see?" I asked.

Tom took a small step back and shook his head.

I looked past him to the crowd of Loyalists. "What would *you* like to see?"

I heard several answers, "Sunset on Riel." "Twilight on Uma'One." "The rains on Ruebyn."

I saw the girl with the pretty smile. She was sitting with her parents. "Do you want to see somewhere special?"

"My birthday on Unarrah," she answered shyly.

"When were you born?" I asked stepping closer.

Her face pinked and she shook her head.

Her mother answered, "During the Harvest."

I nodded and shut my eyes. This scene wasn't as easy to form. I needed to remember things from my run: the pink clamshell-like substance that made up ninety percent of Unarrah's surface, how the suns looked as they set over it, the aroma of the vegetables that only grew at night in the light of its eighteen moons, the sound of the ghostly white crickets that called like children trying to sing a song they didn't quite know, the rhythmic movement of the jaquope with their long tails and sharp ears, and the vibrant purple and green cryptomundo that filled the skies.

Unlike my re-creation of Uma'Three, this time, as the vision solidified, people came forward to test it. Then they began to bow to me, and thank me, confirming their belief in me. I nodded as politely as I could for the endless stream of Loyalists. My re-creation of Unarrah held strong through it all.

Finally, the family with the young girl stood before me.

"This is Nora," Samantha said as if she might be repeating herself.

"Hello Nora." It was the girl's mother.

"I want to thank you." Nora bowed low, not even fully erect from her first bow. "Unarrah is where Aria was born," Nora waved towards her daughter who was lying a few paces away in a patch of velvety soft, emerald green grass. Her father lay next to her. The girl giggled as she rolled from side to side, leaving indents of herself in the growth. "But we had to leave before she was more than a few weeks old," Nora said. "She has never seen her home before today."

I heard the father explaining about the beautiful little flowers that bloomed in the later summer months. I couldn't help myself. With one thought I had both father and daughter surrounded by the small blooming plants with their long bright violet petals.

The flowers looked like a tangle of spindly seaweed with a bunch of hooroop feathers caught in it.

"Oh Papa!" the girl exclaimed as the father wiped his cheeks.

"Thank you again." Nora bowed one last time then hurried away to join her husband and daughter.

~ ~ ~

"Aren't you tired?" Phillip sat on the sofa next to me in my private sitting room. Samantha was busy clearing away the dishes from our meal. The cook had taken the liberty of bringing along as many lu'umon berries as he could. I realized the ones I'd conjured up with Andrew paled in comparison to the real ones.

Collin and Mitch sat on the other sofa. I'd been amusing myself sneaking glances at Mitch. When he thought no one was watching he would stare at Samantha.

"I'm not that tired." I stretched out leaning into Phillip. I felt very awake.

"But it's late," Phillip said.

"Yes, it's late for Turlyn. But for Tem it's early."

"But surely all your adventures have left you tired," Samantha said.

They had tried to ask what I'd done in the tunnels. I'd told them I wasn't ready to say. I could tell they were disappointed but no one complained. I wondered if I never told them would their disappointment eventually fade or would it remain the way I saw it had for Tom?

"I'm really not tired," I said again. I felt too awake, like I was supposed to be doing something. Like I was supposed to be going somewhere — I just couldn't figure out where that *somewhere* was. Gredd and Morris had set up a meeting in the morning to plan our next move. Morning just wasn't coming fast enough.

"Well, even if you aren't tired," Samantha was finished cleaning, "we are." She tried to stifle a yawn, unsuccessfully.

"Oh," I sat up. She wasn't the only one who showed signs of exhaustion. "Oh, please, by all means you should go. Put yourselves to bed. Tomorrow will be here soon and I have a feeling it's going to be a busy day."

"What makes you think that?" Collin leaned forward.

I shrugged, "Not sure, just a feeling."

"I trust your feelings." His face seemed a little greener than before. "Very well," he turned to go. Mitch only hesitated until Samantha had passed him then followed her out. I caught his thoughts; he was admiring her backside.

I smiled to myself, then realized that Phillip hadn't budged.

"Shouldn't you go with them?"

"I probably should." He looked over his shoulder. Mitch was just moving out of sight. "But I kinda wanted to talk to you alone about something."

I didn't like his tone — too ominous. He sat up a little taller. I did the same. "About what?"

He rubbed the back of his neck, "It's about Jef…"

"Oh no!" I was on my feet. I glared down at him, "No! Not you too. Everyone has been treating Jef like a shark and it's gone on long enough. Just because he's from Uma'Three... which, by the way, happens to be the exact same planet I'm from!" I put my hands on my hips. "So, if he's *Fish-Boy* then I'm your Fishy-Princess!"

Phillip looked green, a deep green, deeper than Collin's green. "But Danay..."

"But what!"

He shrank from me.

I sighed and threw myself on the sofa, "What?" I tried to sound less frightening.

"We don't hate him because he's from Uma'Three," he seemed to rethink his words. "Well, most of us don't have a problem with that. It's just... well, we don't trust him. Remember, he almost killed you."

"He did not. All he did was give me my medicine which..."

Phillip cut me off by putting his finger to my lips. "He was only trying to do what he thought was best for you. I know that's what he said. It's just that," his finger stayed pressed to my mouth, "what if..." he shifted.

I was completely distracted by not only his finger, but by how close his shift had brought him to me. It was almost as if we were back in the air pocket trying to fit on the shelf that was only big enough for one of us.

"What if he wasn't really doing it for *your* best. I mean he's not a Loyalist. He's not bound by Magic like we are. And..." he hesitated.

"And what?"

"Well, there are a lot of people who think the doctor should have known better. He should have known that you wouldn't have been able to handle the medicine he'd made. I mean, he ran tests on you."

Phillip was right! I pulled away.

He let his hand drop to his lap and stared down at it. "He's been your doctor all your life, right?"

I nodded.

Even without looking, Phillip seemed to know I'd nodded. "He should have known better. The medicine shouldn't have," he swallowed and looked up. "...we just don't trust him."

"But Jef didn't know that." I didn't trust the doctor either. But I *did* trust Jef.

"No... well, we don't know if he knew. And... and," Phillip's eyes stared into mine. "And we just don't trust him."

"But I trust Jef. He's been my friend all my life and he's been protecting me all that time."

Phillip grimaced. "I know you trust him." His tone implied he had something more to say.

"What else?"

"Well," he shifted again, bringing himself closer to me again, his knee was pressed against my thigh. "He hasn't been here all evening."

"Yeah, he wasn't feeling well," I said.

"Okay, that would explain why he went to the doctor after your training. But when Rith brought your food he said Jef was still with the doctor."

I closed my eyes. If he'd spent the entire evening with the doctor that could only mean one of two things: either Jef was really sick or he was conspiring with the doctor. As much as I hated the idea that he might be sick, I really hoped that was why he'd stayed with him for so long.

"Danay?"

I opened my eyes. Phillip's face was a finger's width away from mine. If I wanted to kiss him, all I'd have to do is lean forward. If I wanted him to kiss me back, all I'd have to do is tell him to. It was tempting.

I pulled away. "Thank you."

"I'm sorry." He sounded sincere.

Chapter Thirty

Royal Trouble

After Phillip left, I was even less tired than before. I felt restless. I wanted to talk to Jef. I was worried that he was hurt... but what if he wasn't? What would I ask him? How could I know if he was telling the truth? *I didn't want him to think I didn't trust him — but all of a sudden I wasn't sure if I did...*

I drew myself a bath and spent a long time in it. Long enough for the water to chill. The chill stayed with me as I got dressed in a nightgown. Still restless, I walked through my suites. The ship felt like it was too still. The emptiness of my chambers pressed in on me.

In my kitchen, I poured myself a glass of cool water and stood by the counter gulping it down. A movement in the next room caught my eye. I figured Samantha had come to check on me.

"May I enter?" It wasn't Samantha.

"Jef?"

"I'm sorry it's so late. It's just," he stood in the doorway a goofy grin on his face, "I couldn't sleep."

"How'd you get in? How'd you get past my guards?"

His smile grew, "It was easy, really. You commanded that no one should stop me from being with you." He came towards me like he was going to give me a hug.

I put my hand up, "I only meant that for Mitch, Collin, Phillip and Samantha."

He stopped a pace from me, "Huh, I guess to these yeah..." he caught himself, "Loyalists, a command is a command no matter who you mean it for." His grin doubled.

I frowned.

"What's wrong?"

Lots. Mostly I was realizing I'd have to be more specific about who I was giving my commands to. But also, Jef, here, after being with the doctor all afternoon... "So you're feeling better?" I asked.

"Not just feeling better. I *am* better."

"What's that supposed to mean?"

"Danay," he spread his arms apart and asked, "do you notice anything different about me?"

I bit my lip.

"Don't do that." Jef pinched my bottom lip until it came loose from my teeth. "Please, it's not becoming of a woman of your stature."

"Woman?" I scoffed.

My lip had slid free of his hand. Instead of dropping it he brought his fingers to my cheek, "Yes, a young woman. Remember, you are of age now."

"And a princess." I sucked my lip back between my teeth.

"Please Danay," his finger tugged at my lip harder this time.

"Why?"

He let me go, "Because when you do that you remind me of my sister."

"Oh." I felt myself redden.

His hand slid to my cheek again, "And I don't want to think about her while I'm with you."

"Oh...?" my reddening was a blush this time. He moved closer, the same way Phillip had, only I knew that I wouldn't have to order Jef to kiss me if I wanted him to. "Jef?"

"Yes?"

I stared at his lips. I hadn't realized until now how different people's lips could be. Jef's were darker, plumper, moister looking than Phillip's. Yet, it was Phillip's lips I wished would be so close to mine.

"Yes Danay?"

I blinked a few times to gather my thoughts, "What did the doctor do to you?"

"Nothing." He leaned even closer.

"Then why were you with him all of this time?"

He pulled back sharply. "Who tol…" he let his hand drop. "Never mind, it doesn't matter."

"It does to me."

"No," he shifted, "it doesn't matter who told you — they're all against me." His shoulders sagged and he sighed. "Don't you notice *anything* different about me?"

I moved back to get a better look. After a moment trying not to bite my lip I said, "You are the same Jef I've always known."

"But I'm not." His grin was back in place.

"You're not?" I moved a little farther away.

"No." He stepped closer. "Look harder.

I looked.

He leaned closer, "Come on Danny, really look at me."

I shifted back an arm's length until my back was against the counter. I searched his face. His soft brown-green eyes stared back, waiting for me to see what I was clearly missing. His face was almost as familiar as my own. I looked at his round cheeks, significantly less rounded since the last time I'd really looked at him. He'd also lost his double chin. Though, he still had the same crooked teeth that I'd always liked.

My gaze traveled down to his chest. It wasn't nearly as defined as Phillip's, but it was far more defined than anyone else who came from Uma'Three. More defined than most of the men on the ship even.

"Here, I'll give you a hint." He slid his feet in front of mine and took my hand, pressing it against his shirt. "Still don't see?"

I shook my head. He was Jef — that was all he looked like to me.

Under my hand, I could feel the heat coming off him. His ribcage was firm and muscular. I could feel the thump of his heart. He unbuttoned his shirt and put my hand against this skin, "Danny?"

My lip was trapped between my teeth again.

"Danay?" His face was near mine again. His heart was racing and mine was trying to catch up.

"Jef, what am I missing?"

He leaned even closer so his nose slid past mine. He stopped as his lips reached my ears, "I'll tell you what I'm *not* missing," he whispered, "my water-suit."

"Your..." my hand flexed. "Your water-suit! Don't you need it?"

He shook his head, "Not anymore."

I pushed him back so I could look at his face. "What did the doctor do to you? Whatever it was..."

"Not the doctor," Jef laughed, his head tilting to the side. "You." His eyes locked onto mine as he leaned in. I knew what he intended to do. I had a split second to stop him — I didn't.

Jef's lips covered mine slowly. Hesitant, like he was ready to pull away if I told him to.

Again, I didn't.

I closed my eyes and enjoyed the feeling of his lips as they pressed gently to mine. He was kissing me. He wasn't kissing me because I needed him to. He wasn't kissing me because I'd commanded him to. He was kissing me because he wanted to.

I never thought anyone would want to kiss me.

Jef tasted salty and sweet. It reminded me of everything I loved about home. I was drawn to the familiarity of it.

His arms wrapped around me and pulled me tight against his bare chest. My hand stayed trapped between us. I could feel the contours of every muscle. There were more there than I remembered. As I ran my fingers along his chest I wondered if Phillip's would feel the same way.

"Danny?" Jef asked in a hushed voice. His hand was cupped lightly around the side of my chest. He was asking for permission to move it closer.

Part of me wanted him to.

"No," my voice came out breathy.

"No?" Jef brought his lips to my neck, planting kisses along my collarbone.

I had to think. The part of me that wanted this was screaming *yes*. His lips sent cascades of tingles down my spine. Yet, as great as it felt — and it felt really great — it wasn't right.

Because, even though they were Jef's hands and lips, I was imagining that they were Phillip's.

"No," I sighed.

He let his hand drop to his side and pulled away. "As you wish." He took a few minutes to get his breathing under control. Then he turned to me with a smile on his lips. "As you wish."

"I do wish..." I sighed again and sucked my bottom lip between my teeth

He just nodded. "Maybe another day." He took my hand and kissed the back of it. Then he bowed and left me.

Now I was tired.

~ ~ ~

I had barely fallen asleep when I awoke with a start. Before I was fully upright, I knew I wasn't alone. I pulled the curtains to my bed back, and found... Andrew. I jumped back and the curtains dropped.

"Sorry," he said climbing through them without making them move.

"What's wrong, Andrew?"

"I need your help." He held his hand out to me.

I didn't hesitate. I took it and the next thing I saw was Turlyn as it disappeared under us.

We appeared in a familiar looking room. Kit was there, in the tub, along with some other girls. Girls I now recognized from every part of Quista — all chained to their beds.

Kit was the only one in a tub; however a few paces away from her stood an empty glass tank. The sides were covered in a sort of red film.

All the girls were emaciated, scared and vacant, like they'd lost their souls.

"What's going..." I turned to ask Andrew but he was gone. "Kit?" I went over to her, "Kit, can you hear me?" Her attention was on a girl at the far end of the room.

I looked over.

The girl was writhing and whimpering on her bed. She pulled against her binding so that her wrists were raw. With a jolt, she arched her back and let out a howl that pierced the room. I moved my hands to cover my ears, but my spirit hands were useless at keeping the sound out.

Her cries cut through me as if they were sharp blades.

The girl in the bed next to Kit's tub leaned over as far as her bindings would allow her. "She's close now."

Kit bit her lip, "Maybe she'll make it."

The girl next to Kit had hair as red as fresh blood and bright green eyes that looked like they would shine in the dark. She was tall with sunken cheeks. She shook her head sadly and put a hand on the small bump at her belly. "There's no hope for her. One way or another tonight will be her last."

"Sorren, you can't know that." Kit frowned.

Sorren looked over at the howling girl, "But I do know." She hugged her belly tighter. "It's happened too many times not to know," she said, quieter like she was talking to herself.

I looked back at the girl. She'd kicked her sheets so they created a wall along one side of her body. She rolled and lay on it panting. Her short violet hair clung to her purple face. Sweat dripped down it. She had a bulge over her stomach that was twice the size of Sorren's. With a great effort, the girl rose up to her knees and moaned. Her hands, stretching her binding, pulled so she could press a palm on either side of her rounded abdomen, as if she was trying to keep it from splitting in half.

Sorren looked down, "He makes strong babies. If she doesn't birth it soon it might just climb its way out of her belly button."

Kit gasped, "Has that ever happened?"

"No, but perhaps it might be better if it did."

"How would that be better?" Kit looked like she wanted to be sick.

Everyone in the room watched as the girl continued to birth whatever grew inside of her. She went through several more contractions that hurt to watch, and yet I couldn't seem to turn away. No one could.

"You're doing good, Kay," a girl close to her said as Kay fell limp after another long contraction.

"Just kill me now." She sobbed. "Why don't they come? Why won't they kill me and take it?"

"Because it's too soon," the first girl said.

"And they like to see me suffering," Kay said. She pulled herself to her knees; her face turned a deeper shade of purple with the effort of pushing. "Too soon or not, this baby is coming."

The girl continued to birth her child alone. Her moans were becoming more desperate. Every other girl in the room was silent. Most everyone had tears streaking their faces.

Then they came.

The shadow creatures ghosted into the room from several sides all converging upon the girl in labor. Of course, I couldn't see them, they were cloaked in shadow. But like flashes, their arms and their tentacle-like fingers, would appear. Wherever they stood they created an empty spot. Most of Kay was obscured by the several that stood around her.

As they touched Kay they left cuts and bruises, but she was far beyond noticing.

I didn't see it being born, but I heard it.

"No! No! Leave her!" Kay screamed as the creatures leaned in close to investigate.

"Bad child," one creature said. Kay was hit across the face; four long gashes were left in her sunken skin. "Bad girl! Not supposed to kill master's child." Another slap.

"Leave her!" Kay screeched louder still. "She's mine! Leave her." She reached into the fray and pulled out something that she quickly bundled into her loose sheets. She was covered in welts and bruises from the creatures as they tried to take the dead baby from her.

"You be making master mad!" One hissed — or they all hissed at once.

Kay ignored the creatures. She sat staring down at the child. "She would have been beautiful." Her voice was soft. "The Emperor would have been proud. I'm sorry."

At first I thought she was talking to the stillborn.

"I'm sorry," she looked up into the shadows, "I'll do better next time."

"No!" The creatures said. "No next time. One time — only one time to be right."

"But I didn't know what I was doing. Now I know. I can do better. I will do better. Just look, she is beautiful." She held the dead child out.

"Beauty is nothing," the creatures hissed.

"Believe me, your master is very concerned with beauty."

"No matter. Too late. Dead. Child dead... soon you be dead too."

Kay pulled the stillborn to her chest. Between its blood, the blood that had seeped into her sheets, and the blood from fresh cuts the creatures continued to make as they scolded her, the scene was too much. I turned away.

"Time for us to take sweet child."

My stomach knotted. Something told me *sweet* was referring to its taste.

"No! Leave her! Don't touch her! Leave it! Please!" Kay's voice was cut off.

I didn't look. Instead I stared at Kit, her eyes were wide like she was trying to turn away but couldn't.

"Please, please leave her. Please don't take her." Kay's voice was only a sob now.

Other girls from all around the room started to shout at the creatures, telling them to leave Kay and her stillborn alone.

"That is quite enough." This new voice caused a hush to fall through the room. There were no more sobs, not even a sniffle. No one dared to breathe. Even the creatures seemed to become still.

I turned to see Emperor Zigel standing at the foot of Kay's bed. I could almost make out the creatures as they stood near him. They had a body like a hoorup, round and hairy, only the hairs looked like sharp needles. And instead of legs, they had an eel's tail. Which held them up as they curled and coiled it about themselves.

"What have you got for me my pets?"

I stared at the Emperor in awe. He was tall with a face that was almost too good to look at. His dark hair was combed back. His eyes compassionate. His tone filled with kindness.

As he took the bloodied stillborn into his hands he cradled it tenderly. "Oh my, what a beautiful girl this would have been." He smiled down at Kay.

She smiled back then looked sidelong at the creatures and smirked.

"What a shame that you killed her."

Kay's smile vanished. "I... I... I tried. I'll do better next time."

"You did your best," he said agreeing. He put the child back into her waiting arms. "But clearly your best isn't good enough."

"I can do better." She looked pleadingly at the Emperor. "Give me another chance."

"I'm sorry," and he sounded it. He sounded like he was hurt most of all by this. "There will be no next time. No second chances. You failed me once." He turned away, tears shone in his eyes. "Once was once too much."

Kay's body began to shake with soundless sobs, "But I did everything you told me. I loved her. You told me loving her would be enough! Please. I love her. Please!"

The Emperor turned back towards her, "Kay..."

She was staring down at her child, rocking it, tears falling to mingle with the blood and gore.

"Kay," his voice rose. I could see the disgust in the set of his mouth.

She didn't respond.

"Kay!"

"I'll do better. See how beautiful your daughter would have been. I will make you an even more beautiful girl."

"You weren't making me a daughter." The Emperor was staring at the blankets with an almost hungry longing. "You were supposed to make me the perfect sacrifice."

I gasped.

The Emperor looked in my direction. Squinting like he was trying to see me. I quickly hid behind Kit. I felt his eyes follow me, but as he stepped closer, he wasn't looking through Kit. He was looking at her. "Hello my newest bride." He slid another pace closer to her, "How are you enjoying your accommodations?"

"Well, seeing as you asked, it's a little cold here."

Sorren gasped and moved as far from Kit as her bindings would let her.

The Emperor ignored Sorren and took another step closer.

"And dark. You wonder why all your creations are dying?" Kit held her hands at her side in fists. "How could anything survive down here?"

"My, you are a brave one." He came closer still.

I backed up to the wall.

"Shall we be teaching her more about being afraid?" One of the creatures had moved next to the Emperor.

He inclined his head towards it, "Haven't you been teaching her since she arrived?"

"Yessss, master."

"Well if she hasn't learned by now I'm not sure she can be taught." He seemed to regard Kit with greater interest. "But perhaps that will turn out to be a valuable asset in the end. It is something the others seem to be lacking."

His next step brought him within reach of Kit. He put his hand on her chin, pulling her face closer to his. She bared her teeth.

"Yes, this may prove the very thing I've been lacking." He scowled towards Sorren who cowered away.

He turned to leave, "Warm up her water and bring in more lights."

"And what of the other?" the creatures asked.

He slowly looked over to Kay. "Kill her."

"Have pity!" she screamed.

"I do pity you," his voice was calm. "Your death will not be swift nor will it be painless. But you deserve nothing less after murdering my creation."

Rage swelled in my chest. I stepped out from behind Kit, "You are the murderer! You murdered your entire family!"

"What have we here?" The Emperor looked directly at me.

I knew I shouldn't have said that. I shouldn't have said anything. I shouldn't have stayed. Why Andrew had brought me here, now, I couldn't understand. But I shouldn't have said anything. And I shouldn't have allowed the Emperor to see me. Yet all I could think about was how angry I was. I was angry and I wanted to use it to hurt him.

"Hello my pretty," he said.

Now everyone's eyes were on me. Everyone could see me. *What had happened?*

His eyes slid to Kit, "You never told me about your friend, my little Water Lily."

Kit paled, "Danay," she said my name like it was something bad.

"Danay," Emperor Zigel smiled. "What a lovely name. How did you come to be here, even if you are only here among the shadow world?"

I stood frozen to the spot.

He continued to regard me. "Surely not a leftover spirit, I had all of them dealt with." His eyes slid to Kit, "But you know her? How long has she been keeping you company?"

Kit's jaw snapped shut. She wouldn't say. Emperor Zigel's eyes bored into her but I knew she wouldn't back down even though I saw her hands shaking.

The Emperor saw her shaking too. "Why does this frighten you?"

Kit's eyes slid to me, her frown doubled. "Danay, get out of here!" She kicked out towards me, sending a wave of water in my direction. It was instinct. I moved to avoid being splashed. The movement was all it took to send me spiraling away. Away from that horrid room. Away from the Emperor. Away from Kit.

Then it stopped. I was back on the ship — but something was wrong.

The ship was moving: tipping… and it wasn't just the ship. It was Turlyn. The whole moon had shifted. Like stepping through water, the movement rippled outwards. I felt the shudder echo through everything.

I was on my feet and dressed in moments. From beyond my door, I heard alarms sounding. Already the shift was having disastrous effects. With each passing moment, Turlyn was sliding further and further out of its proper orbit.

It had to be fixed. I had to fix it — now.

I sat down on my floor with the bag of planets open in front of me. I willed them into the air. They obeyed without hesitation. For a moment, I stared at the formation of Quista suspended in the air around me. I stood up and tried to find Riel.

But I couldn't. So I took a deep breath and focused on Turlyn. She immediately showed herself. There was nothing wrong. She was exactly where she was supposed to be… then the bigger picture came into focus — Turlyn was where she was supposed to be in comparison to Riel and the rest of the worlds, however, the rest of Quista wasn't where it was supposed to be. All of Quista had shifted out of orbit.

Fixing the solar system was easy. Too easy. It really wanted to be fixed. I just let the Magic move things back to where they belonged. The ship shuddered and settled quickly. The alarms cut off.

I was proud of myself. Probably a little too proud. That's when I figured out that it had been a trap. By fixing Quista I'd shown the Emperor exactly who I was… and where.

Chapter Thirty-One

Busted!

"Hello, little Royal one," The Emperor's voice echoed through my room. "Where do you hail from?" I couldn't see him but I had the impression that he could see me.

I scrambled to my feet.

"You can't be my brother's child. I had his wife killed before she could bring her children into the world." His voice implied that he was studying me. I could imagine his black eyes raking up and down my body. "You must be Zoe's girl. Makes sense, I can sense her Magic in you."

I felt dizzy as I imagined him circling me.

"I never thought my sister to be that cleaver." He chuckled and a cold chill raced up my spine. "But, I guess I owe her my thanks. And you my little niece because without you my plan would have never succeeded."

"Show yourself or leave!" I demanded.

"Such brave words for such a frightened child. Fear not we will be face to face soon enough."

He was gone.

I fell to my knees trembling. When I could finally speak I said, "I need to see Gredd, right now."

There was no one to hear me yet somehow I knew he'd come.

He arrived within minutes with Tom and Morris too. The three bowed as they stayed in the doorway to my bedroom. Somehow their bowing didn't bother me as much as it used to.

"Stand up." I said, "We must make haste."

"What is it Princess?" Gredd was the first to straighten. He made a move like he was going to enter my room but stopped.

"What?"

He bowed low again, "Begging your pardon, but I'd feel more comfortable if we took this meeting in your sitting room."

I followed him to it.

"Princess, why did you summon Gredd?" Tom said before anyone else could talk. He was disheveled, like he'd been woken, and yet he still made me feel like I was the one who was un-presentable.

I bit my tongue to keep from giving my first response — *I'd summoned Gredd not you, what made you think you had any right to be here.* Instead I said, "Because the Emperor was here."

"Here?" Morris looked even more green than normal.

"How?" Tom asked as if he didn't believe me.

"Princess, are you okay?" Gredd asked.

"I'm... fine," I stumbled over my response, not expecting that question. "He was here in spirit," I said to Tom.

"He shadow walked?" Morris's shade deepened even further.

"Are you sure you're okay?" Gredd asked.

"I'm..." *I couldn't remember why I ever didn't like Gredd.* "I'm okay. But soon none of us will be. He knows I'm here. He knows who I am. We have to leave — immediately."

Morris bowed, taking my words as a command. Tom stayed standing, his eyes narrowed.

"Are you sure you're ready for this?" Gredd asked. Something about his tone or the look in his eyes told me he wasn't challenging me — he was concerned *for* me.

"I'm sure I have to be." I said. "The Emperor will be preparing himself for an attack with every passing moment. If we don't strike now all will be lost."

"Princess, if you need, we can continue to hide you. We can find a new—" Gredd stopped at the shake of my head.

"You and I both know that the time for hiding is past. I will be ready."

"How can you know that?" Morris asked.

"I know it because I know," I said, "and I have a plan. But I will tell you later." I didn't want to say it aloud in case my uncle was still listening.

Both Morris and Gredd bowed. Tom still stood staring at me. *What was he waiting for now*?

"Forgive me Princess, but how did he discover you?" Tom asked.

I debated not telling. After all, it had been my fault. "I… I visited the Royal planet. I was in the palace."

"You went there? How?" Morris asked.

I didn't know how to explain. "With… with my spirit, I think."

"So, you've learned to shadow walk too?" Tom nodded, his lips pressed together to form a thin white line.

Gredd however, was smiling. "This is something only the most powerful of Royal's can do," Gredd's grin widened, "was this your first time?"

"I…" again I debated keeping this information to myself but only because I didn't want them to know how much I could do. It was pointless — all would be revealed before the morning was up. "No, I've done it before."

"How… When…?" Morris stammered. He seemed upset. "Why didn't you tell us this before now?"

"That isn't important. Right now what I want," I reconsidered my words, "what you are going to do, is prepare to leave." I turned to Gredd. "Assemble your men. Ready them for battle. Have everyone gather within the hour at the practice ring in the center of Dustata."

"I beg your pardon, Princess, but we need to ready the ship and load supplies first," Gredd said.

"No," I stared Gredd in the eye, "what you need to do is exactly as I have said. All fighters and the supplies they need must be in the practice ring in one hour. That is a command."

"As you wish." Gredd bowed but it was clear he wasn't happy about it. All three started to leave.

"Tom?"

He turned back.

"I need Jef…"

His lips turned down before I had the chance to finish.

I ignored it and continued, "I also need Phillip, Samantha, Collin," as I was about to say Mitch's name I got a funny felling, like he shouldn't come to the fight. "...I need them sent here immediately."

"What about Mitch?"

"Not him. I don't want him to come."

"Princess, is there something wrong with Mitch?" His eyes seemed to search my face.

"I... I don't want him fighting with us."

"Is there a reason for this?"

"I..." I sighed. "I have a bad feeling..."

"A bad feeling about him?" Tom cut me off. "Is this about his refusal to be Pledged?"

I wanted to say it wasn't — yet it felt very much like it was.

"Princess?" Both Tom's eyebrows were arched.

"It does."

"Very well," Tom gave a curt bow, "as you wish."

~ ~ ~

Mitch showed up anyway.

"Please Mitch," I begged. "Please, I need you to stay here with the ship."

He stood resolutely beside Samantha, "I go where Samantha goes and there's nothing you can do that will stop me."

I could command him. Instead I tried honesty. "But I fear for your safety."

"I fear for Samantha's."

"Idiot." Samantha looked daggers at him.

He returned her stare with just as much determination.

Collin looked from Mitch to Samantha to me, and then asked in a shaking voice, "So, what's the plan?"

"I'm going to do something that the Magic Weavers used to do."

"What's that?" Jef asked.

I still didn't want to say it out loud. I was still fearful of being overheard. "All I can tell you is that it's risky and I haven't heard of any Royals being able to do this, but I'm sure I can."

No one spoke.

My eyes slid to Mitch, "And if any one of you doesn't want to come," I was being hopeful.

"I'm coming," Phillip said. "I will follow you anywhere, even if it's into the great beyond."

Jef snorted.

"Now that would be an adventure," Collin said. "But I know you can do it."

Collin's words helped my confidence grow — I hadn't realized how afraid I was.

"I believe in you too," Samantha said.

My chest swelled with assurance.

"I've already said that I will go wherever Sam goes." Mitch crossed his arms.

I wondered if I should order her to stay.

The room was strangely quiet. I realized everyone was looking at Jef. "You couldn't stop me from coming even if you commanded it," he said as my eyes met his.

Chapter Thirty-Two

The Breath Before the Plunge

"Samantha?" I asked once we'd picked the closest thing we could find to a form fitted suit for me to wear. It still had a long flowing skirt but the leggings under it reminded me of my wet'skn.

"Yes Princess?"

"If I asked you and Mitch to stay behind would you?"

"You don't want me to fight with you?" She pulled her hands back from my hair where she'd captured it to put it into a scarf.

"I... I don't want you to get hurt."

"Then you needn't worry." She recaptured my hair and started wrapping it.

"But I have a feeling..."

"Princess," Samantha came around to look at me, "I promise you, I will be fine." She tucked a strand of hair into the scarf, "Okay?"

I nodded and we made our way to the door of my bed chamber.

Collin, Phillip, Jef and Mitch were there waiting, "Ready?" Phillip said holding out his hand to me.

Jef brushed his hand aside and stepped closer. He asked quietly, "Can I have a minute with you alone?"

Phillip watched with an anxious gaze as I followed Jef back into my bedchamber. He shut the door.

"Okay, we're alone. What is it?" I said realizing that to open my door I'd have to go through him.

He didn't turn around. "It's about Phillip."

"What about Phillip?" I crossed my arms, feeling defensive. We didn't have time for this now.

"You know he likes you, right?" Jef turned and watched my face.

"Yeah, they all do. Haven't we already been over this, it's a Loyalist thing!"

"No, Danay," Jef shifted closer, still half a pace away. "He really likes you. It goes beyond being a Loyalist." He held my gaze. His voice got quieter, "Danny, he loves you."

"No," I shook my head, "no, he's a Loyalist — he can't love..."

"You know for being this all-powerful-Princess you really are blind when it comes to him. How can you not see it? *Everyone* else does."

"They do? He does?" I smiled in spite of myself — then my face fell, "No, Jef, you're wrong. He can't love me." I felt my smile wilt. "At least not the way I love him."

Jef opened his mouth like he was going to argue but he shut it, narrowed his eyes, then said, "Danay, he does." When I started to shake my head he said, "He really does."

I stared down at my hands. I felt the tears stinging my eyes. "He's not allowed to. The same Magic that binds him to be faithful to me also makes it so he can't love me — not like that."

Jef stepped closer, "No, just listen to me. Phillip likes you, more than any Loyalist should. And his feelings are getting in the way of him being loyal. His feelings are going to get you hurt," Jef leaned forward so he caught my eye, "and possibly him too."

I didn't speak. The thought of Phillip being hurt in any way was too painful.

"Danay, you have to order him to stop loving you."

"What?"

"You have the power to stop this. Command him to stop being in love with you."

"But he's not..."

"Fine, if he isn't in love with you then there won't be any harm. But if I'm right then you need to do this before we go into battle. Before we fight."

"I..." I didn't like what he was telling me to do. But if I were being completely honest, a part of me wanted Jef to be right. I wanted Phillip to be in love with me — to *be able* to be in love with me. If there was even the slightest chance, I didn't want to command it out of him.

"Danay?"

"I'll think about it." I said.

Jef nodded and stepped back.

~ ~ ~

As we left the ship, Phillip asked, "What did Jef want?"

"Nothing," I lied. "Just wanted to be sure I was okay."

"Are you okay?"

We entered the ring and I took a steadying breath. I gazed around at the nearly three hundred Loyalists who'd gathered. That was sobering.

Each was wearing the same look of fear for the battle ahead. They were all committed to fight for me — to die for me. And though I couldn't know the future I was sure that before this day was done some would do exactly that. *How I wished they wouldn't have to.*

I sighed as I walked to the center of the ring where Gredd, Morris, and Tom stood waiting. "Is this everyone?"

"We are all here," Morris answered.

I looked around again, wondering whose face I was looking at for the last time.

"Fear not, there will be more once we get to the Palace," Gredd said, "Several Loyalists are waiting for us there. And once news spreads, more will come."

"More would be better," I said. I knew that for every one of my Loyalists, loyal to me, the Emperor would have hundreds more. *I wondered if my plan was wise...* but wise or not, now that my uncle knew about me, it was the only hope we had.

Gredd held his hand out, "Would you like to address the crowd before we board the ship?"

"I would. But first, just so you know, we will be departing from *here*."

"Pardon?" His hand tightened around mine.

I knew he'd heard me and understood, still I repeated myself. "I will be teleporting everyone from here to the Royal planet."

Morris's face turned a sickly green, "Princess…" his mouth hung open as his muscles twitched in an attempt to find words.

Gredd cringed. It looked like he wanted to protest.

"Princess," Tom said, "I'm not sure…"

"Do you doubt me?"

Tom's lips came together to form a hard line. "Not you."

I wasn't convinced.

"I'm just wondering if you've thought this all the way through."

"Princess," Gredd said, "we don't doubt your abilities. I have seen how your powers out measure any other Royal known. However, teleportation with people is not the same as your displays yesterday. The Royals who have managed to learn it have not been successful in moving *anyone* but themselves."

"My uncle was successful at least once." I watched Tom; waiting for his face to confirm my guess.

Morris and Gredd also looked at him. He turned away and said, "I was commanded never to speak of it."

I nodded, "Of course he would have commanded that." I continued to nod.

"I'm sorry Princess," Gredd moved closer, "what are you talking about?"

"Have you never wondered how Tom was able to get into my mother's chambers on the night he was sent to assassinate her?"

Gredd turned to look at Tom.

Tom stood staring at me. A strange expression on his face. His mouth was partly open. His tongue curled up to the roof of his mouth. His eyes almost appeared crossed.

"My uncle teleported him there."

"Is this true?" Gredd asked.

I wondered what part of *he was commanded never to speak of it* Gredd couldn't understand.

Tom shut his mouth but nodded once.

Gredd looked at me. "Forgive me, Princess, but your uncle's powers work differently than yours."

"Besides, teleporting one person you don't care about is easier than teleporting the nearly three hundred strong we are now," Morris added quietly — he might have just thought it.

"I would not do this if I wasn't sure I could." I put my hand on Gredd's arm, feeling his energy, so similar to his son's yet so different. "The Emperor knows about me. I'm sure he's figured out we plan to attack him. He will be expecting our ship. This is the only way to make sure we have the upper hand."

I could tell Gredd wasn't convinced. All three weren't. They were trying to form their objections. Finally Gredd spoke up.

"Princess, if this doesn't work you could end up on the Royal planet alone. We would be left here, unable to defend you."

"Or worse — halfway between," Morris said without meeting my eyes.

"Trust me, I don't want that either. You are my Loyalists, I do not wish to lose any one of you. And I especially do not wish to be the cause of it. I am not doing this with a light heart. I wouldn't suggest it if I didn't know that I could do it."

There were no more protests but they still looked skeptical.

"About my uncle," I said, "now would be a good time for you to explain to me how to fight him?"

"You will not be fighting him," Tom spoke sharply.

"Not you," Gredd said looking horrified. "No Royal is allowed to bring harm to another Royal. No, *we*," he looked at Tom then Morris. "We have been commanded to defeat him."

"Commanded by whom?" I asked, but I was sure I already knew.

"By your mother." Gredd bowed. *Had I seen tears in his eyes*? "And the true High Emperor, Emperor Zandr."

Morris also bowed his head. Tom turned away closing his eyes.

I bit my lip. Suddenly it made sense. That's why they knew to look for me. "What do you need me to do?" My respect for them had grown.

"Your job is to take control of the planets so they don't spin out of control," Gredd said, his eyes still wet looking.

That I could do. I smiled, relieved that I wasn't the one who would have to face my uncle.

"Princess?" Gredd looked around the arena filled with my Loyalists. They were growing restless. "I think you should address the crowd."

I nodded.

"May I advise you not to expose your full plan to everyone?"

I nodded again, looking at all the eager faces of the fighters who'd gathered. It would be better not to explain it, but rather just to do it. That way there'd be no time to worry.

Gredd called everyone closer.

Phillip, Jef, Collin, Samantha, and Mitch took up their posts around me.

I knew I could do this… still it felt like a nest of eels was in my stomach.

My eyes were drawn to Mitch's hand tightly wrapped around Samantha's.

Morris stepped closer and whispered, "Where do you intend to deliver us?"

"Where would be best?"

He closed his eyes for a moment, "I suspect your mother's throne room…"

Tom also leaned closer, "Are you sure you can…"

I cut him off by raising my hand. I looked into his eyes, "I will be successful."

"Fine," a muscle bulged in Tom's jaw. "Princess," his look wasn't quite a scowl, "when we get there, it would be best if you don't speak and, if you can help it, don't touch anything."

"Why?"

He blinked once, "Because, the walls will recognize your presence and that would alert the Emperor."

I nodded again. It was time. Everyone was hushed and waiting.

I climbed to the top of a stack of crates. Phillip looked up at me and gave a smile and nod. It didn't matter if he loved me or not. All that mattered was he had faith in me, as did Jef, Collin, and Samantha… and me.

"I know that I am your Princess, and it is my job to lead you." I tried to look at every person, tried to see each of their spirit colors. In a moment, I'd be responsible for every one of them. "I want you to know that I care about you, each of you." My eyes were drawn to Jef. He smiled and gave a bow. Most everyone followed his lead.

This was it. There wouldn't be a better moment.

I closed my eyes and imagined everyone's energy mixing and blurring together, like paint in a cup, swirling towards the center, towards me. I could not feel anyone separate from the other... they all felt like they were a part of me. I could only hope this meant I wouldn't leave anyone behind.

Before I opened my eyes I knew I'd done it. We were in the throne room — my mother's throne room. I recognized its feel, so similar to my suites on the ship yet with a different gravitational echo. Despite the battle ahead, I felt instantly safe here. It felt like I'd come home.

I opened my eyes.

Chapter Thirty-Three

The Battle

Jef looked up and let out a gasp, "Danay?"

"Hush!" Gredd cautioned and ran to the main doors at the end of the room. He shut them with a loud crack.

Heads rose. Eyes opened. Confused murmurs broke out.

"Hush!" Gredd ordered as he returned.

Tom and Morris closed the other open doors.

I tried to see if anyone was missing. I hated not being able to ask.

They were all looking around. Most didn't recognize where we were. Those who did seemed to display a mixture of awe and fear. No one had prepared them — they weren't ready. I felt miserable about that. Then I realized everyone was looking at me. They were waiting for me. I couldn't talk. I was useless.

Gredd started barking out orders. "Form ranks! Take up your arms." Everyone listened and soon there were three groups of Loyalists armed and ready to go. Gredd looked over at me nodding, "Everyone is accounted for." There was no mistake; he was impressed.

I sat down on the crate I'd been standing on.

Phillip leaned next to me, "You are amazing."

I nodded.

"Something wrong with your tongue?" Jef asked, standing on the other side of me.

I just shook my head.

"She shouldn't speak," Phillip said. His eyes glanced around the room.

The purple and gold walls were coated in dust. The floor, what I could see beyond the dirt I'd brought with us, was dull as if no one had stepped on it for Royal Years. The ceiling was covered in cobwebs. Uma'Three didn't have spiders. I'd only seen them in books. I tried to find the creatures that had made the webs.

I couldn't find any. Looking beyond the webs I saw a mosaic like the one in my suites on the ship only this one had scenes full of different people.

I recognized the green and violet tinged skin of the people from Unarrah; the eery white teeth of the people from Riel; and the charred looking people from Ursala. There were also mer-folk from Uma'Four and the chubby men from Uma'Three. And more, so many more, some of whom I hadn't seen, not even on my run.

I tried to concentrate on the ceiling. I tried not to look at the stage where my mother's throne stood. It was inviting me. It called to me worse than the waters during a Popling Festival.

I took Jef's hand and squeezed it.

He squeezed my hand back, "You okay?" When I didn't answer he asked, "Why can't she speak?"

"The room will know her," Phillip answered. "If the room recognizes her then it won't take long for the Emperor to know she's here."

"You speak like the room is alive."

I shook my head, feeling even more useless. I wondered if I could whisper. But thankfully Phillip said what I'd been wanting to, "It's not the room. It's the Magic."

"Weird." Jef looked around again. "If this Magic can feel you, does that mean you can feel other people? People like," his grip tightened, "Kit?"

My eyes filled with tears.

"Can you feel if she's here? Can you feel if she's okay?"

I shook my head. I hadn't tried. I didn't want to. I didn't want to know if she wasn't okay. I didn't want to be tempted to find her. Not now. I didn't need the extra temptation, it was already too hard to stay put while everyone bustled around us.

"No?" Jef's eyes shone. "No to what? No she's not here? No she's not okay?"

My lips parted.

Phillip smacked Jef's shoulder, "Quit bugging her. Now is not the time. She has bigger things to worry about."

Jef turned away. He brought his free hand up to his face. When he turned back, his eyes were clearer, "Yes, sorry, forgive me."

"We're ready." Gredd stood in front of me, his eyes locked on mine. "You stay here. We will find the Emperor and subdue him. Once we do, you should be able to take the planets from his control. And once you do that, we will be able to end him."

I nodded. When I'd heard I wasn't supposed to fight my uncle I'd felt relieved. Now, however, I wished it *was* me fighting him. I was worried for each of the warriors I'd brought here. I could still feel them all like they were now a part of me. *How many had I brought to their deaths*?

"How will she know when she can take the planets?" Jef asked.

"She'll know." Gredd's eyes searched mine.

I nodded. I'd know. I'd feel it.

"But how?" Jef's fingers flexed around mine.

I moved his hand so he looked at me.

"It's part of the Magic," Phillip explained before I could try. "She's connected to it. She'll know." When he glanced at me, he looked frightened.

"I don't understand this Magic stuff." Jef looked away at the three groups that had formed.

"You don't need to understand it," Phillip said. His eyes dropped to Jef's hand holding mine.

If Phillip had been closer, I would have taken his hand in my free one.

He stepped away, looking over at Samantha, Collin, and Mitch. "We are ready."

Gredd nodded, "There shouldn't be any trouble here. But just in case I've assigned Efiln, Tezel, Mac, and Rith to stay with you." He looked at me with a smile and gave a quick bow.

The four of them were neither very muscular nor tall, but I could tell they were trained. If it came to a fight they'd be ready. All four had short dark hair though it ranged in color from brown to black. They held their heads high, shoulders back, and their eyes were keen and watchful.

Gredd ran over to the group that had formed closest to the doors he'd closed. He exited. They followed. Tom took the group on the left and Morris the one on the right. I watched them leave, then listened to them make their way up the halls. As the noise of their travel faded, I listened to the silence that followed. It felt like the inhale before the dive.

Samantha came to stand closer to me, Mitch stood just off to the right of her. Collin came closer too. They were nervous. They stood alert trying to be ready for… for anything. Efiln, Tezel, Mac, and Rith situated themselves ten paces out on all four sides of the boxes where I sat. They were at the ready too. But other than that I could feel we were all alone.

Something clicked near Phillip. He pulled a thin object out of his pocket, "Yes?" he whispered into it.

"We've made it to the High Connection. So far we haven't run into any security," Morris's voice said. Then Tom's voice came through the device, "we are through the Second Connection. Same here."

"Magic my ass." Jef rolled his eyes.

Phillip smirked. "All stays quiet here."

My eyes darted around the room. The hairs on the back of my neck prickled like I was being watched.

"Good to hear." That was Gredd. "We've found the first group of hidden Un-Loyalists. Word is being sent to the others."

"There are Un-Loyalists here?" Jef said.

"Of course there are." Phillip shook his head. "You didn't expect us to attack the Emperor with only three hundred fighters."

"Actually I did."

Phillip didn't hear Jef. His communicator had crackled, "We've been attacked!" Morris shouted. "In the High Hall." There were other sounds that came through with Morris's voice. Weapons firing. People yelling. People screaming. And a strange high pitched squeal from… something. *I was sure I knew what that something was.* I imagined the shadow creatures and shuddered.

I squeezed Jef's hand; shifting to get up.

"Danay?" Jef put his free hand on my shoulder.

I tensed. I'd felt it. We had casualties. People were being hurt. People were dying. People I'd brought here. With each passing second, I felt them leaving.

"Stay put Princess," Samantha said. She moved closer to me.

Princess... the word seemed to be echoing through the walls. But I was smarter; I knew what had said it. Everyone looked around not seeing where it was coming from.

I could see them — or at least I could see the shadows they cast. "Behind you!" I called.

The Princess. This time it was the walls, or the Magic in them.

Rith looked at me. The Emperor's creatures were converging on him.

"Can't you see them?" I tried to get up.

Phillip pushed me down and held me there.

"The Princess," Rith's smooth features were contorted into hard lines. "Protect the Princess!" he shouted. He disappeared behind a creature. When I could see him again he was covered in cuts. "Tezel, Mac, Efiln, protect the Princess!" he gasped.

"From what?" Mac said swinging his gun in a wide arc trying to find a target.

"Where are they— aaaaaah..." Efiln let out a growl as he fell. The creatures circled him. He was completely obscured in shadows.

Samantha's eyes hardened as she drew herself closer to me. Collin's nostrils flared. Jef pulled his shoulders back. Phillip's hands clenched as he continued to hold me.

Tezel and Mac had their weapons raised at the ready. Their heads turned back and forth. Their eyes shifting, trying to focus on the unseen.

"They're surrounding us!" I yelled as more and more blurs closed in.

No one could see them.

Phillip let me go and turned away raising a knife. Collin, Mitch, and Samantha drew their own weapons. Jef raised his fists.

"Tezel at your back," I said.

He turned and fired.

He hit the creature. It howled like a beast not ready to admit defeat. Black sludge oozed from the creature's mid-section. They couldn't see the creatures — but they could see their blood. Its wound gave it away. Tezel didn't need me to tell him to fire again. He aimed his weapon and shot the creature until it stopped writhing.

Mac fired his weapon in a wide circle, hitting several more. He hit the three who were lapping at Rith's body. He hit two that stood over Efiln. Efiln was still fighting. Having clear targets made it easier. Mac hit four more that were paces from us. But he'd missed one. I hadn't even seen it until it had its tentacles around Samantha.

She shrieked as she was yanked away just out of my reach. Red welts sprang up on both her arms where the creature held her.

"Let her go!" Mitch lunged towards Samantha.

"Mitch! The Princess!" she yelled, breaking free and swinging her knife trying to hit her invisible attacker.

Mitch didn't listen. He ran to Samantha's side and jabbed his knife into the space around her.

The creature lashed out, hitting Samantha in the face before it moved out of reach.

Samantha fell to the floor.

I'd felt it, as if I'd been slapped across the face. I wanted to go to her but Phillip blocked my way. "Stay here." It wasn't a growl, but it was close.

Jef moved closer to Phillip so they were shoulder to shoulder. "Danay, I will tackle you to the ground if you try." Jef wasn't kidding.

"And I won't stop him." Phillip added — also not a joke.

I sat back on the boxes and watched helplessly as Samantha pulled herself to standing. Mitch tried to hold her — to check her wounds. She pushed him away, "You idiot. Protect the Princess." She started towards me. Mitch followed her.

Mac had killed four of the nine wounded creatures. They lay in heaps less than five paces from where I was. Efiln was fighting with another two. Black blood sprayed off one of them as it tried to get its tentacles close enough to Efiln to cause damage. Tezel was wrestling with one. They rolled blur over man on the floor.

The last two had moved back. They stayed pressed to the outer wall. I narrowed my eyes trying to see if there were more — trying to see how many more there were.

A sound came from right behind Samantha that reverberated through me. It was a sickening crunch. I hadn't just heard it. I'd felt it. I didn't need to look — I knew it was Mitch. A creature had grabbed him and snapped his neck.

I gasped for air. For just a second my lungs had forgotten how to work.

Mitch was dead. His body crumpled to the floor. His eyes stayed open staring blankly to the ceiling.

Samantha turned and gasped, "No!" She fell to the ground using her body to shield him. "No, no, no, no."

The creature that had killed Mitch was still there. It was reaching for Samantha. No one could see it. No one but me.

"Don't touch her!" I commanded, jumping to my feet. I pushed past Phillip and Jef.

"Danny no!" Jef caught me in a hug.

"Let me go!"

"No." Jef kept me close. Phillip glanced at Jef and nodded.

"Samantha needs me!" I gasped.

"Let Tezel take care of her." Jef squeezed tighter.

Tezel had won against the creature he'd been wrestling. He got to his feet and looked about.

"They can't see…"

The communicator in Phillip's pocket crackled, "Phillip, the Emperor… he's gone. We almost had him but he disappeared. Stay alert he might be coming your way."

Before Phillip could respond, he was yanked away. The creature that had killed Mitch — the creature I had stopped from getting Samantha — now had Phillip. Its tentacles slid around his neck.

"No!" I yelled struggling harder against Jef.

Jef had a good hold on me. He could have kept me pinned. Instead he spun me so I was behind his back.

The Emperor wasn't coming — he was here.

Chapter Thirty-Four

Introducing High Emperor Zigel

High Emperor Zigel stood over Samantha. "What have we here?" His eyes moved slowly to take in the whole scene as if he had all the time in the world... as if there wasn't a battle raging all around the room.... as if several of his creatures weren't lying dead or too wounded to fight. Finally he stared down at Samantha who was weeping over the crumpled form of Mitch.

"Don't hurt her!" I tried to lunge out from behind Jef but he stepped back, trapping me between him and the boxes.

The Emperor locked eyes with me. He smiled an evil grin. "I think I will."

Jef tried to step back even further crushing me against the wood.

"Don't." I struggled with Jef while I glared at the Emperor over Jef's shoulder. "You can't!"

"Oh, I assure you, child, I can."

Tezel, Mac, and Efiln were busy fighting with the Emperor's creatures. Jef stayed in front of me. Phillip was on his knees, the creature's tentacles tight against his throat — squeezing so his eyes bulged. Collin moved closer. His hands shook as he stared about like he didn't know what to do.

"Collin, help Phillip."

"Yes Princess." Collin charged at the invisible creature and started hacking. Black blood spouted from it like ink from an inking squid. Soon the creature's outline was defined; its round body, its coiling eel-like tail, its long arms which split into four tentacle fingers holding tight to Phillip.

"Snap her neck," the Emperor said sounding bored.

The space above Samantha blurred, she gasped as she was pulled to her feet. Nasty red welts sprung up where the creature's tentacles touched her. It lifted her so she dangled in its grip. Her legs kicked feebly, never making contact with it.

Mac brought another creature down. It lay in a heap with at least five others. Mac continued to shoot at the creature on the ground until his gun was empty.

"Mac, get that one," I ordered pointing towards Samantha.

He turned to locate her while loading a new clip in his gun.

The creature was wringing her neck but mercifully Samantha wasn't dead yet. It tried harder. If it didn't break her neck it was going to pop her head right off.

Mac was taking too long.

Samantha locked her eyes on me and mouthed something I couldn't understand.

Mac finally had his gun loaded and aimed at the space around Samantha. He took three shots missing the creature each time. Before he was able to take his fourth the Emperor turned to him and said, "Stop."

Mac stopped. So did Efiln and Tezel, as well as Collin. Even the creatures stilled, hanging on their master's word.

The Emperor's face broke into a wider grin. "Good. Now bow."

Mac, Efiln, and Tezel fell to their knees without hesitation. Collin bowed, but more slowly. He'd left Phillip with the creature still squeezing his neck. Phillip slashed at its tentacles without any success.

"Phillip," I moaned. *I didn't want him to die.* Surely if he couldn't breathe soon he would.

Jef pushed me back harder. "You can't help him," he said through his teeth.

My lips trembled as I realized how much I couldn't help any of them.

Emperor Zigel surveyed the room with an air of someone who knew he'd already won. His gaze fell upon Mac. "Time to die."

Mac's eyes rolled into the back of his head and he fell. I felt it too. My sides ached like I'd been punched. Mac was dead.

"You are a monster!" I tried to step out from behind Jef but he moved with me. He kept himself between the Emperor and me. *I had to stop the Emperor* — but how?

The Emperor seemed amused. "Release the girl," he told his creature.

It dropped Samantha to the floor. She fell with a thud that seemed to echo around the room.

"Get up," the Emperor said.

Samantha shook her head and crawled to where Mitch's body lay. She leaned close enough to kiss his forehead and whisper something in his ear.

"Get to your feet girl," the Emperor commanded.

Efiln and Tezel were still bowed — frozen in submission but I could see Collin was trying to fight it.

The Emperor bent closer to Samantha. "Didn't you hear me? I said, rise."

"Leave her alone," I shouted at the Emperor. I wanted it to sound like a command but it came out more like a child trying to tell their parents what to do.

A wicked grin lifted the corners of the Emperor's mouth. He put his hand on Samantha's shoulder, "I am the High Emperor, you will obey my command. Now — RISE."

She was on her feet. Tears clung to her lashes.

"Kill the Commoner." The Emperor was looking at Jef.

Samantha's knees buckled as she fought against his command.

"You will do as I command: kill him. That is an order."

Jef hesitated. I bolted out from behind him and took up a spot in front. "No!"

"Interesting." The Emperor took a moment to regard me. Then he leaned even closer still to Samantha and whispered something in her ear.

Her face paled. She took one step, then two, then three. Each was painstakingly slow as her muscles fought the movement. "I can't...." Her lips trembled. "I can't stop."

Efiln and Tezel were still frozen in their bows, they couldn't help. Collin was still struggling against his.

Samantha's feet brought her closer.

"Stop this," I choked. I wasn't sure who I was talking to, my uncle or Samantha — perhaps both. My uncle's eyes danced.

Jef tried to pull me back behind him. "Danay, what are you doing?"

From the corner of my eye, I saw Collin had finally broken free. He stood looking around.

"Collin, run." I commanded him. "Get help."

He was already running. "As you command."

"Stop!" The Emperor called but this time Collin didn't. He made it to the doors and was gone.

"You don't have to obey him," I told Samantha trying to catch her eyes. "I am your Princess, you pledged yourself to me." She was only a pace away. "Samantha?"

Tears were streaking her face as she shook her head.

"Samantha? Sam, please," I said with a shaky voice, "please stop."

She took one more step but stopped. She looked at me with wide eyes, "Yes, Princess."

"No!" The Emperor roared, "I am the High Emperor!"

Samantha didn't budge. She kept her eyes on me.

I turned to Phillip. He was still pinned by the wounded creature. But he was able to kick its coiling tail and slash at its arms. Then, with a final thrust of his leg, the creature crumpled, its arm still clasped to Phillip's neck. He brought his blade across it and the arm came off landing next to the creature's writhing body.

My heart surged with hope… We might be able to hold the Emperor off until help arrived.

Phillip's hands balled into fists as he turned to my uncle.

"Well done, now kill the Commoner." The Emperor smiled at Phillip.

Phillip flinched like he'd been struck. He turned back to me.

"You heard me," my uncle said with a sneer. "That Commoner is a danger to your Princess. Kill him."

Phillip jerked his head like he wanted to protest as his feet obeyed.

Samantha stepped in front of Phillip with her arms raised. "Listen, the Emperor is wrong. He's lying. Jef isn't a danger and you know it. Jef…"

"Move." Phillip said through his teeth.

"No Phillip, you don't want to do this."

Before he could tell her to move again Samantha was yanked off her feet by a new creature. It wrapped its tentacles around her face so she couldn't make a noise. Then it retreated behind its master, Samantha held in its tight grasp, but I couldn't do anything about it — Phillip had made it to me.

Phillip's throat contracted with a hard swallow. His eyes narrowed as he calculated a way to get around me to Jef.

I reached out to try and touch him.

"Danay!" Jef wrapped his arms around me trying to pull me away.

"Don't ever touch the Princess again you... you filthy Fish-Boy!" Phillip grabbed Jef by the collar and lifted him off the ground. Jef let me go pushing me off to the side where I landed on the floor.

Phillip continued to hold Jef up choking him. Jef swung at Phillip hitting him square in the jaw but Phillip didn't flinch. He held Jef higher, squeezing his neck so Jef made a garbled sound.

The Emperor watched with a satisfied grin.

"Phillip!" I scrambled to my feet and grabbed his arm.

He didn't even acknowledge me.

"Phillip," tears stung my eyes. I pulled on his arm — practically hanging from it. Phillip didn't let go.

Jef continued to gag, his fingers scratching at Phillip's hands.

"Phillip," I put a hand on each of his cheeks, "Phillip, please, if you truly love me you will stop this."

I watched Phillip swallow again, and then his eyes found mine. "I do," he dropped Jef, pulling his arms to his side.

Jef lay on the floor gulping for air.

Phillip's arms stayed rigid; blood trickled from the long scratch marks Jef had made. "I do love you," he said.

"What!" The Emperor bellowed. He took a step closer, his voice shaking, "How dare you!"

Phillip's eyes hadn't left me. He brought his hands up to my wrists trapping my hands against his cheeks. "I do love you, Danay."

Before I knew what was happening... before I could think about it, Phillip leaned down and put his lips over mine.

In that moment there was no battle, my uncle wasn't there, Mitch hadn't died, Samantha wasn't in peril. There was just Phillip and me and our love. I loved him and he loved me back not like a Loyalist, but like I'd always wanted him to.

"Phillip?" the Emperor's voice was softer now, but it commanded more authority.

Phillip pulled away.

"Are you not a Loyalist?" the Emperor stepped closer so he was just two paces away.

Phillip lowered his gaze to stare at the ground.

"Get on your knees boy!"

Phillip obeyed.

"Don't," I tugged on his shirt. "Please Phillip, get up." My voice shook. "You don't have to listen to him."

"Yes I do." Phillip said but his hands came around me.

"Unhand the Princess!" the Emperor snapped.

Phillip's hands made fists and he let me go. "Get her out of here." He pushed me back toward Jef.

Jef wrapped his arm around my waist and picked me up.

"No!" I yelled as Jef started to carry me away.

The Emperor stood over Phillip. He placed a heavy hand on his shoulder, "It is forbidden for Loyalists to love Royals."

Phillip nodded his head continuing to stare at the floor.

"It is a killing offence."

Phillip nodded again.

"No! Phillip, get up." I screamed. "Fight him! I command you to fight him!"

The room behind them blurred with several of the Emperor's creatures. I couldn't see where one ended and the next one began. The Emperor let go of Phillip and stepped back. Samantha was raised over a creature's heads.

"Run! Phillip!" It was too late. The creatures had converged on him — obscuring him in their shadows. "Fight! ...Noooooooooo!" My voice broke.

"Its okay, Danay." Jef had almost reached the exit. "Its..." Jef stopped, dropping me sharply to my feet.

I pushed Jef aside and started running back. *I had to save Phillip.*

"Faster!" Jef was at my back pushing me.

"What?" I said almost tripping.

"The Emperor."

I looked to where I'd last seen the Emperor. He wasn't there anymore. His creatures were retreating, leaving the still bodies of Phillip and Samantha on the floor.

"Danay, keep going!" Jef gave me another push.

I couldn't see the use.

"Danay! The Emperor!"

I looked back at Jef. The Emperor was right behind him, his arm stretched out, his fingers almost clasped around Jef's loose shirt.

I turned to face my uncle.

Jef ran past me but I heard him stop.

My uncle stood towering over me with murder in his eyes.

I didn't budge. *I wasn't afraid of my uncle.* I knew he couldn't hurt me — he'd already taken everything I cared about.

"I won't let you hurt her." Jef jumped in front of me trying to shield me with his arm. Reminding me I did have something else to lose.

"No Jef!"

"I have no intention of harming my niece," the Emperor said as he patted Jef's head.

"No!" I tried to push my uncle away but it was like I hit an invisible wall. The backlash caused me to stumble to the side and fall to the floor.

I stared up as my uncle brought his hand to Jef's chest and patted it twice. Jef staggered to his knees.

The Emperor laughed — a high, evil sounding laugh. "Now, you, my child…"

"I am not *your* child!" I said getting back onto my feet.

His grin doubled, "Just a saying. You *are* so very much like your mother."

I took a step towards him. I wanted to hurt him but all I could do was glare.

"Da—nay," Jef gasped holding his chest.

"What did you do to him?" I said, knowing in that moment my uncle had won.

"Oh," his face made a fake frown, "I just set him r…"

Something flashed in the Emperor's face.

I didn't understand as I watched him fall to the ground and stay there.

Was he dead? No, he couldn't be. I would have felt it if he had died. I continued to stand over him, staring.

"Princess," Collin called. He was running towards me, "get back." Collin put himself between me and the Emperor.

Morris passed us to stand over the Emperor, his weapon at the ready.

"What are you doing?" I asked.

His gun was aimed at the Emperor's head. "I am guarding him."

"Quickly." Gredd and his men entered the throne room. The men fanned out creating a circle around me and my unconscious uncle. "Princess, you must take your throne," Gredd said approaching me.

Tom came through the doors the creatures had exited, running past Phillip and Samantha without a second glance. *Like they were just some unknown causality of war*. Like they meant nothing to him. Like they didn't exist anymore.

"Are they…" the lump in my throat swelled.

"Princess," Tom snapped, "you must take the planets before they spin out of control."

The planets?

"Come." Tom tugged on my arm.

I let him guide me away from my uncle. Jef followed behind us, holding his heaving chest like every breath took an effort. As we ascended the stairs to the throne platform I stared over at Phillip and Samantha again.

Tom pushed me towards the throne, "Princess, please, you need to sit."

I couldn't take my eyes off Phillip.

"Princess, have you taken the planets from your uncle yet?" Morris still held his gun trained on my uncle.

"Danay," Jef moved in front of me, "Danny?"

"I can't." I felt panic twisting my throat. *Without Phillip nothing seemed to matter*. I shifted to see past Jef to where Phillip lay. Someone was kneeling next to him. "Is he…?" I couldn't bring myself to say it.

The man looked up, "Unconscious, Princess."

Relief flooded through me.

"Princess," Tom's voice was gruff. "The planets! Quista needs you."

I closed my eyes and tried to block out everything that was distracting me. But I could still feel it all: Jef — anxious. Collin — protective. Tom — conflicted. Gredd — raging. Morris — fearful. Everyone else — nervous, relieved, scared, hopeful, in awe, confused, excited. Yet I couldn't feel who I wanted — Phillip. Even though he was laying twenty paces from me it was like he wasn't really there.

My stomach swooped. My eyes shot open. I wasn't in my mother's throne room any more. I was in some strange place where the light felt distorted. My uncle stood before me.

"Princess Danay," his grin was wide.

"What have you done?" I wanted to charge him but my feet felt stuck.

"Nothing," he sounded casual as he looked around the strange place. "Nothing yet," he turned back to me with a sparkle in his eyes. Before I could react, he'd reached out and grabbed my shoulders.

A painful spark rippled through me making my stomach plummet as he disappeared and the room, with everyone in it, reappeared before me.

"No!" I could hear my uncle screaming.

"He is subdued." Gredd stood over the Emperor's unconscious body with an empty syringe in his hands.

"What did you do?"

Gredd looked at me, "I…" he looked at the syringe, the Emperor and back to me.

"It is okay Princess. The Emperor can't hurt you now." Morris left my uncle lying on the floor and made his way over to me. Gredd followed him.

My uncle lay completely unattended. No matter how much *they* thought he was subdued I didn't think leaving him unattended was smart. "Someone should…"

"Kill him," Jef finished for me.

I glanced at Jef only briefly then went back to watching my uncle as if my eyes alone could keep him pinned to the ground.

"Princess," Tom was scowling, "you must sit on your throne."

"What if he wakes up? What's to stop him from commanding all of you to die?" I said.

"That is why we drugged him," Gredd said, not even giving my uncle a second glance. "He should not wake for a very long time. And we will be administering his next dose long before then."

Jef's mouth popped open. "Isn't someone going to kill him?"

"Not yet." Tom answered. "Princess, please sit." He gestured towards my throne.

"When?" I asked glancing at Tom then Gredd and Morris before I looked back to my unmoving uncle.

"Once you have secured the High throne," Tom said through his teeth.

"Who will kill him?" I asked, my eyes finally leaving my uncle, "Will you?" I looked at Gredd.

He paled. "I— I can't." He shook his head. "Not— not without being commanded to… and even if…" he shook his head.

All three were looking at me. *Was I supposed to command one of them to kill my uncle*? I hoped not. I couldn't let my first command be to end my uncle's life — no matter how much he deserved it. I turned away to where Phillip and Samantha were. I bit my lip. I should have felt relief when I saw the rise and fall of their chests, and yet it only made mine ache. *He was supposed to be here beside me. I needed him… and Samantha too.*

"Princess," Gredd came closer still, "Princess? You must claim your mother's throne. You must become the Empress you were born to be."

Chapter Thirty-Five

Empress of Quista

The moment I touched it, my weariness evaporated. I felt the Magic. It flowed into me. It flowed through me.

"Princess?" Gredd's voice came to me as if from far away. "Do you have Quista? Are you in control of the worlds?"

"Um…" It was as if I were being suspended above the universe. I saw her. Every planet. Every moon. The suns. Every part. I didn't have her — she had me. She held me up like a mother swinging her child in her arms. I didn't need to 'take' the planets. The planets were exactly where they were meant to be. Between my uncle letting go and now, nothing had really changed.

I could see that in eight Turns Uma'Three's moon would collide with Uma'One — but I didn't need to worry about that for eight Turns. And in eight Turns I would fix it. I also saw that in one Royal Year Riel and Unarrah would have a close pass. I'd need to watch over them when that happened. But for now, there was really nothing I needed to do.

But for Gredd's sake I nodded.

"Good," he whispered with an audible sigh. Then I heard him inhale, "all Hail Empress Danay!"

His words were echoed by everyone in the room. I heard Tom's low voice, Collin's higher more juvenile tone and Morris's: it sounded heavy with sorrow.

All Hail Empress Danay, was chanted three times and just like that I was Empress — there was no going back.

I opened my eyes. Everyone in the room was bowing.

Well, everyone but Jef.

"Can you find Kit now?" he asked.

"Absolutely not!" Tom growled. "Now is not…"

I blocked his voice out because I knew I could. And *now* felt like exactly the right time. It took just one thought, *Kit'Una* and I was there — right where she was.

The room was empty. She was the only one in it. No other girls. None of the creatures. The beds lay unmade and empty. It felt like they might have left in haste. However, Kit's tub was as full as it could be. There was a light set up over it and as I neared I could feel it was giving off heat. Kit lay back, still in her undergarments. Still in shackles. But at least she had enough moisture and warmth.

"Kit?" I said as I stepped closer.

Her eyes opened. Her head jerked up. Then she saw me and the surprise was clear. "Danay? What are you doing here?"

"I— I came here for you." After everything, Kit was the truest reason I'd come to the Royal planet.

"For me?" She seemed a bit groggy. She raised her hand and made a soft fist which she tried to bring to her face. When the chain stopped it she leaned her head up more until she could grind her knuckle into her eye. "Are you really here?"

I was unsure how to answer. "I am here — mostly. I'm just shadow walking." I used the phrase Morris had used.

She shifted to sitting. The water in her tub made soothing sloshing noises. "Shadow walking?" She leaned down to push her knuckles into her eye again. "Is this a dream?"

Something felt off about her — she seemed too dazed.

"Are you okay?" Panic fluttered in my chest. Did she need a doctor? I'd left our doctor and Sue on Gredd's ship on Turlyn.

"I'm—" she yawned, "I'll be fine. I'm—" another yawn, "just tired."

I looked around the empty room. "Where are all the other girls?" *Why had she been left alone.*

Kit's shoulders rose and fell, "I don't know." She also gazed around the room. "They were here earlier." She blinked then looked around the room again. "They said something like I wasn't — wanted." She swallowed. "I think they left me here to die." She lay her head back against the tub.

Had they poisoned her? Anger coursed through me. *How could they do that to Kit.*

"Get up." I reached out — but of course my spirit hands slid right through her.

She jumped to sitting. Her eyes narrowed on me, "You are just a dream." She bent forward to cup her face in her hands.

"I am not!" I wanted to scream. "I am here in spirit. Now get up! We need to get you out of here."

I'm not sure she actually believed me, but she tried. She sat taller and pulled on her chains, "How?"

"Is there a key?"

There was! And, naturally, it was on the farthest wall from her. Right next to the open door. I went to it and tried with all my might to pick it up. I even tried to levitate it. It didn't work. I hadn't expected it to: spirits couldn't do Magic.

I ran back to Kit. "Get up!" She was lying down again. "Get up and get out! And pull your tub to the wall!"

She did. She got up. She got out. But after a lot of pulling, pushing and even one attempt at lifting she'd only made it three finger widths closer to the key. And she was spent. She stood, looking at me, her lips were turning blue. She shivered from being too dry.

"Get back in the tub," I said. *I'd have to figure out another way*. I bit my lip thinking about sending Gredd's men to find her. *If I knew where to send them*… I started to go to the door.

"Don't leave me," Kit moaned. Her eyes were wide, her knuckles white as she held the sides of the tub.

I couldn't leave her. I nodded and turned to come back but a voice tickled my ear. A soft, hissy voice.

"Surely Uma girl being gone by now," it said.

I could feel the creatures. Several of them. They weren't close — yet. Still, I didn't have a lot of time.

"Wishing she'd just go." it said, or another one had… or they had all said it together. I couldn't really tell. "Master wanting her gone."

My teeth clenched. *My uncle had ordered Kit to die*! I hated him so much in that instant I think I could have ordered his death — first command or not.

"Danny?" I felt Jef's breath on my neck as he whispered into my ear. "Did you—" his voice broke, "—find her?"

"Empress!" Tom snapped, "This is..."

I held my hand up to silence Tom and I realized I was back in my body, though I could still see Kit too. I didn't hesitate. I blinked.

At first I thought I'd failed. I could see Kit, in her tub, just a few paces from my throne — but no one else could.

Then Kit opened her eyes and jolted upright displacing enough water to splash to the floor.

"What the..." she tried to stand too quickly and slipped causing more water to be displaced.

Everyone had turned to look.

Jef was the first to reach her. He fell to his knees and scooped her from under the water. He pulled her to his chest.

"Jef—"

Others were quick to follow. Tom, Efiln, Tezel and others whose names I didn't know. Their reactions weren't as kind. Tom had raised his gun to Kit's head.

"Stop!" I jumped from my throne almost into Collin and Morris who had stayed close to me. Stepping between me and the rest.

From the corner of my eye I saw Gredd bent over the Emperor, a needle held poised in his hand. He'd frozen along with the rest.

"—what's going on?" Kit finished.

"Oh," Jef said pulling his shirt off and covering his sister's exposed front with it. "Danay's the Princess — Empress, I guess now."

"The *what*?" She turned to me, shock written across her face.

I nodded.

Tom glared, his gun still poised on Kit's head.

"Lower your gun," I said locking eyes on him.

"But—" an expression flitted across his face that I didn't understand: concern? mistrust? worry? "—how did she get here?"

"Me." I'm not sure why it bothered me that Tom still doubted me. *Hadn't I just taken control of every planet in the galaxy*! Though I wasn't really in control of them... *but he didn't know that*. Actually, the moment I'd stood I'd felt the connection between me and the worlds diminish. With a quick breath I reconnected to them, though it took slightly more concentration now. Again, I could see they were okay without me until those two events that were ages away.

I looked up at Tom. "Tom!" It was just his name, but I'd said it like a command.

He took one last look at the gun, still held to Kit's head, "How do we know it's not a trick?" he asked but he did lower the gun. From the corner of my eye I saw Gredd lower the needle.

I stepped between Collin and Morris, closer to Kit, "Because I did this."

Tom backed away, "Sorry, Empress," he said with a nod of his head.

Kit looked back and forth between Tom and me, "Danay, you're really a..."

"Empress Danay!" Collin said while Jef answered, "She's an Empress."

Kit kept her eyes on me — staring at me from head to toe and back up again, "Our Danay?" She shifted closer to Jef sloshing the water about.

"We have to get you out of that tub," I said dipping my hand in. The water had gone tepid.

"And into some clothes," Jef added still holding his shirt over her front. But the material had become almost translucent with the moisture.

Someone found Kit a blanket but without a wet'skn she would have to settle for staying in the tub. I had Gredd's men move the tub closer to my throne — where Gredd had convinced me to stay while they made sure the palace was secure.

While we waited, Gredd explained that Phillip's kiss and profession of love had been wrong — just as wrong as my uncle had made it seem. These *were* killing offences. No one could understand why Phillip wasn't dead, though Gredd seemed relieved about that. However, as soon as he woke up he'd be spoken to and given a choice: either he could stay my Loyalist and then I'd have to command him to stop loving me; or he could choose to love me and I'd have to command him to stop being a Loyalist.

My heart broke. If he chose to love me he'd have to be a Commoner and he'd lose his purpose.

"What do you think would be best for him?" I asked Kit after Gredd had moved away.

Jef had kept his eyes far from me and Gredd while we spoke. He glanced over scratching at his wet shirt. When I caught him he looked away again.

"Neither." Kit said. She had a plate of food Collin had brought her from the supplies Gredd's men had unpacked. "He should never have fallen in love with you."

I nodded. "I can't believe he actually did."

"I can." Kit took another bite then quickly swallowed, "What I can't believe is that you are a Royal… and tomorrow you'll be the High Empress!"

I had to concentrate just to swallow.

"It's not that hard to believe." Jef smiled.

"I can't believe you knew and you never told me." Kit cuffed Jef the way I'd seen their mother do from time to time.

"Ow, hey, it's not my fault…"

I looked past Jef to where Phillip and Samantha lay. The rise and fall of their chests was a good thing. I'd been promised several times that they should wake any moment. Every moment that passed made me more nervous. However, I guess things could be worse. My eyes moved beyond them to where Mitch lay. His chest didn't rise or fall. Someone had covered him with a blanket so only his shoes showed.

"Empress," Collin said climbing the stairs to the platform my throne was on. His hands were cupped around a bowl of lu'umon berries.

I took them and started eating. After my first bite I heaped as many as I could into my mouth in a very un-empress sort of way. I didn't care — I hadn't realized how hungry I was.

Kit laughed at me, "Okay, maybe I should have figured it out. No one can eat so many lu'umon berries and live unless…"

"They aren't poisonous," I grumbled around my last mouthful, thinking about how Phillip could eat them. I rested the empty bowl on my knee and looked over at him again.

A little ways away from Phillip, Gredd stood with Tom over the unconscious form of my uncle.

"I say give him a double dose," Tom said his eyes shifting around my throne room. "I don't trust the last batch and until the doctor gets here to make him his own — I say more is better."

"But more could kill him." Gredd stared down at my uncle with a sour expression.

Good, kill him, I thought as I glanced at Kit. After everything he'd done to her — and the other girls — my uncle didn't deserve anything less. But before I could call over to tell that to Tom he spoke to Gredd.

"Then give me the needle and I'll do it. If he dies I will only be fulfilling Empress Zoe's command."

"Aren't you getting ahead of yourself?" Gredd pulled his hand with the needle away. "I know I wasn't there when she gave you that command but I would think she'd want the assurance of her daughter taking the High throne before you did something to our only other Royal."

Tom frowned, "Empress Danay *will* take the High throne tomorrow. If *High* Emperor Zigel dies tonight I can only assume that will help in our cause."

"I'm not so sure." Gredd glanced over to me.

I looked away again. I didn't want them to know I could hear them.

"Besides," Gredd continued, "there are a great many more things you need to assist Empress Danay with. If you take *High* Emperor Zigel's life in haste you will be removing your chance to do this."

Tom stared at Gredd with a sour expression.

"Do I need to remind you that our former High Emperor Zandr made a new resolution that any Loyalist who kills a Royal will share in the Royal's fate?"

Tom shook his head, "No, I have not forgotten that. That is why I am not suggesting this in haste. *I* do not think that a double dose will do the *High* Emperor any harm." Tom put his hand out.

Gredd pressed his lips together.

Tom sighed, "Captian Gredd Dis'Hyroo, my friend, you have always known you could trust me. I assure you, that hasn't changed. I am only trying to act in our new Empress's best interest."

Gredd slowly handed the needle to Tom. "Fine."

Tom nodded then bent down next to my Uncle.

Thinking about my medicine as I watched Tom administer it made my stomach plummet. Thankfully Tom was swift. As he removed the needle he looked up, meeting my gaze. His look was impassive but I suspected dislike behind his cold eyes.

I blinked, wondering if Tom would ever think I was good enough. Not that it mattered — Tom would be dead as soon as my uncle was... was that why he hated me so much? In order to make things safe for me he'd been commanded to kill my uncle — but that commandment came at the price of his own life.

Collin jumped to his feet. "Phillip's awake!"

I copied him.

"Empress," Gredd came towards me as Tom made his way over to Phillip. "Empress," he stood in front of me, "please, give Tom a moment."

I nodded and sat back down.

Phillip sat blinking around the room like the light hurt his eyes. As his gaze met mine his face fell... or maybe it was a coincidence? Tom was kneeling next to him, no doubt telling him about the choice he had to make.

He looked at me again, then quickly away, nodding at whatever Tom was saying.

Samantha gasped, her back arched then she rolled to her side. "No!" She turned to look at Mitch. "No, no, no!" She crawled her way over to him. "No!" She fell onto the blanket burying her face in it.

Phillip looked from Samantha and Mitch over to me, and then back to Tom. He nodded again.

Kit leaned over as close to me as she could. "He'll choose you," she said.

I was sure Gredd had heard her. He didn't react, making his face look as impassive as Tom's could be. I wondered what he'd want for his son.

Jef, however, did react. He shook his head.

Kit bit her lip, "He just has to choose you."

My eyes wandered away from Phillip to Samantha. She was now sitting by Mitch's feet, tears streaking her face. Her one hand clinging to the toe of his shoe so tightly; like to let go would hurt her. That's where love had gotten them.

Maybe it would be better if Phillip chose Loyalty.

Tom nodded to Gredd.

"You may go to him now." Gredd bowed and left me.

Tom had left Phillip. Phillip turned to stare at Mitch. He never turned back.

I slowly got to my feet.

Collin copied me. So did Jef. Kit too, water dripped from the blanket wrapped around her.

I didn't go over to Phillip. I was a little too afraid to find out what he'd pick. Instead I went to sit next to Samantha. Tears pricked my eyes. I opened my mouth to tell her how sorry I was, but I couldn't get the words past the lump that had formed in my throat.

Jef knelt next to me. He inhaled sharply and said, "Sorry about Mitch."

Collin and Samantha both stared at him.

"I mean, he was a jerk to me, but he didn't deserve to die."

Samantha finally let go of his shoe, "Yeah, he was an idiot." She took a deep breath as we all stared at her, "Don't get me wrong." She wiped at fresh tears, "I loved that idiot."

"And he loved you." Phillip had shuffled over to us. He glanced at me then away.

"Yeah," Samantha said rubbing at her eyes, "idiot."

I finally was able to get my voice to work. "I'm sorry too."

"Don't be." Samantha and Phillip said at the same time.

As I met Phillip's gaze he didn't turn away.

I had shivers in my stomach — was he going to choose me? *Did I want him to choose me*?

Phillip brought a hand to his neck to rub it. I had seen him do this many times before but I wasn't sure if it was out of habit or because his neck was sore. The welts from my uncle's shadow creature looked painful.

"Oh, hey," Jef leaned towards Phillip, "sorry about your arms."

Phillip stared down at them. They had long scratch marks all the way from his elbows to his wrists. "Thanks. I — guess I should say sorry for nearly choking you to death."

"Right," Jef stretched out his neck. Deep bruises had set in. "I was going to apologize for decking you — but you kinda deserved that."

Phillip just nodded while he rubbed his jaw.

Gredd stepped up behind Phillip, "I believe it is time for the Empress to be taken to her suites."

I nodded and stood. Phillip, Collin, Samantha, Jef and Kit all copied me.

The way Gredd watched, I was nervous he'd say I had to go alone. But he didn't say anything to us. Instead he just called his men over. I followed Gredd, Efiln and Tezel with Kit and Jef on the right of me and Collin and Samantha on my left. Phillip followed a pace behind with the rest of Gredd's men.

The halls were made of stone blocks. They reminded me of sand stones only much lighter. Bone white. Oddly I wondered if the sand to make these blocks had come from the beaches on Uma'Two.

The walk to my suites was very short. Once there Gredd bowed and left me with five guards outside of my door and two, Efiln and Tezel, inside.

I had expected my suites here to be similar to the ones on the ship.

I was pleasantly surprised at how wrong I was.

My front room wasn't so much an actual room, but more like a meadow. The ground was covered with a dark, lush, thick, soft growth. It hugged my feet as I walked — the sandals were ditched instantly. Tall trees grew along all four walls. Off to the right was a waterfall that fed into a lake... m*y front room had a lake...* and a stream with a bridge over it. I started towards the bridge.

"Danay, please..." Kit was cut off.

"Empress Danay." Both Samantha and Collin corrected her.

Kit made a face, "Yeah, anyways, can we just stop here for a moment?" She edged closer to the lake.

Her lips were starting to turn blue. The blanket draped around her was almost completely dry.

I nodded and followed her over.

She didn't hesitate. As she reached the edge of the lake she dropped the blanket and cannonballed in. Jef, who had his hand on his chest like it was itchy, did a shallow dive after her.

Kit came up shaking her thick hair out of her face. "The water feels different," she leaned back to float and stare at the ceiling, "but it's nice." She looked over to me, "You should try it, *Empress* Danay."

I dipped my fingers in. The water did feel smoother.

"You know I just remembered something." Samantha came to stand next to me.

I stared up at her, "What?"

"Well, Phillip once told me that even though you are a Royal — you are a person too."

Before I could ask what she meant she pushed me in.

The shock of it was enough to make me squeal.

"Samantha!" Phillip looked less angry and more amused. His face changed when he was the next she pushed in.

He came up sputtering next to me. His hand slipped around mine under the water. "I choose you," he leaned close enough for his breath to caress my neck, "I will always choose you."

"Don't you have until morning to decide?" Jef said from somewhere behind us.

Phillip leaned closer, his lips tickling my earlobe, "My decision will be the same in the morning."

I squeezed his hand. I was happy and sad at the same time.

Samantha was chasing Collin screaming something about how it was his turn. Only he duped her and she was the next to be dunked. She splashed so close to me and Phillip we had to jump away, our hands breaking apart.

Kit thought this was hilarious, "I see you're still afraid to get splashed." She laughed again, "I guess some things will never change!"

"Oh yeah!" I splashed as much water as I could in Kit's face before I dove under the surface to get away.

Kit was right. Some things hadn't changed. But she was also wrong — some things had. I had always been a Royal, but I had never known it. Then when I'd found out, I didn't feel ready. Now I did. I was ready to take the High throne and rule all of Quista. And I knew I'd be good at it as long as I had Kit, and Phillip and Collin and Samantha and Jef there to help me.

~ ~ ~ ~ ~

~ ~ ~

~

Acknowledgements

To be honest there aren't enough pages in this whole book to list all of the wonderful people who've helped me to make Quista a reality. I will try, but I know so many names will go unmentioned.

The top of that very long list goes to my amazing, supportive, patient, encouraging, cheer-leader, best friend, love of my life, husband, Dave Harold. Thank you for putting up with being a writer's widower from time to time. Thank you for listening to endless stories about people who only exist in my mind (until I can get them onto the paper). Thank you for making sure all my books could become a reality.

Second place goes to the rest of my family. They are my biggest and most devoted fans. My sister, my children, my mother, my aunts, my baba, my cousins, my husband's parents (thank you Mrs. Harold for being one of my first beta readers for almost every novel I've written). Thank you all for believing in me; for encouraging me. And for asking the most important question: what comes next?

And speaking of next; I'd like to thank my teachers — especially those who had the prodigious task of teaching me English. Thank you to all the teachers who saw past the beastly spelling to embrace the story. In particular I'd like to honor my grade three teacher (wish I could remember your name) along with Mrs. Lilly and Ms. Unchiyana (from Kitsilano High 1989).

I'd also like to thank friends, old and new. I may not have been blessed with many from my elementary years but in my teens and into adulthood I made up for it. There are too many names to recount them all. I know who you are — you should know too. Be assured that even if you never heard a word about my books you were always inspiring me in ways you may never imagine.

And a huge thank you to my editors! So many. You have the courage to take the hot mess of letters and words all muddled up and comb them straight as well as keeping me on track and toning my story. First, to Ella Beaumont for being better than a friend. Better than an editor. Your love for Quista and all the characters in it goes beyond normal — thank you. For Allister Thompson — you have challenged me yet again. As much as I dislike the feeling of that, I am thankful that you do what you do to create a better me (on paper at least). And to Toria Spencer. You were not an official editor but your honest breakdown was worth more than ten beta readers combined.

I'd also like to thank my publisher, Brian Hades. It is always a gamble to pick up a new author. I know you've seen something in me that I may never understand. Regardless, thank you for taking the time to see it. And especially thank you for making this book a reality.

And lastly I'd like to thank my fans. Without you I would not be read. An author un-read is like a dog that is never walked — sad. Thank you for taking the time to read my book. I hope you've loved it as much as I did creating it. Feel free to let me know by leaving a review.

~ ~ ~

Biography

Aviva Bel'Harold has been making up stories all her life. She just never thought she could be an actual author — what with her raging dyslexia and spelling malfunctions. Happily she was wrong.

After writing her first novel 'Safe', for her suicidal daughter, Aviva jumped into the world of self-publishing with both feet and no parachute. With three self-published novels under her belt she then ventured into the realm of traditional publishing and was picked up by EDGE Science Fiction and Fantasy Publishing with *Blood Matters*.

Now Aviva is known not only for her novels but also her presentations and the classes she gives. Aviva is a firm believer that if she can do it — everyone can.

Life is hectic for Aviva. Her time is divided, unequally, between taking care of her family, her speaking engagements, bringing up a pack of Dachshunds, and more reptiles than you can count between all your fingers and toes. However, in amongst inspiring the masses, making dinner, cleaning messes and chasing crickets, Aviva still finds time to return to her childhood worlds — capturing them in words on paper for everyone to enjoy.

~ ~ ~

Need something new to read?

If you enjoyed Quista, you should also
consider these other EDGE titles:

~ ~ ~

Terminal City

(Book One in the Terminal City Saga)

By Trevor Melanson

Mason Cross never wanted to be anything like his father

Mason Cross never wanted to be anything like his father, a famous professor who, it turns out, was also a necromancer. But death changes people.

Now Mason is following in his dead dad's footsteps, down a dark, solitary path between two competing lives: one as a student at Terminal City's top university, the other as a necromancer.

But will he find the answers he's looking for? Or will he find only death, caught in a hidden war between necromancers and a religious inquisition?

As the gravity of both worlds bears down on him, Mason will need to discover not just new power—but what a human life is really worth.

Praise for Terminal City

Riveting read from start to finish. Highly imaginative romp into the dark side with complex characters. I found myself liking the bad ones as much as the good ones; indeed the lines between 'good' and 'bad' were often blurred. Action packed, and never a dull moment; the author paints incredible pictures of an alternative Vancouver (Terminal City) as well as other layers of the necromancer's reality, and the flow back and forth between the two. I can hardly wait for the next two books of this trilogy, and highly recommend this book; you will not be able to put it down. This would make an incredible movie. It would be visually stunning; Mason is such a believable character, very multi-dimensional, a reluctant hero! Amazing entrance into the published literary world for this fresh, new author!!

— Linda Nickerson

The book opens with fairly standard coming-of-age material in a world very like our own but with just a touch of the fantastic. The first third is setup, and the rest of the book is page-turning payoff as Melanson subverts the tropes he's introduced and plays skillfully with the reader's expectations. Clearly familiar with authors like Neil Gaiman and China Mieville, Melanson's first novel sets forth into similar territory and proves he's learned from those who've trod that ground before. As a first novel, it's comparable to Gaiman's Neverwhere - strong potential, with excellent writing and imagery that compels you to keep reading.

Melanson's built himself a world to play in, and I can't wait for the next book. I only wonder what that bridge ever did to the author to deserve what he did to it.

— Eric M Gauf

~ ~ ~

The Occasional Diamond Thief

By J. A. McLachlan

What if you learned your father was a thief? Would you follow in his footsteps, learn his "trade"? If you were the only one who knew, would you keep his secret?

When 16-yr-old Kia is training to be a universal translator, she is co-opted into travelling as a translator to Malem. This is the last place in the universe that Kia wants to be—it's the planet where her father caught the terrible illness that killed him—but it's also where he got the magnificent diamond that only she knows about. Kia is convinced he stole it, as it is illegal for any off-worlder to possess a Malemese diamond.

Using her skill in languages – and another skill she picked up, the skill of picking locks - Kia unravels the secret of the mysterious gem and learns what she must do to set things right: return the diamond to its original owner.

But how will she find out who that is when no one can know that she, an off-worlder, has a Malemese diamond? Can she trust the new friends she's made on Malem, especially handsome but mysterious 17-year-old Jumal, to help her? And will she solve the puzzle in time to save Agatha, the last person she would have expected to become her closest friend?

Kia is quirky, with an ironic sense of humor, and a loner. Her sidekick, Agatha, is hopeless in languages and naïvely optimistic in Kia's opinion, but possesses the wisdom and compassion Kia needs.

Praise for The Occasional Diamond Thie:

"The Occasional Diamond Thief" offers just the right combination of unusual setting, relentless plot and multifaceted characters to satisfy readers of any genre."

— *Jean Mills, Waterloo Region Record*

"J. A. McLachlan is a terrific writer — wry and witty, with a keen eye for detail. I've been following her work with interest and delight since 2003. In a world where young-adult fiction is booming, The Occasional Diamond Thief propels McLachlan to the front of the pack."

— *Robert J. Sawyer, Hugo Award-winning author of FlashForward*

"Thought provoking humor: " You need your good dreams to make you want to go to bed and some bad ones so you don't grow overly fond of being there." The author's accurately detailed description of Westminster Abbey and London had me searching the internet for further historical insight on many of the facts included in the telling of this unusual story. Fascinating and entertaining!"

— *Amazon Reviewer*

"J. A. McLachlan is a remarkable creator of worlds, a remarkable creator of character, a master of suspense. In short, a remarkable storyteller. You don't have to be a young adult to love this book."

— *Sheryl Loeffler, Writer, A Land in the Storytelling Sea*

~ ~ ~